KT-143-257

READ WHAT THE WORLD IS SAYING ABOUT
THE *MAESTRA* SERIES BY

L.S. HILTON

'Funny and clever, entertaining and well written, with smart, knowing references to everything from *Grazia* magazine to the Italian baroque painter Artemisia Gentileschi . . . Destined for the bestseller charts'

Louise France, *The Times*

'Set to be the "it" book of the year . . . Judith Rashleigh is a love-to-hate anti-heroine with a screw loose who could give *Gone Girl's* Amy Dunne a run for her money'

Hannah Britt, *Daily Express*

'A blockbuster and a half. It's a gripping story . . . it's going to take Britain by storm'

Kate Williams, *Mail on Sunday*

'Outlandish and entertaining . . . smart and scathing'

Stephanie Merrit, *Observer*

'Fantastically good fun . . . L.S. Hilton can write. She can even make you think that popping along to a sex party is quite a good idea . . . She knows about history. She knows about power. She knows about money, sex and power. And she knows about pleasure'

Christina Patterson, *Sunday Times*

'A decadent tale of lust and lacy underwear . . . Sharp and extremely well written'

Jan Moir, *Daily Mail*

'Hilton can both actually write and plot . . . an entertaining and thoroughly escapist romp with a commanding femme fatale at the helm'

Lucy Scholes, BBC

'A deliciously decadent chase through international capitals, with bodies dropping as fast as the mention of designer labels . . . a glamorous and racy adventure'

Sunday Mirror

'You'll love it if you liked The Talented *Mr Ripley*'

Cosmopolitan

'Set to be the beach read of the summer, tracing the rise of art house assistant Judith Rashleigh as she embarks on the summer of a lifetime. Murder, sex, deceit, designer wares and devious men, it's all there in abundance'

Hannah Dunn, *Red*

'A pacy, sexy thriller set in the decadent world of the super-rich with a resourceful heroine at its heart'

Fanny Blake, *Woman and Home*

'Brimming with scandal, intrigue and mystery, this is a book that everyone is talking about'

Heat

'A first-class psychological thriller . . . Read it now before the entire world does'

Glamour

'A spectacular act of revenge on the English upper class . . . coldly furious, exuberant, wish-fulfilling'

Catherine Brown, *Standpoint*

'In a cat fight Judith would walk all over Anastasia from *Fifty Shades*. She's feisty, independent, hard-nosed and figuratively always on top. And the sex scenes, whisper it, are really rather good'

Metro Book Club

'*Maestra* is already being touted as the new *Fifty Shades of Grey* – it's not, being a thriller which is far cleverer and immeasurably more skilfully executed'

Liadan Hynes, *Belfast Telegraph*

'*Maestra* twists and turns to morph into a crime thriller packed with . . . nail-biting antics and scandalous seductions'

Marie Claire

'A psychological thriller set on the French Riviera, rather like Patricia Highsmith crossed with *Gone Girl*: unsurprisingly, there's a film deal in the works'

Harpers Bazaar

'A fast-paced romp with an amoral and immoral heroine . . . *Maestra* lives up to the hype'

Red

USA

'This year's most erotic novel makes *Fifty Shades* look like the Bible . . . Bound to be the It beach book of the summer'

New York Post

'A shopathon travelogue thriller that has billionaires, art world scheming and a sociopathic heroine who can unfasten belt buckles with her tongue'

The New York Times

'What makes a woman who'll do anything to get what she wants so threatening and thrilling? . . . It's Judith's modes of retaliation that make her a radical heroine. She deploys a uniquely female arsenal . . . weaponizing femininity . . . It's hard not to feel vicariously empowered by a woman unapologetically in pursuit'

O, The Oprah Magazine

'Maestra will be one of this year's most talked-about novels . . . Judith may well be a more interesting character [than Patricia Highsmith's Tom Ripley] . . . More mayhem, more art – and certainly more sex – lie ahead for insatiable Judith and for all those consenting adults who will delight in her endless ups and downs'

The Washington Post

'Jubilantly mordant. . . . Already optioned for the big screen by Amy Pascal, [this is] the story of a twenty-first-century femme fatale as lethal as Tom Ripley and as seductive as Bacall'

Vogue

'A taut, meaty thriller that's certainly on par with those bestselling 'girls' in terms of intrigue, surprising twists, and unputdownableness, while Judith Rashleigh's single-minded and self-centered quest for wealth and acceptance could well be the most compelling since Patrick Bateman's'

Chicago Review of Books

IRELAND

'A glamorous, witty and adrenaline-fuelled romp – if you like your heroines sexy, vengeful, amoral and lethal, *Maestra* delivers in spades'

Declan Burke, *Irish Times*

'One of the books of the year . . . This is Jackie Collins crossed with Jo Nesbo. Irresistibly entertaining'

Edel Coffey, *Irish Independent*

AUSTRALIA

'Shocking? Yes – but also completely unputdownable'

Sue Turnbull, *Sydney Morning Herald*

'It's a killer of a book . . . an all-nighter dripping with blood and glamour . . . lewd, luscious and lowdown . . . it ups the ante way past any Scandi dragon girls'

Peter Craven, *The Australian*

'A wild ride – this is not for the faint-hearted'

Elyse Pickens, *Brisbane News*

EUROPE

'This story is terrific . . . Hilton's heroine is beautiful, intelligent, dangerous and very pleasure-oriented. The result: in *Maestra* you will find not only murder but also plenty of very hot sex'

Freundin

'This thriller is pure suspense, with real pace and a little taste of art history combined with extensive sex scenes and an extraordinary heroine'

Buchmedia Magazin

'A sparkling surprise from the first page to the last, high-quality entertainment from someone who knows how to write'

La Repubblica

'A mix of eroticism and adrenaline, and – at last – a smart character. The intertwining of sex and power is the strong point of the whole novel'

Il Fatto Quotidiano

'The first volume in a trilogy that will become a Hollywood film, but will first be a literary sensation: if you can resist being scandalised, you won't put it down until the last page'

Vanity Fair (Italy)

'The book you should be reading right now is a hot thriller, crackling and well written'

Gioia

'A literary blockbuster'

La Gazzetta dello Sport

'Not *Fifty Shades of Grey*: L.S. Hilton can write. This is colourful, elegant and to the point'

De Morgen

'*Maestra* is an extraordinarily accomplished first part of a trilogy that earns Judith Rashleigh a place on the list of memorable female characters in the world of thrillers'

Hebban.nl

'Judith is sexy, smart and very dangerous . . . Great plot, juicy sex scenes, a stylish and fierce femme fatale – finally, the perfect thriller'

Cosmopolitan (Poland)

'Once you start reading, something becomes clear: once you start, it's impossible to stop . . . The quality bestseller is back – and, this time, women have the power'

Vanity Fair (Spain)

'The new publishing phenomenon that's sweeping through the bookshops . . . Addictive from beginning to end, *Maestra* tells a tale that combines suspense, violence, sex, luxury, art and fashion'

Glamour (Spain)

'A story that hooks you from paragraph two'

El País

DOMINA

L.S. HILTON

ZAFFRE

First published in Great Britain in 2017 by

ZAFFRE PUBLISHING
80-81 Wimpole St, London W1G 9RE
www.zaffrebooks.co.uk

Copyright © L.S. Hilton, 2017

All rights reserved. No part of this publication may be reproduced, stored or transmitted in any form by any means, electronic, mechanical, photocopying or otherwise, without the prior written permission of the publisher.

The right of L.S. Hilton to be identified as Author of this work has been asserted by them in accordance with the Copyright, Designs and Patents Act, 1988

This is a work of fiction. Names, places, events and incidents are either the products of the author's imagination or used fictitiously. Any resemblance to actual persons, living or dead, or actual events is purely coincidental.

A CIP catalogue record for this book is available from the British Library.

ISBN: 978–1–78576–085–3
Export Paperback ISBN: 978–1–78576–301–4

also available as an ebook

1 3 5 7 9 10 8 6 4 2

Typeset by IDSUK (Data Connection) Ltd

Printed and bound by Clays Ltd, St Ives Plc

Zaffre Publishing is an imprint of Bonnier Zaffre, a Bonnier Publishing company
www.bonnierzaffre.co.uk
www.bonnierpublishing.co.uk

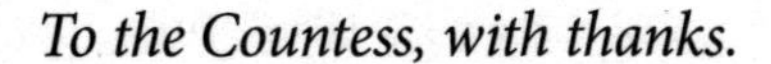

To the Countess, with thanks.

Prologue

I only wanted to get it over with, but I forced myself to go slowly. I closed the shutters at all three windows, opened a bottle of Gavi, poured two glasses, lit the candles. Familiar, recognisable, comforting rituals. He set down his bag and removed his jacket slowly, hanging it on the back of a chair, watching me. I raised my glass and took a sip without speaking. His eyes played over the paintings as I let the silence between us lengthen until he fell into it.

'Is that an . . . ?'

'Agnes Martin,' I finished for him. 'Yes.'

'Very nice.'

'Thank you.' I kept the small, amused smile playing on my lips. Another pause. The thick stillness of Venice at night was broken by the sound of footsteps crossing the *campo* below, we both turned our heads towards the window.

'Have you lived here long?'

'A while,' I answered.

The cockiness he had shown earlier in the bar had vanished; he looked awkward and painfully, terribly young. I was going to have to make the first move, obviously. I was standing, holding my glass with my elbow crooked across my body. We were two steps apart. I took one, holding his eyes with mine. Could he see the message there?

Run, it said. *Run now and don't look back.*

I took the second step and reached out to caress his stubbled jaw. Slowly, still keeping his gaze, I bent forward to his mouth, nuzzling him, letting the sides of my lips brush his, before his tongue found mine. He didn't taste as bad as I'd expected. I pulled out of the kiss and drew away, throwing my dress over my head in one movement and dropping it to the floor, followed by my bra. I brushed my hair off my shoulders, drawing my palms slowly over my nipples as my hands fell to my sides.

'Elisabeth,' he murmured.

The bathtub was positioned at the foot of the bed. As I held out my hand and led him around it towards my Frette sheets, I felt a stifling wave of weariness sigh over me, an absence of that which had once been so familiar. There was no rage left in me, nor any flicker of desire. I let him get on with it, and when he was done I sat up with a giggle in my voice and my eyes all starry. I couldn't have him dozing off. I flopped forward on the dampened sheet, dropping the limp condom with its sad little weight of life onto the floor, and reached out for the hot tap.

'I feel like a bath. A bath and a blunt. Shall we?'

'Sure. Whatever.' Now we'd fucked he'd lost his manners. 'You wanna do those pics?' I'd managed to dissuade him from taking selfies when we'd had drinks earlier. He was already fumbling in his discarded jeans for the sodding phone; it was a miracle he hadn't tried to Instagram his own climax. I'd forgotten, for the few moments he'd humped away inside me, what a total dick he was. This suddenly felt so much easier.

'Snap away, lover. Just a second though.' I trotted naked to the dressing room and scrabbled in a drawer for a packet of Rizla, pausing to connect the Wi-Fi scrambler as a precaution. No more real-time updates for him. I added some cold water and a dollop of almond oil to the bath and opened the heavy antique linen press for a couple of towels. The sweet scent of the oil rose around us in the steam.

'Hop in,' I said over my shoulder as I busied myself loosening the tobacco from a cigarette. My Hermès scarf, the turquoise-and-navy Circassian design, was knotted around the strap of my handbag. I crossed behind him as he eased into the water.

'Just getting a light,' I murmured. 'Here.'

I put the joint between his lips. There was nothing in it, but he'd never know that. While he inhaled I got the scarf round his neck and pulled it up tight beneath his ears. He choked instantly on the smoke, splashing his hands into the deep tub. I braced my feet against its edge and leaned back against the bed, pulling harder. His feet flailed in the water, but there was no purchase on the oily porcelain. I closed my eyes and started counting. His right hand, still absurdly holding the sodden roll-up, was straining to grab at my wrist, but the angle was wrong and his fingers merely fluttered against mine. *Twenty-five ... twenty-six ...* Nothing but the anaerobic fizz in my muscles as we struggled, nothing but the deep rasp of my own breath through my nostrils as his body thrashed. *Twenty-nine, this is nothing, thirty, this is nothing.* I felt him weakening, but then he managed to work a finger and then a fist between the scarf and his Adam's apple and catapulted me violently forward, but the release sent him under and I twisted over the rim of the tub, getting my left knee on his chest and pushing down with all my weight. There was blood in my eye and in the steaming water, but I could see bubbles popping at the surface as he thrashed. I let go of the scarf and reached blindly down for his face and neck. He was twisting his jaw, the yellowed overbite snapping at me. The bubbles stopped. I slowly got my breath back and my face relaxed from its rictus strain. I couldn't see his face through the pinkish milk of the bathwater. I was gingerly easing my pelvis forward when the water slopped up in a wave just before he reared up at me. I fell against him in a straddle as his head strained desperately upwards. I managed to take him under again with my elbow, then manoeuvred myself so that I had one leg on each of his shoulders. We stayed like that for a long time, until a teardrop of blood from my face plopped into the bath.

Perhaps it was the clarity of that one, tiny sound. Perhaps it was the mist of almond oil in the swirling steam, or the cooling scurf on the water's surface. *That cold afternoon, that endless silence, that first dead thing under my hands.* The fault-line inside me split into an engulfing crevasse, and with a force that seared the breath out of me, I was there. Time was suddenly compressed, the past condensed and returned to me. I had left her so long ago. *She had never been part of the life I had told myself, but I was seeing her as though for the first time.* Numbly, I reached again into the deep water, but I found only a stranger's flesh. This had been necessary, although I couldn't now remember why. His hand bobbed up and I paddled the fingers with my own, a watery little tune. It might have been a few minutes that I watched the ripples, it might have been an hour. By the time I came back to myself, the water was chilled.

When I eventually hauled him up from underneath me, his eyes were open. So his last sight on earth would have been my gaping cunt.

His slippery skin was pinkish, puffed out like new bread, the lips already tinged grey. His head lolled back; in the candlelight his throat seemed unmarked. Gripping the side of the bath, I climbed out, legs shaking. As soon as I'd let him go he slid back under and I had to fumble for the plug beneath his bobbing hair. While the water drained, I hunched in one of the towels. When his chest was clear, I rested a hand against his heart. Nothing. I rolled up from the waist and stretched. The floor was soaking, the rim of the bath smeared with blood and specks of tobacco. More hot water to clean him down.

I had to embrace him from the side to heave him over the edge of the bath. His corpse was limp and floppy. When I had him laid out, I covered him with the other towel and sat next to him cross-legged on the floor until he was cold.

I peeled back enough of the towel to expose his face again, bent in and whispered in his ear.

'It's not Elisabeth. It's Judith.'

PART ONE

REFLECTION

1

Eight Weeks Earlier . . .

While I dressed, I played Cole Porter's 'Miss Otis Regrets', the Ella Fitzgerald version. It made me smile. I had turned the bedroom of my flat in Campo Santa Margherita into a dressing room, lined with glass-fronted Molteni wardrobes, my shoes, bags and scarves, and dresses and jackets always companionably visible. That made me smile too. The flat was on the *piano nobile*, looking out over the square with its ancient white-stoned fish market. I'd taken out a wall in the drawing room to form one broad space, with the bathtub positioned at the foot of the bed on a thick green marble plinth, in front of one of the three arched windows. My bathroom, lined in antique Persian tiles, had been installed behind the dressing room, in what had once been a stairwell. It was one of the many joys of Elisabeth Teerlinc's home. The architect had grumbled about supporting beams and permits, but in the nine months since I'd arrived in Venice I'd discovered that the wages of sin make an awful lot of things possible. I'd hung the pictures I'd acquired in Paris – the Fontana, *Susanna and the Elders* and the Cocteau drawing – and added another modern piece, a small untitled Agnes Martin in white and cloud-grey lines that I'd acquired through Paddle8, the online auction house in New York. My other French pieces had joined me too, with the exception of the headless corpse of one Renaud Cleret, which remained hammered down in an art depository near the Château de Vincennes. Whatever the architect thought, I did occasionally worry about leaks.

The handwritten invitation for my first show was tucked into a corner of the mirror. *Elisabeth Teerlinc requests the pleasure of your company at Gentileschi Gallery* . . . I scanned the words yet again as I fastened up my hair. I had done it. I was Elisabeth now. Judith Rashleigh was less than a phantom to me, barely more than a name on the unused passport which lay in my desk drawer. I smoothed my hand over the neatly ordered rack of dresses, relishing the slither of jersey and the supple weight of good silk. I'd chosen a fitted inky shantung Figue dress for the opening, fastened at the back with tiny turquoise and gold buttons like a cheongsam. The deep colour of the fabric glowed as it twined under my fingers. Standard gallerist severity was the look I'd gone for, but somewhere deep inside me a baby unicorn was tossing its mane. I gave my reflection a slow smile; Liverpool was a long way away.

One of my mother's short-lived jobs had been as a cleaner near Sefton Park, the confident Victorian enclave of trees and glasshouses near the centre of the city, three buses from our estate. One day, when I was about ten, I realised at the end of the school day that I'd forgotten my key so I went to find her.

The houses were huge; masses of red brick and bay windows. I pushed the bell several times but no one came, so I nervously tried the door, which was on the latch. The hallway smelled of wax furniture polish and faintly of flowers, the floorboards were bare around a bright square of rug and the space between the doors and the wide curve of the staircase was filled with shelves of thick, heavy-looking books. It was so quiet. Once I'd shut the door softly behind me, there was no hum of tellies, no staccato bawl of couples fighting or kids playing, no revving engines or scrapping pets. Just . . . silence. I wanted to stretch out and touch the spines of the books, but I didn't dare. I called again for my mum, and she appeared in the tracksuit she wore for going cleaning.

'Judith! What are you doing here? Is everything all right?'

'Yeah, I just forgot my key.'

'You gave me the fright of my life! I thought you were a robber.'

She rubbed her hand wearily over her face. 'You'll have to wait. I'm not finished yet.'

There was a big chair at the bottom of the stairs with a tall lamp beside it. I put the lamp on and the room condensed, gleaming around me, so calm, so private. I shrugged off my school backpack and set it neatly under the chair, then went back to the shelves. I think I picked the book because I liked the colour of the spine; a zingy, shocking pink with the title picked out in gold. It said Vogue, Paris, 50 ans. *It was a fashion book, reproductions of women in extraordinary clothes and jewellery, their faces perfect masks of make-up. Slowly I turned a page, slowly another, entranced by the rich, delicate colours. One picture showed a woman in a bright blue ballgown with huge skirts, racing through traffic as though she was running for a bus. I was enthralled. I turned and looked, turned and looked. I wasn't aware of how much time had passed until I realised I was starving. I got creakily to my feet and was putting the book carefully on the seat of the chair when the door slammed open, startling me, making me look crouched and guilty.*

'What are you doing here?' Sharp, a woman's voice, with an edge of fear in it.

'Sorry. I'm sorry. I'm Judith. I forgot my key. I was waiting for my mum.' I gestured vaguely towards the door that had swallowed my mother what felt like hours before.

'Oh. Oh, I see. Is she not finished?'

She indicated for me to follow her down a passage to the back of the house, which opened into a big, cosy kitchen.

'Hello?'

Beyond the table was a sofa whose bright cushions had been tumbled to the floor to make room for my mum.

'Hello?'

I thought I'd seen the wine bottle on the floor before she had, but the resigned tone of the lady's voice soon told me that this wasn't the first time. My mum must have pinched it from the fridge.

'Jus' havin' a little lie-down.'

I was a freezing coal of shame. The lady marched over to the sofa and helped mum to sit up, firmly but not unkindly.

'We've spoken about this before, haven't we? I'm sorry, but I think this had better be the last time you come, don't you? Your daughter is here.' In the emphasis she put on the word, I heard that she was sorry for me.

'I'm sorry, I was just . . .' Mum was dragging at the tracksuit, trying to right herself.

'That's fine.' More tightly now. 'But you had better leave. Please fetch your bag and I'll get your money.' She wasn't being a bitch, that was the thing. She was embarrassed by what she was doing, and that controlled, professional voice was meant to cover it, to push us out onto the street where we could keep our nastiness to ourselves.

I went back and stood by the door with my schoolbag. I didn't want to listen any longer. As the lady handed my mum two twenty-pound notes she must have seen my eyes pull back to the book.

'Why don't you take it? A present?' She bundled it at me, not seeing me anymore. She gave it to me as though it was nothing.

'Fucking snobby cow,' my mum was muttering as she hauled me to the bus stop.

When we eventually got back, she gave me her key and got off first, at the stop by the pub. I thought anxiously of the forty pounds. We wouldn't be seeing them again. I did myself beans on toast and took out the book. The price on the inside cover was sixty pounds. Sixty pounds for a book, and the lady had just given it away. I put the book carefully under my bed, and looked at it so often that in time I knew the names of the photographers and fashion designers by heart. It wasn't that I wanted those clothes, exactly. I just thought that if you were the sort of person who had them, you would feel different. If you owned things like that, you could choose who you wanted to be, every day. You could control your inside with your outside.

I gave my tall heels a rub with their shoe bag before I stepped into them. Maybe the only thing Elisabeth Teerlinc had in common with Judith Rashleigh was that she didn't employ a maid. Becoming Elisabeth had taken so much more than an expensive wardrobe, in the end. Armour only truly protects if it's invisible, and that was where the real struggle had lain. Not just the studying and the exams, but maintaining the conviction that I could win. Getting out of the miserable estate where I'd grown up. Not allowing myself to be subsumed into the squalor of my mother's life. Resisting the taunts, the insidious daily whisperings of 'slag' and 'bitch' that hissed after me along the school corridors just because I'd wanted more. I'd taught myself to hate the girls at school, and then to ignore them, because what were they going to be in a few years but flabby pram-faces in the bus queue? That was the easy part. The difficult bit was eliminating every trace of the gaping prole I'd felt like when I'd finally won a place at university, because people can see it. Not just the sad kid dreaming under the duvet over her precious book of fashion plates and her little collection of art postcards, but the sorry, striving heart inside. Once I'd taken the train south from Lime Street, no one was ever going to see that girl again. Slowly but surely I had erased my accent, changed my manners, learned my languages, shaped and smoothed my defences like a sculptor works marble.

Even that was only the beginning of Elisabeth's demands. For a while, when I'd landed a job at a prestigious London auction house, I'd believed I had made it, but I had no money and no connections, which meant I was never going to rise further than departmental dogsbody. So I took a night job in a hostess bar, the Gstaad Club, because surely a better suit and a nicer haircut would make it come right? I was disabused of this touching belief when I discovered that my boss, Rupert, was involved in a faking scam. He'd taken less than five minutes to show me the door. One of the club's clients, James, had offered me a weekend on the Riviera, and from there things had become a little . . . untidy, for a while. Though ultimately highly profitable, since I'd located and sold the fake that got me fired, and used the money to set up as an art dealer in Paris. Admittedly there had been a few casualties. James hadn't made it back to London, though that hadn't been entirely my doing. And neither had the dealer from whom I'd stolen the fake, Cameron Fitzpatrick; my old school chum, Leanne; Renaud Cleret, an undercover policeman; or Julien, the conniving owner of a Paris sex club. Relocating to Venice as Elisabeth Teerlinc had been a practical necessity. Not least as I wanted to avoid the attentions of a certain police inspector, Renaud's colleague, Romero da Silva. It had taken quite a lot of polish to obscure all that. But Elisabeth's façade had become pretty good, its gleam reflecting only what people wanted to see. It's true what they say – in the end, it's what's on the inside that matters.

2

'Miss Teerlinc? Elisabeth Teerlinc?'

'That's me.'

'I'm Tage Stahl. I hope you don't mind me gate-crashing, but I couldn't help being fascinated by the pieces.'

'I'm delighted.'

'Have you had the gallery long?'

'Not really – just since the spring.'

'Well, it's a wonderful space.'

'Thank you. Please enjoy the show.'

The client drifted off into what felt like a crowd, though Gentileschi only held about thirty people. My space may only have been fifteen paces long, but every stride I took across it belonged to me. The gallery was on the ground floor of the disused naval buildings at the very bottom of the island, near the San Basilio *vaporetto* stop: plain nineteenth-century functional architecture, which contrasted with the glorious view to the east of Giudecca. The beauty of Venice is a bore's topic – one can say nothing that hasn't been said better already – but I liked my gallery better for that, its gesture towards the origins of this city whose enchantments were built on ships and sweat and spices.

My first Italian presentation was a group show of Serbian artists, the Xaoc Collective, who worked out of a squat in Belgrade. The pieces – embroidered collages and canvases set with whimsical found objects – were folksy and deliberately apolitical, undemanding and easy on the eye, as were the prices. And they were selling. They were actually selling. I'd decided to start with a modest August opening. Elisabeth Teerlinc had managed to meet many of the people she needed to know as the Biennale caravan passed through Venice in the spring, but she was a long way off being established. The relatively quiet months around the film festival, when the city belongs mostly to tourists and the dwindling number of Venetians who serve them, had been a perfect time to cultivate my contacts and new identity in preparation for its next arrival.

I'd spent weeks writing the invitations for the viewing, assembling a short press release, choosing the exact grey linen papers for the catalogue and negotiating with a painting firm to re-whitewash the gallery's walls. (Buyers of contemporary art expect white walls the same way they expect works to be confrontational, ambiguous or subversive.) Not much different to the busywork I had done back at my day job at the House in London, but the difference was everything. For a start I had a proper desk, a Poltrona T13, based on the 1953 Albini model, which impressed Italian visitors if no one else, and I could actually sit at it without being harangued for idleness. I didn't have an assistant yet – I'd rounded up a few students from the university to hand round prosecco and take jackets – but they referred to me as 'Signora Teerlinc', rather than 'Er'.

Just for a moment I wished that I could reach back, pull apart the web of all that had happened and show my younger self my future. These guests and these glasses were real, as were the handwritten labels which the students were fixing one after another next to the pieces to show that they were taken. Standing there, poised, polished, confident, even I felt real. My success might have been relatively modest, but it didn't make me feel humbled. It made me feel delighted.

Across the room the Scandi-looking guy, Stahl, was flipping idly through my carefully written catalogue. I watched him signal to one of the students and reach for his wallet. He was buying. I made to walk over, but someone laid a hand on my arm and I turned back. An older man, serious in a proper tweed jacket despite the heat. I assumed he must be a lost tourist, or maybe a professor from the Ca' Foscari university nearby, but the accent of his first careful words of English said Russian, so I nervously tried 'good evening'.

'You speak Russian?'

'Not much, unfortunately.' I switched to English. 'Can I help you?'

'You are Elisabeth Teerlinc?'

'Indeed.'

He offered me a business card, formally, with a little bow. It gave his name, Dr Ivan Kazbich, and the address of a gallery in Belgrade, Serbia. He must have heard of Xaoc then.

'Good. I have come to speak with you on behalf of my employer. Do you have a few moments, please?'

'Oh. Well, certainly,' I answered, intrigued.

'I should prefer to speak with you alone.'

I glanced at my watch. Seven twenty-five. 'Of course – if perhaps you wouldn't mind waiting a little. The show's just about to end.'

He glanced around the walls. Stahl had obviously bought the last three pieces, as every one now showed a 'sold' label in deep crimson ink.

'You must be very pleased.'

'Thank you. If you'll excuse me a moment.'

I went to speak to Stahl, who was lingering as the last of the guests congregated at the door, exchanging goodbyes and plans for dinner. He asked if I would care to join him at Harry's Bar, which ought to have told me everything I needed to know about him right then. If Venice is the greatest masterpiece our species has ever produced, why would one wish to dine in the only place without a view, where the only thing to look at is the joyless grotesques of the clientele? I bit my tongue, explained that I had an appointment and guided him politely but firmly out onto the quay, where the sky was just beginning to mist from sapphire to honeydew. I thanked the helpers, who had stacked the catalogues and tidied away the bottles and glasses, paid them in cash and closed the door behind them before joining Dr Kazbich.

'Forgive me for keeping you waiting.'

'Not at all.'

Kazbich explained that he worked for a collector who was interested in a valuation of his works, which were housed in France. Did I do such work? I hadn't, for a while, but I had valued pieces back at the House, some with surprising results. It was a . . . significant collection, he continued. I knew what that meant. I asked if his client had considered using one of the experts at the IFAR, the International Foundation for Art Research. There was no question of provenance involved, he batted back, with a twitch of a smile that indicated we each knew the other knew what they were talking about. It was merely a private valuation. Dodgy then, but we both knew that too. The kind of offer no respectable girl should take, at least not until she knows how much it's worth. On cue, the mystery employer was offering expenses, naturally, and a 20,000 euro consultation fee, with a further 100,000 on submission of the report. I would make an initial visit to assess the works and would then have two weeks to complete the valuation.

'I could be very interested,' I answered immediately.

I didn't think someone who offered that kind of money would be impressed by time-wasting hesitations. Whatever the client wanted to do with the valuation was very much not my business. Dr Kazbich handed me a thick envelope, the colour of new butter, and waited expectantly while I opened it. Inside was a draft made out to Elisabeth Teerlinc, drawn on a bank in Cyprus, for the first sum, and another slip of paper with just a name. Pavel Yermolov.

For a moment, I stared dully at the name. Overwhelmed doesn't happen to me very often. But Pavel Yermolov. I could see Pavel Yermolov's pictures. Or rather, Pavel Yermolov thought I was good enough to see his pictures. I think Kazbich knew that I would happily have handed him back the money draft with the names reversed for the chance he was giving me.

Yermolov's collection was a mystery, a matter both of legend and greedy rumour. A second-generation oligarch, he was reputed to be a very serious buyer, but he didn't appear in the showrooms himself, preferring to acquire through a series of interchangeable and anonymous intermediaries. He had been connected with successful bids for a Matisse, a Picasso and, less predictably, a Jacopo Pontormo in the past five years, whilst a Pollock had definitely been bought in the name of one of his company trusts. And then there were the Jameson Botticellis.

Named for the American robber baron who had taken them dubiously out of Italy in the nineteenth century, the whereabouts of the Botticellis spun swiftly from rumour into conspiracy. Twinned medallion settings of an *Annunciation* and a *Madonna and Child*, the pictures had not been seen by the public for a hundred and fifty years. Some websperts doubted their existence, claiming that they had been destroyed in a fire at the Jameson property in upstate New York and fraudulently reinsured to augment the family's dwindling assets, others reported sightings in Qatar or Korea. Yermolov's name had been associated with them in a murky sale a decade ago out of Zurich, but no one knew for certain if he owned them.

'The answer is yes. Please tell Mr –'

He cut me off with a theatrical finger to his lips. 'My employer expects total discretion.'

'Of course, forgive me.'

'Not at all, Miss Teerlinc. You have my card. When you are ready to travel, please contact me and I shall make the appropriate arrangements.'

He wasn't wearing a hat, but as the gallery door closed behind him I was sure he had tipped it.

A short while later, in my flat on the Campo Santa Margherita, luxuriating in the bathtub with a glass of Soave, I was clutching the card like a talisman. I loved lying there in the early evenings, listening to the children playing in the square below, the girls swinging a washing-line skipping rope, the boys with their footballs and skateboards, as the market vendors packed up their boxes of squid and *moleche* and the cafés filled with tourists and students. It felt . . . neighbourly.

I was trying to visualise the pieces in Yermolov's collection. The only thing I missed about my job at the House was the pictures themselves. So far, I had managed to avoid handling anything for which I felt actual contempt, but I couldn't pretend to myself that the works Gentileschi had just sold were very much more than specious pieces of crap. I missed not only that initial sucker punch of beauty, but the privilege of spending time with paintings, the almost erotic anticipation provoked by their slow revelations, the way one could swoon into a picture, look and look again and still be moved, or disturbed, or astonished. My first visit to the National Gallery as a schoolgirl had changed my life, and ever since, paintings had been the only things that had never let me down. And fags, I suppose.

Thinking over my plans for the autumn, I realised Yermolov's offer was not just extraordinarily flattering, but perfectly timed. The profits from the Balkan show would cover the gallery's expenses for a while, but my flat and the work on it had eaten just over half of my available funds. Being rich is so *expensive*. I could have rented something when I arrived in Venice nine months ago, but the hunger for a place – a home, even – that was at last unassailably mine had been too powerful for prudence. The flat was owned by Gentileschi, paid for in cash through the gallery's bank in Panama. I hoped to move eventually into the secondary market, selling good pre-owned pictures, but for the present I lacked the cash flow to deal anything other than 'young artists', under the 100K mark. Still, new work, which had no value beyond its status as currency, could be extremely lucrative if fashion was on its side. So I needed something splashy for the new season, a discovery that I could buy cheap and sell high next spring.

There was a Danish girl who interested me; I'd seen her graduate show at St Martin's in London online, and there was a series of simple graphic canvases, strangely compelling gold-ish orbs on sombre backgrounds that I thought would show very well against the syrupy light of the lagoon. Maybe a private view at dusk, if I could get them . . . Then there was my Russian to plod on with; it had seemed a practical language to have in my trade, now that so many Russians were buying art in the West, but it now looked as if I would need it sooner than I'd thought. I didn't delude myself that Yermolov and I would be conversing in fluent Russian (if he even deigned to be present), but the sounds of the language were beginning to gel, and I thought I should make the effort to manage the basic courtesies.

I'd found a retired opera singer, Masha, who lived in an actual garret behind La Fenice, where she gave Russian lessons. My tutor was a born Venetian, the child, so she said, of a couple of Russian opera singers who had escaped the Soviet Union while on tour to Italy just after the Second World War, but she still spoke Italian with a thick accent, and her dim studio, up six flights of ever-narrower stairs, looked like a stage set for an amateur-dramatic production of Chekhov. Icons squatted on every surface that wasn't draped with heavy fringed piano shawls. There was a real samovar, shelves of Russian poetry and a faint miasma of boiling pork fat. Masha must have been nearing eighty and had never set foot in Russia, but she presented herself as pure White, describing scenes from her parents' lives back in Petersburg which could only have been gleaned from novels, and sniffily correcting the inflections of the presenters on the Russian radio stations she tuned into to help me practise. '*Off*,' she snapped in crisp disgust, rolling her eyes beneath her brioche of dyed black hair, 'not *ovvv*. A tragedy, a tragedy,' as though the combined evils of Stalinism had been distilled into the mispronunciation of a patronymic. Altogether she was a fabulous old fraud. Maybe that was why I liked her so much.

3

As it turned out, I had plenty of time for extra classes, since arranging the Yermolov valuation took over a month. Time for the rich is scalar, as I'd learned from my friend Steve, the hedgie whose boat, the *Mandarin*, had proved both my refuge and the launch pad for my gallery. The rich are immune to the directions of their implicit inferiors; the calendar shifts or stretches only according to their own needs. Dr Kazbich had given me the number of a Madame Poulhazan, Yermolov's assistant, who briskly scheduled and then rescheduled the meeting over the following weeks. I was relieved when she told me he would put his plane at my disposal, but twice I made the trip to the airport by water taxi only to learn that Yermolov had cancelled. He was in São Paulo; in New York; at an emergency meeting in London; he was no longer available.

I used the delays to assess the potential of the collection, noting the last recorded sale prices of pieces Yermolov supposedly owned, checking them against comparable sales on Artprice Index and adding background on the movements of pictures known to have been released in the past decade. By the time the day of the trip finally crawled around, I felt I was as ready as I could be. My research had thrown up that Yermolov owned four planes, and even by the standards of Marco Polo airport, his Dassault stood out. Not for its colour, a nice discreet navy blue, but for the four uniformed cabin staff waiting patiently on the tarmac to greet me as though I was on a state visit, the two hostesses gamely adjusting their neat little caps in the runway wind.

I declined vodka, champagne, caviar with blinis and cold-pressed kale juice, accepting with just a slight wince an Armani-branded water as we took off. Until we broke the clouds, I watched the glorious pink rock of the Dolomite mountains swooping beneath me, their heights decorated with the first snows, then settled back to review my notes on the assiduous hostesses' boss. Everyone knew about Yermolov, but what I knew was what everyone knew, which was essentially nothing. Yermolov fitted the boilerplate of the new-school oligarch: early training in what used to be the KGB, extensive interests in minerals and industrial agriculture, close ties with the government, officially resident in Russia though with homes in France, London, Anguilla and Switzerland. A feature in *Architectural Digest* on the sculptor Taïs Bean showed a chandelier she had created for Yermolov's ski house. I had been surprised at first to learn that he was also a politician, a regional governor in his native Caucasus, but cross-referencing with his peers suggested that this was a not-uncommon way of demonstrating loyalty to good old Mother Russia. *Forbes*, *Spears* and the *FT* threw up nothing controversial, and I had also tried back numbers of the *Rossiyskaya Gazeta* and the Russian financial journal *Vedomosti*, but despite my efforts with Masha my Russian still felt rudimentary, and it had been hard going to turn up anything unpredictable. Yermolov attended the usual charity balls and occasional think-tank wankfests, pitched up in Davos and Yerba Buena, had inevitably been photographed with Elton John and Bono, but compared with his predecessors in the last generation of post-Soviet cowboys, he was distinctly unflamboyant. His wealth was officially respectable and solidly undisputed. The collection might be a mystery, but since Yermolov did not appear to attend any of the major biennales and had not been photographed hobnobbing at the Garage in Moscow, I was forced to conclude that he might actually like pictures.

When we landed at Nice, the hostesses fussed me towards a waiting Maybach, navy like the plane. The door was held open by a standard issue Shrek-in-a-suit; holster and platysmas bulging. I appreciated his familiarity, we might well have been old friends, but I did wonder whether a bodyguard as well as a driver wasn't a little excessive. The muscles sat in the front as the car peeled along the autoroute towards Toulon, turning off just past Saint-Tropez. We paused at a pair of gates for the driver to enter a security code, then set off again along an avenue lined with plane trees, gold-dappled in the heaviness of early autumn. We dipped and climbed; ahead I could see the faint thrilling sparkle of the Mediterranean. Another pair of gates loomed, but this time the driver swung off the road and down a concrete ramp, where a garage door was already rising to admit us. We continued down in sudden bluish twilight, until another door slid up and the car pulled up in a tight, low concrete box. The driver opened the door and directed me to a round glass booth set in an alcove in the wall.

'In here, please, madame. Just a moment.'

The curved door of the booth swung shut and a light hummed and buzzed in the ceiling – some sort of X-ray scanner? I was released and the driver solemnly put my bags through the same process before carrying them to a lift in the opposite wall. The three of us rode up in silence, until the doors opened on a view that made me giggle with joy.

We stood at the top of a shallow slope, with a gravelled sweep stretching down to Yermolov's villa, framed in pine and poplar, with the sea beyond. The house was pale pink, nineteenth century, overblown and frivolous as a wedding gâteau, a house for a Colette courtesan, for jasmine-scented trysts and borrowed beds, the kind of house that would once have been staked on the turn of a card at the Monte Carlo casino. After the slightly sinister security proceedings below, its absurd prettiness wafted a delicate, exquisite scent of a vanished fin de siècle dream world. As we made our way to the pale lime double doors, set with a huge brass lion's head, concealed spigots beneath the gravel began to play over the lawns on either side, so that we passed through a fountain of rainbows. I half expected to hear a waltz. Sometimes vulgarity can be so delightful.

A suitably ponderous butler showed Miss Teerlinc to her room on the first floor. More double doors opened into a small octagonal antechamber lined with rosewood boiseries, a balcony on one side and the bedroom on the other. But I barely noticed the surroundings as a burst of heavy lily-scented air tumbled towards me and it was all I could do to mutter my thanks before I sank down on a bed which could have been in another room, long ago, a room where I had waited next to a swollen body suddenly vulnerable in death. Now I waited again for my blood to stop its whistling and churning in my ears.

Maybe I'm shallow that way, but I don't spend a great deal of time thinking about the past. Contingency and reaction are what I understand. Yet that same thick reek had pervaded the room at the Hôtel du Cap where I had found James's corpse; I had not thought of that place for so long, yet the huge arrangement of parchment-petalled calla lilies made me believe, for a moment, that I had never really left it. Was I really still mired there, trapped forever with my shaking hands in a dead man's wallet?

I noticed a familiar heavy cream envelope next to the vase on the nightstand. I opened it with my teeth and one hand, while the other began methodically breaking the flower heads from their stems, unfastening the chain to that moment with every snap. The stamens released orange dust clouds, which stained my cuffs as I read:

Miss Teerlinc,

I hope that your journey was pleasant and that you are comfortable. Please do not hesitate to ask should there be anything you require. You will be shown the collection when you are ready, and afterwards I look forward to your company at dinner. My thanks for your visit.

Yours faithfully,

P. Yermolov

My eyes wandered over the page several times, before the last lily fell to the floor. That woke me up. My pretty silk Chloe blouse was irreparable. 'Fuck, Judith,' I said aloud. 'Sort it out.' But then I stopped myself. There was a mess on the rug, but this was my new world. Someone would take care of it. I was no longer the girl who had struggled for control in that airless room. I was rich, I was independent, I was free, and I was here. On my own terms, as a professional. Wasn't I living proof that if you just believe in yourself and follow your dream you can be anything you want? The dead proofs it was perhaps best not to dwell on. I was all about the power of now, me. No use for history, and Proust and his aunt's linden-blossom tea could screw themselves. I found the bathroom and ran cold water on my wrists, busied myself showering and changing, cleaned my face and pinned back my hair sternly. I had got this far, and it was going to take more than a remembered perfume to throw me off. Time to go to work.

By the time the grunt accompanied me through the villa's grounds to the stark modern cube where Yermolov housed his art, I was feeling quite like myself. I had chosen a black Max Mara shift with stout Marni clogs – hideous, but, I thought, suitably artsy against the plain silk. I had a measuring tape and a record of dimensions in my briefcase, along with a flashlight and magnifying loupe – it's surprising how many fakes have been passed off because experts neglect the basics. I also had an old-school Polaroid, since I didn't imagine I would be allowed to use my phone to take pictures. I was handed over to a disapproving Frenchwoman in a skirt suit similar to those worn by Yermolov's plane staff. This was Madame Poulhazan, the assistant with whom I had been dealing. Her tone was efficient and civil, but the long appraisal she gave both my legs and my briefcase made it plain that she hated having to admit me. Was I too young, or just insufficiently awed? Tinted glass doors slid open once she had gone through a complex procedure of iris recognition and security codes, then we stepped down into a crepuscular lobby smelling of ozone and varnish.

'*Alors*, mademoiselle. This is a non-disclosure agreement. You will sign here, and here, and here, please.'

The document was three pages, in English, so detailed that I had to sign away not only my right to discuss or communicate in any form whatsoever the contents of the collection, but practically promise to erase them from my memory. Still, I scribbled Elisabeth's signature. Madame then scanned me all over with an illuminated device that looked like a luxury vibrator, poked dubiously among my papers and triumphantly ejected the Polaroid.

'This is not permitted.'

'I'll need it for the assessment.'

'You don't trust your eyes?' she sneered.

I could have said it was Yermolov's I had no faith in, but that wouldn't have helped, so I suggested politely that she telephone to the house for permission, and had the pleasure of her disgust when it was granted. Yet another pause while she entered a lengthy code for the final lock, and we were in.

The floor was malachite, but the sound of my clumpy heels on its glassy surface couldn't have given me more pleasure had it been beaten emerald. If I had been disarmed by the clutch of anxiety evoked by the scent of lilies in my bedroom, now I recalled the miles I had trudged down the endless corridors of the House, the months of tedious errands, crossing and re-crossing London's pavements, a tapestried path that led back to the first time I had really *seen* a painting, in the National Gallery, and which had carried me here, professional, independent, respected even. It's rare to know, in a given moment, that you have exactly what you wanted, and for a few seconds I felt weightless, lifted on a coil of time, effortlessly present in my own accomplishment. *Not bad, Judith. Not bad at all.* I opened my eyes to see Madame staring at me enquiringly. I wouldn't give her the pleasure of seeing that I was impressed, but though I had seen quite a few extraordinary spaces, I had never seen anything like Yermolov's.

The room was long and high, as softly lit as though by candles. Two Breuer sofas in toothpaste-white suede stood back to back in the centre, with a few other seats – harp-back Regency chairs in glowing beech, a Louis XIV bergère in grey silks grouped about them – a conversation piece waiting for characters. Without taking another step, I recognised the Pollock and the Matisse – the *Maison à Tahiti* which had caused a sensation in New York when an anonymous buyer had apparently walked in off the street and bid nearly forty million dollars for it five years previously – three Picassos, a Rembrandt, two Breughels, a Cézanne, a Titian – fuck, a Titian; who actually owns a Titian? – Pontormo's *Young Gentleman in a Red Cap*. It was dizzying. I had to repress the urge to run between the pictures placing my hands above their luminous surfaces to absorb the thrill of them. The left wall was Russian artists, a swirling Vrubel dragon, a Grigoriev, a Repin, merging into a Poussin, then a series of Klimt landscapes.

'And here, the drawings.' Madame was pointing a remote at a panel below the Klimts. A hatch slid open with the gentlest whirr, and a steel container like a giant old-fashioned CD rack emerged. As she manipulated the controls, they flipped past, a Ferris wheel of charcoals and aquaforte, every one of them a major piece in its own right.

My elation turned as bitter as a caviar martini. I'd expected the responsibility to be daunting, even been excited by the challenge of it, but this was impossible. There was just too much, and the too much was too good. I needed a team of assistants, ladders, gloves, Christ knew what equipment. I hardly dared to touch these things, let alone attempt to value them. What was Yermolov playing at? Why would a man who owned a collection like this even consider using a solitary, unknown gallerist to value works whose beauty abruptly felt like a taunt?

Madame had seated herself primly on one of the sofas, her lipsticked mouth twisted in a tight, expectant little smile. *Show no fear.*

'I understood that there were some Renaissance works?' was the best defiance I could manage.

'Naturally. This way.'

I followed her along the gallery, my head drooping now she couldn't see it. The end wall was blank, which somehow only emphasised the treasures leading up to it. Madame set her palm against another concealed panel and a tiny door slid open, as though we were stepping into a medieval monk's cell. Inside, I didn't bother to conceal my astonishment. The tiny room was a copy of the famous *studiolo* of the Duke of Urbino, entirely panelled in intricate wood intarsia, the trompe l'oeil images interspersed with the classical philosophers the Renaissance revered. My eyes bounced over its swirl and gleam. And then, so close I could have reached them both with a single stretch of my arms, two medallion settings, two luminous enamelled faces, two touchably moulded chins beneath inquiring grey eyes, two blond heads veiled in gauze so delicate it seemed to float towards my astonished face. The *Annunciation* and the *Madonna and Child*. They were here. The paintings I had studied but never seen, that hardly anyone living had ever seen. The Jameson Botticellis. Now I began to see the point of Yermolov's paperwork.

'Are those the Jameson Botticellis? The real ones?' I couldn't keep the awe from my voice.

'Quite so,' Madame responded. She was warming up a bit; perhaps I shouldn't have bothered with the blasé routine. Only a fool could fail to be dumbstruck. It was as much as I could do to remain standing. The third picture, facing us, was covered with a heavy green velvet curtain. Gingerly I tugged it aside.

'Oh.'

I had named my gallery for Artemisia Gentileschi, the painter I had fallen in love with when I was in my teens. Artemisia had painted her way over prejudice and poverty, even over rape, had chosen boldness, had refused to submit to a world which had defiled and dismissed her. In 1598, when Artemisia Gentileschi was still a little girl, her father and teacher Orazio spent many wild nights in the company of his friend, a northern Italian painter named Michelangelo Caravaggio. They were good times for bad boys in Rome. Caravaggio and his friends peacocked about like rackety rock stars, picking fights, running whores, swaggering sword-side through the taverns of the Roman underworld high on wine and white lead. Caravaggio, named for the armed archangel, made a picture that year of remorseless virtuosity, shattering pagan luminosity. It was a gift from his patron, Cardinal del Monte, to Ferdinando de' Medici of Florence, a self-portrait as the Gorgon Medusa. The painting is a convex poplar-wood shield, a rendering of the bronze weapon Perseus used to reflect the Gorgon's petrifying glare while he killed her. To look directly into the enchantress's eyes would have turned Ovid's hero to stone. Caravaggio gave the monster his own face, Medusa's last agonised awakening as her sleeping head was struck from her body by Perseus's sword. But Caravaggio intuited somehow that space curves as sinuously as the mink bristles of a paintbrush, it cannot stand still, and that time speeds or slows according to its position within gravity. On the Medusa shield, the concave shadows of the writhing, snake-crowned head belie the convexity of the surface. This is where the two planes intersect, where, momentarily, time falters. At the coincidence of our eyes with the Medusa's, Caravaggio freezes the universe to capture the moment of death, screaming his defiance of the laws of art. We are safe; we can look away and look again at this work which transcends a painter's depiction to become, in a superlatively arrogant display of bravura, the thing which is painted. This is the Lombard nobody in his tattered cast-off finery proving he could play God on a piece of wood. Hold this, painter tells patron, and you stop time.

'Oh.'

Even the copy was breathtaking. If I hadn't seen the real thing in the Uffizi, I would have believed I was looking at the genuine Caravaggio. *Could Yermolov . . . ? No, surely –*

'It is a copy of course,' Madame added helpfully, before I fell any further down the rabbit hole. 'Mr Yermolov wanted a third piece for the room.'

'It's still wonderful.'

'For the present.'

I covered the picture, opened the curtain again, Medusa's face snatched at my heart. I turned slowly and looked back into the gallery. The little room was the core of a flame. Beyond it, the colours of the paintings danced and shone.

'Thank you,' I said sincerely. 'Thank you for showing me this.'

It was hard to wrench myself away from those pictures, yet I was more curious than ever to meet Yermolov. What kind of *will* did it take to acquire such a collection? To own the Jameson Botticellis and keep them hidden? Moreover, why had he really asked me here? When I had met Dr Kazbich we'd both known the private valuation wasn't kosher. It happens in the art world all the time – even places like the House produce dubious valuations, often for insurance or tax, but as far as Yermolov knew I had no such background. I presumed Kazbich had been led to my gallery by the Belgrade connection – his business was there, as were the Xaoc Collective. Perhaps Yermolov had demanded someone in a hurry and I'd just been lucky. The hope of seeing the Botticellis – not to mention the money – had been enough to persuade me, even if I hadn't been selected for the most respectable reasons. Yet, after seeing the quality of his collection, that felt much less plausible. Somehow I believed that a person who *loved* art the way Yermolov clearly did would go to the finest in the business, as his pictures merited.

The butler told me that Mr Yermolov was expecting me for drinks on the terrace at eight, but I changed hastily and was down by a quarter to, hoping to catch him selling a nuclear submarine perhaps. In fact, my host was doing nothing more thrilling than reading *The Economist*. Yermolov was tall, narrow-shouldered but strong-looking, with fair hair and colourless northern eyes. He was dressed in that nondescript manner that only very rich men can afford to affect: plain shirt and navy chinos, a cheap digital watch. Yermolov rose to greet me with an odd look – questioning, slightly amused, as though we were already familiar. While he pulled out my chair and offered me a glass of champagne, I noticed that there was something sedate and controlled about his movements; a graceful calm which might have been charming, were it not for his hands. Long and delicate, they spidered around the stem of his glass, picked at the seams of his linen napkin, twitched the little dishes of olives and cornichons into spiral formations. Combined with the military echo of his blond buzz cut, the hands unnerved me; they conjured airless interrogation rooms, yellowed files twitched from battered cabinets, pencils poised to strike out a life in Siberia between sips of tepid bitter coffee. Their restless energy belied his physical poise, something greedy in their endless clutching.

'Welcome, Miss Teerlinc. I'm so glad you could take some time away from the cut and thrust of the art world.' He smiled at his own attempt to be funny. I gave my best version of a silvery laugh.

'I'm delighted to be here.'

Yermolov seemed to be appraising me quietly as we drank the aperitif, making small talk about my journey and the view. Later we moved to a summerhouse overlooking the water for dinner. The servants came and went with ceviche of sea bass, then langouste baked in filo pastry, while the waves fluttered politely against the shore three hundred feet below. Candles flickered along the path towards the terrace, over Yermolov's right shoulder I could follow their glow to the shore, down a staircase carved out of the sheer face of the rock. Yermolov smoked, which was jolly, his conversation was effortfully courteous and the Chassagne-Montrachet was excellent, but I felt somehow uneasy. I couldn't square that feeling with my knowledge that here was the man who had acquired that *wunderkammer* of beauty, humming in its pale box just down the hill.

I stuck to form for the first courses, business only once the plates are cleared, so we discussed the best seasons to visit Venice and the Caribbean, the renovation of the French house, which he had owned for five years, the new architecture of Moscow, on which I'd read an article before I flew down. Groups of citizen vigilantes were now patrolling the city centre at night, hoping to catch arsonists who were destroying old buildings to make way for developments. And then we talked of Lermontov, since as he was from the Caucasus he loved Lermontov, and he quoted a long passage from *The Demon*, in that disarming way that Russians can, and I began to rather like him. The hands twirled and played as we were served a pudding course of tiny violet crèmes brûlées, which neither of us touched, and I stayed silent then, waiting for his questions.

'So – I believe you spent time in New York before moving to Venice. Or was it Paris?'

I froze. Elisabeth Teerlinc had never set foot in Paris.

'I'm from Switzerland actually.'

'Forgive me. My mistake.'

I was suddenly conscious of how isolated we were, far from the house, far from anything. I hadn't told anybody where I was because – well, there wasn't anyone to tell. *Nothing to be anxious about, he's a busy man. You're basically staff. Why shouldn't he make a mistake?* I lifted my wine glass.

'Do you feel you have had some time to begin considering my collection?'

'It was a privilege to see it, yes.'

'And you think you can evaluate it?'

I put down my own glass.

'Mr Yermolov, I should be honest. I'm extremely flattered that you have asked me to come here, and I'm very grateful for your hospitality, but a collection like yours – I wouldn't really trust myself to value it. I think it would be better if you were to commission one of the major houses in London or New York.'

If he was displeased he didn't show it, except perhaps that the quavering hands knotted themselves together and were still.

'You consider yourself . . . unqualified? But why? Your gallery seems successful.'

As I began to answer him my eyes were suddenly distracted by a movement on the cliff path below. A flash of blonde hair caught in the candlelight, the sheen of a woman's bare shoulder. Yermolov did not turn his head, but spoke sharply in Russian from the side of his mouth and I couldn't help jumping as a bodyguard ghosted from behind one of the summerhouse columns and began to descend the steps. I'd had no idea that he was there and I didn't know if that made me frightened or relieved.

'Forgive me. We are sometimes troubled by trespassers here.'

'It's such an irresistible spot.'

I didn't believe him. The place had better security than 10 Downing Street. What trespasser could have got so close?

'You were saying?'

'Of course. You are very kind, but I would hardly describe the gallery as especially successful – yet.' I paused, fiddled with my spoon, fudged. 'Quite simply, I only . . . took over . . . at Gentileschi about a year ago. And we deal mostly in contemporary work.'

'I had understood you were also knowledgeable about Old Masters.' He caught my eye inquisitively.

What did he mean? Nothing. Stop being paranoid.

'I'm trained, but by no means an authority. The breadth and value of your pieces is exceptional, as you know. I wouldn't feel confident in attributing an accurate market value to them.'

'But you would consider doing so nonetheless?'

I did consider. Now I knew what was there, I could go back through the sales reports for the past few years, consult Artprice, compare projections for similar works, the kind of thing I had done all the time back at the House. Daunting, but not impossible.

'If you are troubled about authentication, the provenances are all impeccable. It is only the valuation that I require.'

'I would –'

There were voices nearby, speaking Russian, a woman and the bodyguard. I heard her hiss, 'I want to speak to him,' and then the man's deeper voice, the tone soothing, something I didn't understand and then the word 'impossible'.

'Excuse me, Miss Teerlinc.'

Yermolov rose unhurriedly and disappeared into the purple night. He didn't raise his voice, but I heard him speak clearly.

'Get rid of her. I'll deal with it in the morning.'

He didn't know I could speak a little Russian, but then again he hadn't asked. I wondered if the night-time stroller even realised how dangerous her walk could have been, and not because of the gradient of the cliff. The fact that I hadn't yet seen a Kalashnikov didn't mean they weren't there, and after seeing the gallery I could understand why they might need to be. There was something in the icy calmness of Yermolov's voice that suggested he wouldn't hesitate to use one personally.

'Again, forgive me.' The hands picked up his napkin, hovered, placed it back down.

I realised that what made Yermolov scary was his sheer lack of scariness. He didn't need to be intimidating. The calm was not a disguise for ruthlessness, simply a confirmation of it. I was annoyed at how sexy that suddenly made him.

'Where were we?' he asked.

I was sure that, given time, I could do a fair job. Yet something about the quality of the pictures made me resist. They deserved the best, and loath as I was to admit it to myself, the best was not me, not yet.

'Mr Yermolov, may I ask why you chose me for the valuation?'

'Dr Kazbich suggested you. He buys for me.' He had become impatient at the slightest hint that I was wasting his time.

'Mr Yermolov, you can be assured of my discretion. And I am honoured to have seen your works. But I simply don't believe I am the right person for the job. It would need a team of experts, assistants . . .' I trailed off. In just a few words, I had bored him. As I expected, he made a few more desultory remarks, then excused himself, explaining he had calls to take. I was of no use, therefore of no further interest.

The next morning Yermolov did not even trouble to say goodbye. I never imagined I would see him again, nor did I have any idea how much I would come to wish that had been the case.

4

Like most of the stupider things I have done, Ibiza was my own decision. I hadn't paid much attention to Tage Stahl at the view in August, but he'd persisted in calling and messaging. It turned out he was Danish, something to do with ships. Then he threw a house party on his private island off Ibiza's north coast; I asked him for the hell of it if he would send the plane, and he said of course, so then accepting felt like a point of style.

After my trip to meet Yermolov, La Serenissima was frankly not feeling all that serene. I didn't regret my decision – indeed my choice not to value the collection felt like a form of loyalty to my true self, whoever she was. I'd kept my faith with the paintings by refusing to become involved in whatever Yermolov was planning. But the way I'd handled it rankled. I hadn't felt so awkward and wrong-footed since my days at the House. A smart party was just what Elisabeth Teerlinc needed to restore her plumage. Besides, I was irritated with my flat. Usually just being there among my beautiful things calmed me, but I seemed to be misplacing stuff – cups and glasses cluttered up my customarily immaculate kitchen and I'd apparently bought a bar of chocolate by mistake. I found it in the cupboard next to the spices. Ninety-eight per cent cocoa, with almond flakes. Weird. I hated almonds even more than I hated dark chocolate.

I arrived on Ibiza mid-afternoon. A nippy dark van zoomed me across the tarmac to the concourse; from the state of the crowd in the airport it didn't seem to be the happiest time of day. Homeless huddles of sleeping revellers twitched beside shrink-wrapped wheelie cases, a group of girls whose flowered face paint had smudged to bruises quarrelled feebly at the easyJet counter, two implacable cleaners in hairnets and turquoise overalls pushed wide mops through a spreading pool of apricot-coloured vomit. David Guetta, a malevolently Ray-Banned dictator, stared down from everywhere. I found Stahl's driver, who loaded me into an open black Jeep which wheezed and rumbled through exhaust fumes and chirruping cicadas, past the turn-off for the white citadel above the port, past pizzerias and yoga studios and hoarding after hoarding promising DJ Nirvana, until the motorway narrowed and we began to climb through soft green hills with low white fincas on their brims. It was my first time on the famous island, and I could see that it really must have been lovely, once.

I began to get the point of Ibiza even more when we finally stopped at a sign for a beach named Agua Blanca, pulling up in a dusty car park full of more Jeeps and mopeds. The driver carried my bag down a steep track which opened on to a milky bay, where naked children played in the long shallows between tall columns of reddish rock. I slipped off my flats and felt that little surge of pleasurable freedom that always comes with sand between the toes. Further along the shore, a group of dreadlocked jugglers, also naked, were spinning batons, while sunbathers caked in drying white clay roasted above the surf line. I picked my way through them to a jetty, where the driver was untying a grey dinghy, and we set off, bouncing a little as we hit the current, towards the smaller island, its two green and white cliffs opening like a butterfly's wings, which broke the horizon.

Stahl's spanking new villa may have been done out like a tiki bar, but that view over the strait to the Agua Blanca beach was surely the best that money could buy, which presumably was why Stahl had bought it. Stacked over the hillside in cubes of steel and limed glass, every room of the villa seemed open to the sea. There were no other guests in evidence when I disembarked, apart from an emaciated woman in a Norma Kamali caftan poking dispiritedly at what had to be an egg-white omelette at one end of the huge curved terrace. A maid showed me to my room and began unpacking for me while I rootled awkwardly around her busy hands for a bikini and a pair of cut-offs. On the terrace, the caftan had abandoned her eggs and I took an apricot from the debris on her tray, sliding my teeth through its chalky juice while I watched the pale shore a kilometre away. A wooden staircase carved with grimacing Polynesian heads descended to the deserted pool, a huge oval basin of pale grey marble. The water looked deliciously smooth, but before I had a chance to try it, Stahl appeared fresh from the tennis court, and something about his tanned height, the hardness of his torso and his lapis lazuli eyes reminded me of a happy Scandinavian afternoon two summers ago. I had been living very quietly indeed in Venice after all, so that deal was sealed in his vast Balinese bed with enthusiasm, if not much skill on his part, by the time everyone else had finished their early-afternoon breakfast. The world seemed calmer after that. Altogether, I was quite set for a jolly weekend.

The house party were reviving themselves with rosé and joints around the pool when my host and I reappeared, and Stahl introduced me to the usual combination of greying men and hungry women, a mixture I was familiar with from my first jaunt around the Mediterranean. I declined both weed and wine, but plunged willingly enough into the talk of where everyone had been and where they were going next, until I was interrupted in a discussion of the relative merits of Pantelleria over Patmos by a hand on my shoulder.

'Hi, darling. I'm Alvin.'

It wasn't the ubiquitous 'darling' that bothered me. More the fact that, unlike the other men, Alvin was close to my own age, maybe younger even, and that there was something sly and insinuating beneath the friendliness of his American accent that sent a feather-brush of ice across my skin.

'Elisabeth Teerlinc. Hi – I don't think we've met?'

'Not in person.'

'How intriguing.'

'We're friends on Facebook.'

'Oh, right.'

Judith Rashleigh didn't exist online, but Elisabeth Teerlinc, successful gallerist, kept up a dutiful connection with social media. Dissidence would have been too conspicuous, so every few days I spent a reluctant half-hour accepting and posting, anodyne stuff mostly, no personal pictures, and always related to Gentileschi. I wasn't too vigilant about accepting friends – refusals would be more conspicuous. Alvin was gangly and red-haired, with an unattractively soggy mouth; I didn't recognise him, but then I could see why he mightn't use a personal picture for his profile. He had the slightly mangy look of the wealthy stoner.

'You have a space in Venice, right?'

'That's right.' I smiled cautiously.

'I just finished a year at the Courtauld. My dad works with Tage.'

'Lucky you. The Courtauld Institute, I mean. Though I'm sure your dad's delightful.'

When he returned my smile I saw that his teeth were discordantly unpatriotic, snaggled and thickly furred with plaque around the gums.

'Yeah, it's cool, but I'm not really into that museum stuff, you know?' I had an ominous feeling that he was about to start telling me about the about the app he was working on, so I excused myself for a refill of iced tea, but somehow the shadow of that lupine grin stayed with me all through the length of the hot afternoon.

Tage's 'party boat', a bronze-hulled Razan 47, ferried us back to the mainland that evening, where we were to join another house party at a villa for dinner. After the flattening, creamy heat of Venice, the Ibiza air felt clear, and though the cicadas' humming was drowned by the thump of a Garrix track as the Jeeps climbed into the hills, the music couldn't swallow the pine resin of the maquis or the honeysuckle breeze from the low white walls of the house. The wedge-heeled women leaned delightedly on the men's arms as we crossed a gravel courtyard filled with more Jeeps, a huge open-topped Bentley and a red Ferrari.

I was irritated to note that there was a part of me that remained surprised and excited to find myself within such a tableau, or at least without a tray in my hands. But old habits die hard; if you're not entitled, be prepared. Just as I had done back at college, I'd looked up the right things to know about Ibiza, so when I recognised the remodelled farmhouse as the style of Blakstad, an architect who was imitated in the most expensive builds on the island, I could compliment our host on his taste as Tage introduced me.

'This is Elisabeth. She sold me the Xaoc pieces I have in Copenhagen.'

'You are a dealer?'

'Only modestly.' I smiled. 'Very much a beginner.'

'She has a fantastic eye!' enthused Tage, squeezing my hand.

Our host was another Dane, ponderous and balding, with a signet ring and an American wife at least twenty years his junior. 'You guys are just adorable together!' she squeaked at Tage, who didn't look displeased by the misunderstanding, 'How did you meet?'

'Oh, a little while ago. In Venice,' I offered.

'I love Venice – oh my God how romantic. We always stay at the Danieli – you know the Danieli? I love Italy so much. We went to Sardinia last year – where did we stay on Sardinia, Sveyn?'

'On Tage's boat.'

'Oh, sure we did. No, I was thinking of Tuscany – where did we stay in Tuscany?'

It seemed we might remain in that conversational loop until we got to the Austrian border, so I drew her gently away and admired the flowers, braided arrangements of orange blossom looped around black figs stretched across the centre of the long table.

'These are so clever!' I trilled. 'You must be exhausted.'

As a rule, I found the richer the husband, the more exhausted the wife. It was a safe gambit.

'Oh God, you know, I've been doing this dinner for, like, a week. I told Sveyn, I told him, I am doing absolutely nothing after this, you know? Nothing. It's been crazy.'

I looked past her along the table, set perpendicular to the pool, which dropped off the cliff between two huge driftwood sculptures, white-painted. Four servers in dark jackets were setting out ice boats of sushi; another was lighting bronze fire bowls at the rim of the deck. Two more were pouring champagne and rosé, another was handing round tiny rolls of Ibérico ham and pickled ginger. She must have been knackered.

'I mean, I like to keep things simple, you know?' She was giggling now. 'I mean, this is Ibiza, everyone is really chilled, but still –'

'It's a lot of work, making things beautiful for other people,' I finished sincerely.

'My God, you just get it, don't you, Elsie? Total girl crush!' she squealed at Tage, who had kindly come to rescue me.

There was no placement at dinner, because of it being so chilled; Tage sat next to me, with a woman in a pompommed Vita Kin sundress on my other side. She talked across me to Tage for some time without introducing herself, asking detailed questions about the Ibiza Polo Club, lots of mentions of *patrons* and whom she had seen at Cowdray. We were kindred spirits, in style if not execution. It was only when Tage fed me a piece of ahi tuna with white truffle while nuzzling my neck that she got the point, and in fairness didn't miss a beat, shoved her henna-tattooed hand into mine, took a game slug of rosé and told me that her house had just had all its cisterns refitted with golden water.

'I'm sorry?'

'Well, you know the swirls on a snail's shell? They represent the golden mean – it's found everywhere in nature. That's how water's meant to be, not still and static like it is in the tap. So there's this machine that scientifically rearranges the molecules in your water according to the golden mean –'

'Like the, um, Hadron Collider?'

'Exactly. And it makes the water so much more hydrating. You can really taste when fruits and vegetables have been grown with it – you know, you can taste their happiness. It's really mathematical, but also spiritual.'

'Holistic,' I just about managed, biting the insides of my cheeks.

'Yah. You can get one for your bathroom, anywhere. They're waiting for FDA approval, but you know, there's like so much red tape and bureaucracy. Hang on, I've got a card.' She began fishing in her snakeskin Gucci tote. 'I mean, it's changed my life.'

'Thanks so much. I'll, er, definitely look into it.'

'My pleasure, honey.'

As the guests drifted away from the table, the servers were lighting tiny coloured Moroccan lanterns in the trees. Dried lavender had been thrown in the fire bowls, sending billows of scent into the soft, salty air.

'Taking a risk with the old *vigile*, aren't you, Sveyn?' an English guy with a single button fastened on his blue linen Vilebrequin shirt was asking the host, who laughed drily.

'Yah, they fine you ten thousand euro if anyone reports a naked flame. Half the hillside at San Juan went up last year. I find it easier,' Sveyn confided, 'just to give them the 10K in *advance*.' Both men laughed conspiratorially.

Tage led me to a teak sofa draped with delicate ikat shawls, an arm draped possessively around my shoulder, and introduced me to a Swedish architect who had the commission for next year's Serpentine Gallery Pavilion and his wife who had an impressive-sounding job in medical research in Stockholm. I doubted she had much call for golden water. They were clever and charming, and more than politely interested in my plans for Gentileschi. As I sat there with Tage, the ice cubes melting tiny flowers into my rosé, I could look across at the gleaming walls of the house and the dark promise of the garden and rejoice again in Judith Rashleigh's banishment. Spirituality aside, this was where I had wanted to be, wasn't it? And the best thing was, I was answerable to no one. I caught sight of Alvin, lolling in a hammock with two girls, and raised my glass in acknowledgement. Despite my disappointment over the Yermolov valuation, I felt optimistic, even – maybe – happy.

Afterwards, I saw that was the last time I could pretend that things were going to end well.

5

They started to go wrong at dinner the following evening. I had woken in my room alone – I hadn't moved my things into Tage's Balinese boudoir, as I don't like actually sharing my bed unless strictly necessary. I had been for a run round the island, ending with a swim in the cobalt surf, where fat grey fish played around my feet, then spent the day with the rest of the party, lounging by the pool. Tage had organised a boat trip to the nearby island of Formentera, but as the September heat banked and shimmered over the mainland, I preferred to retreat to the cool of my bed, reading and dozing until it was time to change.

The girls retired to dress at about nine, and from the sounds of giggling and feet pattering between the bathrooms I guessed they were also enjoying a little pick-me-up. I took a long shower and dressed in a simple black georgette maxi dress from Isabel Marant with plain leather sandals, adding a pair of antique earrings I'd picked up on Murano; flaming lozenges of marbled glass set in gold filigree. All suitably relaxed and bohemian. When we reassembled for drinks, I was startled to see Tage turned out in a garment that could only be described as a party caftan, but I didn't need to get involved with that if I didn't want to, and the maids were setting down bowls of flatbread and delicious-smelling *albondigas*. I offered a dish to the woman next to me, whom I recognised from earlier as Egg White, but she pinched me playfully on the thigh with a familiarity that should have been grounds for murder.

'Eating is cheating, Elisabeth! Have a dib dab.'

She proffered a tiny cloisonné bowl of MDMA and stuck the tip of her little finger encouragingly in my mouth. I swallowed my irritation rather than her digit and muttered something about needing carbs to get started, but looking down the teak table, draped with a narrow Turkish rug set with silver coins, I wanted to cry with anticipated boredom. Why is it that the people who can afford all the fun in the world have discovered only such limited ways of having it? I'm not anti-drugs exactly; it's just that I prefer the doors of my own perception to remain firmly bolted. The maids were imperturbably laying out a baroque still life of food, which the guests were equally impassively ignoring, gleefully dipping away at the white grains. This was going to get very messy very quickly, and I wondered how long it would take for them to get so bombed that I could retire discreetly to bed. I grabbed a glass and a fag and wandered to the edge of the terrace, where one of Stahl's friends was gazing out to sea with the wistful sorrow of Sylvia Plath contemplating Lyonesse.

'It's almost time for the closing parties, you know,' he whispered mournfully. So I left him to that and beetled back to the table, hoping to score a meatball, but Egg White intercepted me and pulled me towards her with a scraggy mahogany arm. Then Tage's club-standard sound system started up, the music banging so loud that Egg White practically had my earlobe off with her veneers as she began a pasty-breathed explanation of why I really, *really* needed to *understand* Ibiza, because it was such a special creative place, and I *really* needed to understand that, because for people who were free and creative like us there is just *nowhere* like it. As her eyes flared nearer and nearer to my own I wondered what would happen if I ground a handful of powdered happiness into her pupils with both my thumbs, but our little love-in was interrupted by Stahl, who had accelerated from nought to sixty in an astonishingly short time, leaping onto the balustrade and from there clambering onto an upended whitewashed canoe artfully trailed with purple bougainvillea. He swayed as he caught his breath, then reached for one of the lighted bamboo torches which burned away the twilight along the walls. Red-faced, pores gaping, teeth grinding, I could barely recognise him. The considerate, rather attractive man I had known the day before had morphed into the Beast of Beefa. Minding the sequinned hem of his caftan, he held the torch aloft in the direction of the shore, where two white Jeeps were roaring up from the dock at which I had arrived earlier, driven by white-shirted men in Ray-Bans.

'Ladies and gentlemen,' he slurred, 'the fuck trucks have arrived!'

The crowd made a fair shot at going wild as the vehicles drew nearer, fists pumping the air in time with the blaring horns. There were six or seven bikinied girls in each, standing up on the seats, twerking their arses as best they could without knocking one another out onto the road. Stahl turned back to his audience, and on cue the music faded as he slowly mimed pushing a head down to his crotch, thrusting his pelvis towards an imaginary mouth. 'Boys and girls, the fun starts here! Let's goooooo!' He hopped down and led off towards the pool, where the first carload of stilettos was clattering up the steps. Regret isn't a thing I go in for much, but as I trailed after him I was disgusted by my own lapse of taste. What had I been thinking? Thank Christ we'd used a condom.

'Ready to party?'

It was Alvin again, clutching at the fabric of my dress. I tugged it sharply away but he was holding tight, and as I moved it tautened between us until I couldn't go further without ripping it.

'I don't know whether I'm quite ready for Ibiza.'

He unsnapped his fingers smartly. The dress fluttered back against my body.

'That's not what I heard, Elisabeth.'

'Maybe you heard wrong.'

I turned my back on him and walked past the abandoned dinner table to my room on the first floor, scooping a mound of quinoa and pomegranate salad into a flatbread on the way. The bedroom faced the hills at the back of the house, which mercifully absorbed some of the pounding music. I lit a fag and opened my work phone. Sure enough, there was Alvin, profiled under a witty photo of Michelangelo's *David*. We had been 'friends' for about a month. I'd never bothered to look at any of his posts, but now I scrolled through, scanning the pictures. Alvin at White Cube in London, Alvin scarfing a come-down kebab in Dalston, Alvin weedy in board shorts next to a better-groomed female version of himself on a beach in the Hamptons, caption: 'Congratulations, Big Sis ☺!!!!' Big Sis was flashing an engagement ring, next to her – presumed – fiancé, who, judging from his pallor and the crumpled pink shirt open over his shorts, was English. Next to the fiancé, hip kicked artfully to the camera, blonde hair trailing to her bikini straps, was Angelica Belvoir. I had sensed immediately that Alvin was bad news, but why had I then ignored my instinct that the this whole trip was clearly, horribly, bad news? When was I ever going to learn that Joining In really, really wasn't my thing? I threw the fag end out of the window and lit up again.

Angelica Belvoir. Fuck. The no-mark Sloane who had been given my job, back when I'd been fired from the House in London. Back when I'd discovered my old boss was involved in a faking scam and I'd dumbly poked my nose in it. Before – everything.

Before I'd learned that everything I'd been taught to believe about merit and talent and hard work was a useless load of crap. Before I became complicit in a system I despised. Before I took off from London to the Riviera, before the blood and the bodies, before I made myself adamantine on a diet of rancour and rage. Before James and Cameron, before Leanne and Julien, before Renaud. I had come so far. I had thought Elisabeth Teerlinc was done with all that, but still it pursued me, sure as that scent of lilies in a quiet room, still their streaming arms scrabbled at me, to pull me down until the waves of the past closed inevitably over my gasping head.

I shook myself. This was really not a moment for nostalgia. Was Angelica the reason Alvin had friended me? Had she identified me? I flipped back through Alvin's connections, but there was no way of telling; our mutual friends included five art people I'd never met, apart from Tage Stahl. But I had to get off this sodding island and put a country or two between me and Alvin immediately. I didn't want my face in any of his fabulous Ibiza snaps if there was a chance Angelica might see them. I saw I had been getting slow, complacent, and balls-ups like this were what came of it. That's what happy does for you.

I took a few pointless paces around the room, the vibrations of the party fizzing through the floor, feeling suddenly caged, breathless. *Calm down, Judith. This is nothing.* Was Alvin really a risk? He was creepy, sure, but he didn't strike me as anything other than lecherous and none too bright. Almost certainly harmless, yet he provoked a sensation I hadn't felt in a long while, had hoped never to feel again: the claustrophobic adrenalin clutch of pure fear. Irrational. It wouldn't do to look scared. Elisabeth Teerlinc had nothing to hide, even if Judith Rashleigh had plenty. I'd put in an appearance at the party, I thought, keep my distance, and leave first thing in the morning. Nothing I couldn't handle.

When I returned to the terrace Stahl's soirée had accelerated from naff to grotesque. The circular white beds around the pool were covered in jerkily syncopated bodies, each man surrounded by two or three writhing women. The tarts were directing operations with all the conviction and enthusiasm of motivational dancers at Hieronymus Bosch's Bar-Mitzvah, rearing up to shake their hands to the beat before plunging back to insert a tongue or a finger into a waiting body. The female houseguests were performing a more complex psychological manoeuvre, chemically stiffened faces simultaneously attempting Up For It and Cut Above the Sluts. Stahl emerged from the melee and approached me, sliding an arm around my waist.

'Having fun, honey?'

'Not exactly.'

'Wait until you see this.'

The maids were still moving among the group, changing ashtrays and filling glasses with champagne. How they must pity us, I thought, how they must pity us. Stahl clapped his hands and again the music faded.

'Boys and girls! Come on! Time to stop fucking each other's brains out for a few minutes!'

The women abandoned their activities with suspicious alacrity, lolling on the beds like a trawl of tanned sardines. Stahl was rooting in the pocket of the caftan.

'First of all, a big hand – ahem – for these lovely ladies who've come out to entertain us tonight! And now, the challenge you've all been waiting for . . .'

Christ, what was the man on? He was brandishing a tightly rolled wad of familiar pink notes. 'Ten thousand euros, yes, ten grand in cash, for the girl who can give us the best impersonation. What's it gonna be?'

A few people called out suggestions – celebrities, historical figures. What was this – porn charades? One man called out in Norwegian or Swedish and Stahl cupped a hand to his ear.

'What was that? OK, farm animals! Sounds good! Come over here, girls.'

The tarts gathered around him, adjusting their hair and what was left of their bikinis. Closer up, I had to admit that Stahl didn't do things by halves. Every one of them had a lingerie-model physique, and beneath the layers of make-up their faces were exceptionally pretty. I wondered idly where he'd rented them. Stahl was explaining what was required.

'OK, OK. Are we sitting comfortably? Get yourselves a drink, have a line, Jens. Close your mouth over there and put your dick back in your trousers. First up – what's your name, darling? . . . First up, Stefania here is going to give us – a pig!'

Ten grand, the price of a forest fire. I watched, disbelieving, as in the silence that fell the girl dropped to all fours, wrinkled her face into a snout and began grunting.

'Come on, darling, you can do better than that!'

Stefania was presumably keeping her mind on the money, and I daresay she'd done worse for it, but as she crawled forward, snorting, and buried her head in one of the guy's laps as though rooting for a truffle, I actually felt nauseous. Whoops and howls from the guests. One by one, the girls sank down and became cows, sheep, goats, chickens, bleating and squawking, floundering between the guests' knees in the torchlight. I couldn't watch, but if I needed an excuse to leave right now, I had it. I stepped over the back of a girl who was braying like a donkey while one of the men dry-humped her from behind, and pulled Stahl to one side.

'I'm leaving. Please could you have the boat ready for me on the dock? I'll carry my own bag.'

'Elisabeth! What's the matter? Not your scene? No need to get uptight, baby – just go with the flow.'

'I'm not uptight, I'm horrified. So I'm leaving. Enjoy your party.'

He caught up with me in the doorway of my bedroom. I'd barely unpacked – it would only take a minute to gather my things.

'Darling, I thought we had a nice thing going. Yesterday? You can't just leave.'

'Watch me.'

Stahl's face made an attempt at nasty, but the MDMA had him inanely grinning, which made it really nasty. His conviction that what he had created out there was pleasure was both unshakeable and appalling.

'I don't like girls who are ungrateful.'

'I don't give a flying fuck what you like. Have your skipper get the boat ready now, before I call the police in Ibiza town and tell them you've got enough blow in your sorry little paradise to pay their pensions in rewards for the next five years.'

He looked confused. 'Come on, darling. Alvin told me –'

What could Alvin have told him? Who else had the idiot been blabbing to? What I wanted to do more than anything was slam the heel of my palm into Tage's nose so hard he wouldn't be able to speak to Alvin or anyone else for a week, but I had to get out. Now. I answered him tightly, forcing down the tension that threatened to shake my voice.

'I don't know Alvin. Just get the boat ready. Thank you for the hospitality.'

My case was on the bed and I reached around him to zip it up, but he grabbed my shoulders and pushed me down so my face was wedged between the case and my putty leather Bottega Veneta handbag. He giggled and started to lick my ear.

'Relax, baby. Just relax. Go with it, you know.'

I closed my eyes and let my muscles soften, and sensing it, he nuzzled closer and worked a hand between my legs.

'That's it, honey, yeah, that's it.'

I couldn't exactly blame him. After all, I'd been more than willing earlier. But above the beat of 'Knights of the Jaguar' below us I could still hear frenzied, infantile whinnyings and snorts. Stahl was pulling up both our skirts, I let my thighs loll open as I scrabbled in the bag for my hairbrush. Encouraged, Stahl locked his knees behind mine and began a rummage among the sequins. I inhaled deeply, clenched my muscles and whacked him in the perineum with the Mason Pearson with all my strength. Nothing like pure bristle. He gave a little breathless gasp of surprise and torqued sideways, fell off the bed and curled up, groaning and sniggering. I didn't bother kissing him goodbye.

Two hours later I was sitting in a bar on the port in Eivissa town, the white cone of the old walled city behind me, chasing my second proper drink with my third proper drink, my bags at my feet. It was only about 2 a.m., early for Ibiza. A group of girls in PVC ant costumes shimmied past, handing out flyers for a club, followed by a team of S&M slaves, linked in a complicated human loom of leashes and latex garters. One of them, a beautiful tall black guy, with blued Saharan skin and ice-white hair, blew me a kiss. I'd swapped my dress for jeans, shirt and boots in Stahl's boat. The captain had been a little confused at first, but a pink super-note had convinced him of my urgent need to get into town. I hoped Stefania had won her prize.

I was contemplating drink number four and then finding a hotel for the night when a gang of lads swarmed over the table next to me. 'Lads', definitely. Quiffs, tats, gym muscles, cider tans. I sat up straighter, which took rather longer than I expected. They were looking me over, and I suddenly felt quite happy to look back. The dreadlocked waitress appeared, and they ordered beers politely, despite the fact that her denim hotpants barely covered half her arse. I liked that.

'Ask the lady if she'd like a drink then.'

'Thanks. I'll have a bourbon. Neat.' I liked that too.

They shunted their chairs around to make me part of the group and we chinked glasses.

'What's your name?'

'Liz.'

'All right, Liz. Cheers.'

'First time on the island?' I'd been here all of thirty-six hours myself, but I gave it out like I was an old hand.

'Yeah. Went to Greece last year, but it were shite. Too many little kids.'

They were from Newcastle, which somehow prompted me to let on that I was from the north too, a fact I'd not divulged to the general public for years. We chatted a bit, and I bought the next round, and they smoked a joint, and then one of them was leading me off along the quay, holding my hand, while his mates smiled for him, and we were in a cab, kissing, and his mouth felt soft and sweet and clean. Their apartment on the high-rise strip at Platja d'en Bossa smelled of cigarette smoke and fresh boy sweat. He found a half-empty bottle of sweet white wine and we drank from it while he took off first my clothes, then his own, his tongue entwined with mine. A crimson snake curled up his wrist and splayed its fangs across one smooth shoulder. We sank onto his unmade bed as I stretched my arms luxuriantly above my head, then he angled his body crosswise over mine, pulling my wrists towards him in one hand while his tongue found my cunt. I told him to keep it flat, steady, gentle, and he lapped and probed and got me to the edge, but I bucked him off me and sat up.

'I want to look at you.'

He stood up, back from the bed, and pushed a hand through his hair, eyes down, shy. Beneath the serpent's head, a tumble of black and blue dice spilled across his chest, his waist was beautiful, tight, narrow, the planes of muscle above his hipbones outlined like a sculpture.

'You look like a kouros.'

'What?'

'Doesn't matter. How old are you?'

'Nineteen.'

'Turn around. Lift your arms, put your hands on your neck. Yes, like that.'

I crawled forward across the grubby sheet and reached for him, sliding my hands along the wings of his shoulder blades, somehow so tender and frail. The twin hollows of his lower back were lined with blond down. I dipped my head and licked his buttocks, reaching, probing with the tip of my tongue, deep into the earthy scent of him, until he let out a little gasp, then dropped lower, opening gently until I could lave his arsehole. There was an angry constellation of red spots on the underside of his arse, which made me almost love him. I lapped him until his balls were juicy with saliva, then turned and lay back, spreading myself open with two fingers for his eyes.

'Come here.'

'You want me to?'

'Yes. Yes, I do.'

He slid into me, and maybe it was the weed, or the lovely simplicity of it, but we were both laughing. I held him still inside me for a moment, listening for the throb of his blood, then wrapped my thighs tight round his back, taking his weight on me and slowly circled my hips against him, one, two, three, until he groaned and I thought I might lose him, but he flipped me back over, holding my ankles until I was practically standing on my shoulder blades and then he slammed his length up me in one quick shuddering stroke and kept at it, until I was there again and told him to go faster, and I felt my cum start deep, behind my cervix, and he held me so tight there was only his cock moving and I came the way I'd pretended to with Stahl, head back and screaming for it.

'Where do you want it?'

'On my tits. Now.'

The first gush hit me between my ribs, then I felt the heat of him dripping over my nipples. I rubbed my fingers in it and had a lick, took a palmful and rubbed it over my clit.

'Yummy.'

'Feels like your cunt was made for my dick.'

'Tell me that when you fuck me again.'

So he did.

6

Venice is a city of sophisticated pleasures, but teenage lovers hadn't figured prominently during my time there. By the time I returned to the Campo Santa Margherita, the memory of my anonymous toy-boy had almost erased the contempt I felt for both Stahl and myself. Almost. There had been something uncontrolled and pointless about the whole business, which had only been exacerbated by the irritation of the long journey home, necessitating a ferry to Barcelona, another to Genoa and then a train ride across Italy's thigh. The thing was, I still felt spooky about airport security. The last time I had flown commercial was to Rome, mostly because I had left the dead art dealer, Cameron Fitzpatrick, in the Tiber and skipped the city with a stolen fake. This latest trip had made me stiff and irritable, and despite my attempts to busy myself with the new show, my failure with Yermolov still left me disgruntled. The Danish girl, Liv Olssen, had agreed to sell me all ten of her *Unlikely Bundles* series, and I was looking around for some pieces to contrast – or 'dialogue' – with them. It was necessary to have a handle on the semantics, however much art-speak made me puke in my present mood. None of my usual routines felt soothing. I was jumpy, restless though I'd only just got back. I checked Facebook more frequently, half fearing a message from Angelica Belvoir and then feeling an irrational sense of disappointment when there was nothing but the usual anodyne feeds. I was tempted to get in touch with her, as Elisabeth, but I needed to temper my need for information against the danger of drawing attention to myself. Frustrating though it was, I had to let it lie.

Time was something I generally experienced in practical increments, but though I was running harder, working more assiduously, I felt . . . impatient. I just didn't know for what. About the only thing that cheered me up back then was Masha's company. I didn't mind that her memories were fake. She had invented herself, just as I had, and who could blame her for wanting the world to be more glamorous, more exciting, than her pinched reality? I certainly knew the feeling. I loved her stories, loved her neat black body in its too-big chair, loved the swirls of smoke curling defiantly into her bouffant. I hadn't ever known my grandparents, but maybe I would have liked a granny like Masha.

After my weekly bout with the impossibilities of mutating Russian nouns, we smoked and chatted as we usually did. Obviously Masha liked a gold-filtered Sobranie; I usually picked her up a pack on my way to class. When she had oofed into the easy-chair with her strong milkless tea, I asked her if she had ever heard of Pavel Yermolov.

'He is disgusting man.' We could have spoken Italian, but Masha liked to practise her English, which was clear, if eccentric. She claimed to have picked it up from a famous lover in the 1950s – sometimes he was an English composer, sometimes an American writer. Once it was Stanley Kubrick, but then I think she remembered he spoke Russian.

'Why so?'

'He has done terrible things to my country. Him and those brigands.'

'What did he do? Yermolov.'

'I know for a fact he is killing people.'

'*Pravda, chto li? Is that the truth*?

'In Moscow, years ago. Yermolov was wanting to build new apartment block. All the tenants in the old block, he is killing them. One by one. Every day, one. Until the people were so frightened they gave away their homes for nothing.'

'He offered me a job,' I said thoughtfully. 'I turned it down.'

'This I am gratified to hear. Rapists, all of them.'

I didn't pay too much mind to Masha's accusations, particularly as she'd never actually been to Moscow. The story was the kind of sinister gossip that swirled around every wealthy Russian. I tried to prompt her again, but by then she was away, into all the wrongs that had been done to her beloved people. I was content to listen to her distinctly individual version of European history, punctuated occasionally with a highlight from her past repertoire. Her voice was ravaged by time and fags (she'd gaily taken up smoking when she left the stage), and though even in her heyday she'd only made it as far as the Fenice chorus, I thought she still sounded marvellous.

That evening, as I returned to my flat in the last of the evening's heat, Masha's words returned to me. 'Rapists,' she had said, 'brigands.' Strong words. The almost eerie calm with which Yermolov had dealt with the trespasser, the memory of his arachnoid hands . . . I could believe that he would erase anyone who got in his way. Maybe that was why I had found him compelling, why I was still irritated at my own failure to impress him. My speculations were interrupted by the buzz of my personal phone in my bag. It was Steve, who'd put me in business in ways he didn't even know about. After the unfortunate business with James that summer at the Hôtel du Cap, I'd blagged my way onto his boat on the Mediterranean. In return for my stealing information from the study of one Mikhail Balensky, Steve had helped me to open a Swiss account with the cash I'd taken from poor old James's wallet. Only 10K, but it had felt like a fortune to me back then. The account had been the useful thing really – it was where I had deposited the money from the sale of the fake Stubbs which had lost me my job at the House and started me off as a dealer. I still bought for Steve now and then, so I thought he might be asking after a contemporary piece, but his WhatsApp message read: *Just got tickets for Burning Man! Awesome! Carlotta asked me to invite you to her wedding.*

As far as I could tell from his intermittent messages, Steve the billionaire hedge-funder had recently noticed that it was time to start Giving Back. Or at least he'd finally cottoned on to the tax advantages of philanthropy.

Still, Carlotta's wedding was news. When we'd met on Steve's boat, she and her spectacular tit job had been engaged to a lugubrious German named Hermann. Was he the lucky groom? I messaged back: *Awesome! When and where?* His reply came straight back, unusually, as a single text conversation with Steve could sometimes take weeks: *Monaco. Saturday. Dinner Friday night*. Tomorrow evening, then. Typical of Steve to assume people could just hare between countries the way he could.

As if in reaction, my work phone muttered. Sodding Facebook. Sodding Alvin. *Hey Elisabeth? Where did you go? You missed a crazy-fun party!!! I should stop by your gallery some time. Ciao x*

Why didn't we just wear ankle tags like American convicts and be done with it? That was my evening shot. Lying face down on the kilim I'd brought with me from Paris, I banged my head thoughtfully on the wool a couple of times. It had come up beautifully, considering. It would be laborious to take yet another train via Milan across to Nice, but I would appreciate the time to read, and if Alvin was going to pop by, I had no intention of being home. I messaged Steve for the blushing bride's details, called up the Trenitalia site and booked myself back to the Riviera.

Carlotta's 'rehearsal dinner' was to take place at the Joël Robuchon restaurant at the Hôtel Metropole. Since I'd turned down Yermolov's 100K, a bit of an economy drive was in order, so I'd taken a room in a simple place over the French border at Cap d'Ail, but the taxi driver who took me from the station in Nice warned me that I would be better off catching the bus to Monaco proper, as some weird tax law put the cabbies off from entering the principality between six and eight p.m. Carlotta's dress code was 'Riviera Chic', whatever she thought that meant, and it felt a little odd to be waiting at a scruffy bus stop in a delicate, flower-embroidered Erdem gown. However, the ride itself was a revelation. When the white bus eventually pulled up, none of the female passengers so much as glanced at my full-length ruffles, probably because their collective get-ups made them look like a hen night on the razzle in Selfridges. Monogrammed Saint Laurent purses jostled against quilted Chanel clutches, rainbow-ribboned Alaïa corsetry competed with Balmain gold zips, and no heel was less than four inches. It was only when I began eavesdropping on the pair behind me, an older woman busy on her iPhone and what was obviously her stunningly beautiful daughter, that I realised all of these woman were whores. Second-rank, obviously, since they didn't have apartments in Europe's dreariest tax haven, all of them en route for the night shift. The mother behind me was patently her child's pimp, arranging the evening's programme of jobs in clear, unembarrassed English, while the girl stared placidly out of the window beneath her cape of straight ice-blonde hair. As the bus contorted itself around the high corniche roads

I closed my eyes and listened in to the chatterings of this exotic aviary. I could have been back in London, in my old job at the Gstaad Club, hearing the same negotiations between beauty and money that had once been the backing track of my nights. The difference was that these girls were serious professionals. Across the aisle, two more blondes were discussing the merits of various contraceptive pills to stave off menstruation – 'The thing with the Saudis is, you bleed, you're out' – while a curvaceous brunette cooed sweetly to her john while rolling her eyes and making puking motions at her giggling friend.

That could have been me, I was thinking. *That could so easily have been me.* For years I had trained myself to become a professional *of* beauty, had believed that talent and energy and brains would carry me to a real career in the art world. And then I had learned that it wasn't enough, that the only thing my boss Rupert had a use for was my body. So I had used that, had played the world in which I found myself at its own game. But it would have been so easy for things to have gone the other way; I couldn't dismiss that.

Carpeted corridors and unknown faces waiting in anonymous suites, the trick and the folded bills, the hot-tub grind and the slow crawl home in the searing dawn. I felt my wallet burning through the soft leather of my bag, the neat wad of fifties, the credit cards, the keys to my beautiful Venetian flat, but for the first time those talismans failed to throb with their customary reassurance. I didn't feel grateful not to be part of this world; I felt removed, abstracted, the pale chiffon of my dress encasing me like a shroud. The cheerfulness, the resignation of these girls just left me feeling lonely.

Well, *plus ça* fucking *change*. Pull yourself together, Judith. I had friends, didn't I? Several, in fact. I was going to meet Carlotta and Steve, and I'd never seen Monaco. As the bus released its tottering workers I twitched off the feeling and stumped up the hill to the Metropole, dodging a Ferrari, a luminous orange Bentley convertible and something that could have been Johnny Hallyday to reach the sunken portal of the lobby. Carlotta was attending her guests at the door of the restaurant's private room in a fluttering Pucci slip, slashed down both sides for good measure. The vast rock I recalled seeing on her left hand had been replaced by an even huger arrangement in yellow diamonds. Looking more closely at the bald, bespectacled character bemusedly clutching her hand, I noted that Hermann had also been replaced, possibly by his grandfather. Carlotta blinked at me doubtfully for a few seconds before falling on me like a long-lost sister. We did a bit of screeching and air-kissing, during which I whispered in her ear, 'Who's the lucky boy?'

'Franz,' she hissed back. 'He's Swiss.'

'What happened to H?'

'Oh, he's in prison now,' she trilled airily, pouting over my shoulder at another arrival.

I presented my gift, a set of delicate Venetian lace napkins, which were plonked onto a display table among a pile of branded carrier bags. Whatever matrimony held in store for Carlotta, she was never going to find herself short of an Hermès ashtray.

Steve was peering through the waxy petals of a sinister puce orchid, poking as ever at his phone. His transformation from brutal capitalist financier to New Age crusader was signalled by a move into cargo pants and a thin red leather thread tied around one wrist. Otherwise he looked much as usual – that is, sheeny and awkward. I dodged around an ivy-entrailed column into his sightline.

'Hey, gorgeous,' was his greeting. Back on the *Mandarin*, Steve had known me as Lauren, my middle name, which I'd started using as an alias at the Gstaad Club and then for quite a few other things. I'd been obliged to tell him that I'd changed my name to Elisabeth for professional reasons, to give myself a bit of cachet, but although we'd spent a summer sleeping side by side on his boat a few years ago, I doubted he remembered the original version.

'How's tricks?'

'You know, crazy. I just came back from an Ayahuasca retreat in Peru. Awesome.' Always a bit late to the party, Steve. 'You want to see a video?'

'No, thanks – if we're about to have dinner.'

I couldn't think of anything amusing to say about hallucinatory vomiting, so I asked about his charity. The last time we'd met, at Istanbul Contemporary before the summer, Steve had told me about a foundation he'd started which aimed to lift three million people out of extreme poverty in three years. I wondered if he'd invented an algorithm to keep count.

'Fantastic! We've provided tablets for a hundred thousand children in Somalia!' he replied proudly.

I did think they might have preferred lunch, but I kept that to myself; it would have confused him. I took an exuberant cocktail from a passing waiter, just as another woman reached towards the tray.

'Sorry – after you.'

'No, please, after you.'

We bumped our noses awkwardly into spirals of carved watermelon, before I introduced myself.

'I'm Elisabeth, an – um – old friend of Carlotta's.'

'I believe we've met.'

'I'm sorry, I don't believe so.'

'Forgive me, my mistake.' She looked at me curiously. 'I'm Elena.'

'Are you bride or groom, Elena?'

'I know Franz from St Moritz. My husband and I have a place there.'

'How lovely.'

Elena was a couple of decades off Franz's vintage, and she must once have been beautiful, but her face was a collage of Botox and filler that might have been entitled 'Fears of the Trophy Wife'. Her lips had been pumped so far beyond their natural limits that they threatened to fall off her jaw like cushions from a sofa, while her original cheekbones were lost under two plump apples of plastic that squashed her green eyes into feline currants. From a distance she could have passed for thirty; close up she was ageless as a gargoyle. Hers was a face I had become accustomed to in Venice, peering startled above sable collars or Fortuny foulards, the most shocking thing about its wilful malformation being how ordinary it had become.

When I had last met Carlotta she had been one among a thousand Riviera girls, just a step up from the tarts on the bus, clawing her way to security one shellacked fingernail at a time. Her prospects had improved with her ascent to marital respectability, but I doubted that she was the first, or even the third Mrs Franz, and though the other wives were now obliged to welcome her as one of their own, the question in all their eyes was 'Who's next?'

I dragged my attention back to Elena and asked if she would be attending the reception tomorrow evening.

'Yes, I'll see you at the party,' she remarked as she drifted off. Her accent was Russian, but I didn't feel confident enough yet to attempt any conversation in her language. I rejoined my hostess, who had momentarily loosened her grip on her fiancé.

'Congratulations!' I enthused. 'I'm really happy for you.'

'Well, Franz is seventy, but he's, like, really into me, you know?'

'How could he not be, darling?'

'And he's no bother, if you see what I mean. You should get yourself a nice old one.' She leaned forward confidentially. 'Less trouble. We've got a house in Switzerland – we're there

November through February. You should come visit! And, like, a flat in Zurich, and the beach place here. He's not so bad,' she added speculatively 'And the boat, of course.'

'Of course.'

She took my hand and squeezed it. 'Thank you for being here. You're, like, one of my closest friends. It means a lot to me.'

Looking round the forty or so people picking their way gingerly through the swarm of orchids, I wondered how desperate Carlotta must be for mates if she counted me as a close one. I imagined I'd been summoned just to make it seem she had some actual girlfriends – predators of her type tend to hunt alone. Still, I was quite fond of her, in a way. I admired the honesty of her ruthlessness, if not her taste in restaurants.

However, when we assembled the next evening at Franz's home, I gave Carlotta a silent cheer. Franz's house, set on the shore beneath the famous 'Rock' that incorporated the palace of the Monaco royals, was an exquisite creamy deco pavilion, with a slim entrance hall which cut into a hexagonal drawing room, opening in turn onto a garden overlooking the shore. I clocked a pair of Louis XV marquetry commodes and a Max Ernst from his surrealist period before the harassed-looking wedding planner ushered me upstairs. Carlotta was standing unselfconsciously naked among about ten of the women from the previous night, who were struggling with varying degrees of grace into flesh-coloured Eres body stockings.

'It's Franz's wedding gift!' Carlotta announced, as though that explained everything. She brandished her left hand, now adorned with a gold wedding band.

I did feel that the elastane gussets might inhibit us all from doing him as a present, but I removed my silk beach pyjamas, ruefully discarded my own underwear and began to climb in.

'I'm doing a tableau. Like, Botticelli? Franz is really into art.'

I'm not unaccustomed to remaining socially at ease in a room full of naked strangers, but that left me somewhat bewildered.

'So you've already had the ceremony?' I floundered.

'Oh sure. Got it over with at the *mairie* this morning. Franz and the boys are at the casino right now. I thought a post-wedding bachelor party was, like, more sensible.'

'Can't be too careful in Monaco!' chimed in one of the bodystockings.

'And this is . . . ?' I tried again.

'So, when they arrive, we're going to be arranged in the garden. You ladies are going to be the waves, and I'll be, like, Venus.'

'Venus?'

'The goddess,' Carlotta explained pityingly. 'The one in the painting? With the big shell?'

'Gotcha. Venus. Fabulous, Carlotta. Great idea.'

Carlotta draped herself in a length of white georgette and led us out to the garden. The wives, stunned into obedience, followed meekly. Only one woman, square in a beige skirt suit, appeared to have demurred. Carlotta twinkled her fingers at her as we passed her seat beneath the Ernst. The woman ignored her.

'Who's that?'

'My stepdaughter. I adore her.'

Outside, the wedding planner handed us each a huge fan in a spectrum of blues from turquoise to navy. The bride hoicked herself up onto the fountain, giving us a generous view of her honeymoon Hollywood. We were instructed to arrange ourselves on our side, leaning on one stretched arm, while the wedding planner lackadaisically demonstrated how we were to use our fans to represent the waves. The grass was scratchy and there were definitely ants, but I could see that from the house we would appear as a sea of naked female flesh, with Carlotta-as-goddess floating above us. Quite effective, and unexpectedly touching from Carlotta.

The planner and her assistants were assembling a huge polystyrene clam shell behind the fountain to better frame Carlotta's assets.

'She saw this in *Harper's*,' muttered the woman next to me. 'Ridiculous.' Looking more closely, I saw it was Elena. I had quite a while to look, because we were required to lie there, sweat gathering attractively in the creases of our manmade fibres, while a string quartet picked their way over us to conceal themselves behind the shell. Someone got poked with the spike of the cello, Carlotta had a mid-level screaming fit about the white roses and carnations suspended on invisible fibres, which kept tangling in her ringlets, two water nymphs defected on the grounds that their recent peels couldn't take exposure to sunlight, and by the time the musicians wheezed their way through Vivaldi's 'Spring' to the slightly horrified gaze of Franz and his guests, we resembled less Botticelli's *Venus* than Cranach's. The one with the angry bees.

'People are just, like, so uncreative,' Carlotta grumbled afterwards, once Franz had led his re-swathed beloved down a path of rose petals to the white silk Bedouin tent erected for the dancing.

'Still, Poppy Bismarck had Heston Blumenthal do her wedding cake' – she stabbed at her phone for effect – 'and she only got, like, two thousand likes on her feed.'

7

I had been back home in Venice a few days when things began moving. That is, objects in my flat began to move around. First it was a sweatshirt I used to work out in, strayed from its basket to the bed-head. Next my breakfast cup, a Lalique design of gold leaf on cream porcelain, found on the window seat when I was certain I had washed it and put it back on the shelf before leaving for the gallery. And someone seemed to have been drinking my wine, though I had to admit I was a suspect there. The mysterious chocolate bar I thought I'd picked up by mistake before the Ibiza trip was still in the cupboard. I took a good look at it, remembering that something had felt off in the flat back then. Ghosts are as much a cliché of Venice as masks. Maybe that was why I was so fond of the place; but my own particular phantoms tended to keep to their quarters. I chucked the chocolate in the bin and banged the lid closed, telling myself I was being stupid.

But then it started with the books. I had picked up an order from the Libreria Toletta, some catalogues of Beijing artists and a new biography of Titian, and left the bag on my desk while I walked over to Masha's tiny flat for my lesson. I stopped at a gift shop on the way, the kind that sold dubious Byzantine icons to tourists. In the back they had a small selection of Russian goods, pots of red caviar and scented black tea. I picked up a jar of rose-petal jam, which Masha would carefully spoon into a crystal dish and serve next to dry little sponge cakes after our class. I think I took even more pleasure in that small luxury than she did.

To my surprise, I found Masha seated on a plastic chair in the tiny square in front of her building. She seldom went out, beyond a ponderous weekly trip to the Rialto market. A couple of times I'd gone along with her, to help carry the bags. She was flapping at her face with a large black fan and gripping the arm of a man I recognised as the waiter from the café on the corner. Another woman in a blue nylon housecoat, perhaps a neighbour, was offering her glass of water.

'Masha! *S toboi vse vporyadke?' Are you all right*?

'There's been a burglary' said the other woman, in Italian.

I bent down, bringing my face close to Masha's. Her heavy eye make-up was a coaly mess. She had obviously been crying.

'The signora had been to church,' offered the waiter, 'and when she came back, there was a man in her apartment.'

'My God! Masha, what happened? Have you called the police?'

'They've been and gone. Nothing was taken,' put in the woman. She looked almost disappointed at the smallness of the drama. 'But the signora has had a shock.'

Masha's hands were encased in neat white gloves, buttoned at the wrist. I held them gently, noting that they seemed pathetically frail and tiny.

'Masha, I know you must be very upset, but did you see him? The burglar?'

'*Nyet, nyet.*'

'I'm sorry,' said the waiter, 'but I need to get back to work. I've left the bar unattended.'

'That's all right. I'm one of her students. We can take care of her, can't we?' I nodded to the woman. 'Come on, let's get you inside.'

The neighbour explained that she lived across the *campo* and had heard Masha calling for help. The thief had pushed past her at her front door and escaped down the stairs; no one had seen anything.

'The *carabinieri* are sending a counsellor,' she sniffed.

We helped Masha up the stairs and I called a locksmith while the neighbour made tea. Masha went over the scene again and again: how she had set off on the *vaporetto* to light a candle at San Zan Degolà, how she had known something was wrong when she returned, how the man had pushed her against the wall when she disturbed him.

'Are you sure he took nothing? Did the police check?' Usually the only people who were robbed in Venice were tourists. The locksmith arrived and I let them talk, discreetly paying him in cash as he bent over the keyhole. There was no damage; he agreed with the verdict of the *carabinieri*, that Masha must simply have forgotten to close her door properly and the thief had seen an opportunity.

'Probably one of those Rom people,' put in the neighbour with another sniff. 'We're none of us safe. I said to them – what's the *Questura* doing about all these gypsies?'

I ignored her. 'Do you need to rest, Masha? This gentleman is going to make sure everything is safe. Shall I help you to bed?'

'*Spasibo*, Elisabeth. Such a kind girl.'

'I'll call someone to come and sit with you.' Masha had a whole network of old Russian girlfriends, many of whose relatives had found work in Venice's innumerable hotels. Their lives provided an ongoing soap opera for the *babushki* – Masha was always gossiping about them. She removed a tumble of items from her capacious handbag and eventually proffered a worn diary; in a remarkably short time the stuffy room was filled with old ladies who had crossed the city at lightning speed, equipped with vodka and paper bags of dusty biscuits. Soon the samovar was going and Masha, reclining on her divan in wafts of smoke and Russian chatter, was hosting a party.

'Are you sure you'll be OK?' I didn't like to leave her – she had seemed so vulnerable, but I didn't want to intrude either. Masha patted my cheek, and I made to leave with the locksmith. But as he closed the door, I spotted something. On the wall behind hung one of Masha's many icons, a large waxed print of a mournful, sloe-eyed Madonna. The picture had been hidden while the man was working, but now I could see that the thick paper in its cheap red frame was ripped – no, slashed, the oval of the sallow face bisected by a thin cut. I stared at it for a moment, thinking that perhaps the thief had been looking for hidden banknotes stashed in the frame. I didn't want to distress Masha further by pointing it out – perhaps, given where the picture hung, she might not notice for a while. I closed the door and followed the workman down the stairs.

When I eventually got back to my flat, the books were lying on my bed. Had I left them there? In my concern for Masha, I couldn't remember. One of them, a large illustrated compendium of Caravaggio's paintings, was open at the illustration of the *Medusa*, the wonderful copy of which I had seen at Yermolov's pavilion. Yet I hadn't bought it – perhaps the shop assistant had placed it in the cloth book bag by mistake? I checked the receipt. No Caravaggio. For a moment I considered an absent-minded fit of kleptomania, but lack of control had not been a big feature around my gaff of late. I went and returned it the next morning. Then, when my next Russian lesson was due, I couldn't find my grammar, a tattered old red Penguin edition with the Cyrillic alphabet at the front. I searched, swearing under my breath, but it had vanished in that maddening way that socks do. I had to go along without it, but when I got back home it caught my eye as I unlocked the door, balanced on the curtain rail above the Récamier chaise in the window bay.

That evening felt long; I spent it on the window seat, watching the *campo* with a bottle of Barolo. I didn't much want to leave for the gallery the next day, but I forced myself, and when I got home everything was where it ought to be, and I felt ashamed that I'd taken a different route back before removing my shoes to climb the stairs and working the key silently into the lock before slamming open the door. A few days went by, and then, after I had been to the market and edged inside with my arms hung to the elbows with blue plastic bags of tomatoes, peaches, a kilo of clams, the Caravaggio book was lying in the middle of the floor.

Quietly, I set the bags down without closing the door. I crossed the room and opened the windows wide. I listened for a long time. Three doors led off the back of the main space of the flat: the kitchen, the bathroom, then the dressing room, with a closet behind with the washing machine and wide shelves for household equipment. The drier clicked off its cycle as I checked the cupboard, making me start, but nothing else had been moved. The huge old walnut linen press against the wall opposite the bathtub remained locked – I ran my fingers around the joints, but the key was on the ring in my bag and the hinges were unmarked. I walked around the book on the floor, trying to work out what else was off, why the air in the flat still crackled with interference. All my pictures were askew. Very slightly, as though the frames had been knocked by a duster, but all angled slightly to the left, the right top corner higher. Gingerly I approached the book, squatted down to open it. One of the pages was marked. I didn't need to look to know it would be the *Medusa*. The marker was a postcard, and the postcard was of a painting by George Stubbs. A leafy, romantic eighteenth-century landscape with a horse and three figures – *Colonel Pocklington with His Sisters*. I remembered it well, from my work on the Stubbs catalogue at the House.

I fetched a chair and set the pictures right, sat on it and lit a fag. After a bit I had to get up to fetch an ashtray and I was still sitting there when it was full.

Someone knew.

Knew about the fake Stubbs my old boss Rupert had tried to flog. So they probably knew about his partnership with Cameron Fitzpatrick, from whom I had taken the painting. Knew what I had done to Cameron. There were six people who had any degree of certain knowledge of that story. One of them was me. Three of them were dead – Cameron, Leanne, Renaud Cleret. Which left two people who could betray my story. Rupert, and Romero da Silva of the Roman anti-Mafia police division. It made no sense. Rupert had nothing on me, and even if he wanted to bring me down, he couldn't without ruining his own life. That had always been my safeguard as far as he was concerned. Da Silva was a policeman – if he wanted to question me, arrest me even, there were procedures, official rules. Not this absurd jiggery-pokery. There had to be someone I hadn't factored in. I removed the postcard from the pages and ran my fingers over Medusa's frozen scream. Caravaggio. Yermolov?

Perhaps things might have gone differently with Alvin if he hadn't called at that particular moment.

'Hello?' I answered my work phone cautiously. I didn't recognise the number.

'Hey, Elisabeth. Elisabeth, is that you?'

'This is Elisabeth.'

'It's Alvin – I'm in Venice. I thought I'd stop by, see if you were around.'

'Well, here I am.'

'I'm just passing through. I came on the train. Off to Rovinj.' Croatia.

'That's nice.'

He paused. I was scanning the taut under-shadow of our brief conversation on Ibiza, calculating. '*That's not what I heard, Elisabeth.*'

'Where are you staying?'

'I've just got in. I'm taking the boat, like, super-early.'

Useful.

'Are you calling to ask me for a drink then?' I answered brightly.

'Uh, yeah. Sure. Actually, I am.'

'Good. I really feel like a drink. How about I meet you at the Accademia bridge? It's easy to find.'

Before I left, I checked the times of the ferry departures to Croatia online. Then I called up my bank accounts. I stared at the figures for a moment. From what I hear of love, it's very like money. In both cases, presence and absence are the same – when it's there it may as well not be and when it isn't it never leaves you. And both come with warnings, which everyone ignores. My wariness about Alvin knowing Angelica Belvoir had faded, but now, with the Caravaggio book and the Stubbs postcard on the floor beside me, I knew that my instincts had not been overreacting. Of all the gallerists in the world, why had Yermolov sent Kazbich to find me? Because he must have wanted me to do the valuation, me in particular. And I'd turned it down. So this was – a warning? I could imagine that a man like Yermolov was not accustomed to, or pleased by, being refused. I was tempted to call Kazbich immediately, to ask him what the hell was going on, but I stopped myself.

Elisabeth Teerlinc was real, wasn't she? Her gallery was real, her flat was real, those numbers on the screen were real. Judith Rashleigh was a largely insignificant memory, and she was going to stay that way. Whatever Yermolov might know, I had to deal with Alvin first. Quickly I straightened up the room, sprayed on some scent and brushed out my hair, knotted a scarf around my bag and set off to meet my date.

Over at Accademia we drank an aperitif at the little bar under the bridge. I was just thrilled to see Alvin; at least I was determined he should think so. It was a hot evening, all the more reason to keep my rule about avoiding Harry's Bar, which happened to be the most likely place for Alvin to bump into some random acquaintance. After our drink, we crossed over to find a water taxi to take us across to Paradiso Perduto, a place I liked over by the Ghetto. Aside from having hundred-year-old Delamain licked off your nipples in the Coco Chanel suite at the Paris Ritz, there's nothing like hailing a Venetian water taxi to make you feel rich. Which was how Elisabeth Teerlinc was staying.

On the way, I filled Alvin in on the official biography of Elisabeth, which included an international school in London, a retired father who lived near Geneva and a few vague years in finance before I felt the call of my true vocation as a gallerist. It was a decent enough back story. I'd spent a few days building it up when I first arrived in Venice. The school I'd checked out online, a Nash edifice near Regent's Park where the international rich parked their neglected offspring between ski trips, nowhere that risked locating me in the tight, knowledgeable network of the English system. I'd become quite fond of my old dad, a retired corporate insurance lawyer who had devoted himself to collecting rare books after my mother's tragically early death from cancer. The dead mother usually put paid to any further questions. I had a photo on my work phone of our 'family home' in Switzerland, a solid nineteenth-century villa I'd amalgamated from the pictures in a couple of real-estate catalogues. Dad's study was on the right, with bay windows overlooking the water. My career in 'finance' had involved a couple of internships at consultancy firms, interns being difficult to track down and sufficiently imprecise to follow up without determined inquisitiveness. Anyone who asked more got the word 'Lehmans', which generally elicited a more sympathetic response than my poor mother's demise. Elisabeth had spent a couple of years finding herself in India when she realised a career in business was not for her, including six months on an ashram (now defunct) in Rajasthan. If the cancer didn't put paid to inquisitiveness, yoga guaranteed it.

In turn, Alvin explained that he was thinking of getting into curating, maybe spending some time in Berlin or perhaps LA, where the contemporary scene was, like, much fresher? He showed me photos of a friend's show in Silver Lake, which involved crudely derivative Giacometti-like figures in acid-treated steel with large varnished Japanese radishes laid reverently on top of them. I made some noises about that, while taking note of the passcode on his phone. Then we fell back on the Biennale, which pavilions had been 'amazing' (most of them, in his view), and whether Baku or Tbilisi was the next exciting market (neither, in mine). The restaurant was crowded as usual, people had spilled out onto the quay, a jazz trio was playing and the air was full of excited American voices comparing European adventures. It wasn't until Alvin was on his third white wine that I thought to ask him why he'd friended me.

'Well, there's this girl – Angelica?'

I breathed and listened.

'Her brother's engaged to my sister. He works in New York. They met at Brown. I was looking for some experience in Italy and she recognised your gallery. I'd mailed a couple of others before Ibiza. Angelica helped me. She's, like, really into art. She works at –'

I knew exactly where Angelica worked.

'Anyway, she thought she recognised you, in a shot from a Biennale party, but it can't have been you. Doppelgänger!' He produced the word with some pride.

'And that's why you thought we'd met?'

'Yeah. Sorry about that.'

I pouted. 'You didn't email me for a job?'

'Nah, I'm more into LA now. Cool party though, huh? Shame you had to run off. Tage really knows how to get that stuff right. So this girl, the one you look like, she used to work with Angelica, but she got fired. Had an affair with the boss apparently.'

'Really? That seems a bit unfair. That she should get the sack, I mean.'

'Yeah, I dunno. Apparently she was into some really twisted shit.'

Nice. I wondered where that particular rumour had got started. *Angelica admits she made a mistake. She confused you with someone else, that's all.* I didn't have time to think further than that right now.

'I should be getting back. I'll get the bill.'

'Can I come along? I've, er, got some time to kill.'

'Are you meeting friends in Rovinj?'

'Maybe. You know how it is. I might go to Dubrovnik. Or there's a contact of my dad's in Zagreb – I could go up there.'

'It's such a struggle, getting on in the art business, isn't it?'

'Sure is!' he replied. Without irony. His grin showed me those eager teeth and I felt a shudder of my original distaste.

He walked next to me as we crossed over by the Ghetto and turned in towards the Casino, where I planned to pick up the *vaporetto* to get home. I pointed out the gates behind which the Jews were locked every night by their kind hosts, and the tiny, hidden synagogue built above the ceilings of the once-crowded tenements.

'Awesome.'

We chugged in silence along the Grand Canal until we came to my stop.

'Sure you don't want another?'

Perhaps this is OK. Maybe he can just fuck off to Dubrovnik. But then he pulled out his phone. All evening he had barely been able to keep his hands off it, caressing it anxiously like a mother soothing a fractious baby.

'Maybe a coffee.'

He nodded, distracted with his phone, and followed me down the alley that runs next to the Ca' Rezzonico museum to the nearest café, the canvas backpack of his belongings hoicked over his shoulder as he scrolled through his messages.

'I was just trying to find a picture, of that girl who looks like you. Angelica said it was a dead spit.'

There were a few snaps of Judith Rashleigh in her jolly old university days hanging around online, but after I moved to London there had been nothing. Easy, since I'd not made any friends. Aside from my old security pass from the House, the only recent extant photo of Judith that I knew of had been taken by my old schoolmate Leanne. But Leanne was dead and I had incinerated that picture in the rubbish chute of a Parisian apartment building. *How long would they keep those passes on file at the House? Could Angelica access them if she wanted to*?

Then, just as the waiter came to take our order, Alvin twisted his head towards me and snapped a selfie.

'I'll mail it to her, for a laugh.'

'Let me see it first!' I giggled. 'God, I look awful. We should do a better one. Go on, delete it. You can't do that to me, Alvin!' I let my hand rest, mock pleadingly, on his arm and put quite a different expression into my eyes while his thumb found the little dustbin. Good boy.

He leaned towards me, confidentially. 'You can tell me. Is it you? Angelica was pretty sure.'

'How could it be?'

'Well, you're pretty sexy. So was she, obviously.' *If only he could just let it go, poor dumb fuck.*

'Come on, it is you, isn't it? I can tell you're hiding something. I'm, like, really a people person that way. I won't tell Angelica.'

'There's nothing to tell.'

There was the same arrogant certainty in his eyes now that I had seen on the island.

'So what really happened then? Back in London? Come on, you can tell me.'

He'll do it. If you let him go, he'll say he's found you.

I put a few coins on the table and echoed his gesture, dipping my eyeline below his scurfy chin and cupping my face in my hands.

'Would you really like me to tell you a secret, Alvin?'

'Sure.'

'I'll tell you at my flat. We can take another picture there too, if you like. Maybe – lots of pictures. Come on.'

As we stood, I realised that, the thing was, I didn't want to do this. I just didn't want to do this any more.

8

I began the next day, *like*, super-early. Smudging concealer over the cut on my face, my eyes in the mirror were hollow, haunted. I wouldn't think about the lesions on the inside. Patch up the frontage and get on with it. That had always worked before.

The foot-passenger ferry to Croatia left at 6.05 a.m. for a four-hour trip to Rovinj with a stopover at Poreč. I was on the dock at the San Basilio terminal at 5.30 a.m. with a small bag and Alvin's ticket clutched in my hand. Photo ID is required to collect ferry tickets but not to process them – the steward barely glanced at the paper as he took it from me among the press of passengers. Italians just don't get queuing. I counted ten travellers past me and then made a little pantomime of forgetting something in English, leaving Alvin's phone on the boat, rushed back down the gangplank without catching the busy steward's eye and in ten minutes was back at the flat. Good. Alvin had caught his ferry. No trail. Tucking my fags and a twenty euro note in my sports bra, I jogged through Dorsoduro, over the Accademia bridge and along past the Doge's prisons. I paused on the wheelchair ramp next to the Bridge of Sighs and gently released Alvin's backpack, weighted down with a rather nice pair of Oggetti candlesticks. One must make sacrifices. I ran on to the Giardini at the end of the island, where I went through the undignified motions of my workout, then back to San Marco as the *campanile* sounded, negotiating the first groups of tourists, already slick with sweat and sunscreen in the morning haze. The orchestra had not yet arrived for their shift; the only sounds were the pigeons and the footsteps endlessly crossing Europe's drawing room.

I knew most of the waiters now, from my morning ritual. Taking a table in the shade I nodded to Danilo, who brought my fresh orange juice, brioche and *cappuccio*. The stencil in that day's creamy foam was a broken heart. After a read of the *FT* and a delicious cigarette, I walked back over towards Accademia, plunging into the narrow funnel of streets around San Moisè, idly gazing into the windows of the cluster of smart shops. A pair of Prada sandals caught my eye; black satin on a thin silver sole, with a delightful spray of feathers on the heel, like Mercury's wings. Frivolous shoes, tricky shoes, shoes to splurge your wages on because what was the point of saving for a rainy day if you owned those? Nobody would allow a rainy day to happen to a girl in those sandals. I peered at the price. I could have them, if I wanted, I could have them in every colour. But I didn't want them.

The light on the lagoon still danced in turquoise brushstrokes, the air still smelled of seaweed and ice cream, but inside I was all drains and damp leaves. I took a brisk,

Victorian shower, turning the temperature from tepid to freezing, dressed for a serious day and packed my briefcase with the Caravaggio book and a notepad. I had an appointment at the Marciana Library. The building faces the Doge's Palace, just by the statue of San Teodoro and his anatomically peculiar crocodile. Once there was a gallows between his column and the lion of his neighbour, San Marco, and Venetians still think it bad luck to walk between them. I walked between them. I presented my passport, gallery details and a hastily drafted outline of my 'research project' to the listless receptionist, who waved me through to the main reading room, with its triple loggia and islands of pale wood tables set in red carpet. High above, the fierce air conditioning froze the sunlight on the glass roof and I was grateful for my sensible scholar's sweater. I gave my order to the reference clerk and took a seat while I waited for the material, opening the Caravaggio compendium once again to the Medusa. She wasn't howling me any special message, and I began to leaf through the book, examining every illustration. I paused at *Amor Vincit Omnia*, Caravaggio's glorious portrait of his boy lover Cecco as the god of love. I traced the smooth curve of the adolescent cheek with my fingertip. Even in the flat, shiny reproduction, the laughing anarchy of the composition bubbled out, pulsating with pagan energy. A note beneath the plate quoted a contemporary viewer who had seen the picture in the collection of Caravaggio's patron, where it was always shown last, concealed beneath a curtain of dark green silk. I hadn't exactly needed that to confirm the identity of my poltergeist lodger, but at least Yermolov had a sense of humour.

The name for it is *zersetzung*, a method of 'home intrusion' practised by both the old KGB and the Stasi. A clever and effective means of soft torture. Objects are moved around by invisible visitors, subtly or not-so-subtly. It's disturbingly uncanny – it has been known to drive people quite mad – and entirely deniable. Who's going to believe you have been burgled when the only thing that's been moved is the soap? A popular move, apparently, was leaving pornographic material in the bedroom. I didn't know whether to be touched or insulted that they hadn't tried that one.

What was Yermolov trying to tell me? I knew I should be scared, but what I actually felt was curiosity. This was almost flattering. If he wanted me to reconsider my refusal that badly, why intimidate me? And why Caravaggio?

'*Ecco, signorina*.'

The reference clerk had reappeared, holding out a pair of white cotton gloves and a thick, heavy volume bound between two cardboard covers. I had ordered the manuscript copy of one of the first books on Caravaggio, a biography by Mariani, but I didn't want to swot up on the painter's life so much as examine the notes scrawled in the manuscript's margins. The writing was impenetrably tiny, and the seventeenth-century Italian abbreviations were difficult to understand, but I was enjoying myself. It felt like a long while since I had done any serious research. I muttered the words aloud under my breath, the sound helping with the sense, until I came across what I had been looking for:

'They committed a murder,' Mariani had scribbled furtively 'Prostitute, tough guy, gentleman. Tough guy hurts gentleman, prostitute slashes insult into the skin with a knife. Officers called. They wanted to know what the accomplices – In prison he didn't confess, he came to Rome and said no more about it.' I sat back and stared at the clumped black letters. I had known about the incomplete 'murder note'; it was the source of wide biographical speculation, if you liked that sort of thing, but the slash was news. The *sfregio*, the mark of shame sliced into the victim's face with a blade, often a punishment for women who had been unfaithful to their keepers. I felt a curious little shiver of excitement.

In two of his most famous pictures, Caravaggio invented a new genre. *The Fortune Teller* and *The Cardsharps* each show a scene of illusion, of deceit in action. Two realities play out simultaneously in each. Painting is cheating, the artist shows us; it twists our perceptions as surely as the overconfident marks are duped by their conmen. Beware of what you think you see.

If Yermolov was bothering to threaten me, he must believe I had some sort of power. I didn't hate that. How did we come out, in this? Who was the gentleman, who the whore, who the tough guy? If it was a threat, it was an elegant one.

The rest of the day was spent at the gallery; at about seven I returned to the flat, which was just as I had left it. I was running a bath when my phone rang. Not my work phone, my personal one. Three people had that number – Steve, Dave and my mother – and none of them showed on the screen. I took the call and said, 'Fuck you,' in as firm a voice as I could muster. As I had expected, I spoke into silence.

I had to get out. I was really over sitting around waiting for Yermolov to mess with my head. I needed to feel clean, strong, alive. Time to pay a call on the Ukrainians. I left the heavy wardrobe well alone and ran my hand over the hanging rail in the dressing room. I chose a short flame-orange Missoni dress – at least, a suggestion of a dress – and hung it over the mirror while I bathed. I poured half a bottle of Chanel Gardénia into my bathwater, then dressed in charcoal lace Rosamosario briefs and the silk whisper, adding soft suede flats in the same cream as Mademoiselle's famous flower. Heels are a liability in Venice, but in those it took me just eight minutes to wind across tiny squares and cross five humpbacked bridges to San Polo.

If anyone who went to the Ukrainians' place had ever been sober enough, the apartment might have become a thing, the sort of party hideout breathless journalists get their knickers in a twist about, but even if you were straight enough to find it, you would leave in a state that guaranteed you wouldn't tell. Only Venetians really knew about it, because they know all their city's long secrets. I'd heard from Masha, who did not approve. I bought a bottle of nasty grappa from the Chinese shop next door, which was the form, and brandished it as soon as the low street door was opened. Even for Venice, the Ukrainians' alley was narrow, which perhaps explained the physical type of their visitors. Only the lithe of hip need apply, which suited me just fine, tonight. The Ukrainians (if they had names, no one knew them) were a couple; a raddled blonde and her husband, who claimed to be artists, though mercifully none of their own work was ever in evidence. Their flat was a huge ground-floor apartment hung with rather spectacular nineteenth-century portraits, a water gate opened directly onto the canal, which meant that someone always went swimming, and the mezzanine was a kind of souk, a camp of divans and tattered antique silks, more or less diversely occupied. There was always food, and there were always people, though the guest list could be eclectic to the point of alarming.

The Ukrainian husband greeted me familiarly, sparkling eyes, pidgin Italian, and ushered me and my angry dress along the candlelit hallway. He was wearing an entire 1980s television set on his head, his face poking out where the screen had once been, wires and plugs trailing behind, but I didn't feel the need to mention it. Ukrainian wife was posed by the watergate, her legs engulfed in the foetid canal, smoking a gargantuan joint and explaining something important to a startled-looking German backpacker. She waved at me languidly as I poked among the debris of their dinner party for the least-unhygienic-looking glass. A brunette girl dressed in red lipstick, with wonderfully lustrous skin, scampered down from the mezzanine. 'Has anyone seen Bruno?' she panted in English. She tried again, in French and Russian, but no one had seen Bruno, so she gave it up, plucked a slightly singed shawl from one of the lamps to twist into a loincloth and fell asleep on an armchair. Ukrainian husband poked her shoulder vigorously, but she only stirred a little to shrug him off. He took a moment to twiddle the volume knob under his chin.

'Ket,' he pronounced, with some satisfaction. Once we'd got that settled, he offered me a plate of zucchini frittata. 'How are you, dear?'

We chatted a little in the bits and bobs of languages we shared. I picked gingerly at the frittata, then lit a fag to fumigate it. Once he'd turned his volume down again, I went for a prowl upstairs. I set my glass on the sill of the *oeil-de-boeuf* window above the watergate and settled in for a moment of Venetian contemplation. A faint splash below suggested someone had braved the canal. I hoped it wouldn't cause a short circuit.

'Mind if I join you?'

'Nothing wrong with an old line,' I said, without turning round.

A hand drew round my waist, and I let my head fall back against a shoulder scented with a familiar sharp citrus cologne. We had met here before, once or twice. I felt the harness of a wedding ring as the hand moved up against my left breast.

'Beautiful as ever.'

'Thank you.' The right hand was stroking up my hip, fingertips caressing my skin under the abbreviated dress. I waited for my wet rush of want. Nothing. I turned to kiss her, hard, seeking the pulsing slip of her tongue. Nothing. Confused, I opened my eyes, caught the glow of hers in the misty gleam off the canal.

'Where's hubby?'

'Rimini, with the kids.'

'Lucky me then.'

My mouth was in the hollow of her neck, tracing her collarbone with my tongue, I gripped her waist and moved my palms to the beautiful scoop of her soft ass, she inhaled sharply and brought her hand up to rake through my hair, sucking at my throat. Slowly I knelt down in front of her, tugged her cotton skirt to the floor and let my nails wander on the rim of her lace knickers, pale against her summer tan. Her belly was lovely, puffed out like new bread, I pressed my forehead into its plumpness, then began to tug at her knickers. They were sopping wet. I hooked them to one side as she ground against me, turning my face to stroke my cheek against her neat lozenge of pubic hair, bisected by the hard protuberance of her Caesarean scar, then flicking my tongue to her clitoris, lapping her gently, reaching for the soft slit between her labia.

'Spread your legs, now.'

She straddled a little, her hands still clutching my hair, I kept my tongue flat to her clit and worked a finger up her, then another, gliding through her flesh, pushing against the front membrane, licking a little faster, her juice and my saliva coating my chin, sucking and eating. She made to pull me up, but I wanted her to cum, wanted to bury my whole face in those velvety lips, to feel the spasm of her pleasure twitch against my hand, to find the prospect of my own pleasure in it. She was moaning now; for a moment I pulled back, and saw the silhouette of a man in the flickering candlelight of the stairwell. I didn't mind if she didn't. Keeping my hand deep in her, I reached up under her shirt, stretching to release her nipple from her bra, rubbing it in circles to the same rhythm as my tongue on her clit. I licked harder, faster, felt the first tightening on my fingers and twisted the hard button of flesh viciously as her orgasm took her. She gave a fox's high scream, grating her nails into the base of my skull, lathering my face as she shoved her cunt against my mouth, then a deep sigh of release and she staggered back onto a divan, crucified. I rubbed the heel of my palm against my burning lips, tasting something dark beneath the mineral salt of her cum; nidoric, succulent. I put a finger in her mouth as I crossed to the huge gilt-rimmed looking glass propped beside the low bed. There was dried blood on my jaw, one rusty vampiric dribble.

'Sorry about that.'

'I don't mind.' I smeared it across my chin, gazing dully into my reflection's deep eyes. There was a muted gasp from the stairs.

She giggled. 'Come out.'

The Ukrainian husband appeared, *sans* television, fumbling himself back into his fly. She smiled, glorious, and held out her arms to us both. 'Come here, *cara*. Your turn.'

'I'll be a moment.' I left them and went down to wash my face at the kitchen sink. The brunette was still passed out on the chair, her hair trailing to the floor. I took a grubby velvet cover from a pillow and set it softly over her naked shoulders, then took off my shoes, blurring a bloody fingerprint onto the suede, and quietly let myself out into the alley. I wanted to feel the cool smooth stone beneath my feet. I hoped I had given her pleasure, was glad if I had, but – that was all. There was a sick dizziness in me, as though I had swallowed that whole bottle of bad grappa. I'd been a good sport, got her off, but there was no answering tug of need. I was empty, dull-nerved, absent. Even that then? Didn't I even want that anymore? I wandered home, to check on the ghosts. That was all, I told myself. It was just the ghosts.

9

In every Venetian day there is one moment when the city is made entirely of silver. As the very last sliver of twilight slips beneath the lagoon, stone and water meld into an aquaforte engraving, tints of old pewter, shuddering argentate black and gleaming white gold. You have to look for it, to await its coming, but it is the moment when the city is most entirely and mysteriously itself. That moment was coming earlier now, but the days were still hot, and in the afternoons; the beaches on the Lido remained crowded. One afternoon, a week or so after my visit to the Marciana, I was thinking about taking the *vaporetto* and going for a swim; I was working conscientiously enough in the gallery on the plans for the new show, but by 3 p.m. the dead time in Italy, the day was dragging and I couldn't really think of anything else I wanted to do. I was just about to pack up when I heard the door. I had the 'Closed' sign up, since we weren't selling anything, but the visitor, a woman, from the sound of her heels, moved purposefully across the floor to my desk at the back of the space.

'Elisabeth!'

It was the Russian woman from Carlotta's party.

'Elena. Um – hi. How lovely to see you in Venice!'

Elena was wearing a navy silk wrap dress and high wooden platform sandals, with a stiff-brimmed beige straw hat to protect the remains of her original complexion from the sun. A toning Hermès bag and a pair of huge Tom Ford sunglasses dangled from one hand.

'Are you here for long?'

'Just a few days.' She looked uncomfortable. 'Actually, I came to see you.'

'Really? Well, unfortunately I don't have a show up at the moment, as you can see, but –'

'I thought you might like to take a coffee. We could . . . talk.'

'Oh. Well, certainly. Where are you staying?'

'I'm at the Cipriani.'

'Of course you are. Well, I'm free right now, Elena. Perhaps you'd like to cross over? The gardens there are lovely and cool.' Something about her air of distress made me speak reassuringly, as though to a lost child. She clutched at her throat and swallowed hard, then jerked her head to the right in a stage nudge.

'I would prefer somewhere more – private. My husband is very protective, you see.'

I followed the line of her jaw and saw a besuited pair of thick shoulders and a squat neck silhouetted in the sunlight outside the gallery doors. A tight button-down collar almost concealed the hilt of an inked dagger just below the pit-bull jawline. If that was Elena's bodyguard, I could quite understand why she wanted to lose him.

I gathered my things and took the keys from the top desk drawer.

'Sure . . . I can shut things here for a while. Why don't we go for a walk along the Zattere? Just on the water there. There are lots of cafés – we can choose one of those.'

'*Spasibo*.' She thanked me in Russian and stepped quickly out to the goon, pointing to the left, the direction we would take. He moved off and she hovered while I locked up.

'He'll be back in half an hour.'

We walked side by side towards the Gesuati, Elena glancing round to ascertain the proximity of the guard. After we'd exchanged a few remarks about the loveliness of Carlotta's wedding, I made small talk, starting with the good old weather, then pointing out some of the sights across the channel on Giudecca.

'Do you want to go into the church?' I asked, as we paused outside the white baroque frontage. 'The ceilings are very famous. Tiepolo.'

She assented, and I rooted some change out of my purse to buy two tickets. As we passed through the vestibule into the nave, I noticed that Elena crossed herself right to left, with three fingers folded, in the Orthodox style. I didn't. The church was thick with the perennial scent of incense and damp stone. Neither of us so much as glanced at St Dominic ascending to heaven above us.

'Elisabeth, I am sorry to be so mysterious.'

'That's OK. Just tell me how I can help you.' My tone belied my impatience. What did the silly woman want?

'Also for my English.'

'Your English is excellent.'

'It's Soviet. We can never lose the accent. My husband says we pay three times as much for everything, just for the accent.'

'Your husband?' I prompted. Was she ever going to get to the point?

'My husband is Pavel Yermolov.'

I hadn't seen that one coming.

'And he wants to divorce me.'

'Oh. Elena, I'm sorry about that, but I don't see –'

'You will. Let me explain.'

She had recognised me, she said, when I visited Yermolov's house some weeks ago. She had seen me eating with him. 'I was trying to speak to him,' she said sadly, 'but that – that pig, he wouldn't let me.'

'That was you? On the cliff there? But your husband said it was a trespasser. In your own home?'

'I know. It's pathetic.'

Yermolov, Elena explained, had been planning to separate from her for a while. 'He has women – pouf! What do I care about that? But we have also two boys, at school in England. Harrow,' she added proudly. We had to pause there while her phone was produced from the Hermès and the children duly admired. 'So, then I saw you at Carlotta's wedding. I recognised you. I asked Carlotta, and she said you worked with art. So I did some research.'

'I see.' My hands were folded in my lap. I clenched them tight. I suddenly felt cold, and it wasn't the ecclesiastical temperature. *What does she know? What does she want?*

'I learned that my husband had asked you to value his collection. Did he ask you to undervalue it?'

I hesitated, pretending to be distracted by a tour guide loudly explaining the frescos in German. What was this? Yermolov having another go – trying to get some vote of sisterly sympathy?

'He didn't mention a figure. Anyway, I turned down the job. I considered myself too inexperienced.'

'He won't let you.'

I'd worked that out. Yermolov was fucking with my head, but I'd been a bit busy, I thought, what with one thing and another. Time seemed to get the better of me since Alvin's visit.

'What do you mean?' I asked, trying to focus.

'Have you not noticed anything – odd, since you came home to Venice? Has a ghost moved into your flat?'

How could she know about that?

Yermolov wanted me to do the valuation, Elena went on, precisely because of my inexperience. He wanted the valuation low because, like many wealthy men, he was trying to reduce the official value of his assets before filing a divorce petition, in order to ensure a lower settlement. He would file in Russia, Elena believed, because Russian courts were conventionally more favourable to husbands, as well as more gentle about forcing them to reveal their worth. Yet a few recent cases had attracted unwelcome press, so for a man as rich as Yermolov it would be best if the proceedings were as discreet as possible. If anyone questioned the value of the collection, he wanted someone to blame.

That hurt. It hurt a lot. It was one thing to know that I didn't think myself good enough for Yermolov's pictures, quite another to learn that he didn't either. I thought I had turned him down honestly, and had taken comfort in even seeing the pictures, coming closer to their aura than most others ever would. But he had only wanted a stooge, a straw man. Perhaps he didn't take kindly to being refused, perhaps the antics in my flat were an attempt to bully me, but that wouldn't explain the Stubbs postcard . . . I tried to concentrate on the conversation.

'So it's better for your husband if he divorces you in Russia. Not for you, obviously. But why should he care so much?'

Elena rolled her eyes. It was her turn to be impatient. 'My husband is . . . well placed with the authorities. He wants to keep it that way.'

'I see.' I knew Yermolov had political connections – maybe a foreign divorce would cause a scandal?

'Anyway, I hate him. He treats me like a prisoner, like an animal! And now he throws me away like an old shoe! He says our relationship is no longer "effective".'

From where I was sitting, Elena didn't look much like an old shoe. Her engagement ring alone would have rented a flat in Mayfair for a year.

'I appreciate your confiding in me, and I'm sorry for your situation, I really am, but I still don't see why you think I can help you.'

She looked around. 'This place is giving me the creeps. Let's go.'

I followed her patiently back to the quay, where we both blinked and shivered, blinded by the sudden glare of heat.

'We'd better go back.' She started walking slowly, holding my arm as though we were old friends. Her face was close to mine. I could smell her scent and see the fine feathering of lines around her mouth where the filler was beginning to slip. 'So, my husband thinks he can get rid of me, like that!' She snapped her fingers. 'And he knows that if he does . . .'

'Elena, please be clear. This isn't making any sense.'

She turned and clutched my elbows. 'I have been married to Pavel for many years. Thirty years. I have seen a lot, heard a lot. Without my marriage, I will be in danger. I know this. I need to have something, something that will keep me safe.'

'But you will have money. Perhaps not as much as you feel you deserve, after so long –'

She dug her nails into my elbow. 'It's not money. Do you not read the newspapers? Russia is not Europe, whatever they pretend. If I am not married to Pavel, it will be . . .

expedient – to get rid of me. People who are an embarrassment to the authorities find themselves in prison, or worse. I am under threat, can't you see?'

Before I had time to reply that I didn't see anything except that she was insane, Elena stepped away and, to my surprise and that of the tourist crowd, executed a perfect pirouette in her high chopines.

'I was a good ballerina once!' The woman was utterly mad. 'I will collect you tonight. A little outing, to pay homage to Diaghilev! Shall we say here in front of the church, at 7 p.m.?'

'Elena, please. I don't think this is a good idea. I'm sorry, but I can't help you.'

She turned back, the brittle gay smile wiped from her face. 'Oh, but you can. When I first saw you with Pavel, I assumed you were a –'

'Tart?'

'A prostitute, yes. But when Carlotta told me what you do, I researched your gallery. Nice name, Gentileschi.'

'Um, thank you.'

'Silly of you to have mentioned it to the French police though.'

I gaped at her like a gigged frog.

Morning on the steps of Sacré-Cœur, my last day in Paris. I could smell it, the churned stink of garbage, exhaust from the tourist buses, marijuana, coffee. Renaud's phone in my hand, a whole squad of *gendarmes* waiting at Charles de Gaulle for a girl with a fake passport who never made her flight. *En route. Does the name Gentileschi mean anything to you?*' I'd texted them. Half caution, half audacity, the stupid, enticing compulsion of risk. I'd taken care of Renaud, so how could Elena possibly know? Was she responsible for the Stubbs postcard too? What the hell was happening here?

Elena was clearly taking pleasure in her revelation. I stared past her, along the quay, fighting the urge to shove her into the water along with a sudden sense of strangling claustrophobia, as though the twined circumstances that had brought me here were coiling around me, a hissing, rearing Hydra that could never lie quiet. I'd thought I was safe, clear of the past here in Venice, even if Alvin was still – Stop. Don't think about Alvin. Focus on this mad bitch who's trying to steal your life.

'I have no idea what you're talking about' I said stiffly.

'Oh, but I think you do. I need your help with a picture.'

She leaned even closer, her lips against my ear, as though she was sharing a particularly scandalous morsel of gossip. Somewhere ahead, I sensed the goon was watching us. 'I think you are good with paintings, Judith?'

10

I spent the rest of the afternoon lying on my bed, pinned there by the frozen lead in my heart. Yermolov knew. Elena knew. Why didn't I just take out an ad in the bloody *Corriere della Sera*? It was all I could do to stop myself peering under the bed to see if Romero da Silva was lurking there for good measure. This wasn't going to stop. This wasn't ever going to stop. What was I supposed to do? Pitch Elena Yermolov into the lagoon along with her bodyguard? Quite funny, that. At least, I could hear someone laughing.

I gave myself a mental clip round the ear. I had been right that the *zersetzung* was Yermolov's doing – Elena's use of my real name confirmed it. So who had told them? I replayed my conversation with Yermolov when we had dined in his summer house. Hadn't he said something about Paris? I bit my knuckles in frustration. He'd known before he even asked me there. And I'd been so proud, so delighted. But this was not the moment to cosset my wounded pride. Elena's garbled account about the divorce made some sort of sense. Yermolov had wanted me to undervalue the collection, had thought he could exercise pressure – excruciatingly plausible. But what about the 'threats' to his wife? I didn't set much store by her murky talk, but Elena's urgency suggested she believed her own story. She was prepared to challenge her husband, and she had mentioned a picture. This was, somehow, to do with a picture. So – the next thing. I couldn't protect myself without knowledge. So I had to meet her. Proceed slowly, learn all I could.

By 7 p.m. I had recovered my countenance. At the dock I was handed into a honey-toned Riva to join Mrs Yermolov in the low cabin. Black had seemed the right colour for a trip to the cemetery island of San Michele, silk equipment trousers and a plain round-neck jersey, but at the last minute that looked a bit too Ninja, so I added a heavy turquoise cashmere shawl against the evening breeze on the lagoon. We set off in silence over the milky jade water, admiring the endlessly perfect vistas of the Grand Canal, two ladies on a quirky romantic outing. The goon stood in the prow with the skipper, earnestly smoking. The boat pulled off right towards Cannaregio, and in a few minutes I felt the heavier swell of the open lagoon beneath us. I fancied a fag myself, but halfway through the crossing Elena started looking rather queasy, so it seemed kinder not to. When we drew up at San Michele, she stood for a few moments with her head bowed to her knees, not an easy manoeuvre in a corseted Versus evening dress and four-inch heels.

'The boat will wait for us,' she announced grandly. 'Have you been here before?'

I hadn't. Henry James might have said that Venice was the most beautiful sepulchre in the world, but it wasn't an idea I'd recently felt the need to investigate.

'He's in the Greek section. Come on.'

Unlike the rest of the city, San Michele is neatly kept, bulbs of yew setting off the orange brickwork of the loggias. Elena's stilettos twisted awkwardly on the gravel, but she glided on, holding her shoulders carefully, for Diaghilev's benefit.

'Here it is.'

The monument was cream and ivory stone, its commemoration carved in gilded Cyrillic. Elena sat down cosily on the next grave and produced a bottle of Stoli and three tea glasses from her handbag. 'One for you, one for me, and one for the Master,' she explained, pouring. We toasted the grave and each knocked back a shot before Elena emptied the third glass over the stone. I wondered if it was regular libations of alcohol that kept it so shiny. I lit the cigarette I had been planning and held out my glass for a refill.

'Aren't we going to offer one to Stravinsky?' I remarked conversationally. It seemed in keeping with this deranged cocktail party. 'He's eleven graves along.'

Elena snorted. 'Hah. Old plagiarist.'

Not my most successful gambit.

'So you were a dancer?' I tried.

'Not much of one. For a few years I wanted to get into the Bolshoi Academy, but I wasn't good enough. And then I met Pavel.' She snorted again and drained her vodka. 'I thought we could talk here.'

'Fair enough. It wasn't the first time you saw me, was it, Elena? That evening at the beach house? And we didn't meet at Carlotta's wedding either. You first saw me on Mikhail Balensky's boat.'

Balensky, known as 'The Man from the Stan', was a notorious arms-dealer-turned-businessman who had invited Steve to a party when I was staying on the *Mandarin*. Carlotta had posed as Steve's fiancée while I conducted a little industrial espionage below decks. I have a good recall for faces, and Elena's, deeply tanned and unfortunately made-up, had jumped out at me as soon as I ran the memory.

'Quite right. That's why I assumed you were a – tart, you say?'

The bells of the fat miniature basilica were chiming eight along the avenues of graves.

'Won't the cemetery be closing now?'

Elena smiled wryly 'We are enjoying a private visit, courtesy of Pavel. I might as well take advantage while I still can. So?'

I took a deep breath. 'So. In 2007 Rostropovich's collection came up for auction at one of the big houses in London. The sale was cancelled at the last minute because a Russian buyer purchased the pieces in their entirety for about twenty-five million dollars. He promised to return them to Russia, a patriotic gesture that made him very popular. Shall I carry on?'

Elena hardly appeared to be listening. She was rummaging in her bag again. 'You want to frighten me,' I continued, 'because you are frightened yourself. You want a picture that you can hand over to the Russian state as collateral for your protection. Like the businessman did with the Rostropovich pieces?'

She looked up and smiled, offering me a couple of photocopied papers. 'You are very quick.'

'Either you're quick or you're dead.'

'What?' She looked absurdly startled.

'Nothing. Sorry.'

I glanced at the papers she had produced. Printouts from the online edition of an Italian newspaper; a report on the murder of an English art dealer, Cameron Fitzpatrick, in Rome; a short French article on the ongoing police investigation of a mysterious death in a hotel near the Place de l'Odéon, Paris. I was familiar with them both.

'Looks like we're both pretty good at research. Can we get on with this, please? I'm cold.'

'Have another drink.'

What Elena said next made me choke on it.

'My husband has a Caravaggio drawing.'

She might not have cut it as a prima ballerina, but she had a real talent for theatrics.

'That's impossible. Everyone knows that. Caravaggio didn't draw – he was famous for it.'

'Nonetheless.'

'It must be a fake – it has to be. Whatever he's told you –'

'He has told me nothing. He and Balensky bought it, together. That is the picture I want.'

'I saw a Caravaggio, but it's a copy. A brilliant one, but a copy. Your husband knows that.'

'That's not the picture I mean. This is a drawing. Made here, in Venice.'

'Elena, Caravaggio didn't draw, and he never came to Venice. I don't know what you think you know, but if you think I am going anywhere near this, you are wrong. Totally wrong. I'm sorry about your difficulties, if you really have them, but I'm leaving now.'

I stood and began to walk purposefully towards the dock.

'Wait. I'm sorry. Please wait.' In the fading light she looked like a funeral statue herself, in her unwieldy gown, her hand again at her throat. Something about the appeal in her voice made me pause in the still, greying air.

'Really, I'm not trying to threaten you. I don't care who you are, or what you have done. I know how my husband found you. It was something to do with that man, in Paris.' Elena's voice was wild – it occurred to me that she'd started on the vodka much earlier than I'd noticed. I'd had enough experience with my mother to recognise the signs. She had started to cry, pawing restlessly at her eyes as the tears made tracks in her bronzer.

'Come on, Elena, it's getting cold. We'll go to my flat and I'll get you some coffee.' The flat was the last place I wanted her, but she was too sloppy for a public place. I put my arm firmly around her shoulders, kept my voice firm and gentle as I had so often done, all the times I'd had to haul my mother to bed. 'Come on. Let's get you back.'

Elena knew. Yermolov knew. If I didn't fix this somehow, I couldn't continue my life as Elisabeth Teerlinc. And Yermolov had humiliated me. He had played me, and the thought of it sparked a tiny, long-forgotten flame inside. Since I couldn't plausibly dispose of Elena, I had to use her. If I didn't, Yermolov could destroy me, and she knew it.

She threw up over the side of the launch on the crossing, which seemed to clear her head. I asked the boatman to get us as near as he could to the piazza, and explained to the goon that I was going to help Mrs Yermolov into some fresh clothes, as she was feeling unwell. He positioned himself outside the street door of my flat. I wondered if it was the first time he'd been there. Letting us in, I took a quick, suspicious sniff at the air, but smelled nothing except Cire Trudon's Spiritus Sancti. I asked Elena if she was hungry, but she shook her head impatiently, so I made coffee, adding sugar to hers. I fetched a pair of sweatpants, socks and a jumper and told her to slip them on, then we sat side by side on the chaise. After washing her face, and in the simple clothes, she looked much younger. I saw again how lovely she must have been.

'They have been here,' I began. 'Your husband's people. Moving stuff around.' I wasn't going to let on exactly what stuff, or what message I thought her husband could have been sending.

'I thought so. That's how they work, at first. Him and Balensky.'

'And they bought this supposed Caravaggio drawing together. They're friends then?'

'Friends, colleagues, but not anymore. They made a lot of money in property together back in the day, in Moscow.' I recalled Masha's story about the way Yermolov dealt with inconvenient tenants. Knowing he was involved with Balensky, who had brazened out a fairly foul reputation, made me wonder.

'Go on.'

'They haven't been friends since this.' She used her now bare toe to scoot her handbag across the floor towards us and unfolded the second newspaper clipping.

'This man, the man who died in the hotel room? He worked for my husband. Also for Balensky.'

'I knew him as Moncada.' There didn't seem much point in pretending I didn't know what she was talking about. Especially since I hadn't actually killed him.

'You were there, the night he died, yes?'

I nodded, slowly. 'I was selling him a picture. I took it to the hotel, in the Place de l'Odéon, yes. I left before the – murder.'

'My husband knew that. His people were watching the hotel. There was another picture there; the Moncada man was waiting to hand it over on behalf of my husband and

Balensky. Then this Moncada was killed. But when my husband tried to find the picture, it was gone. Balensky double-crossed him, he thought, with you.'

'Hang on. Your husband thinks I took his Caravaggio? That's why he pursued me?'

'I think so. He thinks you – cheated him. You and Balensky.'

'This is nuts. Besides, I didn't. I really didn't.'

'This is what I know about you. A woman named Judith Rashleigh is questioned by the Italian police in connection with the murder of an art dealer, Cameron Fitzpatrick. The woman sets up an art gallery in Paris, registered under the name Gentileschi. The woman is then seen leaving a hotel where another man has been murdered, carrying a picture. Then . . . pouf! – Gentileschi appears as a gallery in Venice, now registered to Elisabeth Teerlinc. And the picture is missing.'

'How do you know all this, Elena? It's bizarre. I thought you said you and your husband were separated?'

'We are estranged, yes. But officially still married, while he gets things ready. I am permitted –' she snorted the word contemptuously – 'to continue to live in our homes, for the present. But we don't cross over. That evening in France, I had come unexpectedly. I wanted to talk to him.'

'And you found out about this – this business?'

'I am a good spy. I'm Russian, no? When I knew Pavel wanted to divorce me I needed information,' she added with a bitter little laugh.

Startling though Elena's knowledge was, her account left me . . . almost relieved. If Yermolov's scare tactics were aimed at getting me to return a picture I didn't have, I could quickly correct the misapprehension. The picture I had carried to the hotel in the Place de l'Odéon had been a small Gerhard Richter, legitimately purchased at auction by Gentileschi. It was a pity that I hadn't attended the sale in person, as auctions are taped and I supposed that way I could have shown him myself bidding for it, but the provenances were on record; they had to be, as I had given the painting to Dave, who had been my friend back at the House, where he had worked as a porter after leaving the army. Thanks to some connections which had proved very useful to both of us, he and his wife had moved to a pretty village near Bath, where he had retrained as an art-history teacher. The Richter had been sold to fund their move to the country. I explained as briefly as I could.

Elena's hands were uncreasing her clippings again. She seemed to have a talismanic faith in them.

'I accept your story, *Judith*. But I want the Caravaggio. You have secrets – I told you, I don't care about them. Nor, I imagine, does my husband, if he knows you are not a thief. I would like you to offer to find the picture for him, and when you find it, to tell me where it is. That's all.'

'What is this? *Ocean's Eleven*? Why would I do that, Elena?'

'If you do not agree, I will tell him I have been here.' She nodded at the window, reminding me of the presence of the goon beneath us. 'Such a coincidence! Both friends of dear Carlotta. And I will tell him I have seen the picture, and he will kill you first and look for it afterwards. Or I could suggest to the Italian police that they reopen a certain case, ask you why you are living under fake papers. And also – this is the one I like – because I think you will.'

She was threatening me, but she was also offering me a game, of sorts. In a way I didn't dislike the idea of helping her get one over on Yermolov. Not for her sake, but for mine. For now, I played along, if only because I so desperately needed time to think.

'OK, Elena. Checkmate. Though I can't understand why your husband would want to divorce you. You're brilliant.'

'Yes,' she said sadly. 'Yes, I was, once.'

11

I agreed to meet Elena the next day for lunch at the café above the Guggenheim Collection. Most of the night was spent hunched over my laptop. Every now and then I'd jump at a creaking board or the scratch of one of the ubiquitous Venetian rats in the plasterwork, but now that I knew the source of their presence, Yermolov's 'ghosts' no longer troubled me. I had other things to worry about, namely the source who had identified me in Paris.

The night I had met Moncada in the Place de l'Odéon, he had also been working for Yermolov and Balensky, transporting the supposed Caravaggio to them. I already knew that Balensky was dodgy, and it didn't exactly surprise me that Yermolov's past was less squeaky-clean than it seemed. Moncada was Italian mafia; he moved dubious pictures, and a Caravaggio 'drawing' was nothing if not dubious. So Moncada could have informed the oligarchs of his meeting with me at the hotel. But Elena had also said that someone had seen me leave with the picture. That couldn't have been Moncada, because he was in the room on the fourth floor, being strangled by Renaud. The someone else was the person I needed to find, and Elena was a distraction. Simply contacting Yermolov and telling him I didn't have the Caravaggio was pointless. Firstly because he had no reason to believe me, and secondly as, until I discovered the source, I would never be free of the trail left by that stupid text.

The problem with going along with Elena's plan was that the idea of the picture itself was preposterous. All the experts I consulted on Caravaggio were unanimous that he had never drawn – at most he may have pricked pinholes in his canvases to mark out the placement of his models – but there was some disagreement as to whether he had visited Venice. In the online archive of the London Library I found a journal article by a Venetian professor which dismissed the idea, which I copied onto my phone to show Elena. I had to get her off my back, contact Yermolov and explain the misunderstanding, then set about discovering the source. Any thoughts of revenge on the oligarchs were self-indulgence, though I did permit myself a few little fantasies as to what I would do to them as I walked over to the Guggenheim.

Elena had her unfortunate game-face back on and was halfway down a bottle of Pinot Grigio when I arrived at the museum's rooftop café. I poured myself some water, hoping she would follow my virtuous example.

'Where's your friend? Burgling my flat again?'

'Yury? He excused himself on an errand. So I'm celebrating,' she replied defiantly, pouring herself another glass. I took the bottle and turned it upside down in the ice bucket, followed by the contents of the glass.

'Have some water, Elena. You're no good pissed, however sorry you feel for yourself.'

Her protestations were interrupted by the waitress. I ordered mint and fennel bruschetta and a portion of ravioli. I like to live on the edge where carbohydrates are concerned. Elena asked for a green salad, no dressing.

'Elena, I've thought it over,' I explained as the girl set down her depressing lunch. 'I don't think I can help, really. For a start, we both know that despite that – business in Paris, I don't have the picture. I know you believe me. So it must have been Balensky. But there's no way that whatever Balensky did or didn't steal from your husband is worth anything. Even if I could find it for you, it has to be a fake. I was up half the night checking it out online and there's no suggestion of such a drawing existing. I checked it out with the experts. So even if you could get this picture, because you think it represents some kind of leverage, it won't help you in the event that you get divorced.'

Elena was negotiating a rocket leaf. It hung from the side of her mouth as she practically snarled at me. 'Why don't you just kill me?'

I'd already run through about six methods of doing precisely that, but none of them seemed viable without being discovered. Though Yermolov might offer me a reward. Maybe, though, it was the image of the two open faces of Elena's sons underneath their boaters that had made me soft in my old age. I sat there as she champed up the salad.

'I have no idea what you mean.'

She exaggerated her accent, rolling the 'r'. 'What is your phrase? I *know too much*!' She collapsed into a fit of giggles, snorting into her plate.

This was getting boring, but the pumpkin and amaretti in their slippery whorls of pasta were really excellent.

'Stop being stupid, please. Your husband has some extraordinary pictures – the Botticellis, for example. Surely they would be just as good? If you could get those, to give to the state?'

She gasped down her hilarity and finally sipped some water. 'He will give me nothing. I am sure that the drawing exists, that it is real. And I am sure that you will help me. Here.'

Not another newspaper clipping, thank Christ. Elena was holding out her phone, open at a photograph. Or rather, a photo of a photo.

'I took this in my husband's study. It was the day he told me I could no longer use the houses at the same time as him. He had had my things packed up and moved, as though he was sacking a servant.'

I knew that feeling. Maybe that was why I reached for the phone and fanned my fingertips over the screen, expanding, reducing. The original photo showed a sepia-toned drawing room with a large arched window overlooking what was recognisably the Grand Canal, a heavy credenza beneath it, and next to that a stiff-backed sofa covered in what looked like a patterned silk. Above the sofa was a framed picture. I focused in, seeing what seemed to be a portrait of a woman. A bust, slightly turned to three-quarter profile, both elbows propped out as though she was leaning against something. Her hair was bundled messily on her head, her gaze cast down. I magnified the shot, observing both the spare graphic of the line and the intense, tenebristic modelling of the head, which seemed to be done in another colour from the black and white, though in the old photo it was hard to discern. The whole picture looked rippled, though whether that was the reflection from the frame's glass or a quality of the canvas was hard to discern.

'This picture was taken in the 1890s, in a *pensione* here in Venice. That's the drawing.'

'The famous Caravaggio?' I stared hard, held the phone close to my eyes, back, close again. 'It's on cloth?' The unevenness in the surface of the picture looked to be produced by fabric.

'Linen. That's what it said in the notes, but I didn't have much time.'

'Notes?'

'There was a letter, but I didn't have time to photograph that. But the picture shows that it was there, over a century ago, that it's real.' The certainty in her voice was painful.

'Do you remember anything else?'

'It was described as a sketch, in chalk with an oil. I remember that, because the English sounded strange. *An* oil.'

'Elena, I'm sorry, but it doesn't mean a thing. These provenance photos can be faked – it's a classic. There was a couple in Germany who got away with it for years. You mock up a Victorian photo to show that your picture or whatever has been around for a while. And even if the photo is genuine, there's no way this portrait can be real. Maybe it's all in good faith, an honest mistake, but, please, you have to give up on this. Really. Look.' I held out my phone, with the saved paragraph from the journal article:

Despite contentions that Caravaggio visited Venice on his journey to Rome from Milan in 1592 (Provorsi et al, 2001; Filicino, 1990), the hypothesis of such a visit has been definitively dismissed (Raniero, 2003) as indicative of a mere 'fantasy of influence' (Raniero, ibid) with regard to his Milanese tutor Peterzano. Quite simply, no evidence exists of his presence in Venice.

Elena looked into my face for a long moment, then lowered her eyes. I wished I hadn't been so mean with the Pinot.

'I am leaving Venice today. Please, let me send you the photo. And you can take my numbers?'

'I'm sorry, Elena. I really am.'

The booze fell out of her face along with its gentleness. She leaned forward and spoke in a harsh, cold voice. 'No, I am sorry for you. If you don't find the picture, I think you know what will happen to you. You are young, you have many, many years ahead of you. Where would you like to spend them? Here –' she gestured at the view, always familiar, always astonishing – 'or in prison?'

'You have nothing on me, Elena.'

'Perhaps yes, perhaps no. But whatever I can do to you, believe me, you'll be grateful for it if my husband gets to you first.'

I could feel the twitch of my pupils expanding. The clatter of cutlery and multilingual conversations suddenly roared in my ears. There it was, the rushing impulse I had felt with Alvin, that almost ecstatic departure from reality that would last until it was over and I was looking down at what I'd done. I pressed my nails into my palms. Control the consequences. Deliberately I closed my eyes, sullenly I passed her my work phone and let her send the photo across and put her details into my contacts.

Elena was assembling her handbag and sunhat. 'I think you will be in touch. You'll see. Take care of yourself.'

I watched her walk away with the concentrated steadiness of the practised drunk. Ignoring the ostentatious tuttings of an American couple at the next table, I lit a fag. My fingers hovered over my phone like a bloody teenager's. And then, while I waited for the bill, I looked at the photo, then googled a map of the Grand Canal. The view from the window – I noticed that the only boats visible were gondolas – showed what looked like a corner of the Palazzo Grassi, which would place the *pensione* in one of the buildings opposite. Not hard to find. I tracked down the names of the *palazzi*, checked them in turn. All hotels. Maybe it wouldn't be so hard to track down the apartment in that photo, just to ascertain that no such picture could exist? It couldn't hurt. When I contacted Yermolov, it might even prove to be a bargaining chip, the suggestion that his sodding Caravaggio was a fake. A means of getting him off my back. Plus, I admitted, there would be a certain pleasure in imparting the information.

I thought of Masha and her network of old biddies. All of their countless relatives worked in hospitality. Maybe she might know someone who could help me find the hotel in the picture?

Masha didn't respond to her buzzer, so I rummaged in my bag for a scrap of paper and hunched awkwardly on my knees to write a note. But then I didn't like to leave that under the street door, which was kept locked since the burglary, so I buzzed my way through the neighbours until one of them let me in, and started up the stairs.

Silence is not a constant. It has different qualities – the silence of a phone ringing in an empty house, the silence of a room where someone is sleeping. The silence on Masha's landing had a taut feeling, as though the air had been wrung free of noise behind the slightly open door. The silence of an imperceptible lack. She was lying face down on her tatty Persian rug, one black-sleeved arm stretched towards the window. Had she been trying to crawl across the room, to cry out across the rooftops for help? The purpling wound on her right temple was a painted rose on the heavy powder of her pale cheek. She looked so very small in her tight colourful shawl, a broken matryoshka dropped by a careless child. Her skirts had ruched up as she fell, exposing her shrivelled legs in their thick beige tights; there was a sharp stink of piss above the usual fug of tea leaves and dripping. I watched her hopelessly for a few endless heartbeats, but I knew there would be no breath, no stirring. Whoever had done the job would have finished it. And I had seen the crumpled emptiness of death, its subtle inhumanity.

I hooked my elbow under the door handle and stepped inside, pushing it quietly closed behind me. Kneeling, I tugged gently at the hem of her petticoat with my fingertips. At least I could make her decent. She was lying on something hard, partly concealed beneath the black nylon. I tugged it out, then pulled my hand back as though it had been scorched. It was the icon, the Madonna that had been damaged during the burglary. Half the face had been torn away.

I stepped carefully around poor Masha and went to the cubbyhole kitchen, where I retrieved a tea towel to wrap around my right hand. There was a shuddering beneath my ribs but I forced it back like a cough. Using the towel, I carefully opened Masha's bulbous cracked handbag, which sat on a painted stool next to the door, and extracted a worn blue leather diary. I had seen her use it to contact students and note their payments – I always gave her cash, which meant that the only thing linking her to my name was my phone number in her book. Couldn't have that lying around. I was starting to shake, gulping in the close air, but I manoeuvred the diary into my own bag and returned the towel to the kitchen. I hated that I had thought of that, but there was nothing that could help her now. Someone would come eventually, if only because of the heat.

12

And then I ran. Dodging cruise-ship crocodiles, piles of fake designer bags, plastic gewgaws, mask stalls and glass stalls, cursing the impossibility of a cab and the detritus of the Venice streets, I banged out the familiar route to the gallery, my mind keeping pace with my feet, fumbling for my keys as I passed the San Basilio *vaporetto*, slamming open the metal shutters with a desperate heave until the sight of what lay in there knocked the breath back out of me and I reeled back into the street to recover. Then, carefully, I stepped inside and lowered the blinds once more, blinking in the undersea twilight. The floor was a churned mass of papers, glinting with fragments of glass. The top of my beautiful desk. Less beautiful now that it was smeared all over with the new paint for the walls and the deep blue ink I used for handwriting receipts. They hadn't had much to work with – as I said, I like to keep things tidy – but mixed with the fragments were the pieces of the delicate little espresso cups I kept for clients, my orange Venini water glasses and jug, all my kit – tape, hammers, tacks – everything crushed and trampled together. That empty space, which had so recently shone with the pleasure of my own private kingdom, was now sneering in its smallness. Automatically, I stooped and began a futile attempt at tidying, but I soon stopped.

Dislocated and smashed, all my carefully chosen things were reduced to rubbish. I skirted the mess and wincingly opened the bottom drawer of the desk, closed my eyes in relief. The gun was still there.

It had been as quick a job as it looked. Not a search, a scare. Moncada's pistol was where it always laid, underneath the false surface of the bottom drawer. I retrieved it, careful not to mark my arms with the tacky paint, and slipped it into my bag. For a long moment I stood and looked at the wreckage of everything I had thought I ever wanted. I'd seen worse installations. Maybe a better gallerist would have scrawled a title in lipstick over one of the wrecked catalogues, pinned it to the door and flogged the whole mess off, but I had lost patience with knowing art jokes. The dim, artificially lit atmosphere recalled that of the warehouse back in London where Dave and I had spent so much time with the pictures, but the light was the only honest thing left.

It took me a moment to absorb that sharp, astonishing thought. What I felt, looking again at the destruction, was not rage, but relief. Never one to miss a cheap shot, my subconscious threw up another idea. Frankly, I was bored to blisters of Elisabeth Teerlinc. Yermolov's people had smashed her shell, and suddenly, with a surprising sense of release, I could see her for the hollow fake she was. Elisabeth Teerlinc might have convinced a few idiot art buyers, but she'd never really convinced me. Try as I might to become her, her skin had always sat awkwardly.

Elisabeth knew what was expected of her; Judith just hadn't been all that interested in going along with it. The persona I had invented for Elisabeth – sleekly and discreetly Eurowealthy, vaguely educated, monstrously entitled, was the distillation of everything that Judith Rashleigh had despised. It troubled me that my model for my future self turned out to have been Angelica Belvoir all along.

And I'd done a pretty good job. So good that I couldn't stand the sight of the result.

After this, Gentileschi was unlikely ever to be in business again. Nonetheless, I wasn't ready to draw attention to that fact just yet. I spent a while shoving the debris of Elisabeth's career into three plastic bin liners and put them out for the rubbish boat, like a good citizen. I left the shutters down and fixed the 'Closed' sign to the inside of the door. Yermolov's cronies had smashed the locks – just a hammer, probably – but I reached in through the mail slot and shot the bolt at the bottom. From outside, there was nothing to alert anyone to a disturbance.

Naturally, the next thing I did was go to the bank. I cashed a personal cheque for ten thousand euro and a second for the same amount through Gentileschi. I entered the flat barrel first. The 9x21 Caracal F was the gun Moncada had pulled on Renaud the night of the murder in the Place de l'Odéon. I'd planned to dispose of it along with some other evidence – well, to be frank, along with Renaud's head – in a Decathlon sports carrier I'd dropped into the

Seine, but I'd tweaked it out at the last minute. I'd seen to Renaud with a Glock 26 procured for me by useful Dave, and that piece had also taken care of Julien, a one-time club owner, but I'd disposed of it out of the window of the night train to Amsterdam. The Caracal is not too heavy, just over 700g; even better, it has a take-down lever that allows it to be quickly disassembled. I'd kept it ever since, in the gallery, its eighteen-round box magazine fully stocked. Moncada hadn't had a chance to fire a shot before Renaud strangled him. On the landing, I clicked the cartridge column back into place and aimed at the door, picturing a tattooed Russian head coming at me. *Aim and squeeze*. It seemed at first that the ghosts were having a day off. Retrieving my old passport from the linen press was almost calming; at least the spooks in there were familiar. I packed both documents – Elisabeth could come along for the ride, but I would be Judith again, for a while.

I didn't need to pack; there were two bags waiting ready in the dressing room, black enamelled Rimowa cases with four wheels. Rimowas are heavy, but they have a removable zip lining which is handy for stashing things. Each was packed with a versatile capsule wardrobe, allowing me to curate a variety of different looks, along with identical sets of gym gear and cosmetics. One was Med-bunny style, the kinds of things I would need if I was planning to go on the lam with Tage Stahl, the other more sober and practical, at least as near as my wardrobe got to it. I picked the second, lifted the folded contents to slip the gun and the bulk of the cash into the lining and spun the combination on the lock. Then I moved mechanically around the space, fastening the shutters, emptying the fridge, taking down the rubbish, building a mental dam of basic tasks. I paused to send a text to Dave:

I need a grey hat, I wrote, *someone serious, asap. Thanks as ever, Jx*

Dave might have gone bucolic, but he still knew people. I was thankful now that, as things sat between us, we rarely bothered with niceties. I completed the packing while I awaited his reply.

Will do. Give me a day? Hope all smooth. D

I don't have a day.

Soonest then. Hang on.

I wasn't sure if I'd ever see my pictures again, but I could try to save them. I moved the dehumidifier I had bought against the Venetian damp from the drawing room to the dressing room, fetched some cotton garment holders to shield them, then lifted them down one by one, caressing them with my eyes, letting my palms whisper over the canvases. It was when I came to my *Susanna* that I saw the ghosts had been busy after all.

In the painting, the almost nude young woman turns her face away over her right shoulder, in contempt for the two old men conspiring behind the wall against which she cowers. Susanna's story is a triumph of virtue over vice – the two voyeurs lust after her as she bathes and try to blackmail her into sex, she defies them and their attempts at false testimony against her backfire and they are executed. Yet as with many canonised subjects, the depiction of Susanna is usually a pretext for porn. Why show her denouncing her accusers when one could show her naked in the water? The real subject is not vindicated innocence but the anarchy of lust, the skill with which the painter's rendering of Susanna's luscious flesh makes the viewer declare for the wrong side, despite himself. We see ourselves in the elders' plotting, their besottedness, and the knowledge is disarming.

The luminous mirror of Susanna's face was slashed beyond repair. The *sfregio*. Inserted into the gash was the lower half of the Madonna icon from Masha's flat. As if Yermolov hadn't made his point. Removing the scrap of coloured paper, I traced the tear in the painting, which rendered Susanna not only disfigured but lifeless, a flat lump of oil and colour, no longer even an object. The movement of my hands hypnotised me as I gazed at the dark wood of the mount through the hole, my fingers circling its rim. After all, there was nothing there. I watched the fingers insert themselves beneath the shredded canvas, watched it strain and split, watched the varnish crack and flake, until the canvas bubbled and sagged and the fingers closed in a fist as Susanna's body was torn from the frame, the hands scrabbling frantically at her skin, enacting the elders' desires, to strip her to flay her to make her shudder and gape, clutching and squeezing her loveliness into shredded ruin.

After a while I noticed that my nails were torn ragged, and there were long stripes on my arms where they had raked at my skin. There were flakes of paint in my hair, in my eyelashes, shreds and scraps of canvas in a crazed bag lady's nest about me on the floor. The image of Masha hovered at the edge of my brain, and for a moment I considered how soothing it would be to lie there on the floor and let them come, all of them, all the ghosts, to lie quiet as they teased out all that was left of me until I was as hollow as Susanna's frame. No. Not yet. The doors of the linen closet were in my sightline. I jumped to my feet and began to clear up the mess.

Now that I was finished with my preparations, the flat felt like no refuge. I considered a siesta and a bracing wank, but I just didn't feel that way about myself any more. Masturbation can make you feel so used. And I was strangely scared that if I tried, all I would find would be blunt emptiness. Giving a final glance to see if I had missed anything, I left the bags locked inside the street door and trailed off to the *campo* to kill time. I took a coffee outside the flat, but I couldn't keep still, so I walked the canals of Dorsoduro, tourist-blind, clutching my phone and checking the screen every few minutes. Finally Dave sent me a Snapcode and a time: 7 p.m. Good. I sat at another café, ordered another unwanted coffee and a bottle of water, took out my Montblanc and began to make a list.

I needed to know what Yermolov could do if he really wanted to make trouble for me, and if so, how. Most people might think that a dead teacher already represented enough trouble, it was a beginning, merely a signal of intent. The

'Caravaggio' could only be a fake, but Yermolov clearly believed that it was real, and that I had it. Simply telling him I knew nothing about it, even if that were possible, wasn't going to cut it. And from what Elena had explained, Yermolov knew I had been there in Place de l'Odéon, knew that I was connected, somehow, with Cameron Fitzpatrick's death. If the grunts didn't get me first, it wouldn't be long before the police came knocking. What about Balensky? If Yermolov believed that I was in cahoots with the Man from the Stan, surely he would be anxious to dissociate himself also. I had no ideas as to how I could get to Balensky while my throat was still intact, unless he was on Tinder. I found my pen doodling a little dagger on the corner of the page. In the hieroglyphs of Russian crime, a tattooed dagger on the neck signified that the bearer had murdered someone *in* prison. Seeing Yury again wasn't going to happen anytime soon, but I had to know how much time and distance I could buy.

3.30 p.m. sour-mouthed from too much coffee, wandering again. Somewhere near Campo San Polo I heard the siren of the ambulance boat from the canal. It had always struck me as essentially comic that emergencies in Venice were dealt with by dashing boats, but considering where they could be on their way to, it didn't seem that funny anymore. But right now I could only consider myself. Another table, another espresso. At exactly 7 p.m. by the clock back in the square, I entered the code.

'White hats' are coding experts who work legitimately, investigating problems or bugs within systems. 'Black hats' abuse their expertise, sometimes for profit, often for shits and giggles. 'Greys', obviously, sit somewhere in between. Many of them hire out to military outfits, hence my request to Dave. Once my hat and I had connected via the Snapcode, I started immediately with my questions; I didn't introduce myself and nor did he or she.

Thanks for helping me. I need to know if an offshore account can be hacked?

They pinged back. *Not unless you're the CIA, lol!*

Really? Even by someone with serious money to pay for it?

That stuff's for movies.

Even Russian?

Russian? Old school.

Meaning?

Governments can mess with accounts. The systems don't exist outside. That's what people think, but private not advanced yet. They'll just fuck with you.

How?

Usual. Physical.

Nothing like understatement. I suppose I might have described a dead old woman as 'old school'.

What about surveillance?

IMHO (what the hell did he mean? Why couldn't these people just use actual words?) *no worry, unless you're running (:*

Jesus.

Card sensors a problem, even if you don't use them. Watch that.

Thanks. Phone?

Get new burner.

Thank you. If I need you again?

Will message a code.

Thank you.

No problem.

I messaged Dave. *Grey hat v useful. Thanks a million. Where did you find?*

Nairobi. Take care, you x

Kenya. Snazzy.

As I'd thought, I'd have to leave the cards. I felt insecure without them, but I'd managed a surprising amount of my life thus far without plastic. Returning for my bag, I thumbed them one by one into the water, a manoeuvre that greatly interested a group of passing Germans. At the last, I hesitated. A discreet black number with just a twirl of a handwritten name. The Klein Fenyves card, from my lovely bank in Panama. It would be impossibly dumb to use it, after what I'd just learned, but equally stupid to leave myself vulnerable in a real emergency. I returned it to my wallet, then wheeled the case to the *tabaccaio* for some fags and a single ticket for the station boat, walked smartly to the stop, my peripheral vision hyper-alert, though the case alone was a sort of disguise. Venice is full of bewildered women wheeling suitcases. The Caravaggio book was poking out of my handbag, I started reading as the *vaporetto* chugged its way between ugly boatyards and gargantuan cruise ships. On the station steps I refused a porter with his trolley and lugged my bag to the counter, where after a moment's hesitation I bought a second-class ticket. *Welcome back, Judith.* I settled myself as comfortably as I could in a corner seat for the long ride: I had to change at Munich and again at Utrecht.

The altarpiece at Santa Irene in Lecce is by Guido Reni, its subject the Archangel Michael, namesake of Reni's rival Caravaggio. In 1602, Reni left Rome to return to his home city of Bologna, a journey prompted by what he described to a friend as his 'defeat' by Caravaggio. Reni was a painter who believed that pictures should show only a beautiful version of the world, an eternally incorruptible ideal. Like many, he was confused by what he saw as the irreverence of Caravaggio's work, the Lombard's refusal of prettified politeness. It made him nervous. Early that year, Caravaggio had delivered a painting that appeared to show three men having supper in the kind of Roman tavern where artists gathered to drink and gossip; the linen tablecloth is clean enough, but the food is basic – chunky, hard-looking loaves, a bowl of fruit which has seen better days. The roast chicken has clearly lived an athletic life. The men are being served by a stern waiter, who is perhaps wondering whether they are good for the bill. And then, if you look again, you see that this is a painting of a miracle. The young man in the middle of the table is Christ, and this is the supper at Emmaus, when Jesus revealed himself to his disciples after he had risen from the tomb. There is no gold leaf, no crooning angels. The moment is announced in shadow, the waiter's leaning form casts a halo on the wall behind Christ's head, while the lemon and the grapes form an echo of a fish, the first symbol of Christianity, on the starched cloth. The divine hides within the mundane, only available to those who see.

I watched the illustration as the train rolled over the hot Veneto plain, squeezing my fingernails into my palms. The deep shadow cast by the candlelight around the table recalled the dull sprawl of Masha's dress. Again and again I traced the figures in the picture, the wide gaze, the stretching arms. I wanted to cry for her, but the tears wouldn't come, even when I forced my memory into a slow fly-crawl over her corpse. *It's not your fault, Judith.* None of this was, and all of it was, and as the raw-eyed hours moved past in the throb of the sun on the window blinds, the emptiness of the carriage felt like the only mercy I would ever know in the world.

And then it was too dark to see and my legs had gone to sleep long ago. Hopping with pins and needles, I inched through the almost-empty carriages to the buffet car. I couldn't eat, but buying a banana and a bottle of Tropicana was something to do. My watch read 11.20, still the whole night to sit through. As I was paying for the juice, a young guy opened the door that led to first class. Jeans, white shirt, heavy navy cashmere sweater. Not bad. He nodded politely at the waitress, including me in his glance.

'*Buonasera*.'

'*Buonasera*.'

He caught my eye again as he paid for a macchiato. Travelling alone, miss? His skin would be warm and satiny, still the colour of the foam on his coffee from a long season of Italian sun.

'*Sei da sola?*' *Are you alone?*

The plastic table rocked a little with the rhythm of the train as I considered his question.

Bossun was a small-time dealer who hung around my school gates, handing out tiny wraps of weed and speed in return for pilfered fivers. He drove an old white BMW, which counted as glamorous on our estate, and he was good-looking, if Nigerian giants are your thing. I never wanted any of his crap gear, but he would sometimes give me a Lambert & Butler and we'd have a chat. Once, during one of Mum's bad times, when the electricity had been cut off again and there was nothing in the kitchen except a scraped-out tub of Utterly Butterly!, he asked if I wanted to do a drop for him. Fifteen quid. He drove me right into town in that lovely warm car, to a big terraced house on Hope Street, near the cathedral, and gave me a battered textbook to put in the plastic carrier I used as a school bag. The stuff was taped inside, over an introduction to the essays of Walter Benjamin.

'Students,' Bossun explained contemptuously as he pulled away. 'Make sure you bring it back.'

The wind pinned my school skirt to my body as I waited for the door, but I didn't feel the cold. I was hopping on adrenalin, could feel it taut in my muscles, fireworking through me. I had never broken the law before. I was convinced that the slightest error would see me hauled to the police station and I was lit with the thrill of it. I held the book close to my coat, trying for a calm, studious expression in case anyone was watching. The guy who eventually opened the door was obviously buying something a lot stronger than weed. He was young, not that much older than me, but his eyes behind matted mousy hair were yellow and as he reached for the book I saw the track marks on his greyed forearms beneath their raggedy jumper. In the hallway I stood between two oozing bin liners while he detached the gaffer-taped package, replacing it with a few crumpled notes and closing the cover carefully. 'Cheers. Um – see you.' I was surprised to hear that his voice was deep, educated.

Bossun seemed quite pleased with me; he gave me an extra five quid. So after that I started delivering for him fairly regularly. The school uniform helped, he explained solemnly: 'Diverts suspicion.' He was always getting hassled by the police; just because he was black they assumed he was a dealer. 'Maybe it's actually because you're a dealer?' I suggested flatly, and for a minute I thought he'd give me a clip round the ear, but he just laughed and told me I was too sharp for my own good. Bossun had his own flat in Toxteth, two manky rooms that smelled of feet and joss sticks, but there was a gas fire and bright-patterned African throws on the crappy furniture, and with the curtains drawn and the music on it felt all right. After a while Bossun said I could kip over if I needed, if I gave him a nice blow job before I went to sleep. And because when you're fifteen and nothing has ever happened to you, when you've been nowhere and seen nothing and the slightest bit of attention or interest can make the world radiant if only you pretend hard enough, I did. I called him my boyfriend, at least in my head, and for a while I was even proud when he razzed up to the school gates in the Beemer. He didn't bother me for anything except the blow jobs, which was just as well as he had a cock like a collapsible umbrella, but once I turned up at his place to find a skinny blond guy in a grubby shell suit next to him on the sofa, with an Indian and a half-drunk pack of beers.

'All right, girl? This is Kyle. Old mate. This is Judy.'

'Hiya.' Kyle didn't look up. He was throwing down chicken tikka with a plastic spoon like he'd never seen food before.

'Why don't you sit here, eh? I've got to nip out.'

Bossun left us in the sound of chewing. After a bit I asked Kyle if he wanted the telly on, but he just carried on eating. I wondered where Bossun had found him, if maybe he was a bit simple. When the last lurid grease was scraped out of the foil, I took the heap of trays to the filthy bin next to the long-retired cooker and cracked him another beer like a proper little hostess. I wondered if it was rude to get a book out.

'Bossun said –' he piped up suddenly.

'What?'

'He said you'd –'

'That I'd what?'

'See, I just got out. Today, like.' He took a long swig, as though that explained everything.

'Got out?'

'Yeah. Prison.'

'Oh. Well, congratulations.' Obviously I wanted to know what he'd done, but that seemed like bad manners. I thought of something. 'So you're staying here?'

'Yeah. For a bit. Till I sort meself out, like.'

'Well, I'd best get going then.'

'But he said.'

And then I saw what he meant, and why Bossun had left, and somewhere in Kyle's pinched face a hope that I recognised. I looked at him and saw how desperately he wanted to touch me, and that the gnaw-nailed hand holding the beer can was ever so slightly shaking, and that what I had under my pleated skirt and my ugly school sweatshirt was power.

That's how they tame us. Because when you're fifteen and you've seen nothing and been nowhere, even the faintest hint of that power will push you over, convince you that all the pop songs are true, that this is love, never mind that it's coercion, or worse. So you do it, and ten years later you wake up with three kids and some overweight no-mark in the bed next to you and you wonder where it went and why you did so little with it. Why you pissed all that strength away on sentiment and need and cheap attention. But I wasn't like that. Even then, I was never like that. Love wasn't for me. I was going to know about what I could make men do, and one day I was going to use it. This was – necessary.

I reached out and touched my fingertips to his mouth. Then I got up and went to the cold bedroom, pulled down the broken blind as far as it would reach and took off everything except my knickers. I got under the familiar Everton duvet and lay still, on my back. When he kissed me, he tasted of curry and hops. He told me I was gorgeous. When he lay on top of me in the damp fug of our thin bodies I wished I'd had a joint, but seconds after his cock stabbed into me he gasped, 'Ah, fuck! Fuck, girl!' and lay still, holding me so tight I could barely breathe, his face jammed between my breasts. He fell asleep like that, and I didn't want to move him, so we were still stuck there when Bossun came back and slid into bed beside us. 'All right, lovebirds?'

I opened my arms and both bodies, dark and pale, turned towards me, two arms twined across my body. We lay like that all night, tumbled like puppies in the orange lumen of the street lamp under that awful blind. I listened to them breathe, their snuffles and moans, and it hurt me how young they were, how clean we could be for a while. The filthy sheet beneath my naked arse was damp, with Kyle's cum and what

I knew was my blood. It hadn't seemed the moment to mention that I was a virgin. For a while, before I too fell asleep, I could see us lying there, how innocent, how ugly.

The guy had raised an eyebrow, confused, expectant, confident. The offer was there in his face and all I had to do was say yes. He could fuck it all out of me while the Alps trailed their snowy tendrils of fog around like bandages around my heart. Easy.

'No,' I replied, indicating the passage back to second class. '*C'e . . . C'e qualcuno.*' *There's someone.*

He finished his coffee with a smile.

'*Allora, buonasera, signorina.*'

'*Buonasera.*'

I went back to my seat alone, and sat out the night as the train rolled on towards the North Sea.

13

Four thousand euro is a lot to pay for a slip of paper, but I couldn't afford to buy cheap. I had considered a US passport, which ranks equally with the UK on the passport index of the most useful documents in the world, but since I didn't trust myself to fake the accent, I'd have to settle for staying British. I had reached Amsterdam midmorning, creaky and grubby from the train, then taken the underground to Nieuwmarkt, where the coffee-shops on the border of the red-light district were already doing business. I wove through red-eyed clusters of gurning stags, trying several of the cheap hotels until I found a dull, efficient room for cash. After a luxuriously hot shower I allowed myself three hours' sleep, then set off for Alex's place near the Vondelpark.

Back when I'd lived in Paris, when I was still dumb enough to think I could get away with stuff, I had started Gentileschi with the profits from a stolen painting. That the painting – a Stubbs – was forged made me feel quite righteous, but the appearance of an Italian cop posing as a bounty hunter named Renaud Cleret saw off any notions of security. We had been lovers, and in a sense friends, at least until I'd worked out that he planned to sell me out to his colleague in the anti-Mafia squad, Romero da Silva. In the interests of fair play, I'd had to take care of that, but Renaud had left me a number of parting gifts, including Alex, his 'cobbler' in Amsterdam.

Renaud had boasted to me of his connection with the expert passport forger, but Alex had been rather a disappointment the first time we met. In Paris, after my friend Leanne disappeared, Renaud, my undercover lover, had sent her passport to Alex and had the original photo replaced with mine. That document wasn't meant to send me anywhere but prison, yet Alex had shown no surprise when I turned up asking for another a short while later. His professionalism was impeccable and imperturbable, it was his premises that were a bit of a let-down. On that first night journey from France, I'd conjured a workshop lit by La Tour, in a cellar perhaps, or reached through a Fagin-esque warren of attics, where crookbacked clerks laboured with tweezers and diamond loops. Alex, a youngish bearded father in slightly tragic skinny jeans and high-tops, in fact lived with his family in a pretty nineteenth-century house in one of Amsterdam's smartest suburbs and conducted his business from the spare bedroom.

Small talk in these situations is an absurd social fault-line, where manners creak at the seams, but Alex and I observed the form of a cup of milkless tea in his Farrow & Ball-ed kitchen and a few remarks about where we had spent our summer holidays, a conversation so innocuous I might have been having it with my coke dealer. We went upstairs and I positioned myself before the mounted tubular camera, but before he took the shots he asked 'How many of these have we done?'

'Two. Well, three now.'

He paused in his adjustment of the lens. 'You sure?'

'Yup.'

'Right. OK, don't say cheese!' He'd made the same joke last time.

Alex's equipment was housed in three square grey steel cabinets, I had no idea what went on in there, but they hummed reassuringly as he copied down the details I gave him.

Cobblers usually assemble fake passports from stolen ones. The market is huge, for those who are skilled enough to get it right. The zone information, the text at the bottom of the passport which is read electronically, needs to match the printed data, spacing is essential to a fraction of a millimetre, the thickness of the pages has to be consistent, no raised edges, not a speck of excess glue. Alex had come good last time: with the thought of Yermolov on my back I prayed this one would be impeccable.

'All done then. You can collect it – oh, say about 8 p.m.? Same place as last time?'

'Sure. Have you got the code for the door?'

'212B.'

'And it's good?'

He gave me a pained professional smile.

'Well, you're screwed if it's not, right?'

I gave him the cash folded in paper tissues and he saw me to the front door, handing me a small key as we said goodbye. Originally I had wondered what his cover was – looked for a fake doctor's plaque or the headquarters of a minor religion – but of course the only premises that pretend to be something else now are lame hipster speakeasies. If you have a laptop, you're a freelance, end of. The key was for a registered letter box on the other side of the city. At 8 p.m. I would retrieve the envelope with the new passport and leave it inside. Until then there was Caravaggio.

The window of my dreary hotel room was hiked as wide as it would go, and as night fell the air smelled of grass and hot asphalt and hormones. An early autumn evening in Amsterdam ought to have been replete with potential – not that the prurient delights of the red-light district offered any particular thrill – but I found I didn't even have the energy to go looking, though surely company wouldn't have been a problem. The Rijksmuseum was already shut. A joint, to take the edge off? *Yeah, right. Face it, Judith. You're a raddled old whore who'll be alone forever.* Glad we got that cleared up. I settled for an early, stodgy Malaysian dinner with my book, but even greasing my arteries with peanut sauce and palm oil disgusted me. I abandoned my plate and set off on foot to follow the canals round to Lauriergracht.

They say that a brisk walk is an effective antidepressant, but then they say a lot of crap. Yet during that walk I sensed a shifting, a lightening, as though all that I had left behind me, in Venice and beyond, had been dropped carelessly into one of those smooth ancient waterways. Not that I didn't have plenty to be scared of in theory; just that I somehow couldn't muster the appropriate level of anxiety. Hanging up my spurs hadn't, I had to admit, proved as amusing as I had anticipated. What do you do when there's no next thing? I wasn't the type for extreme windsurfing or charity mountaineering. *Ennui* might be a romantic disorder, but it's boring nonetheless.

Seated on the edge of the water, my feet dangling over the stone, I lit a thoughtful fag, sucked the delicious smoke shudderingly deep. Maybe I was getting old, but so much of what I had thought I wanted –safety, security, anonymity –didn't seem worth bothering with any longer. The canals seamed neatly between the tall, narrow old houses, a molten highway of money. Stolid, secretive Amsterdam, floating the wealth of the known world along her veins. I thought of the pictures in the museum across town, the heaps of *things* – plate and fans and lobsters, globes, nutmegs, silk drapes, harpsichords, fruit, chests, parasols, purses – all tumbled artfully for the contemplation of the burghers beneath their meticulously painted ruffs. Still-life, framed eternally for display. It bewildered me, that I had stopped, immured myself in Elisabeth like an insect in amber, a dilettante rich girl playing at business. Why had it taken me so long to work out that where I belonged was the edge of the map? I suppose I could blame Caravaggio. We had a lot in common, after all. Murder, for a start. The painter spent much of his life as a fugitive, with a penchant for the Italian coast; he was a chancer with a weakness for flashy clothes, a pragmatist fearless of extremes, who understood that most things, even murder, are forgivable in the cause of beauty. He knew that honour is a language of wounds. But perhaps it would be more accurate to say that most of Caravaggio's problems were caused by an elevated sense of his own status, a contempt for risk, or perhaps an excessive regard for it. Perhaps risk was all I really understood. I had been off my game so long. Too long. And despite my grief over Masha, or maybe even because of it, I was curious to learn if I still knew how to play.

The Hafkenscheid Archive is housed at the Teylers Museum in Haarlem. I found it the old-fashioned way, with a miniature map from the tourist office. The archive was once the collection of a nineteenth-century Amsterdam pigment merchant, and is one of the principal research sources of the gums and minerals once used in mixing paint. I thought that since I had to be in Amsterdam for the passport, I could find out something more about how a Caravaggio "drawing" good enough to fool Yermolov could be produced. Presumably he would have sent Dr Kazbich to glean information before buying it, which could have interesting implications. If I could, I wanted to work out *how* a fraud so extraordinary could be achieved.

Although the breeze from the now-distant sea was fresh over the former port, it was still hot, and I'd dressed carefully, heavy practical boots which gave a gazelle-ish vulnerability to my thighs and a flared denim Margiela MM6 smock with a push-up bra underneath, a few buttons left undone, just for air. I didn't have an appointment, but I guessed that a custodian of antique turpentine mightn't see many visitors, and after I'd introduced myself and my 'project' while gazing at the elderly docent as though he was the only man I'd ever seen, he waved me through. I'd explained that I was a grad student writing on Tintoretto, quoting the *Technical Bulletin* of the National Gallery in London as the source for a question on the artist's use of a particular colour, Naples yellow, which came into use in Italy in the sixteenth century.

Then as now, Venice was a mirage city, its light conjured through so much glass that it shimmered like a vast mirror, an image of heaven on the edge of the world. I had been thinking about the possibility of Caravaggio being there, between his departure from Milan and arrival in Rome. What painter would have wanted to miss Venice, however eagerly he was hurrying along the road to ambition and success? The Venetian professor's confident dismissal was belied by an earlier writer on Caravaggio, Bellori, who asserted that he had visited the city 'where he came to enjoy the colours . . . which he then imitated'. I had lived in Venice long enough to know those colours, that quivering light whose crackle only renders its shadows deeper. No one could paint darkness like Caravaggio, no one else could tease out the extremities of shade that give his pictures' luminescence their lightning shock. So – there was an intriguing gap in the chronicle – he could really have been there. If I knew anything about evidence, it was that the lack of it doesn't mean something didn't happen.

The pigments were displayed in a long room full of cases, each filled with boxes of samples and printed cards with serial numbers and descriptions. Throwing a smile to the hovering docent, which I hoped might imply the possibility of lunch, I started work. Naples yellow, I knew already, was one of the three original colours introduced by 1600 to augment the limited palette of medieval painting. The recipe was first given in a book by Cipriano Piccolpasso in 1556, a work on ceramic making. It required salt, lead, antimony and 'lees', essentially the dregs left at the bottom of wine flasks. I approved of that. Piccolpasso was from the Umbria region of Italy, but he had travelled to Venice, which was the centre for innovation in paint colours at the time, and had actually included a chapter *Colori alla Venziana*, in his text. Naples yellow was one of the colours mentioned, and laser microspectral analysis (whatever that was) had identified its use in several of Tintoretto's paintings. Despite the glum professor's opinion, several of the scholars cited in the book I had studied had suggested that Tintoretto was an influence on Caravaggio, so it was plausible, I considered, that if he had been in Venice, he would have studied not only Tintoretto's great paintings, but their technical ingredients.

I moved along the cases until I came to a selection of chalks. I had thought that if Caravaggio had made a drawing, he would have used chalk, perhaps a combination of red, white and black, the *trois crayons* technique introduced by the French to Leonardo in Milan, where Caravaggio learned to paint, at the end of the fifteenth century. But chalk would not have given the portrait Elena had shown me its curiously hard-edged quality, or its depth of colour; moreover, why would someone have used chalk on linen? Linen was essentially canvas, which required a binding medium, a kind of glue known as *gesso*, on its surface. Chalk was used in under-drawing because once it was sandwiched between the gesso and oil paint it would no longer be seen. To have endured so long on linen, I thought that perhaps whoever made the portrait would have worked directly in the oil, which in turn would have been consistent with Caravaggio's widely known technique.

Moreover, Caravaggio was poor. Despite the many lucrative commissions that his talent lured before his disgrace, he seemed to have had almost a disdain for money. His hand-me-down fashions were notable for their flash, but he wore them to rags, and besides his equipment he owned almost nothing beyond a few pathetic household utensils and the embittered awe of his rivals. He travelled light. Naples yellow would not have been cheap, but linen, as opposed to fine vellum paper, was. Maybe it was possible, maybe, just, possible that there could be more to the "drawing" than Elena's vodka-infused fictions.

I pouted a couple of earnest questions at the docent, and had to endure an enthusiastic twenty-minute explanation of colour-grinding before I asked if the museum had a visitors' book. 'I'd be honoured to sign it. And maybe I could photograph my signature, for my thesis. The examiners are really strict on primary research.'

He produced a fat red leather volume and a Biro. I leafed through curiously, hoping that the archive would be sufficiently under-visited for me to work through the names swiftly. And there it was. Dr Ivan Kazbich, printed in Latin letters, with a signature beside it in Cyrillic and a date in 2011. Bingo. I had a practice at my own new signature and thanked the old chap profusely.

I couldn't resist a shivery thrill of excitement, but I dismissed it. I wasn't exactly planning a relaunch as a Caravaggio scholar. Whether the drawing was real or not, I had to get my hands on it urgently. And if my theory was correct, I was pretty certain that I knew where that drawing was. And it turned out that perhaps I had stolen it after all.

PART TWO
REFRACTION

14

Dave was a man who had faced down Al-Qaeda snipers during his time in the army, but I'd never seen him looking so agitated as he did at the sight of me hunched over a whisky mac in the bar of the Golden Lion, Combe Farleigh. I'd come in on the Eurostar via Lille, another train from Paddington to Bath and then a cab to Dave's new village. I'd been surprised by the sentimental effect England had on me after so long. The dowdy crowds at the stations, Pret a Manger, leering tabloids, pigeons. I had practically wept when the landlord served me the first proper cup of tea I'd drunk in years, but I had to concede that I wasn't doing the best job of mingling with the locals. Naturally it was freezing, so I'd bought a fleece on the St Pancras concourse and was bundled into practically all the other clothes I had. The barman looked dubious at my Rom-chic vibe, but cash had secured me a room and I'd called Dave from the pub's landline.

'What's going on? Why are you here, Judith?'

I winced. Complicity is such a rare quality, at least for me. The feeling that someone understands you without speech, that your shared history is such that no explanations will ever be required. Maybe that's what families have. But if Dave was as appalled as he looked, the entirely inappropriate joy I felt at seeing him once more was one-sided. I'd never been anything but trouble to him really.

'I bought you a pint,' I said, as though that explained everything.

'I've been trying to reach you. What's going on with your phone?' There was concern in his voice, but hostility too, and a kind of weariness that grieved me.

'Will we go for a smoke?'

He relented a little. 'Go on. They've got heaters out the back.'

The Lion wasn't a fancy organic gastro pub. Ugly square fifties brick, football on the telly, microwaved Thai food and a strong whiff of bleach and urine from the prefab toilet block in the car park, where there was also a children's play set, a couple of benches and a mushroom of a heater. I carried the drinks, Dave limped behind with his stick. The only other smokers were a couple of teenagers sharing a spliff at the top of the slide. They nodded at Dave – 'All right' – and sloped off into the dark.

'Not a social visit then?'

'Sharp as ever, Dave.' It felt so good to see him, even like this. I would have told him how much I'd missed him, but it would only have embarrassed him. Green-grey hills, soft rain, the close English sky. *It's not your fault, Judith.*

'Judith?'

I shook myself.

'Sorry, Dave. Look, I hate to barge in on you like this. You know I wouldn't unless –'

'It's OK. I know.'

I took a deep breath. In the end, it seemed best to keep it simple. I longed to discuss the Caravaggio with Dave, not least because of the pleasure I knew the story would give him, but the less he knew the better.

'I had an email.' He interrupted before I could speak.

'What?'

'Two actually. Look.'

He held out his phone. The first one was dated a few days ago, just when I had been leaving for Amsterdam. There was no superscription or signature, and the account address was meaningless, just letters and numbers at Gmail. It read:

'We are urgently attempting to contact Miss Judith Rashleigh. Please reply if you can help us with this request.'

'I thought it was junk – a con, like those ones you get asking you to send money to Nigeria. But then this one came.'

I held the screen closer to my face in the tangerine glow of the heater. Dated today.

'*Where is she, Dave?*' That was all.

15

I'd only ordered the drink for form's sake, but now I was glad of it. Dave looked at me expectantly as I took a long gingery swallow.

'What the fuck's going on?'

If Yermolov had been able to find Dave's email, he had probably also found his actual address. And I doubted that Yury or his equivalent would be killing time in the Pump Room with a Bath-bun and a Jane Austen novel.

'Dave – where's your wife?'

'Now? She's gone to her Zumba – I told her I was coming down the pub to catch the footie results. She'll be back in about an hour. Why?'

'You have to go home. Now. You have to get something for me and bring it straight back here. The case. The case I sent you the Richter in, in the post. Have you still got it?'

'What's it got to do with my missus? I don't want you –'

He didn't need to say it. *I don't want you anywhere near her.*

'Please. If she's not home, it should be fine.' I prayed I was telling the truth. Laboriously he rose to his feet. 'I don't know if I've still got it. That is, when I sold it, I bought a different case, because –'

'Just please go. Now. Try to hurry.' It felt bad to say that. Dave would struggle with his bad leg, getting up a ladder or whatever, but I didn't dare suggest going along to help. His wife might arrive home, and if the place was already being watched, my presence there would do for us all.

'I'm not happy about this.'

'I know.'

'Doesn't seem like I've got much choice though. I'll be back as soon as I can.' He hadn't touched his beer. I tried to keep a reassuring smile on my face as he tapped his way out of the pub car park.

How long would he be? How long would it take for Yermolov to get someone down here? Or were they here already? I wrapped my arms around my knees, squeezing myself smaller, wishing I could just fold myself away altogether and disappear.

I was winding back the possibilities in my head. It had to be the Richter. I had "acquired" the picture – well, stolen back, actually – from Moncada, the sale being the bait that had brought Renaud Cleret to Paris. I had taken the small canvas when Renaud murdered the Italian, and after I'd taken care of Renaud, with the help of a Glock 26 provided by Dave, I had 'sold' the picture to him, enabling him to fund his new life. It was compensation for my having lost him his job at the House, but also, I had to admit, blood money. Dave had never asked what I intended to do with the gun, and I'd never said, but we both knew that his having accepted the painting was a compromise. Yermolov knew

– somehow – about Gentileschi, about my life and identity in Paris, about Moncada's death, so he could equally well have known about the Richter. Obviously he had come to the same conclusion as me. There had been someone else waiting for Moncada that night in the Place de l'Odéon. The person who was supposed to receive the second picture that had been in the case. The Caravaggio. But that person had never taken it, because I had.

I'd thought I'd covered it, taking the hacker's advice, but I might as well have posted my whereabouts on Instagram. *Smart, Judith.* The pub door swung behind me and I flinched. Just a bloke with a packet of Bensons and the *Daily Mail*. He nodded at me and sat down at the furthest of the tables. If Yury was crawling commando-style across the village green, at least there'd be a witness. If Dave had the case, if he got back here, if Yermolov left him alone, just – please, please – left his wife alone, I thought I didn't much care what happened to me.

No Dave. The man with the newspaper left, the barman came out to switch the heaters off. I shivered, calculated, corkscrewed my hands inside my jacket for warmth, but I couldn't bear to move. It felt like a sort of penance, that endless moment in the English cold; if I just stayed there, Dave would be OK. Finally I heard the blessed tap of his stick, behind me.

'Judith? I was looking for you inside,' he said gently 'What are you doing freezing out here? Come on, let's go in.'

'Where's your wife?'

'She texted, said they're going to Wagamama for a meal. Lucky, eh?'

'So you've got it?'

'Come in.'

The bar was now empty, but the landlord still hadn't called time, though he looked disgusted when we disturbed his viewing of Tottenham vs Man City to request two teas. My hands were so cold I could barely hold the cup.

'Where is it?'

'Right here. When we moved down here we got rid of a lot of stuff. It's amazing how much crap you find hanging around when you move.'

The case was lying next to his jacket on the banquette; he'd left it there when he came to find me. He looked so pleased. Christ.

'When you sold that picture – you know, that one – how was it listed in the catalogue?'

'"Property of a Gentleman" of course.'

We both smiled at the joke.

'But when they dealt with you, paid for it and so on – they had your details, accounts, everything?'

'Of course – it was legit, wasn't it?' He looked panicked again.

'The sale was fine, don't worry about that. I'm just trying to work out how they got your address.'

'So you know who these emails are from?'

'Yes.'

'Is it to do with what you needed – the Kenya contact?'

'That's right.'

'And?'

What could I tell him? Dave, who'd only ever been good to me. That I'd put him in danger?

'You're sure there was no one – hanging around when you went back?'

'Listen. I'm not going to ask you what it is. I'm not. But if my missus . . .'

'OK. Do you still have – you know?'

The worry that had been twisting behind his brow eased out and he was suddenly cold, professional.

'I've got a licence for my shotgun, yes. Do a bit of pheasant shooting these days. That bad?'

'Yes. But better now. When your wife gets back, lock up properly. If anyone comes, anyone at all, if anyone asks, tell them you've seen me. Tell them you gave me this –' I jerked my head at the zipped black nylon case on the seat beside me – 'and that I left immediately. Got into a cab that I'd kept waiting. You haven't opened it, you don't know what's inside. And – could you get away for a few days?'

He looked at me, reflecting, then nodded. 'Probably could, yeah.'

I had never been more grateful that the substance of my friendship with Dave was silence.

'Well then. I'll leave first thing. I'm so sorry.'

'I'll be going then. But – are you all right? You know, for money?'

'I love you.' He raised an eyebrow. 'I meant that. But I'm fine, thank you.'

'I've got something else.' He handed me a fat brown A4 envelope, I could feel pages inside.

'I thought maybe you could have a look,' he proffered shyly. 'I've been writing a book.'

'Seriously? What is it?'

'About me, I suppose. I'd been helping at this centre, you know, for lads who were in the services?'

Dave had left his leg in the Gulf. It was typical of him that he should volunteer to help others who had lost even more.

'And one of the – well, therapists, I should call her – she suggested I try to write something. About pictures really. About how they can help.' *Oh, couldn't they just.*

'Good for you, Dave! That's brilliant. I'd love to read it, if you allow me? Thank you. Although – it's probably best if I don't get in touch, for a bit. But I promise I'll read it. And I've got something for you.'

I held out the book I had bought at Paddington station. Dave had a passion for lurid true crime.

'*The Shade by My Side*. New life of Ted Bundy. Old times' sake.'

As Dave was leaving, the TV screen erupted in a roar. I followed him to the door and called after him down the street and he turned towards me in the glow of the lamp-post.

'Man City. They've just won two–nil.'

He gave me a hint of a salute. I watched him go, then carefully carried the case upstairs. Surveying my possessions in the chintzy pub bedroom I felt pathetically badly equipped. I had about fourteen thousand euros left in cash, the case, and fuck all else that might come in useful. My watch, I supposed, my beautiful Vacheron. Looking at it now I could see that it was almost eleven – no point in trying to make it back to Bath and up to London at this hour. In my wallet was the tag for the luggage locker at Lille station, where I'd left the Caracal after disassembling it in a stall in the women's bathroom and stuffing the parts in a plastic Hello Kitty vanity case I'd bought at the Relais H. Which meant that I'd have to go back through Lille. *Quelle* massive shag, but there'd been no way I was going to try to get through international security at a French station with three IDs and a weapon.

Below my room, the pub was quiet; Sky turned off, the faint churning of the dishwasher behind the bar the only sound. I jumped again when I heard a car slowing outside, only too audible in the thick country dark, and moved instinctively behind the door, holding my breath, waiting for the slam of the door, the heavy footsteps on the stairs, but the driver shifted up a gear and moved off again, into the night. I hadn't switched on the main light. I inched across the small room on my knees and twitched the yellowed net curtain. Nothing but the village street, glowing in the orbs from the lamp-posts, the odd window glowing with bluish television haze. I stretched, tried to relax, but kept repeating the wording of those emails. I was missing something. Why would Yermolov have done this? It was too . . . inefficient. If he wanted to threaten Dave, he would just do it. As he had with my flat, the gallery, with poor Masha. The emails seemed like the work of someone with fewer resources, someone trying to elicit information, not someone who could command a small private army. I was glad I had told Dave to take precautions, but something didn't fit. Why hadn't he sent someone to burgle Dave's place? Maybe he thought Dave, if he had the picture, would be intimidated and try to contact me – from what the grey hat had told me, that might allow him to intercept me. What if the emails were a decoy? Meant to throw me off? Maybe even now a car was sliding north up the motorway, towards Liverpool, towards my mother . . .

Zersetzung. He was confusing me, trying to trap me, to funnel me towards him. I couldn't let him. I had the picture now, which meant I had significantly altered the odds. I just had to stay calm, which was about the most irritating advice I could give myself. What did I have to be fucking calm about? I forced myself to take the shower I'd been waiting for since that morning. Binding my hair in a towel, I pulled on a T-shirt and knickers and dried my hands carefully, no cream, before approaching the case again.

It had taken me a while to work out what must have happened, but I knew that the case in front of me was not the one I had taken to the Place de l'Odéon. I had laid the original on the bed in Moncada's hotel room, and he had stooped over it to remove the picture just as Renaud burst in on us. Their struggle had distracted me from seeing that Moncada had moved the picture into the similar case he had brought, the one containing the Caravaggio. I remembered Renaud's stertorous instructions – 'Quickly, all of it . . . Take the picture, too.' I had grabbed the case without noticing the switch. To be fair, what with the corpse and the approaching cops, I'd been a bit distracted.

As I expected, the main section, which Moncada had intended for the Richter, was empty. Using the stubby blade of my eyelash tweezers, I carefully pierced a small hole in the nylon, then tore the case, millimetre by millimetre, along its length, until I was able to withdraw the thin waxed-card package from the lining. The card was gaffer-taped along the join, I boiled the in-room tea-service kettle and wincingly held the tape six inches above the spout of steam to loosen it, then gradually peeled back the plastic. And when I saw what was inside, in spite of the hideous absurdity of my situation, I laughed.

As soon as I woke, I ran. Four, five quick miles under the freezing drizzle, along the arterial road to Bath, in the lorry fumes and the disdainful glares of school bus drivers, pounding the tarmac until my lungs burned and my head cleared. When I dripped back into the pub, the landlord was wrangling a hoover and listening to Radio 2. I ordered a full English – sausages, bacon, grilled tomatoes, syrupy baked beans, mushrooms, fried eggs and fried bread, and used the landline again to book a cab to Bath. An hour later, the Caravaggio and I were back on the move. Near the station, I took myself to Costa Coffee and sat down at a corner table with a burner phone and a horrible caramel frappuccino thing. Cleaning the sugar-dusted table with my sleeve, I set down the notebook in which I had recorded all my numbers before leaving Venice and dialled Kazbich. I didn't expect an answer, and indeed the line buzzed in the long, slow bursts of a European ring tone before switching to automated voicemail. I had rehearsed the message in the cab:

'*Dr Kazbich, you know who this is. I have the item your employer needs. I'll be in touch. Don't look in England. If you do, I'll destroy it. I've seen it, so you know I know how.*'

Across the street, bored country teenagers wandering in their best imitations of London trends, a party of nice American ladies on a tour, clutching copies of *Northanger Abbey*. I texted Dave, whose number I knew by heart:

Let me know if all is well. I'll call in a few days. Thank you, for everything, as ever xxx

I waited, flipping the little phone over like a playing card until Dave texted back.

All clear so far. Take care. xxx

Then I let myself into the loo, with its conveniently low disabled-access handle, wadded the phone in lavatory paper and stuffed it into the sanitary-towel bin. *Good luck finding that, Yury.*

The night Moncada had died, who had known of his presence in the hotel on the Place de l'Odéon? Me. Moncada and Renaud Cleret, and neither of them was talking. Romero da Silva, Renaud's colleague in the Italian police. And whoever was supposed to collect the picture. Who was that person, and who had sent them? Balensky or Yermolov, it had to be. But Yermolov also knew about me, about Gentileschi. Logically that person had to be the link. The witness who had – somehow – made the connection, who had told Yermolov about me. Was it Kazbich then, or someone else? Until I knew, I would never be safe. Returning the picture wouldn't be enough. So I had to go to Paris. Via sodding Lille.

16

Crossing the Tuileries towards Concorde two days later, I remembered the first time I had spoken to Renaud Cleret, on a freezing bench outside the gardens. It's strange, memory, what slips and what stays. Renaud had played me for a mug, and I had paid him out properly, but as my boots crunched over the neat gravelled paths, all I could think of was the good times we had shared – shopping in the market at my old flat near the Pantheon, him lumbering after me on the wet grass of the Luxembourg, reading the papers quietly with the sun carving patterns on the floorboards of my flat. Though since the nearest thing I'd ever had to a relationship ended in decapitation, a therapist might suggest I had commitment issues. I passed the seat where he had wrapped me in his jacket and blackmailed me into helping him. For a moment I stood there in the traffic fumes and let my hand trail slowly across its green wooden back.

As soon as I arrived in Paris, I had provided myself with a new phone and laptop, paying, obviously, from my dwindling stock of cash. I had been familiar with the newspaper reports of Moncada's death well before Elena Yermolov had produced her souvenir file, but I went through them once more. Following the story, it transpired that the police seemed curiously uninterested in the case. The French press merely reported an investigation into the death of an unnamed man in a Paris hotel, followed by reports that he was of Italian nationality. And then, nothing more. The Italian press made no mention of it at all. I had searched coroners' inquests around the date with no success. The cross-border bureaucracy of two nations with a passion for documents was weepingly dull. As far as I could make out from a handy guideline to expatriating the corpses of non-French citizens, it appeared likely that a coroner's inquest could have taken place in Italy, though not necessarily with access to a French judicial file. The paperwork required for tracing bodies was relentless and apparently circular – if your granny died on a coach tour of the Dordogne it was truly alarming how easily she could be mislaid. I had surmised at the time that Renaud's colleague da Silva would succeed in hushing the matter up to protect his friend, and it seemed I had been right.

I hadn't got any further with Ivan Kazbich. Beyond one minimal website featuring the latter's gallery in Belgrade, which dealt in a mixture of orthodox icons and unchallenging contemporary pieces, Kazbich's web presence was a black hole. No images, no information. I was curious that a man who had been an active and significant dealer for so long – big enough to work for the likes of Yermolov – could leave so little trail, but even after wasting hours cross-referencing ever more unlikely terms, I produced nothing. I had returned several times to the Place de l'Odéon, hoping that the sight of the hotel would provoke some memory, some sequence of logic, but if there were any peripheral clues, they were locked up somewhere in my head.

So now I found myself aimlessly wandering around Paris's tourist attractions, with no real idea where to look next. It didn't help that Paris and I were practically no longer speaking. The city I had once loved so much had betrayed me with ghosts. Maybe if you live anywhere for a while it becomes a palimpsest, reinscribed with the shadows of former selves. Dusty, cramped, traffic-gorged, Paris taunted me with older incarnations, all of whom I preferred to my present one. I had lived there briefly as a student, returned to start my gallery there, spent a few intense, intimate weeks with Renaud, my lover and would-be nemesis. However I tried to avoid my old haunts, they still came back to haunt me.

One afternoon, on Rue de Turenne in the Marais, I was idly riffling through a stack of madly priced marl sweatshirts in a boutique when I glimpsed Yvette's reflection in a mirror behind me. Yvette was a stylist who for a time had been a sort-of friend – at least she'd been useful, and she was still alive. She had also been with me at our regular haunt, a swingers' club called La Lumière, the night I'd unfortunately had to shoot the owner. The shop was small and she was between me and the door, languidly trying to persuade the assistant that she was picking up some clothes for a 'shoot'. Yvette's hair was woven into a ziggurat of cobalt-blue dreads now, which matched the tone of the thigh-high Vetements cowboy boots she'd no doubt nicked from a set. It made me smile to think that she was still in business, but I buried my head in the sweatshirts, praying for her to leave without seeing me, which obviously meant she saw me immediately.

'Lauren?'

Like Steve, she had known me by my real second name. I kept my face blank, tugging my coat sleeve down over my wristwatch, the only thing I was wearing that she could just have recognised from those days.

'I'm sorry?' I said in English.

'*Mais, c'est toi, non?*'

'Sorry. I don't speak French.' I smiled pleasantly, the helpless Anglo monoglot.

'Ah. Excuse me,' she answered in her heavily accented English, and turned back to her negotiation. I crossed to the door and nodded to the assistant. 'Thank you!' I trilled gaily, but Yvette gave me a long, calculating stare as I passed her, and I felt her eyes in my back all the way down the street. At least that made a change from all the other eyes I was convinced were on me. My walks around my lost city were twitchingly accompanied by the imagined presence of Yermolov's goons.

I had paid cash in advance for a two-week stay at the Herse d'Or, not far from the Bastille Métro station and the lovely garden at Place des Vosges. The gag on 'hearse' amused me, and it was relatively cheap, around 100 euro a night. My stack of bills was shrinking at an alarming rate and I didn't know how much longer they would need to sustain me. The door of my room had a lock and a chain, but I didn't think they'd be much good to me in the event of a visit from Yury, and the thin walls meant I spent every night in a paranoid sweat, waking every time I heard movement on the landing. Whenever I arrived or left I checked with the Chinese concierge to see if there had been any visits or messages – I imagined perhaps that he saw me romantically, as a hopeless lover waiting for a tryst – while knowing that I was nothing more to him than an irritating interruption to his perpetual games of online poker. My conversation with Dave's guy in Kenya had reassured me, in that I knew logically that the probability of Yermolov locating me was low, but logic is a poor defence against insomnia. There were so many loose ends, so much I still couldn't know. Even Yvette felt like a threat at four in the morning. I tried to assemble some sort of routine – running on the river, walking to the Rue Vivienne behind the Palais Royal to use the computers in the library there, a depressing picnic from the local Franprix minimarket for dinner – but after a few days I was arthritic with angst.

Hence the nice brisk walk through the Louvre, which had ended in me gawping on a bench like the village idiot. I'd come from the library on the Rue Vivienne, where I'd been going through microfiche files of articles featuring the word '*oligarches*' in the French press. It would have been so much easier to sign up for online access, but that was impossible in my present cash-only incarnation. I was trying to get some sense – any sense – of what anyone connected with Yermolov or Balensky might have been doing in Paris when I was last there. I didn't have much hope of finding anything, but one piece in *Le Figaro* – the paper Renaud had been so fond of – mentioned Balensky's name. The Man from the Stan had been photographed last year at a memorial service for Oskar Ralewski, a Polish–Parisian lawyer who had died when his small private plane had crashed on a journey to Switzerland, killing its pilot and Ralewski himself. Also in attendance at the memorial, held at the Orthodox Nevsky Cathedral on the Rue Daru, was a certain Pavel Yermolov. The two men had studiously not been photographed together, but the story made a gleeful point of the fact that Ralewski's firm had represented a number of Russia's new rich. The article quoted a book by a British journalist, a sensational analysis of the penetration of Russian money into the highest echelons of European politics, whose author suggested that Ralewski's death might have been No Accident. For want of much else to do, I decided to stop by the English bookshop on the Rue de Rivoli to see if they had a copy. I stood and stretched, brushing the remembered scent of Renaud's jacket from my neck like a cobweb.

Bruce Eakin's biography described him as a 'freelance web crusader', no less. His book's neon-pink cover promised insider revelations on the 'cult' of the oligarchs, beneath a smoking gun and a tottering heap of euros, in case anyone had missed the point. Flipping through the pages, it didn't seem that Bruce's research had taken him much further than his parents' attic, as most of the 'revelations' were predictable skim 'n' splice confections freely available on the Web. There was an index at least, and I looked up Ralewski to read the relevant passage. The lawyer had been professionally close to both Balensky and Yermolov, as well as to a number of their compatriots, and Bruce eagerly went over the details of the accident. He did his best to make the circumstances sound sinister, but given that the plane had crashed into an Alp in a sudden thunderstorm with zero visibility, I thought poor old Ralewski might just have been unlucky. The photo of Balensky was reproduced; I studied that ligneous face once again. Next to Balensky, shaking hands, stood a taller, grey-haired man. The caption read: 'Balensky with Saccard Rougon Busch partner Edouard Guiche at the Ralewski memorial'. I flipped back to the index, but Guiche was not listed. I replaced the book under the pointed stare of the girl at the cash till and had a wander in the art section. I had used to come here sometimes when I was a student in the city, before the sounds of French around me resolved into sense, gulping as much as I could from the unaffordable books until the glare of a similar girl would drive me away.

What slips, what stays? Guiche was a senior lawyer in the firm that had represented Balensky in France. Perhaps, since Yermolov had attended the service for Guiche's unfortunate colleague, the firm had acted for him too? It wasn't much, but it was the first real connection I had. Back at the till, Bruce got a sale. A hot chocolate along the street at Angelina's, so thick you could stand your spoon in it, and a quick browse online, then I was on my way to the Place des Victoires at the edge of the first *arrondissement*, where the office of Saccard Rougon Busch occupied a Louis XIV townhouse overlooking the statue of the king. The firm was listed in a group of 'magic circle' French lawyers, specialising apparently in 'High End Capability and Acquisitions'. It didn't seem too intelligent to ring the bell and ask if Monsieur Guiche was available without a story, so I settled for lurking outside, interspersing window-shopping in the square's smart boutiques with covert glances at the doorway, which occasionally opened to admit or release a series of more-or-less identical men in well-cut dark suits. After an hour I was rewarded with a glimpse of Guiche himself, speaking with a female colleague as they got into a waiting taxi and pulled away. The temptation to jump into a passing cab and ask the driver to follow was irresistible, but it's impossible to hail a bloody cab in Paris, so I mooched back to the Hearse and continued digging.

After a few tries, I discovered a series of websites hosted by the French Bar Society, from which I learned that Edouard Guiche had been made partner after Ralewski's demise, and that for the past decade his firm had been involved in property transactions through a Swiss company, involving residential buildings in Paris, Clermont-Ferrand and the Côte d'Azur. A bit more trawling and I found that the Swiss company listed Balensky as a director, and that work permits had been issued for its employees by various French municipalities. I tried a few Russian sites, but my vocabulary simply wasn't up to it. It all seemed relatively trivial for an '*oligarche*', though presumably someone of Balensky's – or possibly Yermolov's – wealth and interests would have armies of lawyers on call around the world. I didn't imagine Guiche could lead me direct to the resolution of the scene in the Place de l'Odéon, but in my search for the mysterious witness of that night's events I didn't have much else to go on.

Which is why the following day and the day after that saw me back in the Place des Victoires. About 5 p.m. on the third day, Guiche left the office and set off towards the river, walking briskly with what looked like a serious briefcase. I didn't know much about surveillance techniques except what I had learned from spy novels, but following him wasn't that difficult, especially as his custom-made Aubercy wing-tips were fitted with brass heel taps which clattered on the paving stones like stilettos. It was quite fun really. Guiche made his way towards Hôtel de Ville, then crossed over the Pont Marie to the Île Saint-Louis, bearing left along the Quai d'Anjou. I'd crossed the island the first night I'd spoken to Renaud, and the last time too, when I'd released his head into the current of the Seine. Such a long goodbye.

Guiche paused and took out his phone, tapped, spoke, all the while scanning the street and the river as though he was looking for someone. Had he spotted me? He continued, more slowly now, replacing the phone and taking out a bunch of keys which glinted against the dark cloth of his jacket. So he was going home? He stopped outside a building at the end of the *quai*, towards the top eastern corner of the island, and then something else happened. Guiche put down the briefcase and went to open the plain black wooden street door, when a young man, approaching from the far corner by the Sully bridge, called out to him. Guiche whirled around, clearly recognised the man and waved him away. I drew closer, keeping my eyes on the river and taking out my own phone as though I was a tourist filming the passing boats. I tapped on the Mirror Contrast app and watched the pair over my shoulder.

The man who had accosted Guiche was a boy really, about twenty-one. Dark-haired, viciously lovely face atop a *ballerino*'s body, its taut lines shown off when his jacket (last year's navy Valentino, aggressive studs on the collar) swung away as he tried to turn the reluctant lawyer to face him. In the corruption that played around his overripe mouth there was something that reminded me of Caravaggio's beautiful, taunting Cupid. A gold watch flashed on the boy's wrist, but his trousers and shoes were cheap. Interesting. Guiche turned to speak to him – it didn't seem as though the two were arguing, more that the boy was asking him for something, his expression halfway between wheedling and pleading. Guiche shook his head, opened the door, relented and turned back to say something else. The boy nodded, and walked back the way I had come, on the opposite side of the pavement. The door closed. I turned, put the phone away and crossed towards the apartment building, freezing when the door clicked open. But Guiche had no eyes for anyone but the boy. He hovered in the doorway, watching him leave until he turned left towards the Rue Saint-Louis en l'Île and vanished from sight. As soon as I heard the door shut again, I jogged down the way the boy had gone, turning onto the main street of the island, busy now it was getting dark with homecoming shoppers and early tourists heading for the restaurants, scanning the pavements for the twinkle on the boy's sleeve. He was already halfway across the bridge, heading towards Notre Dame. I sped up, relieved to see he had stopped to light a cigarette, scowling self-consciously down at the Seine. *He knows he's pretty.*

While he smoked, I took out a cheap bright orange pashmina I had picked up earlier from one of the stalls which line the river. I'd planned to use it as a disguise for trailing Guiche. Now if the boy saw me his eyes would register it and I'd be invisible again when I removed it. At least that's what John le Carré says. He finished the cigarette and tossed the butt into the river, checked his phone reflexively and moved off. This stalking business was fun, I had to admit. 'To be at the centre of the world and yet to remain hidden from the world . . . The spectator is a prince who everywhere rejoices in his incognito.' Maybe this was the feeling I liked best, the total isolation of utter anonymity, when no one at all knows who or where you are.

I followed the boy easily to the Saint-Michel fountain, then into the narrow streets of the Quartier Latin, lurid with kebab-shop signs. It was cold now and I was grateful when he turned into one of the stores and I could follow him into the fatty warmth. I pretended to study the menu board as he shook hands across the counter with young guy busy with the chip fryer, who was saying something in Arabic. I waited in the queue as they chatted, oblivious to the increasingly impatient customers, until the server shrugged and made up a chicken kebab with a huge portion of salad and frites stuffed into the pita bread, handing it over with an obvious nod and a wink. As the boy reached for it eagerly, I saw the watch was a Rolex. It looked pretty genuine – so why was a man with a watch like that scrounging shawarma? He took it outside to eat, standing at one of a pair of small high tables, and I watched him pick the kebab apart and place pieces fastidiously in his mouth, clearly trying to keep his clothes and hands clean, while I drank the small coffee I'd ordered. Then we were off again, first to a McDonald's down the road, where he ducked in to use the bathroom, then back over the river, east towards the Centre Pompidou and east again. He was an easy mark, pausing to check his phone every few blocks, but it was a long walk and though my mouth was unpleasantly dry from the espresso I didn't want to lose him by stopping for water. He wandered for about an hour – it was after 8 p.m. when he finally took a chair outside a café in Belleville. It was a part of town I once wouldn't have dreamed of knowing: even the café tables had a look of drawing in their skirts in disdain at what had become of the neighbourhood. Reluctantly, I unwound the pashmina and took my own seat at the far end of the terrace. The waiter was in no hurry to take anyone's order – eventually I was supplied with a horrible Beaujolais and the boy with a Ricard. Good for the breath. I spun out my drink as long as he did, which felt like about a year. He noodled aimlessly on his phone, I read the latest Houellebecq between covert glances and wincing sips.

I was sure he had paid me no attention so far, but there were only two other occupied tables on the terrace and I felt his eyes on me as I turned a page. Looking up, I briefly met his glance – a studied lack of attention might have seemed unnatural. His own thick black lashes dipped and fluttered flirtatiously. I looked down at my book again. A little while later he got up. I had already put the coins for my drink in the waiting saucer, ready to move when he did, but now I paused and gathered my hair into a ponytail, watching him walk purposefully to the street corner. He had been killing time; now he had somewhere to be. I stayed about thirty metres behind him, keeping him in sight, dodging a woman in bright African prints with a churning pushchair, a freezer truck unloading outside a halal butcher's. He turned into a cul-de-sac lined with grey apartment buildings, a brutal modern block forming a perpendicular impasse, skanky even by the standards of the twentieth *arrondissement*. An ancient Arab guy in a dun-coloured djellaba sat at a table in the doorway under a flickering neon strip light, engrossed in a hand of patience. There was an alarming flare of gold teeth as he greeted the boy, who passed into the lobby and descended a flight of stairs to the right beneath an exit sign. Maybe this was where he lived.

The doorman didn't look up from his game.

'You a friend of Olivier?' He used the familiar *tu*.

'Er, yes.' Whoever Olivier was.

'Twenty.'

I handed him a note and followed the boy inside.

In the time when Caravaggio was painting, when all kinds of new worlds were up for grabs, there was one whose currents hummed beneath the surface of everyday life all across Europe, from the Slavic steppes to the tiny brokewalled fields of England. Those who knew called it 'spiery', the shadow-land of espionage, whose methods were often no more elaborate than lemon-juice ink and Latinate codes, their pace merely the speed of a galloping horse, yet whose power could redraw the borders of kingdoms, massacre whole towns, elect a pope or besmirch a queen. We would have made good in that world, I thought later, those of us who sought out *la nuit*. We recognised our own kind, and we kept our own secrets, at least until the morning. I had sought out that world when I first lived in Paris, then Renaud had found me there, and now, here, at the bottom of a piss-stained concrete stairwell behind an abandoned launderette, I was back home once more.

It was a far cry from the flashy clubs where I used to hang out with Yvette, though the place would have been a hipsters' gold-mine in London or Manhattan. Once I'd got past the twin tubs and the unspeakable lavatory, the crappy cellar felt much like anywhere, except that the red flock wallpaper was unironic. I liked the crowd immediately, a mixture of saucer-eyed swingers up from the *banlieue*, slumming *bobos* from Paris proper and gentle, bewildered transvestites dressed like a gaggle of lost librarians, stubble valiantly concealed beneath old-school panstick, size-eleven courts bravely polished, drowning in a culture that suddenly required you to slice your dick off to prove your commitment. Altogether depressing, but I quite liked that too.

The place was obviously more of a knocking shop than a real partouze club: a few nervous-looking middle managers in cheap suits and denial were picking their trade from a goggle of writhing twinks pouting and bitching at the bar. I wasn't altogether surprised when my quarry joined them. He had the look on him. After a while he excused himself from his chums to slip off to what had to be the dark-room with a youngish guy who twisted his wedding ring as he followed the boy through the velvet drapes. They reappeared no more than ten minutes later, by which time I'd discovered that good old 'Olivier' stocked Maker's Mark. The john scuttled off immediately, ready to spark up the Renault for the guilty commute back to the burbs. My boy left soon after. I didn't bother following him; I'd given myself enough to think about. Besides, I fancied another drink. Maybe too many drinks. I thought I could get quite into that role: I'd never considered I had the discipline for alcoholism, but by anyone's standards I had a whole lot of shit to forget.

As I sipped, I considered Guiche and the boy, what their relationship could be. Guiche worked for Balensky and presumably Yermolov, he was clearly doing pretty well out of it if he lived on the Île Saint-Louis, and I didn't imagine that rent boys were part of his usual social circle. When I'd first encountered Balensky, during the summer I'd spent on Steve's boat, I had been aware of rumours about his private life – gossip about parties with boys at the oligarch's home in Morocco. Maybe Guiche was gay, but so what? Russia was notoriously intolerant of homosexuality, but this was France. I ordered another, neat again.

I had to know who it was who had betrayed my past to Yermolov. Kazbich would presumably have told him by now that I had the picture, but I wasn't about to give up my only bargaining chip until I found out. Trying to return it could easily get me killed, and if not, arrested. The boy's link to Guiche seemed to be the only other connection I might leverage. It was a long time since I had felt so powerless, and it was Yermolov who had done it, Yermolov who had thought me too inadequate for his pictures. But I had it now, didn't I, the one he really craved? The third piece to complement the Botticellis in his gallery. The thought of his frustration that I had eluded him so far afforded me a certain pathetic glee. Who was Yermolov to underestimate me? He wasn't the only one who could be ruthless. I raised a wobbly toast to Alvin and knocked back the last of the drink, but there seemed to be something furious in my grip on the glass, which slid out of my hand and shattered on the bar. A drop of amber liquid dribbled into my lap.

'May I get you another?'

I turned. A young guy, about my own age, bearded. His breath was cabbagy. The last thing I felt like was a turn in the dark-room.

'No, thanks.' I tried to curve my lips, but my smile had long since run screaming from the building, so I settled for sliding arse first off the stool instead, which may not have been my best look. The guy kindly held my bag while I sorted myself out, but I was as bored of him as I was of myself.

'I'm juss ... goin' ferra cigarette,' I managed, as I lurched towards the door, choking down a throatful of whisky vomit. I held it until I got up to the street, where it streamed out into the gutter under the impassive eye of the old Arab doorman.

17

I was becoming quite the detective. At least, I had a hangover. I'd rejected the idea of simply calling Guiche's firm and asking to speak to him – even if I got through, he was hardly likely to discuss his clients with some random stranger, and if I told him I had the Caravaggio he would go straight to Yermolov. I had to find the boy; I had to make use of him, see if there was some way of getting close enough to Guiche without arousing suspicion so that I could learn what, if anything, he knew of the night of Moncada's death. If it turned out to be nothing, I'd have to come up with a plan B. I stuck to water when I returned to Olivier's the next night at 11 p.m.

The junior hustlers were clustered once more round the bar. My boy was not among them, but I did recognise one of the group to whom he had been speaking the previous evening: whip-thin in tight white jeans and a natty leather-collared T-shirt, artfully gelled bouffant atop a sulky, smudgy-featured face. I'd picked the lowest-cut top from my meagre travelling wardrobe and worn a push-up bra, trying to look as though I was genuinely there for a bit of action, and I gave him the glad-eye until he joined me at the bar, with only the slightest *moue* of weary distaste at his chums. He looked about nineteen, and there was no getting around it – in his eyes I was basically a cougar.

'*Bonsoir, mademoiselle.*' At least he hadn't said *madame*.

'*Bonsoir*. I saw you here last night.' He smiled modestly, obviously convinced that I had been drawn back for a taste of what he had to offer in the backroom. 'I hoped you might be able to introduce me to your friend,' I continued simply. 'You were talking with him yesterday.' I quickly described the boy as best I could, mentioning the gold Rolex, which provoked a look of recognition.

'What do you want with him?' he asked suspiciously.

'The same thing you thought I wanted from you, of course.'

He made to back away. 'Sorry – I think you've made a mistake,' he replied dismissively.

I set a note on the bar between us. It was more than I could afford really, but I didn't have time to haggle.

'I'd be glad to speak to him – if you could maybe try . . . ?'

He cocked his potato of a nose at me as the fifty shimmied its way into his back pocket. 'I could . . . ask around.'

'Thank you. You're very kind.'

He made his way out of the club, presumably to place a call as there was no reception down in the basement. He was back about ten minutes later; the fresh air had given his face some colour and he briefly looked young and enthusiastic. 'My friend says he can join you in a short while, mademoiselle. Perhaps half an hour?' His eyes were on my bag. I reluctantly extracted a twenty from my wallet and handed it over. He nodded and wished me a good evening. I wondered what kind of message he had sent to my mystery date.

I drank my water and watched the crowd and listened to Jacques Dutronc sing '*J'aime les filles*' and in a while a hand touched my shoulder. There he was.

'My friend said I would find you here. You were looking for me?'

In the cocksure tilt of his head, the smile on those twisted plum lips, I read his swift estimation of my age, my loneliness, the degree of my desperation, and I found myself liking him for the pro he so evidently was, so I offered him a drink. His name was Timothy, he pronounced it 'Timotee', like the shampoo, which seemed terribly funny. He was wearing the same clothes as the night before, with a thin-inadequate T-shirt under the flashy jacket and the watch carefully in evidence. So his lover, or lovers, were rich, but he was not. Excellent. He gallantly offered a second round; I toasted instead with my half-full Perrier.

'Go on, I'm not dangerous.'

'Unless you want me to be. I know, I know.'

We clinked glasses.

'Your heart to your mother.'

'And my cock to the whores?'

I raised an eyebrow. '*Very* good. Where is she? Your mother.'

'I'm from Morocco.' He said it half defiantly, half proud.

'I've never been to Morocco.'

So he told me about it for a while, a picture-postcard description of the sands of Essaouira and the delights of the Jemaa el-Fnaa, and then asked if I'd like to go to the back room.

'That wasn't quite what I had in mind.'

'Oh.'

I wanted to get to know him, to observe him, before I brought up Guiche's name. 'I was more hoping . . . for some company. For the night, as it were.'

He brightened. 'That can be arranged. It will be a pleasure.'

'How much?'

He looked convincingly offended at the question. 'Really, it would be a pleasure to spend an evening with such a beautiful woman. Lady.'

I remembered that game from my nights at the Gstaad Club – never look like you're in it for the money. Though of course you're in it for the money.

'As you like,' I replied. 'Shall we go somewhere quieter?'

'Of course.'

He helped me on with my coat, without catching the eyes of his crowd lurking at the other end of the bar, and in the street he even managed to get the doorman to hail us a cab, into which he ceremoniously handed me. He was pretty good, given that I doubted girls were really his thing. I asked for the Place des Vosges and soon we were installed in one of the late-night bars off the Rue de Turenne, positively cosy on a plastic-shrouded terrace with electric stoves. As usual, it was empty inside. I ordered a bottle of red and topped him up liberally.

As we chatted, I learned that Timothy dreamed of working in fashion, that he'd had a job for a while as a waiter at the Hôtel Costes, but that right now he was 'looking for the right opportunity'. He claimed to be staying with an uncle for the present, over in Aubervilliers. All standard lines for *la nuit*, but it felt so disarmingly pleasant to speak to anyone who wasn't the Chinese concierge that now and again I almost forgot what I was there for. When most of the bottle was inside him, he asked if I'd like to go on to a party.

'Sure.'

We went through the cab performance once more, crossed the river and drove west along the *quais*.

Paris was doing its usual sparkle of night-lumened loveliness, but the city's brightness only emphasised the tar pit in my chest. The party, on a *peniche* anchored near the Musée d'Orsay wasn't up to much more than I was, mostly idling twinks like Timothy and a scatter of screeching fag hags, but I was supposed to be hiring a night out, so I tried to look as though I was having fun, dancing a bit, talking to his friends. After a while the coke came out, with a lot of exaggerated trips to the stinking pothole of a loo, but as usual I didn't indulge. I sat on a damp floor cushion, nodding along to the music and half following as the boasts and thick-voiced confessions became more urgent, as they all talked more and listened less. Timothy had made a few visits to the bathroom and was showing off his watch, explaining that he'd been given it after a super-crazy weekend in Tangier.

'You should see this guy's place!' he was telling anyone who was paying attention, which was no one, except me. 'It's like – a fucking castle – like, walls and guards and shit! And they gave us all one of these –' he flicked the Rolex to the pump of the music – 'sick!'

'Who was he?'

'I dunno, some Russian guy. I mean, they're all crazy rich those Russians. My friend Edouard took me.'

Bingo.

'Edouard?'

'He's this guy I'm, like, seeing? He's a lawyer. He's from a really posh family. He's married, of course.'

'Aren't they all, darling?' I managed wryly. He misread the tone, suddenly pushed his face next to mine, all grinding teeth and exaggerated concern.

'What's the matter? Did you have a story with a married guy?'

'Something like that. They're all the same, aren't they?'

His serotonin rush slipped momentarily. 'Yeah. But that's how it is, isn't it? They think they can fucking buy us. I mean, Edouard, he's actually pretty cool, but sometimes he just treats me like a prostitute, you know?'

'But you are a prostitute.'

That hung between us for a moment, and I thought I might have lost him, but then he started laughing, so I did too, grabbing the nearest beer bottle to hand and raising a toast.

'Fuck 'em!' I yelled. 'Fuck the married guys!'

He gave me a dry, hoppy kiss and told me he loved me before sashaying off to do another line, vanishing into an animated huddle of sinewy guys in tank tops who looked like Abercrombie models down on their luck. I set down the untouched beer bottle and went up to the deck, where people were smoking and talking more quietly. The Eiffel Tower winked at me.

As I had thought, Guiche was Timothy's lover. Better still, Guiche had taken him to a party at Balensky's Tangier home, the kind of party that red-blooded Russian males like Mr Putin might not approve of. Nor might Guiche's partners at Saccard, Rougon and Busch approve of that kind of corporate socialising. It wasn't much, but if I could use Timothy to introduce me to Guiche, that knowledge might be enough to make him tell me what, if anything, he knew about the person who was waiting for the Caravaggio on the night of the killing in the Place de l'Odéon, the source of Yermolov's knowledge of my past. Then I could work out what to do with the picture, presently marking time in the base of my luggage at the Hotel Hearse.

Timothy's tousled mahogany head was poking prettily up from a hatch.

'Hey! Where did you go?'

'Right here,' I answered. 'Do you want to get going?'

I reckoned I could get Timothy to crash at my place for a while. The uncle in Aubervilliers was hardly competition to the charms of the Hearse. Besides, I was paying.

'We're going to your place?' Only the slightest hint of weariness in his tone.

'Sure.' I held out four fifties, rolled discreetly. 'But as I said, I only want company.' I knew by now that women were strictly business for him, but one less practical than me might have felt disappointed by his evident relief. Still, all that mattered was to get Timothy on my side, and for that, I needed a story.

Old hand that he was, Timothy had a toothbrush next to the condoms in his fancy jacket and a blister of Diazepam to take the high off. That night I slept better than I had in weeks. I felt purposeful and alert again, and even his physical presence, which usually I would have disliked, felt reassuring. As much as I was frantic to get moving, I knew I couldn't rush him if I was to succeed in getting to Guiche, so for the next few days I concentrated on becoming his new best friend. My estimate that Timothy was broke seemed accurate – at least he seemed happy enough to scrounge his food and his bed for a while – so we got acquainted over cheap dinners in the eleventh and the odd joint smoked furtively out of the Hearse's window. Not that I inhaled. I knew what he was, but we never alluded to it again, and our avoidance of the subject allowed him a degree of dignity that made him promisingly malleable in other ways.

As far as I could tell, he had been born in France but had grown up in Rabat, where he attended the university for a while. His mother hoped he might become an engineer, but Timothy's looks, and his liking for men, took him to Marrakech, where he lived off the numerous old-school French tourists and English expats who spiced-up their romances with the pretence that homosexuality was still illegal in Europe. One of his johns had brought him over on a visit to Paris, where the uncle – who apparently existed – had fixed him up with a *carte de séjour* and the waiting job at the Hôtel Costes. He talked about saving up for fashion school, but his heart wasn't in it, any more than it was in serving tagines to tourists. He hadn't lasted as a waiter, but he'd met Edouard at the Costes and for a several months they'd lived as partners in the lawyer's apartment on the Île Saint-Louis where I'd first seen him. I heard a lot about that. Edouard took him to parties, restaurants, trips, but had never come through with much more than pocket money. Then, about six months ago, he had told him that he couldn't stay anymore, that his wife was coming up from the country, that he had a lot of work, leaving Timothy to fall back into *la nuit*. Timothy was puzzled by the sudden insistence on discretion. He still saw Edouard, who 'helped him out', but he was no longer allowed to stay over at the apartment. His days consisted of sleeping off the night before, then spiffing himself up to mooch around the boutiques in Saint-Germain or the Avenue George V until the clubs opened. Timothy wasn't exactly unmotivated – he spent longer on exercise and grooming than I did – and he talked a good enough game about fashion, mentioning 'Nicolas' or 'Demna' as though he knew them from anything but Instagram, but he was twenty-one, and like the majority of the generation below mine he was mostly waiting confidently for the moment that he was discovered.

In return, I told him I was in Paris to complete research for a PhD thesis, hence my daily trips to the library. He brightened a little when I said it was art history – Edouard was apparently 'really into' art – but I didn't want him getting curious at this stage, so I said it was technical stuff about colours and materials in old pictures. He was as uninterested in any holes in my story as I was in picking out those in his – I had taken enough of a shine to him to mean that he could sleep for free inside the Périphérique, and he wasn't going to ask any questions. At least I thought so, until after I got back from my morning run I found him on the floor, with all my stuff laid out around him, riffling through the cash from the bottom of my bag. He was so engrossed that he hadn't heard my Nikes on the stairs. *Oh, not again. If he'd opened the lining . . .*

I was bracing myself to kick him swiftly in the face and then improvise, but I glimpsed the intact lining of the emptied bag over his shoulder in time. The Caravaggio and the Caracal were safe for now. Then he gave me a wide-eyed, red-handed shrug and put the money back on the horrible carpet, so I laughed instead. I hadn't been planning on springing my Guiche story quite so soon, but this was obviously the moment.

'You poxy little grifter.'

'What?'

I switched back to French. 'What the hell are you doing?'

'Looking for stuff to steal. Sorry. I wouldn't have really taken it. I'll go.'

'It's OK. You're broke then?'

'Yeah.'

'So you would have taken it?'

'Well, all right. Yeah. I thought you were rich. You have really nice things.' His eyes moved quite sadly over the rumpled pile of leather, cashmere, silk.

'I do, don't I? You should have asked.'

'But you didn't even want me to –'

'Wouldn't you have done that for free?' His wince was genuine.

'Just as well I didn't ask! Look, you're a nice guy, you're pretty good at reading people . . .' I flattered him.

'Sure.'

'So when we met, in the club, you could tell I was sad. I was really drunk?'

'You're English.'

'You remember I told you I had a thing with a guy who was married?' I turned over my scattered possessions until I found Eakin's book, showed him the passages I'd marked.

'That was my boyfriend. We were together for three years. He was going to leave his wife, but . . .' I blinked back a few brave tears.

'And now he's passed on,' he answered respectfully.

'Yes. It's a few years ago now. But when you said your guy? Edouard? Edouard knew –' *shit, what was the Pole's name?* – 'Oskar. I just couldn't believe it. It seemed like – a sign. I'd love to talk to him, just once. I couldn't go to the funeral, out of respect for the family.'

'You need closure.' He'd seen enough reality shows to know his script.

'That's it.'

'There's no such thing as coincidence,' prompted Timothy solemnly. We were both enjoying ourselves hugely.

'So I was thinking – if you'd help me – I could, you know, help you out a bit? 'I let my eyes slide over the pile of notes on the floor.

'I'll help. Of course I will.'

'And then we'll see. Thank you.'

Timothy's empathy might have been contrived, but he seemed convinced enough by my story, so with that satisfactory little improvisation played out respectably on both sides, I encouraged him a bit more by taking him to lunch at Thoumieux and buying him a pair of pointy-toed Saint Laurent Chelsea boots, which delighted him. I put the lid on any mourning for poor Oskar by saying that I Wasn't Ready to Talk About It, which Timothy entirely Understood, and then we toasted the new boots with a kir royale while he messaged Edouard. We sat outside so we could smoke, but the October air was chilly and Edouard wasn't replying.

'How long is it since you actually spoke to him?'

Of course I knew that Timothy had approached Edouard a few days ago, but the meeting hadn't gone that well.

'I told you, a while. He's been weird lately. I'll WhatsApp him.'

'It's probably best if you don't mention me. I don't want to be indiscreet. Just work out when you'll meet and I'll, you know, casually come along.'

'He could be away. He travels a lot.' We'd seen a burgundy velvet blazer in the Saint Laurent store and I could see that he was irritated – if he didn't produce Edouard for our touching scene of reminiscence he didn't have a chance at it.

'No problem. I'm freezing, I'm going back to the hotel. I'll see you there later.'

Housekeeping at the Hearse was not top-flight; the Caracal had been lurking in wait underneath the mattress since I arrived. I used Timothy's absence to check the barrel was clean and lubricate it with the phial of gun oil I kept in my make-up bag, before checking the safety. I was stuffing it back into the bed just as he charged in, beaming.

'He says he can meet me tomorrow!' He sprawled right over the Caracal. 'He called me back and asked me to an art reception – really smart – the Fondation Vuitton.'

'A party? I thought you said he was being secretive recently?'

'Exactly. He's obviously changed his mind. It could be a new beginning, don't you think?'

'So I get to meet him?'

'Well, that too, of course. I asked if I could bring a friend and we're on the list. Me plus one,' he added proudly.

'Brilliant. I'll introduce myself, see how it goes.'

'I'll be there to support you,' he muttered meaninglessly. I thought his mind must be fixed on the blazer, but something in his face was pathetically hopeful.

'Are you in love with Edouard?'

He rolled over onto his stomach. The last light of the Parisian dusk caught his sharp cheekbones.

'I used to imagine the life we could have. You should see his place!' I'd heard so much about the flat on the Quai d'Anjou I could have hosted a dinner party there blindfolded. The modern art, the rainfall shower, the maid's room on the top floor done out as a Moroccan-style smoking room. With ingenuous venality, Timothy had even informed me of the thread count of Edouard's Frette sheets and the full range of Tom Ford cosmetics available in the walk-in dressing room. Edouard's firm was clearly doing very nicely off the back of their Russian connection.

'He knows so many people,' Timothy went on, 'and he's really kind. Thoughtful, you know? He's just been very preoccupied with his work lately. But he said that he had something to tell me, something important. And the party, you know, public. Maybe he's getting divorced?'

I wanted to tell him that they never get divorced, not for two-bit rent boys anyway, but the remaining scraps of my heart weren't quite cold enough.

'Shit, what will I wear?' Timothy was still in the sweatshirt and T-shirt he'd had on three days ago at the *peniche* party, and his Calvin Kleins were looking a little tired from damp nights spent on the shower rail.

'Don't worry, we'll get you some more stuff tomorrow. I really appreciate you helping me out. It means – so much.' I rubbed my eyes brusquely.

He reached up and pulled me into a hug. 'That's OK, Judith. I really care about you.'

For a man who'd been in the process of robbing me blind four hours ago, he sounded remarkably sincere.

18

I made Timothy take the Métro up to the Bois de Boulogne. He grumbled, but shopping for him had left me with only a few thousand in cash and I wasn't yet any closer to whoever had grassed me up. My own wardrobe wasn't a worry. I'd learned by now that looking too polished marked you immediately as a nouv; the important thing was perfect confidence, which is why a duke can go to dinner in an old polo shirt. At least, that was what I'd read in the *Tatler*. Black high-waisted Miu Miu pants with droll, childish buttons and a mannish white Comme des Garcons shirt with flats looked suitable. Only waitresses wear cocktail dresses nowadays. Timothy was resplendent in blazer and boots, with a fresh T-shirt and a Paul Smith foulard for a touch of *style anglais*. He spent a touching amount of time shaving twice and applying just a stroke of Touche Éclat, and the result was, I admit, very lovely. He could have been a model; I hoped that maybe things with Édouard would work out and give him a chance.

Gehry's sequence of overlapping shells, a toppled Sydney Opera House, hovered above the trees of the park as we approached the Vuitton building. The show was commemorating twenty years of the artists of the 798 district in Beijing; the gallery was illuminated in a gold and black display of Chinese characters, morphing in and out of the brand's logo. Walking inside was a step back into my old life, or at least Elisabeth Teerlinc's life. As we approached the greeter, our feet crunched over a path made of shards of porcelain, a reference to Ai Weiwei's 1995 photo stunt, where he smashed a supposed Han Dynasty vase. Waiters in gold Mao pyjamas held out trays of cocktails in teacups painted with Communist slogans. I asked for a water as I warily searched the crowd, prepared to slip into character as Elisabeth if I was approached by anyone who recognised me from the art circuit. Once we had our drinks, Timothy pulled me through the crowd, not even glancing at the exhibits. We made an anti-clockwise circle of the space and then another before he spotted Edouard, in a dark suit and open-collared white shirt. I hung back while Timothy approached him and the two discreetly shook hands. I watched for a few minutes as they talked, Guiche leaning in as though telling a story. Edouard looked the definition of straight-acting – blandly handsome, professionally confident. If I hadn't heard about what they'd got up to in Tangier I would never have believed that the two had anything other than a casual social relationship.

As Timothy steered Edouard away from the murmuring guests, into the shadow of a huge black rubber sculpture of an obese cavorting Buddha, he cued me with a slight nod and I crossed towards them. Timothy turned away to study the exhibit and I approached Guiche.

'Monsieur Guiche? Good evening. I wonder if I could –'

I'd simply planned to ask if we could have a word in private, but Guiche didn't exactly offer the welcome I'd been hoping for. His distracted social smile froze as he took in my face, then he reeled backwards as though I'd punched him.

'Monsieur Guiche?'

He looked over my shoulder and his expression changed from shock to alarm.

'Both of you? Here? What the *fuck*?!'

I was shocked by both the language and the vehemence of his tone.

'I –'

But Guiche wasn't talking to me. He pushed me brusquely aside, and as I turned to follow his gaze I caught a glimpse of a bald head with a familiar smudge of ink beneath the ear, from behind the rolls of the god's pirouetting leg. Yury. My back was to him, and as he moved towards Guiche I dodged sideways, my body moving before my thoughts began to process what the Russian's presence implied. I began to push through the group surrounding the drinks trays at the exit – *no, don't be stupid* – turned back, ducked under the skeletal arm of a chicken-wire concubine wearing a Madame Mao mask and walked briskly, not hurrying, towards the curve of the stairs, where I had seen the waiters emerging. A corridor gave on to a service kitchen, where a brigade of chefs in whites were plating miniature lobster summer rolls.

'*Madame? Les toilettes sont par la –*' one of them called helpfully, but I deposited my water glass and barged past, knowing there would be a fire exit, spotted the red sign –

'*Madame! Vous ne pouvez pas –*'

'*Désolée, excusez-moi,*' I called gaily, pushing the bar on the door down and slipping out into the twilight before they had a chance to stop me. I ran with no sense of where I was going, a strange elation within the urgency. I felt weirdly strong, inhabiting my body for the first time in so long, hurtling over a lawn, wanting to put as much distance between myself and the building as possible. After about twenty seconds I looked back at the open fire door, from which a confused toqued head was protruding. I could see a line of waiting cars, their drivers smoking and chatting as they waited for their clients. The lasers were swooping over the roof and I was caught in their light, the logo travelling across my pale shirt. I crouched, making myself small until they passed, then waddled like a crab towards a copse of manicured trees, ducked under the wire – *did they have guards? No time* – and dodged the trunks until I came onto another road, this time back in the parkland of the Bois. I walked along one of the avenues which cut through the park until I came to a crossroads, peering at the signs, and took the route marked 'Étoile'. The paths were empty, though every now and then a car crawled slowly past, the headlights making me flinch. Trawling for trade, I thought. The Bois had once been the parade ground for the *demi-monde* of Paris, gorgeous courtesans – 'diamond crunchers' lolling in their furbelowed carriages. I passed a gently swaying minivan which suggested the locals were keeping up the tradition. Further on, the road divided; no sign. I looked in vain for a passing cab, chose the right fork at random. Every second that passed I saw Yury crossing the city ahead of me, nodding to the Chinese concierge, mounting the stairs to my room . . .

Stop it. It could be a coincidence. For all I knew, Yermolov might be in the city for the Vuitton event, just another staging post in the art caravan. It didn't necessarily mean anything. Yeah. Right.

It was properly dark now, and with the sweat drying on my skin I was shivering in my grubby cotton shirt. There was an odd smell of sausages, and the juicy odour made my stomach growl. I rounded a bend and practically fell over a plump woman planted in a camping chair on the narrow verge between the road and the trees.

'Oh, I'm very sorry, excuse me!'

'Looking for company, darling?'

'No, sorry. I'm just a bit lost. If you could please tell me –'

She stood, and even though she must have been six two it took me a minute in the shadowy light of the storm lantern on the table in front of her to realise she was a he. A he in full slap, dodgy red nylon wig and a zebra-print minidress straining over a colossal pair of fake tits.

'Lost?'

'I'm just trying to get to Étoile – I'm in a bit of a hurry.' The quickest way to get back to the Marais would be to take Métro line one down to Bastille. As my eyes adjusted to the light, I could see that she had a very neat set-up. On the table was a half-empty bottle of red, two glasses, plates, baguette, silver and a pot of mustard. Next to the table was a camping stove, with a pan of cheerfully hissing merguez. Another minivan was parked under the trees with the back doors invitingly open to reveal a double mattress, a cool box and a small vase of artificial roses taped to the inside handle.

My clutch was only large enough for a wallet and keys, no phone. I rootled inside for some cash. 'If you could possibly call me a cab – I'd be glad to pay for the call.'

'Seriously, darling, did you come down with the last rainfall?'

I really didn't have time for this. Yury was probably having a go on my Crème de la Mer while he waited to kill me at the Hearse. I turned to go, felt a large palm on my shoulder and a snarl rising in my throat.

'Where are you going?'

I straightened up. 'I told you, I'm in a hurry. I don't care if you've got a machete along with whatever else you're hiding in your g-string, you can have the cash, all right? Just leave it.'

She backed away, hairy wrists flicking upwards.

'OK, OK. *Ça va, quoi*. I meant, I'll take you if you like.'

'You'll give me a lift?'

'Fifty euro. I've got a moped round the back.'

'Er, thanks. Sorry for the trouble.'

'It's OK. There's nothing doing here tonight anyway. Some bolloxy party over there, keeps the punters away. D'you fancy a little merguez?'

'Thanks, but I can't. I really have to get going.'

'Suit yourself. I've got a spare helmet.'

While she put a plate over the sausages and stowed away the kit efficiently in the back of the van, she told me her name was Destiny-with-a-y. I did fancy a sandwich actually. Maybe I could just stay here, living in the forest, sleeping in the van, with no one to bother me. I could forage for herbs, do something about that wig, improve the business. It might not be a bad life.

'Here we go. Put this on, darling.' Destiny was wheeling an old Mobylette out from behind a tree.

'I usually leave the van here, more convenient. The police keep an eye on it.'

'I'm going to the eleventh actually. Is that OK?'

'No problem. We'll have you there in a tiny minute.' She was checking her lipstick in the wing mirror, arranging the crisp rolls of nylon hair protruding from her helmet. 'I used to be a cabbie. Hop on.'

It's not every night you get to swoop down the Champs-Elysées with a tranny on a moped and the warm wind in your hair. I might have quite enjoyed the trip if I hadn't felt that every traffic light might be a pause on my way to my own death. As we rounded Bastille I was squeezing Destiny's comfortable hips so hard I feared I might bruise her. I had the crazy idea of asking her to come up with me, but she didn't deserve that, so I had her stop at the corner of the street and gave her the fifty and a cheerful wave as she zoomed off.

I asked the concierge if anyone had inquired for me, but all I got was a grunt. I felt my heart accelerate as I walked into my room, but the panic which had swept over me when I glimpsed Yury had been overcome by that other, more familiar sensation, a stretching of the pupils, a cliff-top adrenalin rush. There might even have been an ugly little smile on my lips. *Hey there, baby*. When had I forgotten that rage could feel so good?

But the room was empty, everything just as Timothy and I had left it, the only sound my own low panting. As I sat on the bed sucking air with my head between my knees I felt curiously disappointed. The high was passing, the fear oozing back to furnish the silence. Fumbling, my palms slick with sweat, I eased the Caracal out from the mattress, shoving it in my waistband. Passports and money stowed, I ruthlessly halved my clothes to make the bag lighter. My mouth was gummy so I swigged a handful of tapwater as I jumbled the contents of the bathroom into my washbag. Odd, when you can buy a toothbrush anywhere, that packing it always seems so important. And then I heard the footsteps. At last.

There was no internal lock on the door, just the keycard, which half the time didn't work, but I didn't think Yury would have had much trouble persuading the concierge to hand one over. Click. Pause. I imagined the red light flashing. I braced myself, back to the wall, facing the door, both hands on the gun to keep it steady. *Aim and squeeze. Click. Release.* I'm not a great shot, but Parisian hotel rooms are tiny. It was just as well for Timothy that he called my name before he opened the door, or I would have blown his head off.

'Judith? Where did you go?' It took him a moment to register that the thing in my hands was, indeed, a gun, and another moment for me to register that it wasn't the first one he had seen. Things back in Rabat had obviously been rougher than he'd made them sound. Ten years crept onto his face as he spoke, slow, thin-voiced.

'Please put that down. OK? Just put it down.'

I considered. 'I think I might not put it down just yet. Close the door. Keep still now.'

He did as he was told.

You could still do it. Watch his lungs burst, watch the fat bubbles of blood, watch him thrash, watch him drown in it. Come on. Grip your forearm and pull the trigger. It's not like you haven't done it before.

Effortfully, I lowered the barrel through a treacly force field. *Not now.*

'Your friend recognised me.'

'What are you talking about?'

'Edouard Guiche. He knew me. Which means one of two things. Either you convince me that you know nothing about this, or I put your face on the other side of the corridor. Take your time.'

'It's to do with that Russian guy, isn't it?'

'You tell me.'

'Edouard was great tonight, at first – he seemed like his old self. He told me that he had to go away for a while tomorrow, but that I could spend the night. He said he had something to give me. That everything was going to be different. And then –'

'What happened then?'

'How am I supposed to know? You came over, then suddenly you vanished – I couldn't work out what was going on. Edouard was talking to that big guy in Russian. He speaks Russian, you know.' The pride in his voice was convincing.

'Whatever. Carry on.'

'So I went to see where you'd gone, and when I got back, they'd left. I tried calling him; his phone's off. So I came back here. It's embarrassing, you running off like that. And he said he had something for me,' he repeated petulantly.

I sighed and pushed the hair off my face. Timothy jerked back. I'd forgotten I was still holding the Caracal. I held it out and clicked the safety on so he could see.

'Sorry. Just sit there for a minute, will you?'

Guiche's reaction when he saw me could mean only one thing. It was Guiche who had been waiting that night in the Place de l'Odéon. Guiche was meant to retrieve the second picture in the case. He'd never taken it, because I had. But back then Guiche couldn't have known anything more about me, about what I'd done. He had failed to produce the picture for Yermolov, and Mischa had just seen us together. Yury was with Guiche right now. Carefully I put the gun aside.

'You should go,' I said. 'Just – get your stuff and go. There's no need for this to have anything to do with you.'

'What is it? Please, tell me why you're doing this. What's going on with Edouard?'

I calculated.

'You said Edouard seemed – affectionate?'

'Yes. It might not seem like much, but the way he looked at me, I could tell –'

I could still use him. If Yury and Guiche were looking for me, Timothy could be a useful barrier between us. A hostage, basically.

'I think Edouard might be in danger,' I said eventually.

'Should we call the police?'

'We can't. I – can't. But I need to see him.'

'Then I'll stay with you. If Edouard's in danger I want to help him.' Maybe that was the first entirely sincere thing he had ever said to me.

'OK. Then we have to leave, now.'

Timothy stuffed his things into the Saint Laurent carrier which had held his finery and followed me with bewildered obedience to the Rue de la Roquette, where after a few more anxious minutes I hailed a cab. I asked the driver to take us to the Pont de Sully, where I had first seen Timothy near Guiche's home on the Île Saint-Louis.

The island was busy, the restaurants and cafés full of people chatting, smoking with their coats on under outdoor heaters. A glance at my watch told me it was early, only ten. I found a table and ordered two glasses of white wine.

'Go round the corner and ring the bell. Text me if he lets you in.'

He disappeared. I wondered if he'd come back with Yury in tow, if he'd come back at all, but he returned a few minutes later, alone, to slide in next to me.

'The lights are out upstairs and no one answered the bell. I tried phoning again too.'

'Then we'll wait.'

'OK. And you can tell me what's going on.'

I thought of Elena, giggling hysterically into her salad. *Because I know too much.*

'Timothy, I really can't. I just think someone might be after Edouard.'

'Is it to do with that Russian bloke, the one he works for? Like your boyfriend that you told me about, in the book?'

'Kind of. Look, I know this seems crazy. But I'm serious. We have to wait for Edouard, that's all.'

I ordered two plates of *moules frites* to pass the time. Timothy ate both, in between popping round the corner to look for any sign of life. We sat as the customers dwindled away, until, after several meaningful looks and some banging with a broom, the waiter started to stack the chairs indoors and set the bill firmly on the table. We moved round to the bridge and sat for another hour on its parapet with our bags, Timothy periodically checking his phone, but no one appeared.

'It's nearly two. This is hopeless,' I conceded.

'He said he had to go away, but he wanted to see me first, remember? Maybe he'll be here in the morning,' he suggested.

'I suppose so.'

We trudged all the way up to the Hôtel Ibis near Place d'Italie, where I had Timothy check in using his identity card. I gave him enough cash for the room. I didn't want to think about how much was left. As before, we both kept politely to our respective quarters after flopping down in our clothes on the meagre double bed, but neither of us slept much. Possibly that was because I was gripping the Caracal. I watched the lights of the first morning traffic build behind the thin blind, weighing incentives, waiting for morning. I had told Kazbich I had the Caravaggio. Guiche was the person who had originally been meant to collect it. I could tell Guiche I had it, offer to give it back, in return for him telling me, if indeed he knew, who was the source who had betrayed me to Yermolov. But who could it be? I twisted under the thin duvet, flailing in my own futility. The names spun round in my head. What was that line from Brodsky – something about the speed of light equalling a fleeting view? Fucking Russians. Masha was dead. Yury was in Paris. He had been looking for Guiche. So, maybe. Fuck.

'Timothy! Get up. Now. We have to go back.'

19

Still gloomy at 8 a.m. but the boulevard was already clogged with traffic. The cab ranks stood defiantly vacant; we jogged towards the river through the postcard smells of early-morning Paris – clouds of buttery baking from the boulangeries, a whiff of ammoniac cheese as an aproned woman opened a delicatessen. Twenty minutes later, as we arrived at the Quai d'Anjou, scuffling through fallen chestnut leaves at the top of the island, the sky behind us was growing light. The river was dark and choppy, scurfed with foam, and the water stilled the noise of the traffic over towards the Hôtel de Ville, but there was the usual amount of ill-natured honking and swearing as the vehicles snarled their way into the square. So when we heard it, it didn't seem all that unusual, a crunching thud, a magnified slap, maybe a cab taking a door off a delivery van or an unlucky motorist forced over the intersection. We didn't stop walking, just glanced over to the roadway. Then the screaming started, a woman, wailing uncontrollably, and, like a speeded-up film, the few pedestrians nearby began to run, carrying us with them along the bank. The screaming went on and on, the sound only faltering when the woman drew breath for her next hurling, hysterical cry. All I was thinking was that someone had been hurt, that they needed help, until I felt Timothy slowing beside me and saw that his face was sweating, gnarled in shock and disbelief.

'What is it? Are you OK?'

He stopped dead and pointed. Then I saw why I hadn't recognised the sound, because I'd never heard a body hit a pavement from six storeys up before.

'Is that Edouard's building?' I hissed.

He pointed again, his mouth moving in spasm.

'Come. Come now.'

I dragged him by his sleeve past the huddle of bystanders, all of them talking at once. Someone was holding their phone towards the body, a man was kneeling, trying to cover it with his coat while another held the screaming woman awkwardly in his arms. I saw a dark jacket sleeve, a gold watch fastened around the wrist. Maybe Timothy recognised the watch; he was still pointing, frozen, his mouth still working silently. I don't know how else he could have known his lover, because Guiche's head had exploded like a pumpkin on the cobbles.

A thick stream of blood pulsed towards the gutter. The woman, I realised, must have been passing just at the moment of impact, she was striped with it from her knees to her forehead, as though she had leaned forward over a fountain. Even her neat, morning-ready hair was delicately stippled with magenta. For a moment we were arrested there, all of us, unlucky witnesses to a martyrdom.

The scene around me was unrolling in slow motion, inversely proportional to the speed of my thoughts. Three things: One, I had been right; Two, we were too late; and three, if Guiche had jumped, odds were his flat would be empty. If he had been pushed, whoever did the pushing was unlikely to be still in there. There was enough chaos to cover us, and the door of the building stood open. I dived for the stairs, pulling Timothy by the wrist, one flight, two.

'Which way? Fifth floor?' I knew the answer. Timothy had told me about the wonderful view. The treads were carpeted in a thick red fabric set with old-fashioned brass rods. We mounted silently except for Timothy's strangled breathing. The double door of 5A was slightly ajar. Guiche hadn't jumped then. I pushed it open slowly, seeing a long parquet hall with doors leading off either side.

'There's no one here, don't worry,' I whispered, though I wasn't as certain as I tried to imply. Timothy was still staring as though he'd had a stroke. I shook him until his eyes dully found mine.

'You know where the kitchen is? Of course you do. Go and get some water, put some sugar in it and drink it. Then stand by the door. If anyone comes, just say you're a friend of – just a friend. OK? You can do that?'

He nodded.

'Good. Edouard has a study, right? Or a place where he has his desk?'

Another nod. Hopeless. I'd be quicker alone.

'Go on then.'

He shuffled to the first door on the right. I heard the tap run.

Timothy had described Edouard's fantastic double drawing room with the river views. That would be on the left, the front of the apartment. I walked softly down the hall, opened the third door on the left, which was a small dining room, from which I could see into the drawing room on one side and what looked like a library on the other. One of the three long windows was wide open, the white linen drape blooming out into the street. The flat was clean and modern, with just a few real antiques mixed with the contemporary furniture; the desk in the library was a compact walnut keyhole, eighteenth century, with a bright Prampolini chromatic above it on the white-glossed wall. Timothy was right to be impressed by Edouard's taste. There was an envelope on the desk, with an initial 'T'. I pocketed that. The room was preternaturally tidy, aside from the painting there was no decoration and the whole back wall was a deep stack of white USM filing cabinets, shelved to the ceiling. I listened. The woman had stopped screaming, but the crowd in the street sounded bigger. The ambulance and the police would be here in minutes. Gingerly I tried the desk drawers. All locked. The mountain of cabinets would be hopeless – there was no time. Secrets? Where would I keep a secret in this ascetic room?

Tempting as it was to start fiddling beneath the desk with a hairpin, I didn't have the space for an ingenious Auguste Dupin routine. Plain sight. The best hiding places are often the most obvious. What would Edouard want to hide? His secret life with boys? Hardly – there was his phone for that. I took a step back, gazing at the smooth clean surfaces. In the furthest corner, though, there was a gap between the lip and the shelf above. I dived at it and the filing cabinet glided smoothly open, filled with binders with names and dates. They were arranged alphabetically, A through D. Presumably Guiche had been disturbed while looking for a file. My eyes accelerated over the labels, locating B, filed under the Russian character, the hooked lower-case 'b': BALENSKY. I manoeuvred the heavy box file onto the floor and shunted the others along so the gap was less obvious, heaved myself up with it under my arm just as I heard the sirens. Counting swiftly along the shelves, I figured that 'Y' was too high to reach, we had to get out.

'Timothy?' I was already moving back down the hall, the unwieldy file crooked awkwardly into my arm. *Shit*. There were frantic voices coming up the stairs. Timothy was motionless in the kitchen, a full glass of water in his hand.

'You said there was a maid's room? The *chambre de bonne*? Where?'

There was a door next to the fridge, I struggled one-handed with the latch. Beyond, a laundry room and a narrow staircase.

'Up. Now. Bring the glass.' I closed the door as gently as I could and pushed Timothy up the dark, narrow stairs.

'Keep going.' The steps to the attic floor were wood, our feet were clattering, but hopefully the neighbours were making enough noise to drown us out as we emerged into the fabled *fumoir* and I tripped over a cymbal-sized Moroccan tin table, sending it rolling sonorously into a heap of kelim cushions. Timothy crashed into me, spilling the water all over my feet.

'Jesus. Just keep still a minute. Breathe. Breathe slowly.'

I could hear the voices below us, moving through the rooms, calling out. Random shouts, not the focused attention of the police. We froze as the kitchen door opened.

'*Allo? Il y a quelqu'un?*' Then, when there was no answer, '*Il n'y a personne. Alors, on attend les flics?*' *There's no one here. Should we wait for the cops?*

'Maybe we shouldn't touch anything?'

'You're right. We should wait downstairs. We shouldn't disturb anything.' Evidence – everyone knows how to behave at a crime scene these days. Thank you, Netflix. I waited until we heard the door close, the steps retreating. I scooted back down the stairs and found a plastic mop bucket, stuffed the box file in it and handed it to Timothy.

'Take your jacket off. Give it to me. Now go down the service stairs – there's a door into the courtyard there.' I pointed through the tiny window, festooned with delicate coloured glass lamps like the ones in the orange trees on Ibiza.

'Walk. Keep your head down. Just keep going the way we came, back to the hotel. I'll catch you up in a few minutes. Can you do that?' Another speechless nod.

I hated to trust him, but if Yury was outside I'd never get away with the file.

'Go on then.'

In his crumpled T-shirt, with the bucket, he would hopefully look like a cleaner. I pulled the velvet blazer on over my own jacket and nipped down the stairs, rooting in my bag for my sunglasses. The main stairwell was empty, but the crowd by the door had swelled, several more ghouls taking pictures. One woman, phone at the ready, dressed in shorts and a purple gilet, was craning to see the body. Tourist. 'What happened?' I asked her in English.

'I think there's been a suicide,' she replied greedily, in a heavy Australian accent.

'Oh God, how awful,' I muttered, moving away.

At the street corner I turned back to look once more at the crowd. The ambulance had arrived but the bystanders were blocking its path; two paramedics in high-vis vests were struggling to get a stretcher trolley through.

'Please step aside,' they were yelling irritably. As the group moved, I caught sight of a dapper older man, standing to the edge, looking up at the open window of Edouard's drawing room. Kazbich. Not a suicide then. I didn't stay around to look any further. I backed slowly down the street, crossed the Rue Saint-Louis en l'Île and broke into an awkward jog. How long before Yury and Kazbich found me? For all I knew, Yermolov could have dozens of goons scouting the city for his precious picture. But the room was booked under Timothy's name, I could stay there a few hours surely – enough time to go through the papers. With that in mind, I slowed to a hurried walk and took a circuitous route, doubling back a few times, alert for any familiarity in the passers-by, any sign that I was being followed. Inverting my game of cat and mouse with Guiche didn't feel so much fun now that I was the mouse.

'It wasn't true, was it?'

'What?' It was the first time Timothy had spoken since I returned to the hotel.

'That stuff about your boyfriend. The lawyer. It wasn't true.'

'Well, you said it. There's no such thing as coincidence,' I replied nastily. The files sat between us in the plastic bucket; I was itching to get at them. While we sat here, the police would be going over the flat, questioning witnesses, going over the footage on amateur sleuths' phones. I really didn't have time for grief counselling. But then I stopped myself. None of this was his responsibility; he hadn't done anything. If I'd been quicker off the mark, we might have reached Guiche, warned him. And now he was dead. *It's not your fault, Judith*. I spoke as gently as I could:

'Look, you've had a terrible, terrible shock. I know I need to explain, and I promise I will. But let's get you into a hot shower. And then you should rest.' If I could get a couple of his trusty Diazepam down him before the tears kicked in, I could get on with my research at least. For the immediate present, the terror of what he had seen had rendered him numbly trusting; I didn't want to think about how it would go if he panicked and tried to leave. I'd have to work out what to do with him once I knew more. When he shuffled into the tiny shower I jacked the window open the regulation six inches and smoked an uncomfortable sideways fag, then found him a brandy in the mini-bar. Checkout was at 11 a.m. I nipped down, still in my bedraggled clothes from last night, and handed over yet more cash to the imperturbable receptionist. I found Timothy hunched and shivering in the duvet. He held out his arms to me and as I embraced him he began to weep, mewling and gasping. Awkwardly, I stroked his hair while I felt for the brandy glass and the pill.

'Come on, come on. It will be all right. Come on now, drink this. Let's find something to help you sleep, shall we? That's right, it's for the shock, come on . . .' I repeated the meaningless, unfamiliar phrases of comfort as he swallowed, sobbing and choking, then held him against me, feeling his flurried heart slowly settle through my T-shirt. It took so long I almost dozed off, but as soon as his breathing was regular I drew my arm from under his body and hopped into the shower myself, first scalding hot, then freezing cold. I was starving. I crammed a mini-pack of Brittany butter biscuits from the bar messily into my mouth while I hauled on a clean sweater and knickers. I covered Timothy with the quilt, spread out the files on the floor and began to sort through the sheaves of papers.

They seemed to be arranged by subject, some in quaint legal French, some in Russian. I worked systematically through the lot, scanning for anything to do with paintings.

I found nothing, and barely understood what I was reading. The first bundles took me took over two hours. Many contained documents of the property transactions I'd already learned about, along with applications for visas or permits. Then, in a separate folder, I found the provenances. A typed summary in English was provided alongside the original documents in French, Russian or another language that I thought might be Serbo-Croat. The first name that stood out was Kazbich's. I'd always had difficulty with his initial in Cyrillic. A photocopy of the provenance for a painting by an artist I'd never heard of, the name all j's and v's, described as a landscape in oils, signed by the artist in 1929 and sold out of a private collection via a gallery in Belgrade in 1997. Serbia – Kazbich's gallery was based there. Balensky had purchased the landscape for fifty thousand US dollars, along with about ten further twentieth-century pictures, all from 'private collections', in the space of about six months. Each group of papers was clipped together, with a photograph of the painting at the top and the documentation beneath. Serbia was at war in the nineties. Turmoil often gives a boost to the art market. Currencies crash, people need funds to escape, they pop the heirlooms. Some of the pictures had been exhibited; there were copies of gallery catalogues and museum pamphlets, receipts, many of them handwritten, dating back to the paintings' creation. The standard paper trail which shows a buyer the progress of a painting through the market and authenticates its value. So Kazbich had been in business with Balensky for many years. One name recurred several times, an owner who had dealt through Kazbich. Dejan Raznatovic. Raznatovic had not only sold, he had bought, not twentieth-century pieces, but several valuable Russian icons. There was definitely a law against that. I made a note of the name.

And then, in the early 2000s, old Dr Kazbich hit the big time. A small Cézanne, another landscape, with Balensky buying at twenty million and then selling the picture on, about a year later, for thirty-five, to one Pavel Yermolov, again with Kazbich as the runner. The same process was repeated with a Giacometti, and a Klimt, perhaps one of the ones I had seen at Yermolov's French home. So Balensky had been flipping pictures to Yermolov. Had the two oligarchs connected over art, with Kazbich as the go-between? Spreading the provenances out on the mangy Ibis carpet, I scanned them clockwise, pen poised, waiting for something to jump out. Rothko. Kazbich had sold a Rothko to Balensky in 2005, the picture having first passed through the collection of an Italian bank and then the collector in Belgrade, Raznatovic.

Timothy slept on. I stretched, paced what there was of the room. So many variables, so many potentialities to consider. *Go slow*.

There was nothing at all unusual about corporations or banks owning paintings. Art was a commodity like any other, serviced by investment funds – pensioners in Dorking might own a square inch of Francis Bacon without ever knowing. I knew from my time at the House that huge warehouses of pictures existed, aureate masterpieces throbbing for years in temperature-controlled darkness, emerging for a few weeks into a sale room only to disappear again – Yermolov's Botticellis being a case in point. Dealers could stack works indefinitely, until the market was ready. But there was something off about the Rothko. I knew it because, back in Paris, as part of his pose as a bounty hunter, Renaud Cleret had told me he was on the trail of a fake Rothko for a client. That had been his cover for blackmailing me into seeking out Moncada. As a consequence, I knew the contents of the Rothko *catalogue raisonné*, the authorised compendium of an artist's works, back to front. I'd needed to check that Renaud was lying. And this Rothko – a two-metre-high panel in tones of black and silver, quartered into overlapping parallelograms – had never been near a catalogue. I looked through the provenances. An Italian bank – the Societa Mutuale di Palermo – had supposedly acquired the picture soon after its exhibition in New York back in the sixties. The name of the Chelsea gallerist was appended, along with a shot of the exhibition notes. The bank had sat on its asset for twenty-five years before Raznatovic acquired it, with Kazbich as the broker, and it had then been sold on to Balensky.

As I had explained to Elena back in Venice, provenance could be faked. Photographs, receipts typed up on old typewriters and the paper aged in an oven, false pages re-clipped into archives, a dud canvas inserted into a job lot of authentic pieces and sold through an auctioneer so it would appear in the daybook – there were hundreds of ways to con the market, because, unlike other commodities, the value of a picture ultimately rested on the perceptions of its buyers. If the provenance is good enough, dealers will often overlook obvious flaws, in good faith or bad. So I knew that Kazbich had shifted a dodgy Rothko, via Italy and then Serbia, into Balensky's private collection.

The next sale was another Italian acquisition, with the same chain of provenance, this time in 2008, the year of the worldwide financial crash. The Palermo bank was obviously propping up its holdings, because this time it had flogged off a work by the Venetian baroque painter Antonio Bacci, for the extraordinary but plausible sum of four million. Raznatovic was clearly a man of impressive means. My hands started working faster through the papers, as though my fingertips knew what they were going to find.

A siren on the street below. I held my breath as its whine receded. I'd paid up the room at the hearse in advance and my abandoned clothes were still scattered about there – I doubted the maid would even notice I'd left. Would the police be looking for the mysterious young couple who'd been spotted at the scene of the distinguished lawyer's tragic fall? I doubted that too. Back to the papers.

And there it was, my old friend. Michelangelo Merisi da Caravaggio, portrait of a woman, on linen. Kazbich was the runner, Balensky and Yermolov joint buyers for a cool 200 million euros. Half the money through a fund in the Turks and Caicos in advance, the other half payable on receipt by the courier. The receipt prepared in three languages, official as you like, ready to be signed by the receiver and the courier. Guiche had already filled in his name, signing in ink with a flourish. The deliverer's signature was blank. Unsurprising, since the picture was zipped securely into its case about a foot from where I was sitting.

Guiche had known they were coming for him. Timothy had said his lover had been distracted and anxious for several months, avoiding him, keeping him away from his apartment. I considered the timings. I leave Paris with the picture last November. Guiche is unable to produce it, naturally. Yermolov believes I have it, waits for me to surface. I open Gentileschi in Venice in spring – *that bloody text message* – but there's no real publicity for the gallery, on or offline, until early summer, when I start producing the Xaoc show. Bingo, Kazbich appears. He and Yermolov fail to trap me. I evade them for a few days. Yermolov has Guiche watched, suspicious of him; I could see how his mind must have worked. I arrive in Paris, apparently with the picture, where I meet Guiche. Guiche continues to protest he knows nothing, but they assume he and I are in cahoots. A 200-million Caravaggio might have corrupted anyone.

So Guiche had just run out of time. I wondered how it had gone. Had Yury simply shoved him out into the air above the quai, or had Guiche been allowed the dignity of stepping to his death? Maybe suicide was more tax-efficient than murder. Kazbich in the crowd, ready to report the job done. Where was Yury now? Looking for me, undoubtedly. But I was safe here, for the moment. I shook off the paranoia and continued reading, and as I leafed through the provenances I couldn't help smiling. I hadn't been the only one hard at work in the archives. The provenances Kazbich had produced for the Caravaggio were practically a novel.

Perhaps it was the Palermo bank's Venetian holdings which had given Kazbich the idea. While most scholars were at least uncertain that Caravaggio had ever visited the city, some were convinced that he had. His first teacher, Peterzano, had been a pupil of Titian, and in turn Titian had been taught by Giorgione, whose influence was agreed to be strong in Caravaggio's works. Like Caravaggio, Giorgione had disdained under-drawing, emphasising colour over design. The extremities of Caravaggio's palette, the crackle of supernatural illumination he burned across his canvases, were attributed to the influence of Venice. In Kazbich's version, the young painter had spent time in Venice en route to Rome in 1592. There was a rumour, cited from several academic papers, that one of Caravaggio's many lost portraits was of a 'woman who had given him lodging' – from which the creative doctor had spun a version of the classic story of the impoverished artist paying his bills with work. The photograph Elena had shown me in Venice was reproduced, along with a convincing-looking inventory for a removal in the eighteenth century in which the picture was described, but not attributed. After this the picture had apparently remained in the same place, sold on as a job lot with the building's contents as it changed hands over the years. For the attribution, Kazbich had gone to town. There was a letter from a 'nineteenth-century traveller', an American art-fancier, in which he speculated to his correspondent that the picture on his hotel room wall could be a Caravaggio. There were then two reports from the International Foundation for Art Research, which provides an authentication service. IFAR reports don't technically constitute a certificate of authenticity, but they are often respected as definitive by eager buyers. However, the foundation is not incorruptible. Experts engaged by the service can choose to remain anonymous, which means that they can create a dubious report without damaging their public reputation – if the price is right. Kazbich claimed that he had been pursuing the picture for years, had obtained it finally through a conveniently deceased relative of the *pensione*'s owner and had then offered it to IFAR.

Ever since I'd first seen the Caravaggio, I'd known it couldn't possibly be real. But this was stupendous. The sheer audacity of it. And yet, such things had happened. Old

Masters did occasionally turn up in attics. A 'Vermeer' made by a faker named Han van Meegeren had famously fooled that well-known connoisseur Hermann Goering. I helped myself to a Coke, took a slug of the viscous sugar syrup and wished I hadn't. What Kazbich, like all art frauds, was clearly counting on was the desire of his marks to believe. The need to possess which ineluctably binds fraudster and defrauded, the victim sealing his faith with money. The more money, the stronger the desire to believe – the very need as priceless as the work itself. Had Kazbich set his price lower, I doubted that a collector as discerning as Yermolov would have been taken in. And yet he had, and, having been thwarted, had already killed two people in the attempt to recover his heart's desire.

So, time to choose. I still hadn't discovered the identity of whoever it was who had traced Gentileschi back to Judith Rashleigh and given Yermolov such power over me. The pieces of the one person who could have confirmed it were being reassembled in the Paris morgue. A bullet in Timothy immediately? And then . . . then what? Kazbich was probably still in Paris – I'd seen him only this morning, so I could leave the picture somewhere it could be safely recovered, take a chance on using my bank accounts and spend the rest of my life waiting for the mysterious witness to knock on the door. Or I could take Elena up on her bargain, hand the Caravaggio over and trust her. But I'd seen enough of Yermolov's methods to think that even if she could be relied on to protect me, she'd be hopeless in the face of her husband's opposition. Or maybe I should just take the Caracal, walk out now and find somewhere peaceful to put the barrel in my mouth.

20

It was getting dark already. Timothy would wake up soon. The only other food the mini-bar had to offer was a foil pack of mixed nuts, and perhaps that was what made me rain-check the suicide option – it would be a really tragic death-row meal. There had to be something else, something in the connection between Yermolov, Balensky and Kazbich. Timothy stirred, turned in his sleep. My legs tingled with pins and needles as I crawled over to my bag, trying not to disturb him. If I was going to shoot him I'd rather do it while he was unconscious. I opened up the laptop I had bought when I arrived in Paris and ran a search linking Raznatovic and Kazbich, but beyond one minimal website featuring the latter's gallery in Belgrade, Kazbich's web presence remained a black hole. No images, no information. Raznatovic, on the other hand, certainly wasn't shy. In fact, if your thing is Serbian ex-paramilitaries-turned-gangsters, he was basically Mick Jagger. Born in 1967, he had served in the notorious Red Berets under the Milošević regime when the wars began in 1991, but unlike his boss had adapted successfully to the post-Yugoslavian state and set up as a gang leader. The Chetniks, as Raztanovic's military colleagues were known, had emerged to dominate the collapsed state with their own brand of brutal and anarchic justice. Initiation into the militia, and later into the ranks of the gangs, consisted of the slow throat-slitting of a (preferably Muslim) victim. 'A little weird the first time,' Raznatovic was quoted by one journalist, 'but afterwards you're happy to go out and celebrate.' From simple assassinations, going rate fifteen dollars a pop, Raznatovic and his crew had supposedly moved into guns, flogging state-issued AK47s at a basic 200 dollars to rocket-propelled grenade launchers for as much as 2,000 dollars. Serbia was ideally situated for moving military contraband into the Schengen Area of Europe, and once inside, there were no pesky border crossings to worry about.

So here was Raznatovic posing with a famous Russian writer, here with his comrades in a mountain camp-ground, here with cigar and standard-issue bikinied lovely in Saint-Tropez – when it was still safe for him to leave the country. Raznatovic was the subject of earnest profiles in foreign newspapers, indexed in think-tank papers, quoted as a national hero and an international criminal. He even had his own Wikipedia entry in English, which mentioned his wealth, his legitimate business holdings and, conveniently, his interest in Serbian national art, specifically icons. He had been a major contributor to a recently established museum in Belgrade and apparently still lived in the city. I could have spent all morning looking at him had I wished, there was enough material for a dissertation, but it was another kind of *matériel* that interested me. Namely the kind that had made Balensky's fortune.

Before he had gone straight by securing his assets in the West, Balensky had been an arms dealer. In the kleptocracy of post-Soviet Russia, where there was no distinction between the gangsters and the state, the military black market had been big business. As Bruce Eakin and his fellow Mafia-theorists earnestly pointed out, the war in Chechnya had essentially been a cover-up for a vast surreptitious arms sale, whereby the state could write off redundant weaponry which had been 'destroyed' – that is, sold. Balensky dealt with Raznatovic via Kazbich. Raznatovic, it was claimed, had also risen to his present position via arms dealing. So what if Kazbich was running something other than charming mid-century landscapes? If only old Bruce had tried a bit harder, I reflected, he might have won a Pulitzer.

The question was, where was Kazbich running them to? The only connection I had was Moncada, but then I thought of the bank in Sicily. So I turned to my old friend Renaud, as I sometimes did. Just because you Google someone doesn't mean you miss them. I'd learned enough from him to suspect money laundering. Paintings are a fairly untouchable way of holding money – the authorities can devalue a bank account, but in order to devalue a painting they have to possess it. Which might be why, after guns and drugs, the third most important black market asset for Italian organised crime is art. The market was estimated at 8 billion euros annually, while the Tutela del Patrimonio Culturale – the Italian body charged with recovering stolen art – had succeeded in sequestering over 600,000 works in just one year alone. It was quite possible that Kazbich was at the centre of a trade of guns for pictures, with Raznatovic and Moncada as the suppliers of the exchange.

Elena was certain that Yermolov had secrets to keep. I'd known about Balensky, but he was old-school, pushing eighty, practically a relic. Yermolov was a new breed, the respectable face of post-Soviet wealth. If he was mixed up in arms smuggling along with his fellow art-fanciers, that might be my point of leverage. Elena wouldn't be able to protect me, even if she had her damn painting, but that could. But how to work it? How to get to Yermolov in a way that kept me alive long enough to blackmail him?

Timothy chose that thrilling moment to awaken. After a few stunned moments before he realised that, no, this wasn't a nightmare, he started crying again. I felt that way about the Ibis myself. I fetched him some water and made some more soothing noises, then remembered the note I had removed from Guiche's desk. It was still in the pocket of my discarded jacket. I handed it over and watched Timothy's face as he unfolded from the single sheet. A sheaf of banknotes, followed by a little shower of coins, tumbled onto the bed. Timothy ignored that, read the paper in silence and handed it over to me.

'I'm sorry,' Guiche had written. *'Thank you for the joy you have given me. Please take this, try to be happy. You should study. Know I believe in you. But please, please, leave Paris. E.'*

He had cared for Timothy then, even down to the mawkish tone of his *adieu*. I gathered the cash and counted it: just under three thousand euro, two thousand in hundreds and the rest in odd notes, as though he had planned it, but had to make up the money hurriedly. Timothy didn't say a word. I watched him for a while, laid a hand on his arm, but he shrugged me off, folding his hands into his armpits, gazing stolidly out into the dusk.

If I'd returned the picture as soon as I'd tracked it down in England, this wouldn't have happened. Guiche would be alive. Timothy might have had a future with a man who loved him.

'Judith?' he said suddenly.

'I'm here.'

'You remember that party I told you about, the one in Tangier?'

'Yes.'

He sat up, earnest, the whites of his eyes gleaming in the dimness.

'So there was this couple there – straight – a boy and a girl. Just tourists. French. Someone had picked them up in the city and brought them there – to perform.'

'Perform?'

'They had sex. In front of everyone. Regular sex. The girl – she seemed quite into it, but you could see it made the boy sad, even though they were getting paid. We all watched them.'

'And?'

'They were together, a couple. Both blond. And I was thinking . . .' His voice thickened, he choked on a sob.

'What were you thinking, Timothy?'

'That the thing that was really sick . . . is that what we were watching wasn't sex. It was love. They were in love. And I was wondering –' he was speaking rapidly now, trying to get the words out before the tears. He sounded high – 'whether he wanted to spoil it. Paying them. The Balensky guy. Because they loved each other, you know? He j-just wanted to sp-spoil it.'

I could see where he was going, I really could, but just then the last thing I needed was poignant tales of innocence corrupted. I put my arms around him.

'Listen. What happened was terrible, horrible. I am so, so sorry that you had to be part of it. But Edouard loved you, he really did. He wanted you to move on with your life. He said so, didn't he? Because he cared about you. So that's what we're going to do. I'll help you, I promise.'

He sobbed harder, and I rocked him. It wasn't Edouard he was weeping for, because it never is, and that was what we had known the first time we had laid eyes on each other. His swagger as he emerged from the backroom at that terrible club, his face looking up at me when I'd caught him stealing my things. I'd always known what he was, and somehow that connection had always been there between us, unspoken. Because he knew what I was too. What do you do when you stare into the abyss of another's soul and the abyss waves right back?

'It will be OK,' I whispered eventually. 'Don't worry, it will all be OK.' I held him tightly until his breathing quieted.

There was no way I could kill Timothy. He was a whole lot more useful to me alive than dead. It appeared that I'd actually made a choice. Yermolov wasn't going to hurt anybody else. Not that that was my motivation exactly. It was more the pleasure I would have in his knowledge that I could stop him. Liability that he was, I needed Timothy for the plan that was scrambling in my mind. I had been used to acting alone, but now I could see that I needed him. And, maybe, I wanted to make things right for him. Touching, that. Any minute now I'd be selling my blood to keep him in Kit Kats.

'There's a lot of money there,' I prompted. 'You could use it – go back to Morocco? Do you want to do that?' I had to let him choose. He had to choose to feel loyal.

He shook his head miserably.

'Stay in France?'

'Are you joking?'

'I have an idea – something we can do. If it works, we can get back at the people who hurt Edouard. Avenge him,' I added, with only a slight wince. Timothy's dramatic temperament would appreciate that.

'OK.'

'But it will be . . . pretty dangerous.'

'OK.'

'And if it works, there's money in it for you. Lots of money.'

'I don't care about money.'

We looked one another in the eye. A wry, venal muscle twitched at the corner of his mouth.

I raised my eyebrows questioningly. 'Enough money for fashion college. And more.'

'Edouard did want the best for me,' he came back, deadpan.

'In the meantime,' I said, reaching for the cash, 'I'm borrowing this. For a bus fare. Start getting your stuff.'

With a slightly sinking heart I turned back to the computer and called up the site for the Paris international coach station. There was a bus to Belgrade leaving at eight, we'd miss that, but the later one departed at eleven, I hoped there'd be seats available. Once we were in Serbia, I could let rip with my card, but it was better to be cautious while Kazbich was still close. Then I turned the laptop camera to face the wall of our dowdy bedroom, nothing to give away our location, and placed a Skype call to Jovana, the leader of the Xaoc Collective in Belgrade.

A PhD in Renaissance studies, Jovana cheerfully admitted to being no artist herself – she claimed she could barely sketch a stick-man – but she was extremely tech savvy and market literate. She ran the co-operative like one of the old Italian production-line workshops – she came up with the concepts and the artists in the group executed them and shared the profits. Like a Serbian Damian Hirst, only clever and with interesting facial piercings. We had met in the Macedonian Pavilion at the Biennale, where Xaoc were showing a huge version of one of the collages they later made for me, thirty metres of hand-stitched quilts set with icon cards and tiny pewter tea pots, and I'd admired her straight away. She talked as confidently of leverage margins and threshold resistance as she did about the influence of Flemish art on Eastern European religious fresco, and during our conversation I learned a lot from her. When I'd worked at the House I'd been naively shocked to find priceless masterpieces treated as investment chips, but Jovana's view was both subtle and unpretentious. She saw the market for what it was, what it had always been, but believed there was still room for beauty and ideas in new work, even if they had to be sneaked in guerrilla-style, invisible to the clients.

There was no response, so I packed while waiting. I also disassembled the gun, planning to drop the bits piecemeal on our journey. I didn't plan on needing it again. On my third try Jovana picked up. When her image bloomed on the screen I saw that she had a tiny plastic statue of Michael Jackson, culled from a key ring, dangling from her eyebrow piercing. I explained that I was going to be in Belgrade and asked what Xaoc was working on.

'Ohhh, Elisabeth ' I could see her rubbing her hands to show her delight – 'something . . . juicy. I've been thinking about – let me say this right – abjection.'

'Abject art?'

Vomit, shit, blood, slaughter, mutilation. Works that seek to provoke disgust and hence to challenge our relation with the beautiful. That's the sales pitch anyway. Or concepts whose vulgar sensationalism are only remarkable for their banality, which is not the sales pitch.

'Veerrry edgy. I've got some footage of some really nasty stuff, tracheotomy patients . . . We're putting it together with some rapeporn images from the dark web and setting the video in little telescopes.'

OK, Jovana. Dark web, rapeporn, gotcha.

'No, not telescopes,' she continued, 'those things that make patterns with sand?'

'Kaleidoscopes?'

'That's it. And then we are putting them in the carnival crackers with lots of little toys' – she leaned forward to demonstrate so that Michael did a jiggly moonwalk above her eyeball – 'so you are opening them and finding some . . . innocent thing – some very, very nasty.'

'So – it's about exploitation and the re-perspectivising of the corrupt?'

'Good words!' She paused to take a sip of Coke Zero. 'You are maybe interested?'

'Definitely. And I have a couple more ideas for you. One is a reworking of an old piece, the other a film installation.

A kind of enactment, sort of a play, with lookalikes. A bit Cindy Sherman.'

'Sounds good. You have a client?'

'Two. Well, possibly.'

'Great. It'll be super to see you again. Do want to crash here?'

'Thanks – maybe. It would be good to get a feel for what you're doing.'

'Sure, sure. You will be in Belgrade when?'

'Tomorrow.'

21

As the coach droned across Europe, Timothy slept and stared. I stared. Somewhere just over the Slovenian border, he asked me dully why we were going to Belgrade.

'Firstly, because it's the last place that they'll look for us,' I told him slowly. I explained that I was going to give a message to a man named Raznatovic, that if I could find him and have him agree, it would convince the people who had killed Guiche that we were serious. 'And we're going to make some art!' I added brightly. I knew that I sounded a total flid, yet the horror of Guiche's death had induced a sort of waking coma in Timothy, a blank-eyed acceptance that I knew what I was doing.

I told him he wouldn't need to do much, yet, that his part would come later, once I'd found Raznatovic.

'Anything I say, just go along with it,' I warned him, but I couldn't be sure he'd really taken it in.

There wasn't much else to say about the eighteen-hour journey to Belgrade, except that it was as cramped, uncomfortable, dirty, and hypnotically exhausting as one would expect such a trip to be. When we reached the White Town I parked Timothy in the Square Nine

Hotel and told him to get his ass to the gym. Maybe the endorphins would cheer him up. We weren't due to meet Jovana until ten that evening, so I took myself off for a look at the city. The thin coat I'd packed all the way back in Venice did nothing to keep off the freezing wind brattling up from the Danube, but there was no way I was wearing the hideous English fleece. Full-length mink seemed to be more the look in central Belgrade. I'd never been this far east before, and it did feel different, though at first I couldn't quite sense why. Many of the buildings were eighteenth- and nineteenth-century standard municipal – grand, with solid-balconied thirties apartments mixed in. I found a hipster coffee-shop, Koffein, on a tree-lined square and drank a macchiato while I located the address of Kazbich's dealership in the guidebook. The menu was printed on brown paper, offering artisanal Balkan breads and dinky lace-topped Kilner jars of berry preserve. Standard beards, flannel shirts and Macbooks; I could have been in Shoreditch. Walking up to the castle district overlooking the river I wove around nut-faced women in approximations of Balkan folk costume selling embroidered tablecloths and lace mats, and implausibly huge men flogging war memorabilia. But for a capital city in the early evening the streets had an eerie stillness to them. Aside from the vendors, every doorway, every corner was crowded with people just . . . standing, with a strange peon-like patience, the wind burling through thick grey hair or headscarves, as though they had long been awaiting something, but had forgotten what it was. Opposite Kazbich's building was a smart modern gallery, showing retouched early-twentieth-century photos of dwarfish children, vermilion bows festooning long-dead black curls. In the middle of the road, plywood hoardings concealed a gaping pit, and when I looked up, the corner of a dull grey office block was clearly pitted with bullet scars. The bus stop beneath displayed a poster for the latest series of the Kardashians, as if these people hadn't suffered enough.

Unlike the owners of Koffein, Kazbich was clearly wise to the fact that his native city couldn't afford irony yet. His space was reassuringly plush and old-fashioned; a bay window latticed in dark wood, a simple black velvet drape cushioning a display of two delicate icons, Byzantine Crucifixions framed in silver net either side of a large monochrome canvas of a naked body builder, massive thighs encircling a marble column. Peering through the door, I saw four similar canvases in heavy gilt mounts, interspersed with more icons; they at least looked like the real thing. It was nearly eight, the gallery was closed, but I stepped back towards the mortar pit before snapping off a few rounds of the display with my phone. Jovana would need inspiration for her commission.

The squat where Jovana and her crew worked was famously the biggest artist-occupied building in Europe. A twenty-storey ziggurat in chocolate concrete, the edifice was all the more intimidating for its air of the amateur. It had once been the architectural pride of the Serbian civil service, and the tropical mural of giant toucans and orangutans in what had once been the lobby couldn't quite exorcise the phantoms of grey-toothed bureaucrats in Soviet suits, of beige plastic and ersatz coffee, of joyless, airless artificiality, a fake headquarters for a fake state whose only currency was cruelty. As Elena might have said, it gave me the creep. The collective's space was on the tenth floor; Jovana had warned me about the broken lifts, and we began to climb.

Timothy was at least looking rather more alert, but the state of the building was clearly bringing on a sulk, even though the slogans on the walls reassured us that punk was not dead. At the end of each flight we traversed a vast, low, graffiti-covered corridor. Why is anarchy always so samey? The silence was all the more oppressive for the faint, strangled wails of electro pulsing from one of the distant floors above. Abruptly, there was a scuffling behind us, and we turned to see a crowd of shapes moving between the scarred concrete walls, hooded figures, running low. Wordlessly we quickened our pace; behind us, the boys speeded up. I shoved my watch further up the sleeve of my arm under my jacket as we rounded another staircase, panting now, feeling them gaining on us.

'How many of them?' Timothy hissed.

'Lots. Run.'

We broke into a sprint, reached the next landing and bolted across yet another piss-stained floor. *Would they have knives*? The corridor ended in a huge pair of steel doors, padlocked, dripping with red-sprayed rage.

'Shit!' We wheeled, panting.

'Maybe we can get round them. Either side. Quick as you can and then go down?'

They were fifty metres away, twenty, their faces hidden, feral.

'Wait until they're really close. Ready?'

And then a door opened off the side and a burst of hip-hop banged off the ceiling. The kids slowed, pushed back their hoods and, grinning, shuffled into the studio. A woman in a neon bomber poked her head out and waved them in. A dance class. They were late for their dance class. One of them gave us the thumbs up and did a little moonwalk in behind his friends. The door closed again, sealing off the music. Jesus.

Timothy was bent double, heaving, head between his knees.

'I can't take this.'

'I know. But it's our problem. They were just kids.'

'I mean, I can't take this. Not anymore.'

I squatted and pulled his face up towards mine. 'Look, it's OK. They weren't going to mug us. We're just paranoid.'

'Really? Why would that be?'

I really didn't have the energy for another pep talk.

'Don't be a dick. We're here for a reason. Just keep it together. You can do that.'

He nodded miserably.

'Come on then.'

I led us off the way we had come, looking for the next stairwell, but I was shaken. Not by the children, that was just silliness, but by the wave of protectiveness I had suddenly felt towards him, the urge to cradle him and tell him it was all going to be fine.

We took a moment to recover before I knocked on the door of the space. A hatch in another steel door, a cheerful face almost hidden beneath a mobile of piercings.

'Hey. We're meeting Jovana. Elisabeth.' I shot Timothy a look, reminding him to keep quiet.

'Sure. Come in. D'you want a tea? We've got mint or violet?'

'Violet would be lovely, thanks, umm . . .?'

'Vlado.'

It seemed colder inside the studio than on the wind-scoured boulevard. Divided into cubicles by hanging sheets, I recognised the wire-strewn space from the collective's website. About twenty people were milling about, most of them dressed in fatigues and metalwork like Vlado, a couple concentrated on canvases propped against the walls, others just smoking and chatting, the majority gathered around a bank of laptops on a large central table. Jovana's candy-pink dreadlocks glowed in the middle.

'Elisabeth! Great to see you again!' Her English was comically accented, but perfect. I put my cheek against the swirl of indigo Cyrillic lettering tattooed around her left eye.

'This is Timothy. He's my intern. From Paris. Why don't you help Vlado with the tea, Timothy?'

He looked blank, so I repeated it in French and he shuffled off.

'So, Jovana. Three things. First, can we take up your offer to stay for a couple of days – from tomorrow? I want to get a feel for the work now I have the chance, and it would be good experience for Timothy. We'll contribute, of course.'

'Sure, no problem. It's not exactly five star though,' Jovana added doubtfully.

'It will be an honour, thanks. Two – I have something here. I need you to make me a design – fairly quick. Tomorrow, hopefully. Just mock it up on your laptop, I only need a screenshot. There's a chance of a commission from a client here in Belgrade,' I explained grandly.

'Fantastic!'

There didn't seem to be much in the way of running water in the studio. But naturally the Wi-Fi was perfect. In a few minutes, Jovana was swinging the shots I had taken of Kazbich's window display around on her screen.

'And then I need you to add – something like this?' I showed her an image of a Venetian icon I'd downloaded at the hotel.

'No problem.'

'Before you start though – thank you –' I paused to take a sip of scalding floral tea from a proffered mug decorated with the Duchess of Cambridge – 'there's the third thing. Quite big. An installation for another client, in Switzerland. Kind of thematically linked with your rapeporn stuff.'

'Cool.'

'But maybe – toned down a bit?'

'Why?'

'It's pretty extreme, what you were telling me about.'

Jovana gave me an appraising look. 'The Prada Foundation are showing the Kienholzes' *Jody, Jody, Jody* soon, in Milan. Have you seen it?'

I had, in photos. I wished I hadn't. Child abuse wasn't my thing, aesthetically.

'So he made that in, like, 1994. You wanna keep up, you gotta be extreme. Just business.'

When did disgust become a measure of artistic value? No one is really appalled to see shit, used tampons or plastic genitalia any more – what else would one expect to find in a gallery? So it follows that if all you have to offer as an artist is offensiveness, then as soon as it becomes predictable you have to push it further.

'But this stuff is really obnoxious,' I objected.

'Exactly,' Jovana said placidly. 'So, do you want to use it?'

'I suppose so. Are you interested?'

'Always.'

I was back at Kazbich's gallery at eleven the next day, the first part of Jovana's work loaded into the phone. My clothes were getting that ratty look of things that have been worn too often, but I couldn't mind about that – I'd pulled a black cashmere crew-neck over the trusty Miu Miu pants and scraped my hair into a high topknot, simple and serious.

'Can I help you?' The girl on the desk looked surprised at a walk-in, quickly shoving a magazine and an ashtray into her desk. She wore a black felt pinafore over a vintage seventies paisley shirt with a pointed collar. Convincing enough, but the bag at her feet was vinyl and her skin was bad. Not a Beograd princess playing curator, most likely a student part-timer.

'Maybe, I hope so,' I answered warily. I half expected Kazbich to appear like Nosferatu from behind a door. I handed over one of my Gentileschi business cards. 'My name is Elisabeth Teerlinc. I have a piece which I think could interest one of your regular clients.'

I clicked on Jovana's montage and handed it over. The girl gave it a cursory glance, her gaze far more focused on the three hundred-euro notes I'd tucked between the phone and its cover.

'So, I was hoping that you might be able to contact him for me. I'm only here for a day or so, and I think he would be seriously interested.' I put the phone and the money firmly back in my bag and let the silence swell between us.

'What is the client's name, please?'

'Dejan Raznatovic,' I answered, all innocence.

Her features scrambled in dissembled shock.

'I-I don't know who you mean.'

I took my cigarettes from my bag. 'Go on, it's all right. You do. It's OK. Dr Kazbich came to my gallery in Venice. I know he works for Mr Yermolov too. Really.' I offered her the pack, which happened to contain another two hundred. The average wage in Serbia is just under four hundred euros a month. I removed a cigarette and lit up, handed her the pack. She took one, stowed the pack in her desk and retrieved the ashtray. I waited a couple of drags, then added that I had tried calling Dr Kazbich but been unable to reach him, and since I was in Belgrade visiting my artists at Xaoc Collective, I thought I'd drop in.

'You know Xaoc?' Her face brightened.

'Sure.' Jovana and co. were pretty big in Serbia, regular rock stars. 'I've just come from their space. They have some pretty crazy parties there.'

'I guess I could have a look . . .'

'Of course you could,' I encouraged her, conspiratorial.

'If I could just see the – er – piece again?'

I raised an eyebrow and handed her the phone in its case. 'Naturally.'

She sat back at her desk and began to make a show of running through the gallery's database.

'They're having a thing this weekend,' I mentioned casually. 'A secret gig. Vladimir Acic is playing.'

'Really?'

'Really. I won't make it, but I'm sure I could arrange for you to go. Just need your name . . .'

Her eyes narrowed, sliding over me, assessing. Had I overdone it? I pretended to be distracted by one of the Renaissance bodybuilders, setting my bag on the desk next to her and letting it fall open so she could see the label.

'These are quite nice. Are you an artist yourself?'

'Yes, I am. Sculpture, mostly.'

Bingo.

'Really? Then you should definitely meet Jovana.' I smiled, in what I hoped was a sisterly fashion. Not a look I'd practised much.

'So . . . er, yes, we do have a Mr Raznatovic.'

'And you can call him? Don't forget to write your name down for Jovana.'

The assistant made several calls – even though she was speaking Serbian I could tell she was nervous – and fifteen minutes later I had a date with Dejan. Leaving the gallery, I thought I would give her name to Jovana; you never knew, she might turn out to be talented, though I had a feeling that Vladimir might be cancelling his gig.

Timothy was less than thrilled about our new quarters, which I felt showed a distinct lack of imagination on his part. At least his sulking was now directed at the grim foam mattresses and sleeping bags that now comprised our bedroom, distracting him from his suffering over Edouard, though I tried to persuade him that documenting the activities at the squat would be a great inspiration for his portfolio for fashion school.

Making my own toilette with the aid of a single cold tap in what had once been an office kitchen was a more immediate preoccupation. I boiled the kettle and took a sponge bath and did my face as best I could with a compact mirror. Eres lingerie in fine black mesh and the one smart outfit my bag contained, a charcoal tussore Lanvin dress with a deep pleat in the back, which I'd had the hotel steam out before we left, did well enough, but I felt irritatingly badly finished. I carried my punched-leather Alaïa sandals barefoot down the nine flights of stairs, and cleaned the soles of my feet with a wet wipe on the faux marble tiles of the lobby before inelegantly drawing my black hold-ups into place. Dejan was nearly fifty, the right generation to respond to stockings.

The restaurant Dejan had named to Kazbich's assistant was on the curve of the Danube, beneath the walls of Belgrade's old castle. What had once been wharfs and warehouses had been transformed into a fashionable drag of restaurants and bars overlooking the water. Just before eight, I joined the swarm of girls teetering determinedly along the quay, all of us ungainly on our heels over the wide cobbles. Serbia's political isolation might have screwed their economy, but it had done wonders on the eugenics front. Most of the girls had runway model figures, hovering around six foot, endless racehorse thighs displayed in clinging minidresses or tiny skirts which paid no due to the weather. They were naturally lovely, at least under the layers of make-up and false eyelashes, but the thing I really noticed was the hair. This was a tough country, and everything that could be done to a hairstyle had been stoically endured. Bleached, blow-dried, backcombed, tongued, teased, spritzed and sprayed, the Cold War might have been long over, but as far as these girls' do's were concerned, the Berlin Wall was still intact. Defiant, magnificent: in the competition for happiness, they weren't going to be bested by a sloppy extension.

Still, apparently I had the hottest date in town that night. When I gave Raznatovic's name to the maître d' at the Peruvian sushi joint, I thought for a minute he was going to choke. He called me 'Madam' at least four times as I picked my way through the crowded room to the table, which was set in splendid isolation on a dais at the back of the restaurant in what looked like a hastily improvised VIP area. I ordered a glass of red wine and lit a cigarette, simply for the dirty pleasure of smoking indoors. Three waiters rushed at me with ashtrays.

'Let me help the lady.'

Even by Serbian standards, Dejan Raznatovic was huge. Six foot six, I reckoned, with shoulders that blocked the light. Before I'd joined Steve on the *Mandarin* two years ago, I'd barely been inside a decent restaurant; since then I'd sat at a lot of expensive tables with a lot of serious men, but the atmosphere Raznatovic projected was like nothing I'd ever encountered. As he greeted me and we shook hands, I realised that the entire company was watching us. Even the obligatory DJ was craning out of his booth. The air felt heavier for his presence, as though his power was squeezed between its molecules. It wasn't just celebrity, or the invisible spore of wealth; it was, I recognised, fear. Apart from his size, there was nothing thuggish about Raznatovic – his navy suit was impeccably bespoke, his cufflinks discreet – but as the chatter around us slowly resumed, I saw that while everyone in the room knew who he was, not one man in there dared to catch his eye. I was hit by a slug of desire so pure that I did actually feel weak at the knees, and I was letting him see it in my eyes when the waiter made a squawking noise, tried to pull out a chair far enough for his giant guest, dropped the ashtray on his foot and caught the tablecloth as he steadied himself, sending a stream of wine across the cloth. The three of us contemplated the mess for a moment.

'Do you like sushi, Miss Teerlinc?' Dejan asked.

'It was very kind of you to invite me here,' I replied neutrally.

He put a note on the table and said something to the waiter in Serbian, then pulled out my chair for me.

'We'll go somewhere else, I think.'

A silver Aston Martin was parked on the pavement, in the pedestrian area outside the restaurant. Dejan opened the door for me, waited until I was seated and then spent a moment levering himself into the low driver's seat. I had a terrible urge to giggle. We pulled away, followed, I saw, by a black Range Rover with tinted windows which had also gaily disregarded the parking laws. His security, I assumed. We began to climb a steep road that I thought must lead up to the castle park.

'It's very good of you to see me on a flyby,' I began. I wanted to see if he knew the term – a flyby is an informal estimate of what a work might bring at auction.

'If the piece is as interesting as it sounds, then it is very good of *you*.' *He was dancing then. Good.*

'Here we are. I hope you won't find the road too steep.' He was looking unabashedly at my legs. *Even better.*

He offered me his arm to negotiate the Alaïas up an almost perpendicular alleyway. My hand looked tiny on the expanse of his sleeve. A young man had dismounted from the Range Rover behind us, waiting for an instruction, then bobbed into a doorway ahead while we followed at cab-shoe pace. Inside the room was lit by oil lamps, with a few wooden booths, green velvet banquettes and a good deal of silver and starched linen, but it didn't feel formal, more as though we had stepped back into an older version of the city. An elderly waiter with a blue-rinsed walrus moustache welcomed us with a silver tray and two tiny chased-crystal glasses of slivovitz. Dejan raised his courteously to the scattering of other customers before swallowing it back. I imitated him and felt the delicious must of plums burn down my throat.

'This is one of the oldest restaurants of Belgrade,' Dejan explained as we sat. He pronounced it the Serbian way, an 'o' replacing the 'l'. 'I think you must try the horse tartar.'

'I'm sure it's delicious.'

He ordered and, once our wineglasses were filled, asked for the photos I'd had Jovana make up. I launched into my pitch:

'I should explain that I met Dr Kazbich in Venice, where my gallery is based. We have several professional acquaintances in common. I understand you are interested in icons, so when this came up, I took the liberty of contacting you.'

'Dr Kazbich gave you my number?' He seemed amused.

'No,' I replied, looking him in the eye. 'I went to his gallery and asked for it. They were very obliging.

'How enterprising you are. You are British, no?'

'My family lived in Switzerland.' Elisabeth's story felt oddly rusty. 'So,' I continued, 'the concept is similar to what the Chapman brothers were doing with Goya – you saw the work, naturally? The icon is thirteenth century, Venetian, exceptionally rare, but badly damaged. It's for sale – privately, through the family who own it. Xaoc plan to divide the fragments and produce a triptych, something like this.' I showed him the series Jovana had constructed.

I didn't know how expert Dejan really was as an icon collector, but I didn't worry that he'd recognise the piece, since it didn't exist. Jovana and I had made a composite image of several of the smaller icons based on the collection of the Ca' d'Oro museum in Venice, a typical dark-haired, sloe-eyed Virgin in a gold-trimmed mantle, holding a bug-faced Christ child awkwardly on her lap. We had inserted the appearance of cracks across the faces and a bad watermark in the bottom left corner. The 'concept' was that Xaoc would slice up the damaged picture and remount it in three pieces, overlaying it with photographic images of the 'client's' choice – we had mocked up several examples based on the Renaissance bodybuilders I had seen displayed in Kazbich's gallery, some Serbian graffiti in marker pen and one of the nastier screenshots from Jovana's 'abject' project. It actually didn't look too bad, though all that mattered of course was that I got the opportunity to meet Dejan and pass on my message.

'It would be a commissioned piece, so of course the details would be – malleable.' Dejan's English was almost flawless but I hoped the word might confuse him slightly. He studied the pictures for some minutes, his thumb hovering over the screen.

'Where is the icon at present?'

'In Venice, at the home of the owners. It has only ever been owned by them. I could arrange for you to see it?' I knew perfectly well he couldn't leave Serbia.

'And there are . . . permissions to use the work in this fashion?'

'None needed. It is in the family's possession, to dispose of as they wish.'

'The price?'

'750K USD to acquire, plus my commission, plus the fee for Xaoc on which I will also take ten per cent. I estimate the resale value to be at least twice that.'

'And to bring it to Serbia?' He was good.

'One of the family will fly to Belgrade, I will accompany him, the sale will take place technically on Serbian soil. No patrimony issues.'

'You have thought of everything.'

'I would never have dreamed of approaching you had I not.'

We were interrupted by the arrival of the waiter, who set down small bowls of dark red meat, capers, parsley, chopped egg and onion, which he mixed in front of us. Dejan showed me how to spread it onto thin *tartines* of toasted bread. I took a bite. The horsemeat was velvety, gamey but with a surprisingly fresh, clean taste of iron.

'Do you like it?' Dejan asked solicitously 'It's not too strong?'

'Not at all. I love it.'

I did. It seemed that I hadn't actually tasted real food forever. We charged through the tartar and a bowl of boiled potatoes swimming in butter and dill and another of tomatoes roasted with paprika and garlic. The waiter changed our plates for little glass bowls of set cream studded with preserved cherries and silver-rimmed cups of cardamom-scented coffee. We didn't speak much.

'I won't buy your piece,' Dejan said suddenly as he sipped the coffee. I had been floating a little, in the wine and the warmth of the restaurant; it took me a second to haul my head back to business.

'I'm sorry to hear that. But we have – other clients. Thank you for such a wonderful dinner.' I made as if to gather my things and leave, though he caught my eye as we both smiled at the feint.

'Wait a moment.' He set a huge heavy paw over my wrist. I felt the heat of his fingertips in my veins.

'I won't buy it,' he continued, 'because, as you say, I am very interested in icons. I own several and I care deeply for them. This piece would – disturb me.'

'You're being polite. You hate it. I understand.'

'Perhaps you would like to see them?'

'You're asking me if I'd like to come up and see your icons?'

He was grinning now. 'Yes. I think they would please you.'

'Well, thank you, that would be – delightful.'

I thought he might kiss me after he had squashed his body back into the car, but he didn't need to, and he knew it. We drove for about twenty minutes in silence, the Range Rover visible in the wing mirrors. Every time he changed gear the car shifted slightly with his weight, I could feel it through my seat. I was so wet I thought my juice must have soaked the back of my dress. We crossed a motorway and turned off onto a bleak straight road, empty except for a ribbon of spindly trees, then turned down another, looping back towards where I guessed the river must flow beyond the city. It was, I thought, a long way out of town. And no one knew where I was or who was with me. Momentarily that felt wonderful.

'This is your house?'

The floodlights beamed up as the gates slid open. I thought I'd seen a fair representation of all the crassness that money can buy, but Chez Raznatovic was – villainous. If I closed one eye it might have looked like a pink plaster version of Chenonceau, with three rounded towers huddling over an artificial lake; if I closed the other it was pure Churrigueresque, heavily iced in festoons of cascading cement. There was actually a drawbridge. There was also a life-size plaster Siberian tiger snarling over the three-metre-high steel security doors.

'Do you like it?'

'It's very . . . powerful, yes.'

He gave me a wry look. 'I had another house, in Montenegro. Much more beautiful, simple, stone. Venetian. Just outside Kotor, on the fjord. You would probably prefer that.'

'Yeah, bummer, that extradition treaty.'

'That's not very polite, Elisabeth.'

'I'm sorry.'

He pressed a button on the dash and I bit my lip as the drawbridge solemnly descended. 'It's what they expect. Not subtle –' he moved us forward – 'but useful.'

Three young men in black combat pants and heavy padded bombers jogged up to the car as we braked in a cramped courtyard. Two of them opened the doors in a smooth, practised movement as the car's engine was still humming, the third advanced to the open door, pointing an AK47 into the night, sweeping the driveway until the steel clicked shut. After my faux pas it seemed more courteous to pretend not to see it. Effectively though, I was walking into a fortress. I remembered the quote I'd read, on Dejan's career as an executioner – *A little weird the first time, but afterwards you're happy to go out and celebrate.* Dejan spoke in Serbian and, after helping me from the seat, one of them peeled off to usher me through a narrow door set in one of the turrets.

'This way, please, miss.' He indicated that I should pass before him up a spiral staircase set with garish mosaics. I came out into a round room where I was surprised to find a wall of books and two rather battered velvet sofas set either side of a lovely but raggedy Persian rug. There was a fire burning, something strongly scented in the logs – apple maybe? – and a quite severe Louis XVI table in mahogany and marble, with a bottle and two plain glasses. Looking around, I could see how pretty the room was – white roses in a blue Chinese bowl, embroidered cushions, limewashed walls tinged with gold in the light from the fire and a huge dull bronze doré candelabra, Empirish. With the rest of the horrible building hidden behind the shutters, it might have been a room from a nineteenth-century Russian novel. Especially when I saw the three icons set on their dulled silver mounts.

'Better?'

Dejan was crossing the room, holding a corkscrew.

'May I remove my jacket?' he asked.

'Of course.' I assumed he already had, downstairs, since whatever had been on his hip in the restaurant was gone.

'This is my private apartment. An ivory tower?'

I cringed a bit but I couldn't blame him.

I took the glass he handed me and pointed to the icons.

'Tell me about these.'

'Tell me if you like this first. It's Georgian, from Kakheti.'

The wine smelled of cedar and cherries.

'It's delicious, thank you.'

'So. These are from Okrid, these two, and this one – the Madonna – from Skopje. They are all thirteenth century, because the thirteenth century was the most . . . revolutionary time for icon making in Serbia. You see, this is when Serbia became an independent kingdom and the holy Saint Sava expelled the Greek bishops from their – seats?'

'Sees.'

'Am I boring you?'

'Not in the slightest.'

'So, the icon painters developed their own style for the first time. Most of the painters were still Greek, but there is a new simplicity. More colour, more – fierceness.'

'They are very pretty.'

'I like this. The wine is delicious, my priceless icons are 'pretty'. That is always how the art people speak. Understatement?'

'Exactly.'

'The more valuable the thing, the more little the . . . ?

'Adjective?' He was right, and the affectation had always amused me too. Back at the House, if you knew what you were doing you would describe a Gainsborough as 'quite charming'.

'Thank you.'

Dejan sat beside me, the old sofa bucking under his weight, and sipped his wine.

'So now?'

'Now?'

'We can fuck and then you can tell me what you're doing here, or you can tell me what you're doing here and then maybe we'll fuck.'

'Then we should fuck.'

He reached over and took the glass from my hand, set it down alongside his own. The scent of the wine was thick on his tongue as he turned to kiss me, lifting me easily with a hand in the small of my back so that I was lying below him. I opened my mouth wide, greedy, pushing my hands under his shirt. His chest was vast, ropey with muscle, and though he was holding his full weight off me, I could feel his cock swelling against my thigh. I opened his shirt, tracing my nails through the thick hair, finding his nipple, squeezing gently. We were necking like teenagers, breathless, a little clumsy.

'Let me take off your pretty dress.'

I wriggled off the sofa and gave him my back, his massive hands dexterous on the row of hooks concealed in the silk, followed by my bra.

'Beautiful.' He stroked his fingers the length of my spine, following them with his mouth so that he was on his knees behind me, both hands squeezing my ass. I was dripping for him, the hot ache in my cunt almost unbearably pleasurable. I stepped out of my knickers and made to bend forward on the table, but he gripped my waist with both hands, standing up in one movement, holding my whole body easily above his head. Tipping his head back, he reached for my pussy lips with his tongue, sucking deep, so that for a second I was weightless, suspended, the hollow of me pulsing, then I set my shins on his shoulders and reached my palms flat against the ceiling to steady us, and began to grind his face as he licked me from my cunt to my asshole. His tongue was inside me there and I pushed on the ceiling, my weight urging him to lick deeper, my body arcing back over his head. I could have cum like that, but this was too good.

'Put me down now.'

He lowered me as smoothly as I had been lifted and I turned and knelt to take his cock in my mouth.

'Oh. Oh.'

God would have made every cock like Dejan's, if only He'd had the money. Thick as my fist, even down the whole length, the circumcised skin drawn together in a little raised trident, delicate as watered silk. I tongued him there first, letting just the flat of it caress that tenderness, teasing and flicking until he gasped, twitched, swelled even more, then grasped the shaft tight in my palm, long dropping strokes, following with my whole mouth, drawing his fingers to the hollow of my throat, so he could feel himself deep there, dipping my head faster, lathering him with spit and letting him hear the wet slurp, pushing down, half-choking myself until I gagged and my throat contracted. They love it when you look . . . uncomfortable. His hand found the base of my skull under my falling hair and he began to thrust at my face as I smeared his balls and perineum with my cunt juice, extending my tongue up and over the head of his cock as I pumped him. And then – slowly, infinitely slowly, relaxing my mouth, loosening, withdrawing my hand until once again there was just the insistent hummingbird flutter of my tongue, all torment, all promise.

He was silent, his face intent far above me. I tipped my head back and gave one last long lick at the whole length of him.

'You can fuck me now.'

I reached my arms to clasp his neck, hauled my body up his thick thighs, kicked my coccyx back, up and over, and settled him inside me, my legs locked around his waist as his hands took their place under my ass. He took a few steps backward, me impaled on him, propping his back against the wall and drove into me, cramming my hips against him. One slow stroke, two, three, until I was screaming inside for the whole length of him, biting at his chest, and he turned and gave me his place and slammed into me with his whole massive weight, over and over, until I felt my cum start, deep through my clit to my cervix and hissed at him, 'Now!' He gave me a few more strokes to take me over and as my head went back and my cunt spasmed I felt the girth of him grow inside me and as his own orgasm exploded he lifted me slightly off his cock so I could watch the gouts of his cum spray up into me, sliding just the head between my soaked and gaping lips, until he roared and released me, letting my whole weight smash down him, catching me at the last moment and grasping me there against him while the last of it poured through me.

We were both shaking; weakly I licked a salt trickle of sweat from the deep hollow between his pecs. Still holding me around him, he carried me to the sofa, knelt forwards and let me roll off him, trembling. He reached for one of the glasses, took a long mouthful of wine then put his lips to mine as I took it from his mouth.

'You are well, Elisabeth?' He sounded touchingly anxious.

'I think so. I don't know yet.' My hand brushed his cock, retreating now into the thatch of his pubic hair. 'That was . . . surprising.'

'You don't really think that.'

'No, I don't.'

He sat up and began pulling on his shirt and trousers. I followed suit, scouting among the cushions for my underwear, and when we were both approximately dressed, he refilled our glasses and turned to me.

'So, now you are going to tell me why you came to find me with your rather terrible picture?'

'You deal regularly through Ivan Kazbich?'

'Yes. You know this.'

'I think you sometimes sell him other things.' I practically saw the ripple of tension run up his cotton-clad arm, a rip tide from elbow to shoulder.

'Perhaps,' he answered tightly.

'I want you to give him a message for me. For one of his other employers. I've written it down, I'll give you the paper before I leave. Kazbich knows I have the thing his employer is looking for, and I will give it to him in Switzerland in one week's time. Assuming he will keep the meeting according to my conditions.'

'And why should I do this?'

I could have said that I hoped I hadn't just screwed him for nothing, but that would have been untrue, not to mention coarse.

'Because Kazbich is flipping fakes and he is risking . . . complicating your other supply chain.'

'You don't know anything.'

'Maybe.' I didn't actually, I just had to pray he'd buy the bluff. Happy ending notwithstanding, the whole point of this trip was to convince Yermolov and Balensky that I knew what they were up to. Only a message direct from Dejan Raznatovic would convince them that I had seen Guiche's papers and made the connection. Assuming I got out of here alive, a communication from Dejan himself would suggest that I knew enough to bring them down. That's why they would agree to the meeting, in just the way I planned to stage it. Of course, tipping them off that I knew about the art-for-arms connection might just inspire them to kill me, but they were planning on that anyway. A conviction of my knowledge could buy me the time I needed to confront them.

'You're very inquisitive.' Dejan sounded disappointed. 'Or possibly very stupid.'

'That's not polite.'

He was right. He wouldn't need to summon help; those huge hands could snap my neck like a cocktail stick. This was the riskiest part of my scheme, which was what made it the sexiest. I stared him down, ventured a cold smile.

'Surely you wouldn't – not after we've just . . .?' I purred.

He smiled back. 'How does it go? You don't think I would have done that before? You are . . . funny. As well as brave.'

'Thank you. But as I say, your . . . private arrangements are not my business. I only want to get the message to Kazbich and return the missing object. That's all. I assure you.'

He stood. 'I will have someone drive you home now, Elisabeth.'

'But will you do as I ask?'

'Maybe. I think so.' He handed me my bag. I retrieved the paper with the instructions. 'I would perhaps like to have spent some more time with you, but you must forgive me. I am very busy.'

'Of course.' It stung a little, the sop to his pride, the renewed formality.

He pressed a bell by the door to the stairwell and I straightened myself up as we heard footsteps ascending. Dejan spoke swiftly in Serbian through the door.

'Zvezdan will drive you wherever you wish to go. Goodbye, Elisabeth.' He bent over my hand.

'Goodbye, Dejan. Thank you so very much for your time.'

I followed the boy across the courtyard, passing another of them, who unlocked a barred gate and accompanied us down a ramp into an underground garage. The Aston was parked there, as well as a Porsche SUV and two Range Rovers, the dark one from earlier, which in the strip light I saw had white interiors, and a white one, with the leather in black. I held my breath. The boy clicked a key and my lungs erupted in relief. The black car, with the white inside. If he'd chosen the other one, it would have meant he was going to kill me. Can't have blood on the motor.

The squat was thumping when the bodyguard dropped me back about an hour later. He held the door for me and gravely handed me my bag before giving a little half-salute and heading back to the city. He wasn't bad-looking, and I was feeling so gleeful that I might have asked him up, if it wasn't for his boss. I removed my shoes again and reversed the schlep to the tenth floor, the cold and the climb burning off the haze of the wine. A kaleidoscope of sounds, mostly house and techno, bounced off the walls; the studios were all open, full of people dancing, drinking, kissing, smoking. A bearded giant rode past on a child's tricycle, waving to me as his friend filmed him on his phone. Two gorgeous Serbian Amazons clomped past in Doc Martens and leather leggings, holding fistfuls of lighted sparklers. I hauled on up to the roof for a chance of quiet and took out my phone, that strange, exuberant city gleaming below me.

First I messaged Carlotta, to take her up on the kind invitation to visit St Moritz she had mentioned at her wedding. Blowing on my fingers, I tried the various numbers Elena had given me back in Venice. First a Russian mobile, which was switched off, then a 44 code – perhaps she was in London. It was after midnight there, if she was awake she'd be unlikely to be sober, but she answered muzzily on the second ring.

'Elena, it's Elisabeth, from Venice. That thing you asked me about? I can get you something better. Way better. Don't say anything. I need you to call me back now, a new number, I'll give it to you. But you need to do it from a different phone. Can you do that?'

'*Da.*' If she was surprised, or confused, she didn't show it.

There were some junkshop picnic tables on the roof. I spent the twenty minutes Elena took to return the call shoving a couple of them together into a sort of windbreak, then I squatted inside it, shivering in my thin dress and bare feet. Dejan's cum had frozen unpleasantly over the tops of my thighs. Then she did call, and we spoke for so long that my hand congealed around the phone and I had to unpeel it and massage it into life as I creaked downstairs to seek out Timothy.

Xaoc's space was as crowded as a club, dense with sweating bodies. I pushed my way to the kitchen, where Jovana was stirring a huge frying pan of scrambled eggs and fag ash. She grinned at me dreamily, spangled. I had a sudden urge to kiss her mouth, but I remembered I was effectively her boss – it might have seemed like harassment.

'How did it go?' she shouted over her shoulder.

I gave her a thumbs down and she shrugged.

'But we're on for the other one!' I yelled. 'Can we go through it tomorrow?'

She nodded, adding Tabasco, tick-tocking her spatula to the mix.

Timothy was dancing in the studio, twirling a girl in an incongruous rock 'n' roll routine. He'd made himself a one-shouldered blouse from one of Jovana's folky fabrics, gypsyish against his dark hair. He had his shine back good and proper, he looked young again, and ingenuously happy. I had never seen him look that way, and it gave me pleasure. What I had in store for him was pretty nasty, but sex was business to him after all. Afterwards he'd be OK, I was sure of it.

I tapped his partner on the shoulder and took her place, letting him spin me as best he could through the snarl of bodies.

'Having fun?'

'I love this place!' he shouted back in his heavy English.

'Good. Enjoy yourself then. We're leaving tomorrow.'

'Leaving?'

I gave him a hug.

'Yes, darling. We're going to Switzerland.'

PART THREE

DISPERSION

22

Although I'd spent most of my life broke, a few years of being flush had caused me to forget how magnificent flush feels. Acts of God aside, I was certain that after hearing my message through Dejan, Yermolov and I had a date in two days' time, so there no longer seemed any need to heed the grey hat's warning that he could track me through my bank card. I even travelled as Judith Rashleigh, for the hell of it. Timothy and I flew business for the short trip from Belgrade to Milan, and after the coach and the squat we thoroughly enjoyed both the hot meal and the selection of complimentary beverages, served by willowy Air Serbia hostesses in natty leather gloves. Timothy was all for stopping off for some shopping in the city, but I was eager to get up to the mountains, so we took a driver direct from Malpensa airport.

The Maloja Pass to the Engadin Valley climbed in a series of switchback bends, through which the driver gyrated the cab with practised aplomb, occasionally pulling aside to allow a creaking bus full of blank-faced Filipinos or alarmed-looking tourists to pass. The snow began about halfway up, stacked two metres high in thick wedges either side of the road. We passed Christmas-card stone farms with swords of ice dangling from their eaves and thick groves of gnarled pine, bent horizontal under their burdens of snow and years of Alpine winds. On the lip of the valley we drove past a long black lake, stiffly adorned with cross-country skiers in neon hats and Lycra, moving ponderously across its frozen waves, then several villages with musical names, Sils Maria, Silvaplana, until the ornate blue-and-white façade of the Kempinski Hotel announced St Moritz proper. I hadn't expected the town to be so modern; its many glass-and-steel buildings looked ugly against the white grandeur of the mountains, but as we crawled through bottlenecks of Porsche and Audi SUVs I had plenty of time to see that rustic simplicity wasn't really St Moritz's thing. Furred up like Pomeranians, tubby women slithered along the pavements in crystal-spangled wedge-heeled trainers, mink ski-bands holding their hijabs in place, peering into watch shops, jewellers' shops, sunglasses shops. Anything that wasn't covered in brand logos was covered in diamonds. One boutique displayed a white fox-fur sleeping bag, another window was hung with padded black satin ski jackets with 'Sexy' in diamanté crawling over the lapels. Perfect for a chilly January in Riad.

We deposited Timothy in the Eiderhof, a hostel-style concrete block by the station. After paying for three nights the two of us went up to his room, single with shower, number 9, and I took a look at the building's layout while Timothy checked the corridors for CCTV. This was Switzerland, and it was clean. Downstairs, I gave him some money. He accepted it with an uncharacteristically dubious look.

'I'll see you later,' I tried to reassure him. 'You should go shopping now. Get yourself some proper gear. There's a Moncler shop over there.'

That perked him up a bit, though he looked very young and alone standing on the snow-blown steps among a group of hearty Swiss ski instructors in red jackets.

I reminded him of what time to be ready that evening, and that I'd be watching. Then I wriggled through the snarled traffic to the waiting cab and embarked on a shopping excursion of my own. First a sex shop I'd noticed at the entrance to the town, conveniently attached to a petrol station and buffet restaurant. So efficient, the Swiss. I picked out a black PVC jerkin and matching hotpants from the men's aisle. The other props for my crime scene included fishing line from a camping stockist, a good old Swiss Army knife, a heavy trilobite fossil from a souvenir shop and a bottle of whisky. Finally the impassive cabbie and I set off in search of Carlotta.

It took a while to find Franz's place above the town centre, mainly because Norman Foster had disguised it as a bit of hill. The house might have been in Architectural Digest, but from the outside it resembled Bilbo Baggins's dream bachelor pad, less a building than a hummock. Still, once I'd paid the astronomical fare and lugged my bag gingerly down a narrow path cushioned with black sphagnum, I had to admit that the interior view was pretty spectacular. Carlotta was waiting for me in the NASA-grade kitchen, whose glass wall gave onto a perfect vista of the peaks across the valley. I was surprised to find her dressed in jeans and a Tyrolean jerkin over a navy cashmere polo-neck, but then her chameleon quality was one of the few things we had in common. After we'd squawked-and-kissed she offered me a cup of tea, though producing a mug and a tea bag from the banks of brushed-steel cupboards left her at a loss.

'Our Filipino's broken,' she explained.

'Oh – um – dear.'

'Yah, I'd sent him to Hanselmann's to get this rye bread that Franz likes and he, like, slipped over on the ice and snapped his leg.'

'How awful.'

'Yah, Franz is really, like, pissed, because we were going to give a dinner tonight, but never mind – we can go to Cecconi's.'

'Is he all right?'

'Yah, Franz loves Cecconi's.'

'OK. Great.'

I settled for a glass of the best tap water I have ever tasted and we sat side by side on a reindeer-hide-covered bench, contemplating the view. It was quite difficult to balance, because the artfully arranged skins kept threatening to slide to the floor.

'It's so kind of you to have me!' I enthused. 'And what a fabulous place.'

'We like it. At least, Franz was all for getting some, like, old stable conversion along the valley in Zuoz, and I was, like, no way, I'm not being stuck in the sticks with a load of old Germans, so we kept this. Fuck!'

'What's the matter? Are you all right, Carlotta?'

Carlotta was squinting at the gold ingot strapped round her left wrist. 'Just a second.'

She disappeared and returned a few moments later brandishing a syringe.

'Bit early for that, isn't it?' I asked rather nervously.

'It's my IVF,' she explained. 'I have to do the injection. Here, you can get it ready for me.'

She handed me two glass ampoules and told me to snap the tops off and mix the contents in the syringe while she hiked up her sweater, displaying a smooth plane of tanned stomach. She stretched the skin between two fingers. I looked away as she depressed the plunger.

'I need some cotton wool. Stick that in the trash, would you?'

I looked round helplessly for the bin.

'I'm trying to get pregnant,' she announced, in case I was wondering.

'Has it been difficult?' I asked sympathetically.

'No. I'm, like, totally able to do it naturally, but this way you can get twins and you only have to be fat once. Insurance policy.' She nodded confidentially. 'He'll, like, totally have to redo the prenup.'

'Right. Well, I hope it goes really well for you both.'

'Yah, except sometimes they have to remove the extra ones, the, like, unviable foetuses, and there was this woman I knew in London, and they took the wrong one out and her kid had, like, one arm.'

'Jesus, Carlotta.'

'I know. It was, like, back to front or something. Gross. Anyway, this woman –'

'Please shut up! Why not just do it normally?'

'I wouldn't mind that much, actually, but that would mean I'd have to get Franz to, like, fuck me, you know?'

'I thought you said he was no bother?'

'Well, no. But he's still a pig. Like he wants me to pee into a glass and then he drinks it while he has a wank. Less hassle but no good for babies,' she concluded ruefully.

'What happened to Hermann, by the way?'

'Ten years. Gross fraud. Bullet dodged.' That newsflash seemed to cheer her up.

'Come on, we should get changed. Franz is at the Cresta but we're meeting him at seven.'

Carlotta's go at Gotha-chic did not extend to eveningwear. She reappeared in a black leather Balmain cocktail dress set off with a rope of emeralds which vanished into her prodigious cleavage and snakeskin Louboutin ankle-boots with a line of spikes around the ten-centimetre heel. My travelling wardrobe didn't extend quite so far, but I managed to convert the somewhat crushed Lanvin into a mini with some strips of tit-tape from Carlotta's bathroom, reluctantly adding black stack-heeled patent thigh boots borrowed from my hostess. Contemplating my reflection, I recalled that this had been my idea of elegance, in more innocent times. I remembered my first trip to the Riviera, how excited I'd been to get all dollied up in a minidress and heels. Had it been yellow, that dress I'd worn to go out with Leanne? I'd been so naive, in so many ways . . . thrilled by a Chanel handbag even.

'Come on, darling!' Carlotta interrupted. She was wrapping herself in something that might once have been a jaguar. I still didn't have a properly warm coat – 'Great, we'll go shopping tomorrow!', Carlotta squealed, so she generously lent me a dark mink jacket from a large collection hanging in the hallway. At least she knew where that wardrobe was; got to have your priorities right in the event of a fire. Franz's driver texted and we teetered over the moss to the ubiquitous blacked-out SUV, grateful for its warmth after the sudden dash through the sub-zero night air.

'So, Franz is bringing a friend for you,' announced Carlotta idly as we wound back into town. Her lip gloss gleamed plummily in the screen-light from her phone.

'Anyone nice?'

'No, Tomas is a total snore, but he owns, like, half of Frankfurt. You should really think about your future, you know. I mean, you have your gallery thing, and that's great, but –'

'I'm not really in the market for a husband.' I'd always known that wasn't for me; I'd never cared for the idea of being owned.

'You don't want to leave it too long. Once you're over thirty, you can forget getting anything decent. Like, do you remember that model we met at that party?'

'Help me out here.'

'You know, in Italy. She was with that TV bloke.'

I hadn't been all that focused on the company the time we dined with Steve on Balensky's boat – I'd had other things to consider, such as not getting dumped overboard by his bodyguards for stealing information from his study – but I did recall a swimwear model hanging off the arm of an American producer.

'Yah, so she was living with that guy, didn't get a ring on it and he left her for some, like, seventeen-year-old. I think maybe it was even a guy. And then the IRS got her and she had to move home to Pittsburgh. Like, Pittsburgh. I saw it on Facebook.'

'Poor thing.'

'Goes to show. You have to be more serious, darling.'

'Noted.'

'She's doing, like, catalogues now.'

I did balk a bit when old Franz ordered an acid-yellow Riesling for the aperitif, but dinner was quite fun. Tomas, who turned out to be of a similar vintage to Carlotta's husband, droned harmlessly about international real-estate prices, intercut with Carlotta's running commentary on the Cecconi's regulars. Proper white-jacketed waiters did some impeccable gliding, and the *gnocchi al cervo* were pillowy and delicious. Afterwards we piled back into the car to go to the Dracula Club.

Back when I'd tried to teach myself about the world I had believed I wanted to inhabit, the Dracula had seemed like a myth. The glossy magazines reserved a specially syrupy sycophancy for the parties in the secret mountain cave, accessible only to the members of the Cresta Run bobsleigh team and their guests. Franz had been a 'ghost rider' since before his current wife was born, so we were shown past a younger group of anxious blaggers to a narrow table near the bar. Black and red drapes hung from the high ceiling, and framed posters of the Cresta and its riders were dotted about, but dwarfs and dancing girls were in short supply. The DJ was spinning – Adele. Waiters carried magnums of Dom Perignon across the floor, sizzling with indoor fireworks, each delivery met with whoops and yells, at the next table a loud group was showing just how craaaazzzeee they were by bopping unsteadily on the banquette. I was only half surprised to recognise Stefania from Tage's party on Ibiza. I gave her a nod and she flashed me a grimace of fake recognition. I hoped she was having a good season. The music was too loud for conversation, but Franz and Tomas seemed happy enough, bobbing their heads like a pair of old turtles, waiting placidly for bedtime. Maybe the Dracula had been wild once, but Gunter Sachs had been dead a long time.

After about half an hour I dragged my jaded carcass to the ladies', locked myself in a stall and messaged Elena.

'Any news?'

'Balensky's landed.' Presumably at the private airfield at Cellerina further down the valley.

'Where are you now? I'm at Dracula.'

'Palace.'

Badrutt's Palace, in the centre of St Moritz overlooking the lake, is one of the oldest and glitziest of the resort's hotels. Elena had told me that Balensky always stayed there.

'On my way.'

Our party had grown when I returned. I was glad to see Carlotta holding court, and equally glad that I couldn't hear her. I was intercepted by an American called Jeff, listening impatiently as he tried to tell me about heli-skiing in Colorado, eventually dodging his high-decibel drone by the simple expedient of turning my back on him and climbing over Tomas to reach Carlotta.

'What are you *doing*?' she screeched. 'That's Jeff Auerbach. He's the CEO of KryptoSocial!'

Jeff had disappeared into a crowd of more eager founder-hounders.

'He seems happy enough. I told you, darling, I wanted to hang out with *you*. D'you want to go on somewhere else?'

'Where?'

'I thought we could take the boys to the Palace for a nightcap? Franz looks a bit tired.'

Franz actually appeared to be asleep.

'Yah, sure, if you want.' Carlotta poked her husband in the chest, perhaps slightly harder than necessary.

'Baby? You want to go have a drink, play some backgammon?'

'We can always sneak down to the King's,' I hinted. King's was the other St Moritz club, in the basement of the Palace Hotel.

Everyone checked their phones as we drove down into town. I had three messages from Elena.

'Still waiting.'

'He's here. Bar.'

'Where are you?'

I replied, then messaged Timothy.

'Time to go. Bar at the Palace.' The hostel I had selected for him was about ten minutes' walk away.

'Ready.'

I was glad of the swagger of the thigh boots as Carlotta and I strode into the Palace lobby. Just now, they suited my mood. Elena was positioned on a chair in the lobby, apparently engrossed in her phone. Since Yermolov would be coming to St Moritz, she would not be permitted to stay at their home, so we had agreed that she would take a hotel, as she had done several times since their separation. I'd asked if Balensky seeing her would be a problem, but she'd scoffed at me.

'Ha! I am old wife! Practically invisible. And it is quite normal for me to be in St Moritz at the start of the season. Besides, you have given him something else to think about, no?'

Elena was in full battle-dress, but seemed quite sober, though I suspected that the clear liquid in her glass was neat voddy. She didn't acknowledge me, just nodded her head sideways in the direction of the bar. Carlotta was making her way through display cabinets of candy-coloured diamonds to the half-empty lounge where Franz, revived by his nap, was opening a backgammon board. I grabbed Tomas's hand.

'I've never seen the bar here. I've heard the view is stunning. Shall we have our drink there?'

Tomas followed me into the more intimate panelled space, with a huge picture window, through which the Alps gleamed again in all their indifferent majesty. I asked for a champagne cocktail, and while the barman mixed it I snuggled under Tomas's surprised but not unwilling arm. Shielded by paunch and jacket, I peered over my shoulder. Elena had really missed her vocation. Balensky was ten feet away.

His gnome's back was half buried in a Deco club chair, but I'd have known that hair weave anywhere. Looking at him, shrunken and wizened, it was difficult to believe that this man had basically been responsible for a series of minor wars. How many lives had he and Yermolov ended between them? Not that I was exactly in a position to judge.

'Here you are, my dear.' I asked Tomas if he had known St Moritz for long, and as he launched into a lengthy anecdote involving the good old days when a young buck could keep a sportsman's cupboard at the Palace, I swivelled my eyes the other way, steering Tomas's body towards me and turning my own for a clearer view. Balensky's bodyguard was to his right, drinking a Coke, with an incongruous leather man-bag plumped in front of him on the low table. To Balensky's left was Timothy's competition, a slender, high-cheek-boned Slavic-looking boy with bleached blond hair and full lips that looked as though he'd been at the hyaluronic acid. Balensky was on the phone, ignoring both his companions, but his left hand lay discreetly on the boy's knee. Tomas, obviously encouraged, was telling me about his own chalet in Kitzbühel now, suggesting that I'd like to see it this season.

'Sounds gorgeous,' I encouraged him, letting his hand brush the gap between my skirt and the dreadful boots as though by accident, watching Balensky intently. His shrivelled little head jerked round when Timothy walked in, wearing black jeans and a fine white cashmere sweater, a new padded jacket with a quilted leather collar slung over his arm, his gold Rolex flashing just indiscreetly enough beneath. He'd somehow faked the glow of a ski-tan, the tips of his perfectly tousled hair just brushing the ruddy flush on his cheekbone. I no longer feared that Balensky would notice me – he only had eyes for Timothy, who ordered a drink before turning to survey the room and making a little mock show of surprise before approaching Balensky.

I had drilled Timothy on his lines on the plane to Milan, but it was crucial to me that I watch him in action. I had to be certain that he would do it right, it being make a date with Balensky in the presence of witnesses. He was to remind Balensky, who spoke French, that they had met before, in the company of Edouard Guiche, and spend a few moments commiserating over the shocking tragedy of his death. Steer the conversation to neutral chat, then mention that he was in the resort with a group of friends from Paris, implying that the 'friends' were throwing a similar sort of party to the one Balensky hosted in Tangier and suggesting that Balensky might like to drop by. Play sad and desirable, a little bit lost but not inconsolable, wounded but still naughty. Tempting. I had counted on Balensky having at least one bodyguard; it was essential that the man see the meeting and Balensky, hopefully, take Timothy's number. Watching him, I was reminded of the Timothy I had met just a few weeks ago in Belleville, the same dirty insouciance, the easy promise of pleasure. I don't know why people consider whoring to be unskilled labour. Within minutes he had claimed the pole position on Balensky's left, leaving the blond in disgruntled silence. Soon Balensky was laying an avuncular hand on his arm and tapping Timothy's number into his phone. Tomas looked rather disappointed when I told him I was feeling tired, but helped me politely into my coat, ready to join Franz and Carlotta. We hovered in the lounge, waiting for Franz to finish his game and Timothy to pass us as he left the Palace, before persuading them to call it a night. Elena was still at her post in the hall, empty-glassed and steady-handed. She held up one hand and a thumb as we crossed out to the waiting car. Six. Elena had informed her husband's staff that she was in St Moritz and needed to pick up a few things from their home before he arrived. They confirmed that he was expected that evening, just as I had planned. So we had until 6 p.m. to set the stage.

At eight the next morning I was swimming laps, naked, in the narrow slate-lined pool in Carlotta's basement, pacing the order of my strategy with the beat of my arms through the water. I worked through the stages in my head, allowing, naturally, for time to select exactly the right outfit.

Showered and dressed in jeans and my heaviest sweater, I found Carlotta in the kitchen, where a maid was pulsing ginger-and-carrot juice and Franz was studying the *FT*.

'Want to go skiing?'

'Skiing?' Carlotta asked, as though I'd proposed something deeply eccentric.

'Yeah, I thought I'd get myself some gear and then go down to the ski school to see if I can book a lesson.'

'Nah, I'm like crazy busy this morning. I've got Pilates and then Franz wants to have lunch at Trais Fluors. We're going to Klara for fondue tonight though!'

'Great. I'll catch you later then.'

'You'll need some keys. Want the driver?'

'No, I should walk. *Ciao*, darling.'

I pulled the loaned mink gratefully around me as I slithered down the hill, the thin mountain air delicious in my lungs. I messaged Timothy to join me at the ice rink at the Kulm and ordered us hot chocolates as I waited, watching three small, exquisitely dressed Italian girls practise clumsy pirouettes with a patient teacher, irrationally jealous of their little white skates.

'*Ça va?*'

Timothy was transformed. The anxious lethargy of the past days had blown away and he seemed ready for anything. Or maybe it was the Kulm, and the view and the deferential waiters with their tiny yellow embroidered napkins and silver chocolate pots. This might be his future, if I came good. It was the kind of future I'd once imagined for myself.

'Has Balensky been in contact?'

He made a hurt face. 'What do you take me for? First thing, *vieux schnoc*.' Old bugger.

'Good. So you're clear – if we have to do it?'

'Yeah, of course, Judith. You've only told me about twenty times.'

'It'll hurt.'

He looked dismissive. 'I've done worse.'

'And if I don't come, Elena will find you. She'll give you the money. It'll be OK, I promise.'

'Don't sweat.'

'You've got something to wear?'

'*Yes!*'

'OK, I'm going to Elena now. Hopefully see you later. Start waiting at six and *don't* leave the room, yes?'

'Sure. I won't. You *told* me. Good luck then.'

We embraced briefly, but I didn't fool myself that there was any warmth in his touch. He might have needed me for comfort in his first shock of grief over Edouard, but from now on we were strictly business. I understood that.

I took a cab outside the lobby of the Kulm to a village called Pontresina, about twenty minutes along the valley. Elena had described the house as a *kottezhi,* a cottage, which in a sense was correct, in that the American millionaires of the Gilded Age had referred to their fifty-bedroom Newport summer houses as 'cottages'. Three glass cliffs descended through the pinewoods, each a window about ten metres high, set in thick cherry-coloured plaster walls. A small funicular rose through the trees, to take goods to the house, with a narrow piste cut through below it, to allow direct access from the slopes. I imagined Yermolov must have had it made specially. I sent the cab off, but Elena was late and my gloveless hands were senseless even in the pockets of the mink by the time she arrived.

'Elisabeth! How wonderful to see you, darling!' she shrilled, for the benefit of the security camera installed in the stone wall which circled the base of the property. As she embraced me, she said, 'I called and told them I needed to pick up a few things. *That* is permitted.' I passed her a crumpled orange Hermès carrier I'd filched from the wardrobe of Carlotta's guest room containing the phone and the leads. Jovana had given me a Huawei P9, the best for the job, in her opinion, and we'd gone over the connectivity set-up several times before I left the squat.

Elena entered a code into the panel set in the wall. A pause, then what I had assumed to be a service door opened to reveal a small lobby and a waiting lift, cut right into the mountain.

'We will need to be quick,' she muttered as the door closed once more and we glided upwards. 'The cameras turn every three minutes.'

'Well, I hope you've been doing your stretches.'

In reply, Elena lifted one booted foot from the folds of her sable and raised it slowly and effortlessly level with her chin.

'*Grand battement*,' she explained with satisfaction. I couldn't help feeling exhilarated.

'You can wait in the hall, darling,' she called theatrically as the lift opened, 'and then we'll go meet Carlotta. I'll just be a moment.'

We were standing in a circular room with a domed wooden ceiling. A mounted row of stags' antlers set off a series of Chinese Gansu-style horse statues jutting out on plinths, beneath the huge, intricate Bean chandelier I had seen in the magazine when I was researching Yermolov's collection. Constructed of more bone and what appeared to be bronze swords, it fell a menacing three metres, the delicate natural forms of the ivory contrasting with the brutal efficiency of the forged metal. It was the chandelier which had given me the idea. We were going to film my encounter with Yermolov and Balensky, but we had to install the device before Yermolov's own cameras picked it up. I hadn't cared for the inclusion of Elena in this, but I couldn't think of a more convenient way to get smoothly onto Yermolov's premises and get it installed. I'd promised her that I was going to push Yermolov into handing over the prize of his collection, namely the Jameson Botticellis, but right now she seemed delighted less about that than the chance to show off.

Elena disappeared up a staircase to the left of the lift and re-emerged moments later, coatless, on a mezzanine gallery that encircled the hall's upper floor, doorways leading off it. Aside from the sound of her boot heels on the wood, the house was eerily silent; I could feel rather than hear the hum of a generator deep within it. This place must gargle fuel.

'I'll just throw these down to you!' Elena paused on the landing. Opposite, a grandfather clock with a porcelain face showed only seconds before noon. I caught her boots, then a flutter of clothes descended, floating slightly on the house's invisible thermals, to land at my feet, all except a flimsy white silk blouse which had unfortunately become impaled on the lighting feature.

'Oh, I am stupid!' cried Elena dramatically. The minute hand moved to noon and the clock began to strike.

Elena hopped neatly over the balustrade with her back to the lamp, holding the rail with both hands like a *barre* as she extended one leg towards the chandelier. *Arabesque.* I counted the seconds under my breath. Her boot caught the antler and pulled the chandelier towards her like a swing as she twisted her supporting leg through a hundred and eighty degrees, drawing her knee bent as she did so, opening her arm over the extended leg. *Second position.* She lifted herself *en pointe* on the impossibly narrow ledge, the rest of her weight suspended by the tense support of her crooked arm as she bent gracefully forward from the waist, pulling the chandelier tight with the flexed leg. The muscles of my core tightened in sympathy; if that thing swung she would break her neck. Holding the lead in her teeth she clipped the phone into place with her free hand, turning the screen face down towards the hall floor. One minute thirty. With agonising slowness, she detached her toe from the tangle of ivory and bone. If her strength failed, she would be whip-lashed to the flagstones. I hoped to Christ she hadn't had a drink. I closed my eyes, waited for her to cry out, couldn't bear it, blinked into the sight of Elena vaulting back to the safety of the mezzanine. Two minutes.

'It's stuck!' she called down, not even out of breath. 'I will have to get someone to fetch a ladder!' The wisp of silk was almost invisible against the pale ivory, but from above the phone was concealed.

'*Prada*,' announced Elena as she came, re-sabled, down the stairs. It crossed my mind that if Balensky or Yermolov killed me, which was a definite possibility, the canopy to my demise would feature a designer label. Somehow that seemed very funny. I don't know what Elena was thinking, but as she caught my eye she started to smile, and in a moment we were laughing so much we had to hold each other up, tears of hilarity melting into the plush heat of our furs.

Elena took me through the entry code twice, then went to meet Carlotta for lunch. I went back to St Moritz, packed my things and set out what I would need for the evening. I messaged Jovana the confirmation; at 6 p.m. the screens in Belgrade would open their eyes. I sent a Snapcode to Kenya.

There was one thing left to do, the hardest one. I had to call my mother. There might never be another chance.

Some of the exuberance I had felt with Elena still fizzed inside me; the fear was building, but still low level, subsumed by the thrill of risk. In that moment, my mother's voice felt more intimidating than the confrontation with Yermolov and Balensky. If I'd had to describe my feelings for her, I might have said 'complex' or 'fierce', but the meaning collapsed in the saying. My mother had never protected me, but then she was barely capable of taking care of herself. I pitied her, in many ways despised her, but I had always tried to be dutiful towards her. Because, for reasons I wasn't prepared to think about right then, I also admired her. She was weak, but she was quick. We were alike, she and I. Good at improvising.

Get it over with.

I lay next to the Caravaggio on the bed and punched in her number.

'All right, Mum?'

'Judy! How are you, love?'

Things came and went all the time in our house. A slow, permanent slippage, a leaking trail with its own centrifugal logic. The Christmas tree would stay up until May, then one morning I'd come down to find the telly gone.

'Fine. Working hard.'

'It's all going well then?'

Once there was a bread machine she'd got on the Tesco stamps. The house smelled like an advert – for a while.

'Really well, Mum. How about you, what have you been up to?'

Sometimes it was stereo speakers so I'd know she'd picked someone up in the pub. I didn't blame my mother for trying to live a bit, even if she wanted to do it to Crystal Gale.

'Oh, not much. The usual. I've got a new couch.'

It was the grotesque carnival of the attempt that I couldn't bear, the swim of scattered clothes on the living room floor, the unspeakable stains on the sofa.

'That's lovely.'

The money I had sent to my mother since I moved to Italy had relieved her of her intermittent attempts at employment. Enough each month to keep her comfortable without arousing suspicion; my plan had been to wait until I'd been in Venice a while, got the gallery established so it wouldn't look too obvious, then buy her a place on Gentileschi's money. In the meantime, I'd asked if there was anywhere she'd like to go, anything she'd like to do, but she seemed happy enough with a bit of online shopping and going down the pub. I'd come, slowly, to realise that she didn't want a new home, she was happy enough in her tarted-up council flat, with no worries and money for booze. It pained and exasperated me that that was all she wanted. But my mum really thought her life was OK.

The vodka and Radio 1 on her old digital clock radio, red minutes ticking down the twilit afternoons.

There was a pause on the line. There were a whole load of things I would have liked to say to my mother, but they would never be said. Never might just be coming a bit quicker, I supposed.

'Weather nice?' she asked eventually. My mum had never gone south of Birmingham. She thought I lived in the tropics.

'Fine, bit cold now it's winter.'

'That's nice then.' I could hear the telly. Busy mums go to Iceland at Christmas! It was barely November. I gulped air.

'Just wanted to see you're OK.'

'Fine, love.'

'Bye then. Best not run up the bill.'

'Yeah. Bye, Judy. Love you.'

She didn't used to say that. She'd learned it, from TV. I wanted to say it back, but my thumb cut the call before the words came. I sat up and looked around the room, but there wasn't much to break.

Why had I assembled this tottering stack of contingencies? To protect what? Dave? To make things right for Timothy? It wasn't that, quite. Yermolov had taken away the most important thing I had ever had. Not money, not my gallery, not Masha. Yermolov had seen through me, through the laboured carapace which had taken me so long to construct. Pictures were the only pure thing I had ever known, but he had scraped away my faith in them sure as a restorer lifts a panel with a razor. I needed to catch him out, certainly, to make all this stop. But I wanted to make him own something ugly, something vulgar and crass and despicable. Something that I had made. He thought he'd shown me up, but he was wrong about me. At least I was going to keep on telling myself that.

Taking the bolster from the bed, I wrapped my arms around it, squeezing and squeezing until the place behind my eyes turned red and my thoughts went quiet.

23

No security, no staff, or no show had been my instructions. The darkened glass of the Yermolov home at Pontresina seemed as still as black ice, yet I paused outside for a few achingly freezing minutes, searching out any sign of an ambush. Without Elena, the huge house felt Gothic, the graceful pine-covered slopes in their sparkling mantle of snow a horror-movie backdrop. Yermolov could easily have positioned a sniper in the wood, but I had to assume he wouldn't be so foolhardy as to take me out without ascertaining the whereabouts of the Caravaggio. The lift was lined with tiny mother-of-pearl tiles. I counted them, their cool lustre, as I rode up. As promised, the house felt empty, though I held my breath and listened again to a silence magnified by my knowledge of the massive peaks outside in the dark.

Entering the hallway at 5.55 p.m., I waited out the last five minutes in shadow. Then I sent a message from my phone to the device suspended in the tangled net of the chandelier. I watched for the tiny red star to illuminate. One of Jovana's tech-artists had installed a modified version of Livestream, preset with a timer which I could activate. Whatever happened could be watched by her and her team through an encrypted link and would also be recorded on film. I was nervous about it, but collaboration had never been my thing. I had to trust her breezy reassurances. The film was an insurance policy, a built-in plan B. Hopefully it wouldn't be necessary.

Once it was working, I fiddled with the complicated system of switches by the lift, raising and lowering the lights until I'd found a suitably dramatic level. I tried to listen for a vehicle on the road below, but the thickness of the walls and the snow padding insulated me so thoroughly that I could hear the low whisper of my own breath. Then, faintly, the smooth whine of the elevator, descending. I had counted thirty-two luminous squares on the climb, one per second, which meant they'd be inside in just over a minute.

There was a small comic struggle between the tall man and the short as they each attempted to exit the lift first.

'Where is she?' asked Balensky in Russian.

'*Vot*,' I answered. *Here*. I switched to English. 'I have the picture, as I said.' Balensky advanced, close enough for me to smell the spicy cologne in the folds of his heavy cashmere coat.

'Where is it?'

'Just hand it over, please, Miss Teerlinc. The sooner we get this charade over with, the better.'

Yermolov's voice was weary rather than angry. Had he and Balensky decided to play good cop, bad cop?

'Before I give it to you, I have some conditions. You are here, obviously, because your . . . colleague Ivan Kazbich gave you a message. From Dejan Raznatovic, in Serbia. I went to see him, as you know. I know that you've been flipping art for arms. I don't give a toss about that, but quite a lot of other people will. What I want is for you to stop fucking about in my life. In any way whatsoever. I'll give you the picture. In return, you' – I pointed to Yermolov – 'will give the Jameson Botticellis to your wife. And you both have my silence. Easy, no?'

Yermolov snorted, which threw me off a bit.

Balensky advanced even closer, the sandalwood of his cologne overwhelmed by the rotten stench of his breath.

'I think it is clear that this is not a joke. You have no evidence for these absurd threats.'

'You're here though, aren't you?'

'We came for the picture. Hand it over. Now.'

He dropped his gaze, I followed his eyes. A snub metal snout protruded from his coat. Not a lady's gun. Oh well, plan B it was.

'You do know that your picture is a fake?' I addressed him, watching both of their faces in the low light. Yermolov looked entirely unsurprised.

He knows. *He knows. So why?*

I was recalculating even as Balensky's face stilled, then exploded into rage. He shouted something in rapid Russian I couldn't follow. Yermolov merely shrugged, those pale eyes calm. I caught the name Kazbich in Balensky's tirade.

'Yes, you might want to ask Dr Kazbich some questions,' I interrupted. 'Only a child would have believed those

provenances. Your picture is a piece of worthless crap.'
Why wasn't Yermolov reacting?

Balensky raised the gun. As planned, I had dressed very carefully for the performance, my black pants and a black Dolce jacket purloined from Carlotta, wasp-waisted with a stiffened kick of peplum, a high, revered white leather collar. Beneath, my breasts were bound tight under linen, but I still figured that Balensky could see my heart pumping. I wasn't scared. I wasn't even thirty either, but I was really, really tired of being fucked about. And having a loaded barrel aimed at one's aorta does awaken a sense of life's rich possibilities, so I did what any girl would in such dire circumstances. I started to take off my clothes.

As the first button fell open, Balensky let out a long, quivering sigh, but it wasn't the prospect of a glimpse of my tits that was doing it for him. Under my jacket, I was wearing the Caravaggio.

The inventories of the painter's works made in his own time include many pictures which have been lost, canvases that disappeared or were ignorantly destroyed. These vanished paintings occasionally resurface – in an attic in Toulouse, a dining room in Dublin – some to be astonishingly authenticated and hung like treasures, and others, unproven, driving their fanatically convinced owners slowly insane. Kazbich had quoted one such inventory in his provenances: 'a picture made for the woman who had given him lodging'. An adaptation of the well-known convention of the artist paying in kind, scrawling a hasty masterpiece on the tablecloth to pay for his wine; in this case, Caravaggio had supposedly drawn his Venetian landlady – perhaps also one of his many lovers – using her loose under-shift as an improvised canvas.

It was the Serbian icons which had explained the last element of Kazbich's forgery. When I had opened the case back in England I had been confused to find that the 'Caravaggio' was on a piece of clothing. But the museum Raznatovic had helped to establish in Belgrade contained examples of ecclesiastical dress from the region's monasteries, copes and surplices hand-stitched by generations of patient nuns. I knew nothing about textile history, but presumably Kazbich had filched one. Gingerly shaking out the garment, I could discern tiny holes where the original embroidery had been carefully unpicked, creating a blank canvas of authentically dated period cloth on the simple sleeveless garment. The folds of the fabric were stiff and liverish, but linen can survive a long, long time. I had guessed right at the chalk at the archive in Amsterdam, and been spot on about the Naples yellow. It was only then, when I saw Kazbich's signature, that I realised where it must be. What had stalled me was how Moncada could possibly have concealed another painting at our meeting in the hotel room. But if it was on linen – a possibility which it seemed Kazbich had also considered – then it could have been carefully rolled into a briefcase, hiding it not only from airport security, but also from me.

Pretty clever. The portrait had been built up to resemble the sly, inquiring head of the girl in *The Gypsy Fortune Teller*, one of the first pictures with which Caravaggio had astounded the sensation-hungry art collectors of Rome. Kazbich had drawn a poetic connection between the face of the forgotten Venetian woman and the playful knowingness of the gypsy girl's features. The ardour of greed, he must have hoped, would do the rest.

Balensky gaped at my forged breastplate.

'You can shoot me,' I continued, 'but you'll never get the blood out. Want to try?'

His mouth was working, but he was still aiming the gun.

'Or I can tear it off. It's very fragile, this old cloth. And then you can shoot me. But you still won't have your picture.'

'What do you want?' He was wavering. 'Money?'

'I don't need money. I want you to stop. Just leave it alone. And him –' I angled my chin over Balensky's shoulder at Yermolov – 'he is going to give his paintings to his wife. The Jameson Botticellis, as I said. I'm going to walk out of here just the way I came in, with this thing on me. When Elena Yermolov is sure of the pictures, you can have it back, for what it's worth. Which is nothing.'

Yermolov appeared to be stifling a giggle, which wasn't quite the reaction I'd been expecting.

'*Ona bezumna*,' muttered Balensky. *She's insane*.

'Possibly,' said Yermolov, in English. 'But not entirely stupid. As you know. Get rid of her if you want. You know the picture's worthless.

Balensky turned slowly to the other man, pivoting like a mechanical toy. Both his hands now hung limply by his sides. He watched Yermolov, who simply shrugged, then looked down at the gun as though bewildered to find himself holding it.

'We need to talk.' Balensky was clearly struggling for composure, but there was a crazed desperation to him now. He wasn't at all intimidating, more absurd. As absurd as an angry geriatric with a loaded gun can ever be.

'No. You really don't.' I put my hands to the collar of the shift, feeling the cloth crackle with the strain. 'Do you want it or not? Shall I count to ten?'

I knew Balensky couldn't shoot me. Even the cleanest aim to the head would drench the picture with my brains before he had a chance to ease it off my body. It wasn't the supposed monetary worth of the thing that would prevent him either. Desire was a currency I'd dealt in for a long time. He couldn't shoot me because of his craving to possess this thing, with a passion whose blindness only rendered it more overwhelming.

Then Balensky shot me.

An echo of stillness before the bullet's report cracked deafeningly off the walls. Something heavy thudded against my chest, no time to feel even surprise as Balensky's skull bounced against my collarbone and the gun clattered to the floor in a crisp tinkle of breaking china. He made a small, gentle sound, the exhalation of old bones rising from a chair. Yermolov was supporting him with his left arm from behind, in his right hand a heavy ormolu ashtray. Balensky's arms swung bonelessly as his knees folded and Yermolov crouched forward, lowering him neatly to the stone. He pushed aside the swirling fabric of his overcoat and felt for the pulse behind Balensky's ear with a practised three fingers. Then there was an embarrassingly long silence.

'We had better call an ambulance,' said Yermolov eventually. 'Mr Balensky appears to have had a heart attack. And I think he must have hit his head when he collapsed. How dreadful.'

Quietly, he set down the ashtray next to the body. Quietly, he picked up the gun.

My synapses were going off like the Fourth of July and my shoulders were in spasm, the whole of my body still twitching in disbelief that the shot had gone wide. The floor was covered in tiny fragments of porcelain. The horse. Balensky had shot the horse, then died of an ashtray. Smoking was allowed indoors then? Yay. *Jesus, Judith.*

'He shot the horse,' I blurted uselessly.

Yermolov held the gun in his right hand. With his left he reached into his pocket for his phone.

'The same –' My mouth was arid, I gathered saliva and tried again, but all I could manage was a high, winded gasp. I squeezed my throat together, controlled my voice. 'The same kind of heart attack Edouard Guiche suffered when your goon pushed him out of a fifth-floor window? The same kind Masha died from? Am I going to have one too?' I was talking too fast for him. He looked confused, but he didn't pull the phone out.

The Caravaggio was drenched in sweat, but I was freezing. I continued, 'You should know that what you have just done has been filmed. Live stream, real time. A whole shitload of witnesses. He's got a wound the size of your fucking fist in the back of his head. Heart attack?'

I didn't feel the need to mention that Jovana and company believed they were watching a mock-up.

Yermolov's hand was clutching my throat before I even saw it move. The back of my tongue was contracting, but I squeezed out the words. 'You can do what you like, but it won't help.'

'What the fuck are you doing?'

'Let go.' He eased his grip but didn't release me. 'You have just committed murder on a live webcam. Do you understand?'

Very slowly, the fingers round my neck relaxed. My heels reconnected with the floor. I sucked air.

Interesting, how rage works. I was pretty familiar with it myself. Yermolov's voice was as cold as the steppe in January, yet his tone was almost conversational. 'What reason do I have to believe you?'

I smiled as sweetly as I could. '*Mr* Yermolov. This is not a job interview. But, OK. I have your picture, despite your best efforts. I found out about your little racket in Serbia. I found Raznatovic, all by myself. And I got you here. Call me a pleaser, but why doubt me?'

'Where is this camera?' he asked slowly.

I took a step back. 'Up there.' I jerked my head at the dangling bones. 'I imagine you're a good shot, you could probably take it out in one, but it's too late. As I said, what just happened was streamed. Not on the Web, mind you. It was, however, taped. So you have a choice.'

The gun hung loosely from his hand, relaxed, familiar.

'What are you doing?' he hissed. 'You stupid little bitch.'

'You can throttle me, or shoot me. See what happens. You murdered two people for your fucking painting. Oh, sorry, three. Well, here it is.'

I shook my jacket to the floor and eased the shift slowly over my head, tossed it to one side. I'd put two sports bras underneath to make it fit. I jerked my head at the crumpled heap of cloth lying next to Balensky.

'All yours.'

Yermolov changed tack. 'I was in no way responsible for the death of Edouard Guiche and I have no idea who is this Masha. I have no interest in that . . . thing.'

'Why should I believe you? Why did you pay for it if you don't want it? Why did you . . . ?'

I was feeling distinctly peculiar, so I lay down on the floor next to Balensky's corpse. Yermolov turned away from me and walked a lap of the room, fists clenched in his pockets, like a bad actor doing a big decision.

'I would very much like a drink. Would you care to join me?'

'Maybe. Yes. Thank you.'

'Perhaps, first, you would switch off the camera, please?' His voice was soothing, coaxing. The kind of voice you would use to a dangerous lunatic. 'You are in no danger. And then I'll fetch you a drink.' We were humouring one another now, each uncertain of the other's next move.

'I'll need my phone. In my bag, over there.' I wiped my hand on my trousers and called the silenced device, which would cut the timer and hence the link. Yermolov watched with interest. Then I messaged Jovana:

All done. Did it work?

Seemed to. Weird stuff! she pinged back.

I know, right? Speak tomorrow, thanks.

I replaced the phone and lay back with my eyes closed. Yermolov was gone so long that I thought he might be calling reinforcements. He could have come back with a rocket launcher and an iron maiden, I wouldn't have noticed. *He knew it was a fake. He knew. So why?* Doors banged somewhere in the depths of the house. I remembered Carlotta, lost in her own kitchen.

'Here.'

I sat up and took the cold glass Yermolov handed me. Elena's favourite.

'Thanks.'

He lit a cigarette and handed me the pack.

'So. Tell me about this film.' He was still using the lunatic voice.

I took a long slug, relishing the frozen burn.

'I commissioned it for you. Either it's an artwork, or it's evidence. It doesn't have a title yet. If you want to buy it, the price is 200K euros. Plus my commission, ten per cent.'

'You said it was live. Witnesses.'

'Indeed. I'm sure you've heard of socially critical photography? The witnesses are artists. They think this is staged – a comment on the power of capital to subvert materiality. Or some shit like that. Surreal.'

'Riiight.' Maybe I did sound a bit mad.

'So you buy the tapes, a unique artwork. The other condition still stands. Your Botticellis go to your wife. Your call.'

'And you are doing this because . . .?'

'I want you to stop – meddling. Leave me alone, as I said to your friend. Stop killing people into the bargain, maybe.'

'Don't be tedious. I did not kill anyone. Not this Masha person, not Guiche.'

'You destroyed my gallery in Venice.' I reached across Balensky for the bruised ashtray.

'Why would I do that?'

'To threaten me. Because you wanted the picture.'

'The fake Caravaggio? He wanted it.'

Balensky had looked terrified, furious, confused, but Yermolov was none of those things. He looked bored. It's difficult to fake bored, one tends to overdo it. So suddenly, shatteringly, I knew that he was telling the truth.

An elevated sense of his own status. Throughout the ramshackle triumphs of his progress, Caravaggio experienced success as confinement. Desire fulfilled became desire disdained. The claustrophobic interiority of his pictures, their reduction of the world to the confines of a single room, they perform their deceits even as they cajole us into believing we see clearly. There is nothing else, so how can we be deluded? And yet, so possessed are we by looking that we blind ourselves to the simultaneous realities of his scenes. *Painting is cheating.* Beware of what you think you see. I let my head fall back on the floor, a brief flash of the kilim in my flat in Venice. *No.* I remembered a line I had read somewhere, that the moment of communication in an artwork appears as a sudden salience on the surface of the psyche. It was all so swiftly, stupidly clear. Ever since that moment in Paris when Renaud had whipped the garrotte around Moncada's neck, I had placed myself at the centre, when in fact I had only ever been a satellite, peripheral to an entirely different materiality. Others – Kazbich, Balensky, Yermolov, Moncada himself – were playing alternate odds. The surface had been muddied, and I just couldn't see.

I groaned. I wished Balensky had shot me. I had been wrong. Wrong about all of it.

24

Yermolov's story took several hours to unravel. As he talked, we lay on our elbows like Romans at a feast. The huge house had seemed so menacing earlier, but now, as we lay on the heated floor with our vodka, it felt cosy, a cocoon in a duvet of snow. All quite friendly. But as he spoke I felt myself shrivelling, desiccated by my own conceit.

'I knew Balensky was a cheat for a long time,' Yermolov explained. 'Him and Kazbich.'

'I worked that out – Balensky took a fake Rothko from him, for a start.'

Yermolov was polite enough to look genuinely impressed. 'You spotted that? *Otlichno.*' *Excellent.*

That might have been the moment to ask him why his opinion of my skills had been so low, but I needed information from him more than reassurance. I ignored the compliment, asked him why he had continued to associate with Balensky.

'We had many connections. We had worked together in the past, in Russia. It was complicated.'

'Of course.'

'But I knew as soon as he came to me with the Caravaggio deal that it was a fake. Only an – an ignoramus would believe that story. But he – he didn't know pictures, didn't love them.

They were just things to him, objects to sell.' He leaned forward confidentially, 'The only picture he really loved was a Safronov portrait of himself.'

'Ouch.' Nikas Safronov specialised in fake-classic swagger portraits. He had done the Russian president as Francois I. 'As Napoleon?'

'Funny. Peter the Great.'

'Double ouch. So why did you go along with it? Why did you agree to buy the Caravaggio?'

'Balensky needed money. He's broke.'

'Broke?'

'It happens. The government in Russia froze his assets. If he returns he will be arrested. Not an uncommon occurrence.'

'One that you've managed to avoid.'

For some time Yermolov had been aware of what I had worked out from Guiche's papers. Kazbich had been dealing more than pictures to Balensky – using paintings as a cover and Raznatovic as a supplier he had indeed also been moving arms. Yermolov was not involved. What I didn't know was that Balensky had become an inconvenience to the Russian authorities. Like many of his predecessors in the post-Soviet gold-rush, his fortune had been too flamboyantly and violently acquired to suit Moscow's new order. And so his assets had been frozen. Balensky was therefore living on credit, desperate for money, hence the Caravaggio scheme, which he and Kazbich had cooked up together. Kazbich would sell the picture, supposedly to Balensky and Yermolov, then Balensky and Kazbich would split Yermolov's part of the fee. Smoke and mirrors. Balensky's pretended 'investment' was supposed to convince Yermolov. Hence Balensky's panic when I announced the picture to be a fake. It had been for Yermolov's benefit. Perhaps he had even frantically chanced that by shooting me, he could still persuade Yermolov the picture was real.

'But if you knew it was all nonsense, why did you go along with it? Why did you come here today?'

'Politics.'

'What?'

'I needed to stay close to Balensky. You know that I have . . . political connections in Russia? They – we – considered that it would be more convenient for all concerned if Balensky was arrested in the West. For fraud. This Caravaggio scheme was a perfect solution – he built his own trap.'

'So that was why you paid over the money?'

'I knew I would get it back. It wasn't so much.' Fifty million dollars. I supposed it wasn't, to a man like him.

I was reminded of a phrase I had read in Bruce Eakin's book: 'For my friends, everything – for my enemies, the law!'

'But – what about Balensky's people? I saw him with a bodyguard last night.'

'There are very few left. He kept up appearances.'

The emails Dave had received. The burglaries. There had been something . . . amateurish about them. *As if I could have run so easily if Yermolov had really been after me.*

Kazbich, ignorant that Yermolov was playing him, had been equally desperate for Yermolov to buy.

'But he had been your dealer. You trusted him?'

'Once, yes. He was no longer of any interest to me. I was to see the thing through with Balensky, that was all.'

'You weren't angry? He'd cheated you. You didn't want revenge?'

'Revenge is not something I have a use for. It's not effective.' He caught my eye as he raised his glass, and a tiny fizz of electromagnetism bounced between us.

Kazbich had known I was in the Place de l'Odéon, and had thought I must know where the piece was. He had suggested the 'valuation', had tried to goad Yermolov into pursuing me, but that had failed when I turned Yermolov down. Yermolov didn't much care about finding the piece itself, as between the provenances and the payment Balensky was already entrapped, but Kazbich had been frantic to go ahead and get Yermolov to hand over the rest of the money. So he had begun exerting pressure – trying to mess with my head. Which, it turned out, he had done, spectacularly. Yermolov thought he must have been responsible for the 'ghosts' in my flat. And then Elena had interfered.

'Elena. Yes.'

'Judith, as I say, I am not without principles. Whatever Elena told you, she is the mother of my sons. I would never threaten her. She is . . . a difficult woman. Hysterical, frustrated. She drinks – impossible. I sent her to doctors, to clinics, but nothing worked.'

'I've seen worse.' My own mother, for example.

'Please accept that there are some things you simply do not know.'

'But you are going to divorce her?'

'Yes. And I am not going to give her my Botticellis, though I must say I appreciate the romance of your request. Elena will be well cared for. But I do not think that you did this' – he waved his hand at the chandelier – 'for Elena's sake?'

'Elena wanted to use me, to get the picture. That's why she's in St Moritz. She had an idea that without it she would be in danger. But because of what she knew, what you both knew, returning it wouldn't have been enough. I needed to know how you had found out, and to have something – something to bargain with. That's why I went to Raznatovic. I thought you and Balensky were in the arms thing together.'

'I knew about the dead men. One in Paris, one in Rome. The Italians? But I also knew that you had stolen nothing, for all you had changed your name.'

'But still.'

Yermolov rolled his eyes. 'Miss Teerlinc –'

'You can call me Judith if you like. It is my name.'

'Judith. This is not a game. I know what people think of us – oligarchs and murderers, locking people in the Lubyanka and throwing away the key. But we don't all go about with our pockets full of polonium. I do have principles. I may not be a saint, which is why, frankly, your terrible past is of little interest to me. But neither am I a cartoon.'

'Yes, well,' I said, looking over at Balensky, 'I can see that. How did you learn about the . . . incident in Paris though?'

'Kazbich, naturally.'

But how did Kazbich know who I was and what I was doing there?

'Elena told me that you were dangerous. And then I thought you killed Masha, smashed up the gallery, killed Guiche. So I thought you were serious. I thought you were coming for me.'

'But why did you think this?'

'Yury. I saw Yury. In Venice, then in Paris.'

'I know Yury. But he works for Kazbich, never for me. I asked Kazbich to have him keep an eye on Elena. When she drinks, things can get ugly. I knew nothing about Masha. I heard Edouard Guiche had committed suicide.'

'Balensky thought he had the painting,' I said slowly. 'It wasn't suicide.'

'Guiche would not be the first man who worked for Balensky who ended that way.'

We were quiet for a moment.

'There's another reason,' I said. 'Because . . .'

'Yes?'

If I had learned one thing from Caravaggio, it was to suit your techniques to your circumstances. 'Because I could. Because I had talked myself into believing that you were pursuing me. Because I was angry with you. I wanted to humiliate you. Because it was – exciting, I suppose.'

'Masha was your friend?'

'Sort of. Yes. Enough for it to matter.'

'Then I'm sorry. I'm sorry about your gallery too.'

'That doesn't matter actually. I'm sorry about your horse.'

'That does, rather.'

We had temporarily forgotten Balensky, the silent guest at our little drinks party. I raised my glass at the pile of cashmere on the floor. 'How come he's not bleeding?'

'I was a professional, once.'

'You and Elena were made for each other, you know?'

'Once.'

Yermolov rose to his feet, stretched athletically. He caught me noticing.

'So now you and your clever artist friends have me over the keg?'

'Barrel.'

Yermolov looked amused. 'You are very thorough. And do you intend to pursue this rather dramatic blackmail?'

'No. But I did promise some money to my artists. I will need that. And to someone else. Elena knows about it.' I pinched the bridge of my nose. I would have time to think about my own colossal stupidity later. 'And we still have to get rid of Balensky.'

'As I said, a heart attack. He was an old man.' Yermolov was pacing, as though the hallway was a cage.

'But your people in Moscow wanted to bang him up. Put him in prison, that is. They won't be too thrilled by this.'

'It is . . . inconvenient.'

'That's where the someone comes in. I think you'll like this.'

'You're telling me how to dispose of a body?'

'Don't get me started.'

Yermolov had driven himself from the airstrip that afternoon in an Audi station wagon, collecting Balensky from the Palace on his way. The Caravaggio came in useful as a temporary shroud – we wrapped it round Balensky's neck and head in a snood to conceal the wound, then fastened his overcoat tightly to prop his head in place. The loose papery skin of the throat was still warm. There was plenty of space for the body in the boot, and after we'd hoicked him down in the lift and rolled him into the car we didn't need to speak anymore as we drove back to St Moritz between thick-walled old farmhouses and modern condominiums gleaming out of the snow like stalagmites. I broke the silence only to give directions to the hostel.

'We'll have to carry him. Get his arms round our necks as we get him out. Make like he's drunk.'

I had done that before, when I had taken care of Leanne in Paris.

'You are sure this is the best way?' Yermolov asked.

'What does your government hate even more than dissent?'

'I don't understand.'

'Homosexuals.' He looked at me blankly. 'You didn't know Balensky was gay?'

'I had no idea.' Pride and, I had to admit, a little disgust were in his voice.

I thought ruefully of my precautions with Dave's grey hat in Kenya. There I'd been casting Yermolov as some kind of omnipotent supervillain, and he was ignorant of stuff he could have read in *Grazia*.

'Well, he was. Wait until you meet my friend Timothy. I think your friends in Moscow are going to be very pleased with you.'

Timothy's room was on the second floor. I took a quick peek into the lobby. I knew from dropping Timothy off that the stairs were on the right, with the reception desk built into a cubicle at a right angle. There were no guests in evidence, just a woman in a thick yellow roll-neck jumper leafing through a magazine behind the desk. The entrance was directly in her sight-line. I had a map-pin loaded on my phone with directions to a house I had randomly selected down by the lake.

'I'm going to go in and ask her for directions. When we get outside, you take him in, OK?'

'No problem.'

I approached the desk and began to explain in the few words of German I had that I was meeting a friend at the hostel and that we didn't know how to get to our host's chalet. Perhaps glad of the distraction on a boring shift, the woman smiled helpfully and pored over the location on my phone, switching to perfect English when I seemed confused. She led me outside and began an efficient explanation of how to get down the hill, bearing right until I passed the supermarket on my left, from where I would see the lake. I switched the phone off in my pocket as we passed through the doors, figuring that the time it took to reopen it once outside would give Yermolov his chance. The two of us shivered on the porch until the screen came back to life. The receptionist traced her finger along the route I should take.

'Thank you so much! I'll just go up and see if my friend's ready.' I could see the hem of Balensky's coat drooping up the stairwell like a dragon's tail.

'No problem! Happy to help' she called as I bounded up the stairs.

Yermolov was waiting for me on the second-floor landing. Even a skinny old party like Balensky must have weighed sixty kilos but he hadn't broken a sweat.

'In here.' I knocked gently on the door of room 9.

Timothy had dressed in lederhosen for his date with Balensky. At least he was wearing the buff leather shorts and embroidered braces, but he seemed to have forgotten the shirt. His hair was combed back neatly with water, gleaming in the bronze light off the cheap pine panelling of the walls. The two men nodded to one another.

'Put him on the bed.'

All the items from my shopping list were arranged on the bedside table. I noted approvingly that the whisky had been opened and two glasses poured. Timothy was going to turn a trick with a john who got over-excited, and be forced to defend himself. Eyeing up the objects, Yermolov got it without my needing to explain.

'How did you know?' he whispered.

'I didn't. Contingency. It might have been you.'

He looked amused again.

'You are very confident.'

'Thorough, as you said.'

'Was I also to have been . . . gay?'

'People can be surprising. Shall we get on with it?'

I unwound the cloth, exposing the base of Balensky's skull where the anemone of his wound was finally beginning to seep. It was a rag now, the picture. A nothing.

I rearranged the props a little, removing some, placing the fossil on the nightstand.

'Get his clothes off.'

Timothy and I did that, Yermolov standing discreetly to one side. From the wardrobe, Timothy produced a plastic bag containing Balensky's get-up. He folded Balensky's clothes over the room's single chair – coat, jacket, sweater, shirt, underpants, socks, vest. There was something a bit unbearable about the vest. We replaced them with the black PVC gear. Like Yermolov, I averted my eyes as Timothy unlaced the front of the shorts to roll a condom onto Balensky's cock. Unsurprisingly, that took a while.

'How much are you charging tonight, darling?'

'Two grand,' Timothy answered. I put the cash in Balensky's pocket.

'OK. Lie on the bed.'

We rolled Balensky over to the wall and Timothy got into position, lying on his front, undoing the buttons on either side of the lederhosen.

'Wait. Did you get the lube?'

'In the bag.'

Timothy sat up, took the bottle I handed him, did the necessary and lay down again.

'Can you reach the fossil?'

He tried with his right hand first, pushing himself up on his elbow, then the left, but the angle required to strike Balensky's wound was implausible.

'And if we were doing it missionary?'

Timothy unselfconsciously lay back, popped a pillow beneath his head and spread his legs.

'No purchase. He's old.' We were speaking French, I could see Yermolov following with detached interest. Bizarre as the scenario was, I had a feeling it wasn't the first time he'd staged a death.

'How about like this?' Timothy moved to his knees in one graceful motion. 'If he was kneeling behind me? Then I could turn?'

'Hold him up,' I told Yermolov, then had a look, 'Yes. Reach for it, right hand, turn under him, he falls – so.'

Yermolov obligingly dropped Balensky, who fell forward, his floppy, mottled arse protruding obscenely from the plastic pants.

'Good. Get the wire. One roll in his jacket pocket. Are you ready? You're sure?'

Timothy grimaced.

'Ready? Do it now.'

The only time I saw Timothy wince was when he swung the fossil true at Balensky's neck. It made a dull *thwock*, like a tennis ball hitting a racket. He swallowed hard. We rolled Balensky untidily onto the floor.

'Hold it. You'll drop it more naturally. Give me the wire.'

'I'll do it,' put in Yermolov. 'He'll fight you.'

I had been sure I could do it, but I was grateful.

'Go upstairs straight away. There's a fire escape from the top floor, wooden. It comes out at the side, so your car will be round to the left.'

'And when will I see you?' he asked suddenly in Russian. An odd moment to ask me on a date.

'Elena is waiting for me at the Palace. It might be a while, so you'll have to put up with each other until I get there.'

'Certainly.'

'I'll wait outside.'

Waiting again. Praying that no one would come, but it was evening in high season in St Moritz; they would all be out doing après-ski, wouldn't they? Flinging down the jolly old glühwein? I flinched as I heard footsteps on the stairs, took out my phone and pretended to study it as a couple in heavy jackets and bright-coloured salopettes over boots came round, speaking German. I nodded at them from my position in the corridor; they returned the silent greeting as they headed downstairs. Come on. *What were they doing*? *Come on*. More footsteps, inside this time, Yermolov passing me in silence. He had removed his shoes.

I banged the door open as hard as I could, holding up my phone, recalling the rubberneckers circling Guiche's body on the Île Saint-Louis. The modern reflex – snap first, scream later. I pressed the screen blindly as I moved forward, once, twice, three times. Then I looked. Timothy was sagged forward on the bed, doubled over his knees as though he was doing yoga. I went closer. His face was purpled, it didn't look like he was breathing. Had Yermolov tricked me? Finished the job, with me next? *Oh, Jesus.* I crooked my arm under Timothy and let him down gently onto his side. I was standing on Balensky's back. I did note that the makeshift garrotte was trailing between his wrinkled manicured fingers.

'Timothy? It's OK. It's finished now. Come on, breathe. Please breathe.'

Nothing. The wire had cut his skin, there was blood on the starched Swiss pillow. I felt a slow gale of panic begin to build in me. The cotton was milky, the colour of dirty bathwater. I wanted to delve my hands into it, to pull his face free; if I could just reach down to her, I could make her safe. *Not that. Not that. This is Timothy.*

'Please. Come on.' I shook him, harder, harder. He coughed. *Oh, thank you.* He was wheezing, gulping for air, still choking, I supported his head until his throat cleared. He gave me a gorgeous, lazy smile.

'*Ça va?*'

'*Ça va.*'

'I'll be in touch. With the money. Take care.'

I knew I would never see him again. Whatever warmth we might have felt for one another, this had only ever been business, all along. Perhaps that knowledge was what had created the trust necessary for our brief alliance.

I kissed him once, tenderly, on his swollen, cyanotic lips.

And then I started shouting.

25

We left St Moritz that night. I had waited until the last possible second, when I heard the receptionist pounding up the stairs in response to my horrified screams, then bolted out the same way I had directed Yermolov. The concerned friend would remain anonymous. I walked down to the Palace, too high on adrenalin to notice the paralysing temperature even with just Carlotta's smart jacket to cover me, and joined the Yermolovs in Elena's suite. I went straight to the bathroom, locked the door and checked in with my grey hat.

All done. $2,000 to upload them?

Understood.

I'll need the account. You'll need to wait until I get to a laptop.

U R good 4 it. I know.

Thanks. Blur out the boy's face. Wait five hours. Then viral.

Consider it done. An unusually elegant flourish, that.

U OK? No Russki hassle?

None. Thanks.

:) Sending new code now.

When the message pinged through, I sent the pictures I had shot of Balensky and Timothy *in extremis*. Timothy's story would hopefully be corroborated by Balensky's bodyguard, more likely since I now knew he was unpaid and likely to be disgruntled. Timothy would explain to the authorities that he had arranged a meeting for paid sex with Balensky. That Balensky had wanted a little Christian Grey action, which Timothy had gone along with until the wire got too tight, when he had struck out desperately in self-defence to save his own life. He would have a rough few days, but Balensky's age would make it difficult to prosecute a manslaughter case, while the nature of the offence would keep anyone in Balensky's family from making a fuss, particularly given his financial circumstances. And Timothy would get his double spread, in the end, when the photos swam up from the dark web. I'd asked for his face to be obscured to preserve his anonymity, but I probably needn't have bothered. Turning tricks was no bar to fame. He'd probably end up with his own reality show. I would give him 500K, which would allow him freedom. It had seemed a reasonable price before; since Balensky's demise had been so useful to Yermolov, I reckoned I could get him to come in to increase it.

In the next room, Elena and Yermolov seemed to be chatting quietly in Russian. I took a long shower and wrapped myself in a quilted bathrobe with a Palace monogram. When I appeared, my hair turbaned in a towel, Elena ran to embrace me as Yermolov opened a bottle of Krug. I couldn't quite see why I was suddenly so popular, but I took advantage to order double cheeseburgers from room service. We gnawed them from our knees, mayonnaise and juice dripping down our wrists. Elena raised her glass in an unsteady toast. I clocked Yermolov eyeing her, but he said nothing.

'Thank you! We have had such a wonderful talk, the first in months, thanks to you!'

I could see why having the chance to blackmail her husband for murder might have cheered her up, but she looked sincerely happy.

'If only we had spoken before, explained,' she continued, 'all would have been so much easier! Nothing to be afraid of.'

I knew where she was coming from with that one.

'I have told Elena that everything will be arranged properly,' put in Yermolov. 'She had nothing to worry about.'

'Sorry about your Caravaggio, Elena.'

'I think it does not matter now.'

The look she exchanged with her husband was rueful, knowing, regretful, loving. Its effect was only ruined by her rolling slowly off her chair and coming to rest on the carpet with a quarter of burger still clutched in her fist. The hidden bottle of vodka rolled out from beneath the cushion which had been assisting her impeccable ballerina's poise. Yermolov and I looked at each other.

'Tell me you didn't.'

'Tell me *you* didn't.'

I turned her over and she emitted a loud snore. 'Jesus,' I sighed. 'I actually thought –'

'So did I,' he cut in.

Then we laughed a lot, until Yermolov asked if I was ready to leave?

'Go back to Carlotta's? Sure. We should get this one to bed though.'

'Not Carlotta's. I am going now to the house in France. Did you think I was going to let you out of my sight before your little artist friends send their "installation"?'

'What makes you think there won't be copies of the tape?'

'Nothing. But then I'm not planning to hurt you.'

The way he said 'hurt' told me how it was.

'I haven't got any clothes,' I stalled.

'Are you flirting with me?'

'Yes.'

'Then you won't need them. Do you have your documents and so on in your bag?'

'I do.'

'Well then. Unless you think that your friend here would mind?'

I looked down at Elena's prone form, considered. 'She isn't my friend. She never was.'

He drove me to the airport naked under the bathrobe, though I waited until we were airborne before I took it off.

Any residue of sisterly solidarity I might have felt with Elena was banished when I saw what she had done to the ground floor of Yermolov's villa. On my previous visit it had been too warm to stay indoors much, but now, in winter, I was exposed to the full horror of gilt on an unlimited budget. They say that you have to be a Rothschild to pull off 'style Rothschild', an axiom proved abundantly by Elena's drawing rooms. We were greeted by Madame Poulhazan, immaculately suited and coiffed, although it was four in the morning. Her face betrayed nothing, but I could feel her opinion of my bathrobe. Nonetheless, when she showed me to my room, I found it full of logoed cardboard carriers.

'I hope the size will be correct,' Madame explained. 'I had to guess.'

'But how?'

'Mr Yermolov called from the flight. He said you were – er – sleeping. He explained you would need some things, so I had some of the boutiques in Cannes open and sent the helicopter.'

'Seriously? I'm very grateful, but it's the middle of the night – they opened the boutiques in the middle of the night?'

'Just a phone call, no trouble at all. I hope you will find the things satisfactory.'

As I got into bed in a pistachio silk Carine Gilson negligee, I rather thought that I did. Before I slept I texted

Carlotta: *Sorry to vanish. Had an offer I couldn't refuse. Thank you so much for a wonderful stay, and love to Franz. Good luck!* I didn't mind abandoning my clothes. I'd been sick of the sight of them anyway.

She pinged back immediately 'Who is it?' I imagined her, hot-eyed in the temperature-controlled bedroom in St Moritz, Franz's sickly old-man odour filling the close space, clutching her phone under the quilt. I hesitated. 'Russian guy. No one you know, but I think you'd approve.'

She sent back a kiss, and an emoji of a diamond ring. Dear Carlotta.

Lots of people confuse sex and love, which is not so damaging as confusing love and understanding. Sex and understanding together though are a potent combination. In the five days that followed, Yermolov and I took care of business in the mornings and spent the short winter afternoons in my bedroom. I had Jovana DHL the old-school videotapes of *Death of an Oligarch* from Belgrade, and Yermolov consented to wire the fee as well as contributing to Timothy's part in the Balensky solution.

On a borrowed laptop, provided by Madame Poulhazan, I checked my bank accounts and went through the backlog of emails to my now-defunct gallery, responding that Gentileschi was closed. I finally began reading Dave's book, when I wasn't following the online progress of Balensky's spectacularly scandalous demise. Dave's spook had done us proud. The pictures had broken on social media and been picked up immediately by hideous Russian anti-gay vigilante groups. Hashtags spawned, human-rights activists twittered, the Swiss police merely said that they were investigating the death of an 86-year-old man. The Russian press splashed the story, complete with thundering editorials on decadence in the conservative papers, which Yermolov translated for me. The source of the photographs was given definitively as an undercover Russian journalist working to end corruption, propaganda that swiftly became truth. I didn't worry about Timothy. A call to Panama had moved his money into a trust that he would be able to access when he returned to France. The password I chose for him was 'Edouard'. I made it 750K. Timothy would get his front-door key to the Playboy mansion, in the end.

'What are you going to do about Kazbich?'

Yermolov and I were sitting up in bed. The fire was lit, the shutters open. Outside, the sky above the sea was a soft dove grey threaded with sudden, surprising phthalo blue. We were drinking Lapsang and munching blinis with black-cherry jam. The smokiness of the tea and the sweetness of the jam tasted of my lessons with Masha.

'I let him know the picture was sadly destroyed when Balensky attempted to recover it. A tragedy on a tragedy. He doesn't know I know. He's in Belgrade. I didn't want him running. He'll be dealt with.'

'Effectively?'

'Indeed.' He kissed my temple, trailed his mouth over my cheekbone and along my jaw.

'So Yury will be looking for a new boss?'

'Maybe. Or shall I deal with him too?'

'Ever the professional. Yes. I'd like that.'

'Revenge?'

'No. Just fair.'

'And what about you, Judith? What are you going to do?'

'Go back to Venice, I suppose. When the delivery arrives from Belgrade.' Not that my flat held much appeal.

There was a moment then, when I thought Yermolov might ask me to stay, but it dwindled along with the blue light beyond the cliffs, and we dozed until it was time to dress and go to look at the pictures. Each evening, before dinner, we went over to the gallery. We watched the pictures differently – Yermolov would choose one of his collection and stand still before it, for twenty minutes or so, while I, I think I swam, like a diver who has dared the black lip of an underwater cavern and emerged in a hidden lagoon of colour. I hadn't looked at pictures like that for so long, not measuring or assessing, calculating what I remembered and what I needed to know, but simply looking, looking with my whole body, my senses entirely deconcentrated. Nothing we had done in my bedroom, not anything I had ever done with anyone, came close to that. The right word is ecstasy. And then we would walk back, hand in hand through the dark towards the house glowing before us, and eat dinner as Yermolov told me about the works, how and why he had acquired each one, fetching books to compare illustrations and read passages aloud, until the table was cluttered with piles of images and we put our abandoned plates on the floor to make more room.

'I knew you knew,' said Yermolov, on what turned out to be my last evening.

'Knew what?'

'When Balensky called me – we hadn't spoken since that thing disappeared – and he said he'd talked to Elena, that Kazbich had had a message and that you would be in St Moritz with the painting. I knew you knew it was a fake.'

'How?'

'Come here.'

He didn't take me in his arms as I expected. Instead he led me to a small cubicle under the main staircase, the triangular wall banked with screens. He flicked one into life – it showed the gallery, the camera moving every twenty seconds from one angle to another, the pictures glowing and dissolving.

'I watched you. The first time. I watched you look at my paintings.'

'And?'

'You know. Your Russian accent is terrible, but you have a good eye.'

'Thank you.'

So he had thought I was good enough after all. I wasn't bitter. Sex and understanding. We could have gone somewhere with that, maybe. Someone uncharitable once said that the synthetic light of mutual self-regard represents the narrowest horizon of the human soul, but nonetheless it was good to feel it, just the once.

26

The installation arrived next morning. According to our agreement, Jovana had copied the film to the tapes and provided three vintage Junost portable televisions on which they could be shown, the 'staged' murder intercut with the close-up shots of Balensky in his PVC panties. Neither of us felt the need to view them. I watched Yermolov overseeing the bonfire out on the cliff as I packed the small bag with which I had travelled from St Moritz. It seemed tacky to keep the clothes, though I had a moment of regret about a particularly beautiful Fendi skirt – cloud-coloured duchesse satin stiffened to a full fifties wheel with buckram. As a travelling outfit, I chose a navy cashmere sweater with grey tweed Chanel pants, Ferragamo ballerinas and the huge, ridiculously swollen Mulberry silk Dries Van Noten coat Madame Poulhazan had chosen to throw over my cocktail dresses.

I rang for the butler, not an activity for which my early education had prepared me, and told him to inform Mr Yermolov that I was leaving. I asked for a car to the station in Nice, retracing the trip I had made months before.

I found Yermolov in his study. I had become accustomed to those fluttering, twining hands, but now, standing in the doorway, I saw them as though for the first time, twisting over the desk in front of him, and they unnerved me once more. Perhaps because they reminded me of myself. Stillness was something for which I no longer had a talent.

'So – time for me to leave.'

He didn't try to stop me. He asked if I needed the plane to return to Venice.

'So you can crash me into an Alp? Thanks, but I'll take the train.'

'You are unkind.'

'So are you. That's why we get on so well.'

'May I call you?' He was only being polite. Our strange, delicious intimacy was over, and we both knew it.

'No need. *Proshchai*, Pavel.' I hadn't called him by his name before.

'*Proshchai.*' *Good luck.*

Once I was in the carriage for the Milan train, I spread out my documents across the table. Judith, Elisabeth, and the last passport I had bought in Amsterdam, which had carried me to France and England and Serbia and now, if the guards could be arsed to check, back to Italy. Katherine Olivia Gable.

I watched the familiar signs as we crossed over the border into Italy. It felt right, somehow, to be making this trip, as it had in many ways been my first. I'd wanted so much, back then. Money, yes, and freedom and independence, but also beautiful things, beautiful views, to prove to Rupert that he couldn't treat me like a no-mark pleb, to myself that all my efforts had been worth it. Admittedly that trip hadn't involved a very coherent plan.

Call me sentimental, but you never forget your first dead body. I had left James slowly softening in the bedroom of the Hôtel du Cap, Cameron under a bridge in Rome, Leanne on another bed, in another city, Renaud – well, at least I still thought of him, and then Julien, that flare of surprise in his eyes, which perhaps Balensky had seen in mine. Masha and Balensky and Moncada and Edouard Guiche . . . *It's not your fault, Judith.* The lights were coming on in the carriages, a steward pushed a refreshments cart with a tinny bell awkwardly down the aisle.

In the spring of 1606, Caravaggio committed a murder. The next four years of his life, his last, were spent more or less on the run. The victim, Ranuccio of Terni, was killed on a tennis court, over a point in the game, a gambling debt, the avenging of an offence, in self-defence – everybody talked, and nobody knew. Caravaggio had flicked his sword, the accessory of his painful striving to be accepted as a gentleman, at his opponent's cock, some said in a gesture of contempt which went wrong when he severed the femoral artery. Others said the killing was the result of Caravaggio's nature, that his wildness caused him to deliberately look for a chance to risk his own neck. If he wanted a thrill, he got it, leaving the city with a bounty placed on the production of his own severed head.

The first picture from his exile was of a whore, a girl named Lena, as an ecstatic Magdalen, in the colours of death – red, white, black. Most of the canvas is darkness. Head thrown back, absurdly luscious mouth parted, a tear creeping beneath her narrowed eyelid the only hint at penitence. The picture fits so beautifully with the narrative of Caravaggio's life that many viewers have been prepared to ignore the fact that he obviously didn't paint it. The rendering is crass, the shadows of the face bungled, working Lena's nose into a snout that grows more hideous the longer you look. People want so badly to see a story, something that makes sense, all Caravaggio's darting, agonised violence of technique condensed into a sentimental narrative of repentance, that they overlook its bathetic feebleness.

What Caravaggio did paint, as the Pope's troops scoured the Roman countryside in pursuit, was a second version of the *Supper at Emmaus*. It is a joyless, shrunken rendering. The innkeeper and his wife are crushed with age. Christ is aged too, so weary he can barely lift his hand above the table in blessing. The meal has passed from meagre to squalid, a scrap of rancid meat, a few stale, crumbled loaves. It is twilight in this picture, and no miracles play in the shadows. The only connection with the picture of Lena is the sidelighting of the figures. Everything else is darkness. If anything at all of the painter's state after his crime can be understood from the pictures, it isn't sexy chocolate-box sorrow. Everyone at that dismal table just looks knackered. Come to think of it, so was I.

Before I got halfway up the stairs to the flat I knew there was someone waiting for me. The smell was a bit of a giveaway. It tumbled down to meet me, a stinking meniscus atop the sodden Venetian air I had let in from the street. I suppose I could have turned around even then, but I quelled my instinct to run. Part of me knew it was already too late and besides, I was curious. Still, as I dragged my bag through the miasma up the last flight, my eyes were hot with unruly tears. This was the nearest anywhere had ever come to feeling like home.

When I turned on the lights, I saw the chair, and I saw the picture. A copy of the *Medusa*, hanging above the bed as though it had always been there. Nice touch. Caravaggio's paintings are cruel to other artworks, always the prettiest girl in the room. Just one will render a roomful of masterpieces invisible. He was waiting for me in the velvet armchair, dragged round so the winged back flared out towards the door, the elbows of his dark linen jacket resting on either arm, watching the painting.

'Hello, stranger,' I said, for my own benefit more than his.

Alvin wasn't looking too good. Six weeks in a wardrobe can do that to a person. I'd triplebagged him, which had held the maggots back, but damp was always going to be a problem in this town.

Whoever had dressed him had rinsed him down first; the reeking bin liners were clumped in the bathtub, a Milky Way of black plastic swirled with some white tendrils of softly rotten flesh. His soft tissues had disintegrated to mulch, the pancreas would have eaten itself, bringing up blue-green blisters on the scraps of flesh that clung stubbornly to the remaining cartilage. I breathed shallow, through my mouth, as I moved around to face him. Methane and hydrogen sulphide. I hadn't shared my flat back in London with medical students for nothing. The head, with its horribly protruding curtain of shredded bright red tongue was hooked over one of my coat hangers, its wires torn into the fabric, with the jacket slung in an approximation of shoulders. The rest of him was piled neatly in a puddle on the seat, his scuffed Sebagos positioned where his feet would have reached. A card was pinned to his lapel with one of the safety pins my dry-cleaner used. I made myself reach out and touch the slimy bone, and we both of us stayed there for a moment, looking at the face of death. When I bent to unpin the card, the coat hanger came loose and Alvin with it, the eyeless head bouncing off the chair, thudding to the floor, rolling up against the bed. I felt the vibrations of its fall like a siren, and when at last they ceased the room was still, so still that I thought I could hear the dust of my absence swirling gently in their wake.

I recognised the card. I'd owned its duplicate once, in Como, where I thought I had so successfully played dumb about the disappearance of Cameron Fitzpatrick.

'Ispettore Romero da Silva, Guardia di Finanza', the print read. On the other side was a number in biro and a miniature message in neat block capitals.

'You need to call me.'

Kazbich had shopped me. Kazbich had known about Fitzpatrick. Kazbich had inadvertently given Elena her crazy plan of blackmail. And there was only one person to whom Kazbich could have suggested Fitzpatrick's death required attention. Da Silva. Kazbich had been working with Moncada, whom both Renaud Cleret and da Silva were pursuing in connection with Mafia fakes. But how were Kazbich and da Silva connected? Kazbich was in Belgrade; obviously da Silva was responsible for my homecoming tableau, but why hang the *Medusa*? Kazbich's dying request, a revenge from beyond whatever grave Yermolov had consigned him to?

'*You need to call me.*'

I had been waiting for this moment for so long. I stepped over Alvin and took a peek into the square. No massed bands of cops with riot shields. Da Silva was going to let me come along quietly.

I showered in my beautiful bathroom for what was perhaps the last time. As I scrubbed my nails, my fingers twisted over my wrists, writhing like eels until I had to pull them apart and press my palms against my skull to still them. That was where the cuffs would go. *Not much longer*. I dressed without looking at Alvin, clean cotton underwear, jeans, a T-shirt and sweatshirt. I picked up the heavy down jacket I had bought against the Venetian fog. I thought I wouldn't be allowed to keep my bag, but I stuffed a few things in it – always the toothbrush, deodorant, moisturiser. A book – would that be allowed? Pulling my wet hair into a topknot, I looked into the mirror. *Hello, Judith*. All done then. I stepped onto the landing to make the call, and heard the trill of the mobile once, below me in the *campo*, before da Silva picked up.

He was waiting at the bottom of the stairs. Taller than I remembered, still the same broad-shouldered, neat physique. He wasn't in uniform, and he was alone. The first time we'd met, I could have embraced him, for the sheer relief that the geyser of tension inside me was stilled. There was a different quality to my resignation now. I touched him on the shoulder.

'*Sono pronta*.' *I'm ready*.

He turned, and his eyes were gentle as they took me in, sneakers to wet tendrils of falling hair. I raised a hand to push it from my face but the hand stopped halfway, inviting. Old habits.

'I said, I'm ready.'

'I thought you might like to go somewhere quiet. Somewhere we can talk.'

'Aren't you going to arrest me?' I asked stupidly.

'No.'

'But –' My hand made a spastic gesture upwards, at the flat. I'd left the light on. Alvin waited behind the shutters.

'As I said, I think you need to talk to someone. To me.' His dark jacket swung open. I thought I saw a holster at his hip, but it could have been a shadow. I nodded.

'I have a boat waiting. Please, come this way,' he added courteously.

On the trip round to the Arsenale, da Silva offered me a cigarette, but I shook my head. I didn't look at Venice, just at my knees, scrunched under my chin, my hands winding and clasping. The driver handed me out at the gates of the naval offices, attended by their two huge white lions, saluting da Silva as he climbed after me onto the quay, a steadying arm at my back. I'd walked past a hundred times; the Arsenale was the second site for the Biennale exhibits, though now in the dark it looked like what it had always really been, a fortress.

'Do you prefer to speak in English or in Italian?'

We sat in a small, brightly lit office, a window open on the canal. We had passed several uniforms in the lobby, but da Silva was still unaccompanied. On the table were two full espresso cups, plastic glasses and a bottle of water, no tape recorder. I thought dully that it must be built into the walls, or maybe there was one of those two-way mirrors? I didn't much care.

'English is better, maybe.' I was too exhausted to think in the formal grammar of Italian. The coffee was acrid in my throat, I poured half a glass of water and gulped it.

'Very good.' Still soft, his voice coaxing. 'Where do you wish to begin?'

I drew my knees up under my chin, squatting in the chair. He waited me out.

'It was the oil,' I began. I didn't know the sound of my own voice. 'I put the almond oil in the bath.'

It was the almond oil. That was how she smelled, of almonds. My sister.

She was born when I was twelve. Katherine my mum named her, for Katherine Hepburn. We had a new place after she came; I had my own bedroom for the first time, and the hospital sent my mum home with a bag of things, disposable nappies and bibs, samples of baby milk, shampoo for her delicate head, and the almond oil, to rub in the funny creases of her arms and legs after her bath. I'd thought of babies as fat, but Katherine wasn't, at first. She was just a little bag of skin and bones, like a monkey, the skin of her tiny round tummy so thin and tight you could see the veins pulsing there. I loved her puffy little frog hands, the way her wisps of hair sang in my mouth. She was my sister and I was going to take care of her, I was going to take her to the park and make her daisy chains, I was going to get her a little tea set like the one in the Milly-Molly-Mandy stories, with real china cups and little patterned plates. My mum showed me how to change her nappy and rub her back when she had drunk her milk. She lay between us on the sofa while we ate our tea and she made us laugh and laugh with her huge eyes and her questing fingers.

My mum was good for a bit. She took Katherine to the clinic on the bus and pushed her to the shops in the buggy, slumped sideways in the tiny pink anorak she'd bought with the family allowance. I knew enough about how babies were made, but I never asked who Katherine's dad was. My mum never talked about my dad, and that didn't matter at all. It was the three of us, and I would rush home from school every day to see her. When it wasn't too cold I'd take her to the swings at the top of the close and set her carefully on my lap while I sang to her, all the nursery rhymes I could remember from when I was little. She would laugh when I did 'Jack and Jill', making the swing fall down the hill, her face scrunching up in what I knew was a smile.

And then my mum wasn't so good. She started going to the pub again, and when Katherine woke up in the night she wasn't there to give her the bottle. I didn't mind. I could do it. I'd mix the formula carefully by the marks on the plastic, then stand it in a cereal bowl of boiling water from the kettle to get it warm enough, testing a few drops on the inside of my wrist like I'd seen my mum do, just like I was a nurse, and when she'd drunk it and was all cosy and sleepy again I'd rock her against my shoulder and open the kitchen curtain and show her the stars and the lights from town, and put her in under the blankets in my bed, curled against me like a comma.

I started to worry about my mum again. In the mornings she wouldn't be up, and there'd be the smell of it on her, that greasy sheen on her skin and her make-up all over the pillowcase. I'd stand by her bed in my school uniform, holding Katherine; I was always missing the school bus because I didn't want to leave unless I knew she was awake to take care of her. I started nipping home at lunchtime, just to check, letting myself quietly into the flat to see if I could hear the telly or the radio, check to see if the buggy was inside the door, or if my mum had got herself up and taken Katherine for some fresh air. Then I stopped going to school altogether, because my mum was hardly at home, and I didn't want to leave my sister, at least until the school rang up and my mum gave me down the banks for skiving. I had to go to the headmaster's office to say why I'd been truanting, but I couldn't say why, because I thought they might put Katherine in a home.

'You're a bright girl, Judith,' the headmaster told me. 'Don't lose your chance. You could go to university.' He wasn't unkind, just puzzled. I looked at the floor when he asked me why I was stopping off and chewed my ponytail and tried to look like all the other girls in my class who bunked off all the time. I said I didn't know, but I was sorry, sir, and he shook his head and said not to let it happen

again. So I had to start going to school, in case they sent the social round and Katherine got taken away.

My sister must have been about five months old when it happened, because my mum had started to give her baby food out of glass jars. Sometimes I would mash up a banana for her and spoon it into her gummy mouth, scooping the dribbly bits back from under her lip. She could sit up, and she wouldn't eat unless she had her own spoon to hold, except she kept dropping it, or poking herself with it, so it took ages to feed her.

That day, when I opened the door, the flat smelled of sweet almonds. It was winter, already getting dark, but there were no lights on. My mum was on the sofa, an empty bottle of white wine and a half-empty bottle of gin beside her. She must have started as soon as I left for school. Katherine wasn't in her cot in my mum's room, or in my bed. The only strip of light came from under the bathroom door. I didn't want to go in there. I made a cup of tea and put it on the floor by my mum, drew the kitchen curtains. I wanted mum to wake up, but she didn't. So then I had to go into the bathroom.

At first I thought she was OK, because she was warm, but when I got her out of the bath I realised it was the water. It was slippery, still tepid. Her face was grey. My mum had put the special yellow towel with the hood next to the bath, so I wrapped her in that. Her head lolled in the hollow of my neck as though she was sleeping. I stood by the sofa, and then I sat down by her feet because my legs felt shaky.

'Mum,' I said, over and over. 'Mum?'

I think she knew before she opened her eyes. There was a long moment when her face woke up, but she wouldn't look at what she'd done. When she sat, she was already reaching out her arms for her baby, drawing back the towel, because she knew.

'I found her,' I whispered.

Mum wrapped the towel back where it was, getting up and fetching her coat, her boots.

'I'll get help,' she said, and she was gone. Her phone was in the pocket of her coat. I thought she must be going out to call the ambulance, but she didn't come back. Not for hours. I thought it was important that I didn't move. I held Katherine against me, stroking the bottom of her back through the towel. I thought it was very important that I kept her head up, so I sat so still that I got pins and needles over and over again. I needed the loo but I knew I mustn't move. I could see the lights going on in the top flats across the way, the flicker of televisions, people drawing the curtains. I held Katherine's head very still, and in a while, I think, I convinced myself that the beating of my own heart was shared.

Mum was sober when she came back. She must have made herself sick, washed her face. She had shopping, which confused me, a bag from the spa with Peperami and orange juice and a tin of beans threatening to split the plastic. I could see it against her jeans in the hall. She was talking to someone – 'I'll get the kettle on' – and I heard the voice of Mandy from down the close who did my mum's hair sometimes, dancing round to Radio 1 with the plastic gloves and the Clairol and a bottle of wine.

'Why are you sitting in the dark, Judy? Are you all right?' My mum was all breezy and surprised-sounding. I couldn't move. I tried but my legs were still asleep, and when I tried to get up, holding Katherine steady, I stumbled. My mum was looking in the bathroom, all concerned. The water must have been cold by then but you could still smell the almonds.

'Judy? Where are you?'

She put the light on in the living room and I held out the towel.

'Mum?'

My mum screamed then. But in the moment before she did, she looked at me and I saw her eyes. I'm a lot like her, I think. Quick. She hadn't brought Mandy to help. She'd brought a witness.

Then Mandy was in the room, and she was screaming too, and suddenly the grey dimness that had disguised my sister's dead face was sharded with light and noise, the siren and the men in their hard jackets, someone was making tea and somewhere Mandy was still crying.

'Let's get her up.'

'Come on, love.'

'She's wet herself.'

'Come on now. Slowly, like.'

'It's the shock,' Mandy's voice was repeating, 'the shock.' But my mum's arms were round me, and when I started choking and fighting as they took Katherine from me to put her body on the trolley she held me tighter than she ever had, her own body shaking but her arms corded around my back so I couldn't speak, my face jammed tight into her belly that had held my sister and she was saying, 'It's not your fault, Judith. It's not your fault.'

I said I couldn't really remember what had happened. The social worker and the police lady and the counsellor all asked me if my mum had gone out when I came in from school, and I said yes. I was twelve, it wasn't even illegal. And I had bathed my sister? I said yes. I had put too much oil in the water, maybe I had slipped. I said I couldn't remember anything after that. I'd watched enough of my mum's soaps to know about trauma. Your brain blocks out things that would kill you if you remembered them. I knew why my mum had done it. She'd have gone to prison and I would have ended up in a home. And between all the questions and the tests and the neighbours standing outside on the day of the funeral, the cards and the bouquets, I thought sometimes maybe it was me after all. I hadn't gone into the bathroom, I had been too scared.

'It's not her fault,' my mum kept repeating, and everyone said how brave she was and asked how she was coping. The council moved us to a different flat on another estate. They said we didn't need the extra bedroom any more, and

I had to change schools. But it had been in the Echo *and someone's cousin went to my old school and it was all over the place after I'd been there a week. The boys started making the sign of the cross as I went past in the corridor, like I was a vampire.*

The counsellor asked me if I was jealous of her. Of my sister, with her wet eyes like flowers.

27

'The oil?' Da Silva was looking at me, patient, curious. I realised I hadn't spoken for some time.

'Please help me,' I whispered. 'I don't know what you want.'

'Two years ago, in Rome, you killed a man known to you as Cameron Fitzpatrick. Do you admit this?'

'Yes.'

'You then took a painting that man was selling and sold it to another man, known to you as Moncada. Do you admit this?'

'Yes.'

'Moncada was murdered some time later in Paris. I believe you were present.'

'I was.'

'You have since been living here, under an – forgive me, my English – an alias?'

'I have.'

'Why did you kill Alvin Spencer?'

I had been responding dumbly, in a fugue state, but this question roused me a little. Surely this was wrong. Shouldn't there be someone else here? Why hadn't he asked me about Renaud, his colleague, his comrade in arms? He had a perfect murder scene, a confession, a culprit effectively in custody. Why hadn't he brought out the cuffs yet?

'Do I need a lawyer?' Idiocy, learned from cop shows.

'Not at present, unless you prefer me to charge you. Please continue. Why did you kill Alvin Spencer?'

'Alvin knew someone. Someone from the past. I thought he was a threat. But I couldn't, I wasn't able . . .' I trailed off. I hadn't been able to get rid of the body. I hadn't been able to get rid of the body because I knew that if I tried, at that moment, then I would splinter. Couldn't have that. So I thought I'd wait, just a week or so, just until I had the strength. But then Elena appeared, and Masha was killed, and I didn't have the strength for it then either. I'd just – left him there.

Da Silva reached into his pocket. I imagined he was producing a formal charge sheet, was about to read me my rights, the scene we all know so well, but he produced a tissue and handed it to me.

'Here.' My face was soaked, and the collar of my jacket. I hadn't felt the tears. I blew my nose explosively.

'There are a great many questions I need to ask you. We can talk in the car.'

'The car?' I supposed we must be going to Rome. Da Silva was part of the Roman division of the Guardia – perhaps he couldn't charge me here. 'Do I have to come?'

'You can accompany me, or I can arrest you now. You can choose.'

The way I felt right then I could have happily lain down on the floor and woken up in an orange playsuit, but it wasn't like I had anywhere else to be.

'I'll come.'

He stepped around the table and pulled my chair back for me politely, as though we were dining in a smart restaurant. As he bent, his jacket swung back. He was carrying a gun. A Caracal F, to be precise. Standard issue for the *Guardia di Finanza*. There had been a demonstration by the police of its capacities at the Futura shooting club in Rome some years ago. Also the preferred weapon of Italian Mafiosi, as evinced by the fact that, to the embarrassment of the Guardia and the outrage of the *Corriere della Sera*, the entire supply of demonstration guns had been diverted in its police van on the way back to the city, never to be seen again. Moncada's gun. I knew the fit of it in my hand, the weight. The gun I had dismantled in Paris, unused. I twitched as a jolt of adrenalin surged through me so sharply that I staggered.

'Are you unwell?'

'No. Fine. A little dizzy. We can go.'

I sank my head into the collar of the coat as I shuffled into the corridor. *Don't let him see*. The question I had buried in St Moritz was unspooling in my mind. How did Kazbich know? I had thought that Kazbich and Moncada had been involved together in the art-for-arms gig, that Kazbich must have heard da Silva's name from Moncada. But what if Moncada and da Silva were on the same side, what if da Silva was a double agent, a cop who worked for the Mafia? What if he'd been involved all along? *Brilliant, Judith. Wrong again.*

All the time da Silva was handing me into the boat, back through the journey to San Basilio, where the only road from Venice to the mainland begins, I dissected it, laying out the pieces.

Who knew Moncada was going to be in the Place de l'Odéon that night? Me and Moncada himself. Renaud. Guiche. Balensky. Kazbich. Da Silva. Da Silva had helped out Kazbich with the 'ghosts'. Da Silva had hung the Caravaggio. He knew.

Art for arms. Da Silva had been part of the same investigation squad as Renaud, charged with recovering stolen artworks in the south of Italy. One operation had ended in the deaths of several of their colleagues in a bomb ambush. I had assumed, had believed, that Moncada's death had been revenge on Renaud's part, acting for the honour of his workmates. I'd led him to Moncada and then he was going to turn me in. But I'd vanished for a while, until I opened Gentileschi in Venice and they'd found me.

I'd sent that stupid text:

Does the name Gentileschi mean anything to you?

That's how Kazbich had tracked down my gallery. Because only da Silva knew its significance. The sight of the gun, the same gun, had made it clear. The reason I hadn't returned the Caravaggio, the person, the witness I had searched for so fruitlessly, was da Silva.

At the docks we were shown to a car, a dark sedan with a driver. Floodlights between the cranes lit it harshly. I saw that the number-plate was Roman. Da Silva indicated that

I should ride in the back next to him, pressing a button to divide the vehicle with a Plexiglas screen, like a London taxi. We pulled away towards the bridge to Mestre and da Silva sat back.

'How's your wife?' I asked him suddenly.

'My wife?'

'You told me about her, when we met in Como. Francesca.'

It was Francesca – Franci – who had led me to Renaud's real identity. I had stalked her on Facebook, friended her, and found pictures of Renaud at her child's christening. To be fair, da Silva didn't show any surprise.

'She's – very well. But now, I think you need to talk to me.'

The problem with the brave choice is it's never the fun choice. I sat up too, and slowly unfastened my hair, spread it out over my shoulders, brushed a fingertip over my mouth. I switched to Italian.

'No, I don't think so. I think you need to talk to me.'

'How so?'

'Does the name Gentileschi mean anything to you?'

'I believe it is the name of your gallery, *Miss Teerlinc*.'

'I asked that question once before. In a text message, sent from the phone of a man I knew as Renaud Cleret. You know that. I want to know how Ivan Kazbich knew. I want to know how you knew what was in my flat. I want to know why you haven't arrested me for murder. Because I think I know the answers.'

The way I figured it, if this little joy-ride was on the straight, he would think I was mad and arrest me when we got wherever the hell we were going. And if he was bent, he could have the goon pull over and murder me right on the autoroute. At present, that did feel like the relaxing option. But I knew that he would do neither.

Da Silva stared straight ahead.

'And your mate? My friend in Paris? Why haven't you asked me about him?'

Da Silva pushed a button and the window slid down to a rush of icy Veneto night. He took out a cigarette and lit up. I declined when he held out the pack; I really hate smoking in cars. He took a long drag, a ribbon of mist unfurling from his throat.

'Let's just say you did me a favour there.'

I sat with that one for a while.

'So where are we going?'

'You'll see.'

From the mainland, the autostrada unpeeled through the night. Once we stopped at an Autogrill, where da Silva asked for my phone before I used the bathroom. We stretched and smoked and drove again, and as I began to doze I saw that we had crossed the invisible line that squiggles across Italy, where the olive trees begin. After that I rolled my jacket into a pillow, hunched my body away from da Silva's and slept, waking to the warmth of daylight against my eyelids, but I kept them shut, sensing the movements of the car, feeling it pausing more frequently through an occasional rumble of traffic. I twisted stiffly and buried my face in the pillow until we slowed, stopped. Da Silva touched my shoulder.

'We're here.'

Unfolded, we stood on a small concrete dock, gusts of engine oil and remembered fish lapping our faces, the thick damp of Venice replaced by a bright sea breeze. Behind the dock, a concrete promenade, two sorrowful desiccated palm trees, a row of scruffy concrete apartment blocks encrusted with junkyard balconies and peeling paint crowded a locked white stucco church. The driver was taking our bags from the boot, I hovered uselessly next to him.

'This way.'

Turning towards the little town, I saw that it was banked in by high arid hills, from one of which what looked like an unfinished motorway protruded like a rotten tooth.

'Where are we?' Alice in effing Wonderland, that was me.

'Calabria. I'll explain. We'll get some coffee first.'

Da Silva gave some directions to the driver, who set off with our stuff. I followed da Silva along the promenade. An old man stared at us indifferently from a balcony. Away from the front, the town abandoned its efforts at seaside gaiety: most of the shops were empty except for a supermarket, a slot-machine parlour and a place selling electronic cigarettes. Cerise tinsel bunting was strung between the lamp posts. We turned into a deserted bar, TV blaring a game show, smell of fresh coffee and brioche and lemons and drains, and took a table at the back. Da Silva nodded at the bartender; he seemed to know him.

'Are you hungry?'

'No,' I answered rudely. But the bartender was hovering, so I ordered a cappuccino. When we were alone I scraped my spoon across the froth, back and forth.

'You knew then, all along? You knew it was me, in Rome?'

'I was uncertain. Your performance was pretty good. But then you turned up in Paris and – let's just say there was a great deal else going on. Which you had walked in on.'

I had believed that I was playing one game, whose rules were of my own making. Yet I had wandered into another, a game begun long before, the rules of which I could not even see.

Da Silva and Moncada. Art for arms. All along.

'So yes,' he was continuing calmly, 'I know some things. I imagine you have many more to tell me. We have time.'

Suddenly I felt breathless, choking. I took a gulp of the coffee but it spluttered over the tabletop. The bartender looked around in irritated concern.

'I'm sorry, I need to get some air.'

'Of course. As I say, there's time.'

I stood in the doorway, looking down the street. A group of children came past, thickly bundled, though it wasn't cold. They were carrying packages from a bakery. Some of them had already torn off the thin wrappers to cram the treats into their overfed faces. Marzipan. Tiny vegetables, carrots and aubergines, bundles of grapes, a miniature panettone studded with drops of dye. They make them for

Christmas, in the south. I wandered down to the front and looked at the sea for a while, but the water had nothing to tell me. There was nowhere else to go.

Da Silva was waiting for me outside the bar. He took my arm. 'We'll go this way.'

For a while we walked along the main road, leaving the little town behind us. A few cars passed. Perhaps their occupants thought we were a couple, out for a festive stroll. After about twenty minutes da Silva directed me along a dirt track which sloped down towards the sea. Plastic bags and drinks cans snagged in the thorn-bushes on either side. Then we came out into a shingled cove, more rubbish marooned where the waves touched the shore, though their swell was muffled by the churning of machinery. A concrete platform was built into the water, housing what I took to be a water purification plant, as from the squat breeze-block structure on the platform a red pipe thicker than my body stretched into the swell to a tanker moored about a hundred metres off the beach. It swayed in the sea like the tentacle of a monstrous squid. I scanned the decks of the ship, but they were as empty as the beach. Da Silva guided me to the land-side of the plant, out of sight of anyone on board, and where the sound of the turbines was loudest. I smelled oil and piss and somewhere, as the breeze shifted, the faint scent of almonds.

I'd got the idea before he produced the Caracal.

'So, I'm offering you a choice,' he began.

'Yeah, yeah. I've worked out you're bent, so now you'll kill me. Nice spot you've picked. Close to your mates, Calabria.'

'Exactly. Or –'

I'd believed I was playing one game, which turned out to be entirely another. The thing is, I don't like rigged odds. Twisted loner that I am, I do have this idea about things being *fair*. Until I'd seen how things were, I had been feeling a certain sort of bewildered indifference, an echo of the lassitude that had seeped into me when I drowned Alvin. Meek little Judith, paralysed by trauma. Except now I felt angry. Really fucking angry.

'So what do I get to choose?'

I took a tiny crab-step towards the edge of the platform, then another. He followed the move with the gun.

'Don't think you're going swimming,' he muttered. 'The current out there will wash you up in Gallipoli by tomorrow morning. Why do you think we're here?'

'Because you lack imagination?'

'Either we stop here or you come back to town with me and we see if we can work together for a while.' His hand was as perfectly steady as his voice. Odd, that I'd spent months thinking someone was trying to kill me, and now someone actually was trying to kill me it felt like a let-down.

'"Work together"?' I hissed.

'I have something I want you to do. And then you'll be free to go, Judith.'

I could have thought of my sister, or of my mother. Of all that I'd done, of all that had happened to bring me here, of all that I'd been and all that I'd become. But I didn't.

'Go on then. Do it. Do it. Go ahead.'

So he raised the gun and aimed it at my heart.

TO BE CONCLUDED

Acknowledgements

My thanks to The Tosh, to Errikos for the hats, and to my amazing editors, Joel Richardson and Tara Singh-Carlson, for their immense patience.

Dear Reader,

I'm thrilled that you have picked up *Domina* and hope that you'll enjoy it.

Maestra introduced the character of Judith Rashleigh, an ambitious junior art expert who discovers a fraud at the auction house where she works. She is fired for her curiosity, and when, in desperation, she accepts a trip from one of the customers at the bar where she moonlights as a hostess, she learns a very different way of fulfilling her dreams . . . *Domina* opens as Judith is established in her own gallery in Venice, but her past is about to catch up with her.

When I began Judith's story, I was interested in playing with the conventions of noir fiction, and in creating a very different kind of anti-heroine. I wanted readers to find themselves rooting for her despite her criminality; to be caught up in the glamour and danger of her world even as they recognise how flawed she is. *Maestra* has provoked some pretty strong responses, both positive and negative – some readers find Judith an empowering character, whilst others, well, really hate her. Strangely, perhaps, I find both reactions exciting, because they suggest that readers are really engaging with the book. I wonder whether *Domina* will change the way Judith is perceived? In developing the narrative, I began with the phrase "the end of desire is death". What happens to Judith when she actually gets what she wants? And when she is forced to protect it, possibly at the cost of her own life, does she even want it anymore?

Domina was huge fun to write, not least because I had to do some pretty fascinating research. I interviewed web hackers and a bona fide arms dealer, I travelled to Belgrade and Venice, and I spent a lot of time with Caravaggio, one of my favourite painters. I even started to learn Russian – admittedly with fairly pathetic results! It's a fast, energetic, dark and sometimes comic story that, I hope, will keep surprising readers right until the end.

Domina's mood is very different from *Maestra*, and I'd love to know which book you prefer, or where you imagine the story will go in the third and final book. So do get in touch – you can visit www.bit.ly/LSHilton to become part of the LS Hilton Readers Club, where you will find lots of extra material, from background on the artworks to a travel guide based on Judith's adventures. Bonnier Zaffre will keep your data private and confidential, and it will never be passed on to a third party. We won't spam you with loads of emails, we'll just get in touch now and again with book news, and you can unsubscribe any time you want.

I look forward to hearing from you and sharing your reactions to *Domina*.

With all best wishes,

Lisa

Find out where it all began . . .

MAESTRA

THE NUMBER ONE BESTSELLER

GLAMOUR'S WRITER OF THE YEAR.

WHERE DO YOU GO WHEN YOU'VE GONE TOO FAR?

By day Judith Rashleigh is a put-upon assistant at a London auction house.

By night she's a hostess in one of the capital's unsavoury bars.

Desperate to make something of herself, Judith knows she has to play the game. She's learned to dress, speak and act in the interests of men. She's learned to be a good girl. But after uncovering a dark secret at the heart of the art world, Judith is fired and her dreams of a better life are torn apart.

So she turns to a long-neglected friend.

A friend that kept her chin up and back straight through every past slight.

A friend that a good girl like her shouldn't have: **Rage.**

Available in paperback, ebook and audiobook now

IF YOU CAN'T BEAT THEM – KILL THEM.

Judith Rashleigh returns in

ULTIMA

The gripping final instalment of
the Maestra trilogy

Coming 2018

'I want the next LS Hilton with an aching,
selfish yearning I do not feel for
the Man Booker list'

Stephen Bayley, *The Amorist*

Read on for an exclusive first look . . .

From the terrace at the top of the riad, I had looked across the harbour to a long crescent of sand, framed by tall, modern hotels. Between the buildings and the Bay of Tangiers stretched a palm-flanked promenade, clogged with the lights of early evening traffic. From that that viewpoint, Tangiers was a city like any other, but from down here, in the sinuous alleys of the Kasbah, it was almost impossible to believe it even existed.

As I walked uphill, between the white walls and bright-painted doorways, women in djellabas and sandals filled plastic containers at standpipes, illuminated by the crazy web of improvised electric wiring that trailed like creeper between the houses.

Grubby, half-dressed children streaked busily past me; a man pushing a handcart loaded with a luridly patterned velour sofa spat thickly as he laboured up a flight of shallow steps. The shadows were moth-soft with tumbling, skinny cats. The higher I climbed, the quieter it became, and the layered scents of the air – diesel, sewage, lemon, jasmine, cumin, sweat – peeled away until as I came out into the square, I could smell only the clean ozone of the Atlantic.

The Club Maroc looked incongruously smart against the stillness of the crumbling, ancient citadel walls, gleamingly restored Spanish colonial balconies shut in with spruce green blinds. A doorman in a white shirt waited outside. As I approached, a chunky beige Mercedes taxi pulled up and he held the door open for a tourist couple in linen jackets.

"*Bonsoir*, Madame," he said as I followed them in,

Inside, it was the twenty first century again, the standard version of Morocco peddled from Barcelona to New York: dark red walls, low brass tables, intricate lanterns and embroidered cushions. I asked for the bar and was directed across a courtyard strewn with rose petals to a roofed terrace furnished with stolid leather club chairs. I took a seat and a waiter appeared with a small brass bowl and a long handled jug, from which he poured orange flower water over my hands before handing me a starched linen towel. I asked him for a *kir framboise* and sat back, watching the smooth dimming of the sky.

"Miss Rashleigh? Judith Rashleigh?"

The voice came from behind the high back of my armchair. It was the kind of voice I had become unaccustomed to hearing since I left my job at the House in London; a relic of a voice, marooned somewhere between D-Day and the Suez crisis, though its owner couldn't have been more than sixty.

"May I? Thank you. Jonathan Strathdrummond. Drink? Oh – very good, I'll take a gin and tonic, there's a good chap."

"Thank you for meeting me, Mr Strathdrummond."

"Oh, please call me Jonny. We don't stand on ceremony out here, you'll find."

Jonny wore a crisp pale suit, gleaming Church's brogues and what I strongly suspected was *not* an Old Harrovian tie. If he'd taken down the accent and removed the signet ring he might have passed, but then presumably the reason he lived in Tangier was so he didn't have to.

"Found the place easily enough?" He took a long swallow of his drink.

"Yes, thank you. I had a wonderful walk."

"Game girl. Have to have your wits about you in the old Kasbah."

I was tempted to add that I'd forgotten my parasol – and would he send his bearer for it, *chop chop*? But I didn't think he'd laugh.

"As I explained in my email –," – Jonny winced a bit: perhaps it was chipping away at the old colonial dream to mention technology – "I'm interested in Mikhail Balensky's house."

"Quite. Rum business, what?" *Christ, was the man ever going to let up?*

"I understand it's for sale."

"That's about it. Do you know Tangier well?"

I could see that Estate Agent hadn't perhaps been Jonny's optimal career choice, but I was going to have to move things along a bit. Aboubouker had messaged me on my latest burner phone to tell me they were waiting at the property with the truck, but he and the boys wouldn't stand around all night.

"Would you care to see a menu, Madame?"

Jonny looked at me hopefully. Close up I could see the foxing on his shirt cuff, the grease in the carefully pressed seam of his trousers. I was rather sorry for him. Momentarily.

"Thank you, I don't think we have time." I turned back to Jonny. "The thing is, my client wants to buy the house, and so I need to see it as soon as possible."

"Really?" Any wistful longing for a pigeon tagine forgotten, Jonny was all business. He reached into his jacket for his diary. "Well, how about the day after tomorrow? Got a few things pencilled in but I daresay I could bung them back –"

"I want to see the house tonight, please. Perhaps you could ask them to call us a cab?"

"Now? But, well, it's dark."

"That's not a problem." I leaned forward and laid a confidential hand on his arm. "You see, the thing is, my client is a very busy man. He tends to get . . . distracted. If we both want our . . . commissions, Jonny, we need to move on this."

"Understood." He rose to his feet, signalling eagerly to the waiter. "I'll have to stop at my office for the keys."

"Of course. And naturally I'll take care of the cab. Please allow me to offer you the drink, too. I'm so grateful for your understanding."

I had bought a beautiful soft leather bag in the Medina earlier that afternoon. As I reached inside to extract my purse, I caught a brief glimpse of the handcuffs and the hammer, gleaming dully in the soft light of the tiny lanterns.

ULTIMA

Coming 2018

Pre-order now, and join the conversation

#DominaBook
@lshiltonauthor
@BonnierZaffre

Want to read
NEW BOOKS
before anyone else?

Like getting
FREE BOOKS?

Enjoy sharing your
OPINIONS?

Discover

Read. Love. Share.

Get your first free book just by signing up at
readersfirst.co.uk

For Terms and Conditions see readersfirst.co.uk/pages/terms-of-service